Welcome to Aberdeen

by

Jules Hahn

Welcome to Aberdeen

Cover Art by *Diana Carlile*

The Wild Rose Press, Inc.
PO Box 708
Adams Basin, NY 14410-0708
Visit us at www.thewildrosepress.com

Publishing History
First Sweetheart Rose Edition, 2020
Print ISBN 978-1-5092-3039-6
Digital ISBN 978-1-5092-3040-2

Published in the United States of America

"Does my presence bother you?" He tucked a strand of her hair behind her ear.

His fingers brushed against her flesh. Lily's heart thumped. *Hell yeah.* Maybe if he was located a town or two away, she wouldn't be bothered. Seeing as she'd taken a vow for him never to know her real opinion, she'd just keep her thoughts to herself. She did have pride, after all, and the last thing he needed was an ego-stroke. "No." She lifted her chin. "I just don't appreciate the gossip."

Another smile flitted across his face. "In a place this size, we're bound to be seen together on occasion." he cupped her elbow.

Warm electricity shot through her veins. "What are you doing?"

"It's raining." He tilted his head toward the front. "I thought I'd give you a ride home."

Lily glanced out the broad expanse of window. Sure enough, rain poured from the dark sky. Her lousy luck in action, again. "I'm not made of sugar. I'm sure I won't melt."

Praise for *WELCOME TO ABERDEEN*

"Witty humor and entertaining characters create this lighthearted pleasurable romance that pulls the reader into a simpler lifestyle in this small town."

~Judith C.

~*~

"A guilt-free read of when fate and coincidence spark a true romance worthy of a permanent place on my "read again" and again…shelf."

~Allyson B.

Dedication

For my parents…

Acknowledgments

I would like to thank my parents for their love, support and encouragement through the years. When I was just a little girl and wrote my first story, "Goober the Squash," my mother told me I was born to write. Thank you, Mom, for giving me the courage and belief that I could. To my father, thank you for passing your amazing creativity to me. Without you, this book would not be possible. To my mother-in-law Marge Setzer, who was excited about my writing every time we spoke, thank you. To my father-in-law Ron and his wife Susan for being my cheerleaders, thank you.

To all my friends through the years who have encouraged me every step of the way. But I would especially like to thank Kathy Giles, Jodie Byers, Johanna Imperial, Lana Hakari, Laurie Little, Becky Berhow, Candace Clark, Debbie Breecher, Lori Miano. Each of you have stood by me, believed in me, and cheered me on. Thank you. Thank you. Thank you.

To Brenda Nelson and Karen Hefflel, the very first readers of my book. Thank you for telling me to submit it and giving me the encouragement to do so.

To Toni Lopopolo who took the time to read my contract, to advise me and to offer her help. Thank you.

To my sons, Alex and Nick. You two are the best. If I could describe my greatest creation, it would be you. I am nothing without you. You are both a blessing in my world.

And finally, to my husband, Ron. Thank you for your love, for listening to my weird ideas, and for giving me insight into the minds of men. I love you.

Chapter 1

"This doesn't look good…" Lily stared at the scene outside in her rearview mirror.

The long, black road, slicing through the tall pines, spruce, and maple trees, stretched out behind them. Between her stopped car and the last curve they'd whizzed past sat the object of Lily's worry and Peri's obsession.

Tilting up her sunglasses just a bit, Peri studied the view outside the rearview window. "He looks good to me."

Lily couldn't argue with Peri's assessment of the officer, who with a determined stride, headed in her direction. Tall, broad-shouldered, and from all appearances muscular—if the way his leather jacket stretched across his chest and his pants strained against his legs were any indication. Of course, her attention wasn't centered on the shoulders wide enough to belong on a linebacker, or the powerful legs encased in crisp, perfectly ironed pants. Her gaze locked on the gun holstered against his hip before shifting to the badge tacked on the front of his leather jacket.

Slowly, her gaze made the long journey upward, taking in the dark hair peeking out from his official silver motorcycle helmet to his perfectly proportioned, perfectly sculpted face with just enough chin stubble to make a girl think dangerous thoughts.

She wasn't the only one staring. Peri's attention remained glued on the officer, which wasn't exactly a surprise. Men were like candy to Peri. So many to choose from, so little time to try them all.

Peri didn't need to worry, though. *She* wasn't the one who took her gaze off the road for one teeny, tiny second, causing her car to swerve *while* speeding. Worse still, Lily made the mistake right in front of the hottest cop she'd ever seen, and all because of the ridiculous bet she'd made with Peri.

With a shaky sigh, she hooked her arm around the back of her seat and grabbed her purse. "Grab my registration…" she hissed, all the while keeping her gaze fixed on her rearview mirror.

While Peri searched the glove box, Lily dug in her purse for her wallet. Finding the wallet wasn't an easy feat, considering she kept glancing at the rearview mirror at the approaching officer. How embarrassing. She considered herself an impeccable driver. She stayed within the speed limit, always wore her seatbelt, and never left home without her license…

Until today.

Dropping her head against the back of the seat, she closed her eyes. A groan of frustration rippled from her lips. Didn't it just figure she'd leave Buffalo without her license. Three hundred endless miles of highway behind them, countless twists and turns, climbing ever upward, on the winding mountainous country road, and her wallet was M.I.A.

She opened her eyes and peeked at the side view mirror. The approaching officer carried himself with an air of authority of a man used to getting what he wanted, and right now, he wanted her.

Lily's stomach clenched. *Not a ticket. Please, not a ticket.* Her mind scrolled through the mantra over and over. She wasn't opposed to a ticket, per se. After all, wrong was wrong. However, she could barely afford the impromptu vacation with Peri as it was. The added cost of a ticket, plus a rise in her insurance premiums would wreak havoc with her savings account. Especially now since her job had ended disastrously not two days past and with no future income in sight.

Frantic, she dug through her purse. Only, no errant license was tucked in a forgotten pocket. "Did you find my registration?" Her words rushed out in a choked whisper.

"No. I did find a ton of tampons, though." Peri waved a hand. "I'll tell you what, I know where I'm going the next time I need one."

Lily ignored her sister's stupid comment. "Are you sure my registration isn't in there?"

"Positive."

Great! No license or registration. Pasting on a whatever-did-I-do-wrong smile, Lily powered down the window.

Cool mountain breezes mingled with the pleasing scent of spicy cologne, warm sunshine, and early morning air. Lily scrutinized the officer. Up close, he was even more attractive. At least she thought he was. She wasn't positive, though. She was too busy noticing the fear in her eyes reflected by his mirrored sunglasses.

"Humanah…humanah…" Peri whispered. "Now I call that criminal justice."

Lily ground her teeth. Now was not the time for Peri's flirtations. She glanced downward. A pile of tampons covered the floor, exposed for anyone's perusal. "Put them away," she hissed, waving a finger toward the mess.

"What?"

She had no idea why she bothered with Peri. Her twin was too busy gearing up for possible flirting, not cleaning. Lily snapped her attention to the officer and gave him a hopeful smile. His face didn't soften an inch. Her smile wavered before fading. "Can I help you, officer?"

"Step out of the car, please." Opening the door, he stepped aside for her to exit.

She glanced at Peri. Her sister returned her look with a half shrug. Pinching her brows together, she faced the officer. "May I ask why?"

"Suspicion of driving under the influence."

A bubble of laughter welled up. She searched his face, praying for a glimmer of humor from him. Instead, his expression remained hard and implacable. Her stomach squeezed just a tiny bit and her laughter disappeared. "It's barely ten in the morning," Lily protested, flicking another quick glance in her sister's direction. "I assure you I'm not under the influence."

"Then you won't mind taking the test…"

Lily opened her mouth for a brief second before she snapped it shut. Tilting her head, she clenched her fingers around the steering wheel. Actually, she did mind. "And if I don't?"

His frown deepened. "Then I'll arrest you."

The knot in Lily's stomach tightened. Didn't it just figure? One ridiculous bet with her sister and she was stuck taking a stupid sobriety test proving her innocence. She had two options—comply or be arrested. She didn't relish either choice. "Fine. I'll take the test." She jabbed a finger at the latch of her seatbelt. As she stepped from the car, her lips formed a thin line.

She passed the test with flying colors. A smile of victory crossed her face as she slipped back into her car seat. "See, I told you I wasn't drunk."

"May I see your license and registration?"

Lily looked up from fastening her seatbelt. The knot in her stomach twisted a bit more at the hard, uncompromising look on his face.

Peri leaned over. "If I were you, I'd flirt," she whispered.

She narrowed her eyes at Peri. Her sister's suggestion didn't surprise Lily. At the ripe young age of ten, Peri had earned her first degree in flirting. By sixteen, she'd earned her second degree in perfecting the art of partying. Her third degree, and she assumed Peri's future career, was in Communications. Although, the kind of communication Peri excelled at was social discourse at parties which included flirting with men.

With a flick of her hand, Peri sighed. "Fine. Cry."

Lily clenched her jaw. Cry, and act all feminine and weak? No way, but even as she rejected the thought, a bubble of tears pooled in the back of her eyes. She forced them back, refusing to let them escape. Taking a deep, shaky breath, she faced the officer. "I think I left my license on the table at home."

His mouth thinned into a hard line. "I assume the table isn't in Aberdeen?"

The quaint little town where they were headed resembled in no way the exotic foreign location of the same name. The vacation town did have a lake, though, which Lily planned on enjoying while lounging on the sandy beach with cool, refreshing water lapping at her toes. Not through the bulletproof glass window in an airless jail cell. "Buffalo…" Her words trailed off.

The muscle flexed in the officer's cheek. Shifting his head, he glanced at Peri. "Do you have a license?"

A smile burst upon Peri's face. She batted her lashes and nodded. "I sure do."

Lily rolled her eyes at Peri's antics. Her flirting wasn't lost on the officer.

A flicker of a smile formed as he studied Peri. "Can I see *your* license?"

"Well…you see…" Peri gave the officer another winsome smile as one manicured nail made lazy circles on the dashboard. "I think mine is on the same table as hers."

"I see…" The smile disappeared and his mouth pinched into a hard line. With fingers beating a rapid tattoo on the pad of tickets, he studied the two women. He shifted his attention, his mirrored gaze landing on Lily. "How long will you be in Aberdeen?"

"For the summer." Lily swallowed back her nervousness. At least, she hoped she was here for just the summer. She didn't know if they could lock her up for not having a license. However, if they could, she was certain she'd be toast in a matter of days.

He studied her for a second longer. "Can someone send your license and registration here?"

Lily let out a shaky breath. "My mother."

"I'll let you off with a warning—" he began.

A burst of exhilaration and relief shot through Lily. She gave the officer a broad smile. "Oh, thank you." Her words rushed out. "I promise I've learned my lesson, and I'll have my mother send both right away. As soon as I arrive in town, I'll call her." She pressed the power control for the window,

Thrusting his hand on the open window, the officer stopped her action.

Lily's heart thumped, and a chill of fear slid down her spine. "Did you want something else?"

A brief smile flitted across his lips, disappearing as quickly as it arrived. "I'll allow you to drive, but only to town. Once you produce your license and registration, I'll lift the restriction. Do you understand?"

Gripping the steering wheel, she stiffened. How the heck did she move about without her car? "But—"

"Do you understand?" His face remained stern, without a hint of emotion.

A car whizzed past. The breeze ruffled her hair. With an impatient swipe of her hand, Lily shoved the strands out of her eyes. A smile twitched on his mouth. She ground her teeth together. "Yes, fine. I understand."

"You can bring your license and registration to the Aberdeen Police Station." Switching his attention, he waved his pad in Peri's direction. "No driving for you, either."

"Yes, sir." Peri batted her eyelashes.

The officer dismissed the action without a second glance. He turned, and with long strides, returned to his motorcycle.

Lily alternated between embarrassment with her sister's renewed attempt at flirting and fury at the officer's uncompromising attitude. For goodness sake, she'd made one small mistake. She wasn't a criminal, and she wouldn't let an egotistical, power-hungry, misogynist, small-town cop treat her accordingly.

She watched him drive onto the highway. Without

thinking, she whipped out her hand and gave him the finger. She smiled in satisfaction. His brake lights flashed. She whipped the smile off her face, ripping her hand back into the car.

"Oh my God, he saw you." Peri's laughter filled the car.

Closing her eyes, Lily dropped her head against the back of the seat in defeat. Talk about a terrible week. First, she discovered her boyfriend, Eric, boffing her roommate Janelle on the brand-new couch she'd just bought for the office, and then she lost her job. Of course, losing her job was a given, seeing as Eric was also her boss.

At the time, she hadn't thought her week getting any worse was possible. She was wrong. "Great. Now I'm stuck here with no escape." Lily started the car, taking extra care when she maneuvered onto the highway. She didn't want another run-in with the officer. "This vacation will be the worst ever."

"Are you kidding me? A hot cop stopped you." Peri's gaze remained fixed on the departing officer. "Now, that's a nice welcome to Aberdeen."

Chapter 2

On the drive to town, Lily made her decision. If that cop thought she'd allow his reprehensible behavior, he was in for a rude awakening. She'd already dealt with one man who was a cad. She wouldn't accept the same behavior from another. Even if that man was a cop. "As soon as I arrive in town, I'm going to the police station."

Aberdeen. The town time forgot. Small. Quaint. Old. Exactly as she remembered. Ubiquitous antique shops, family-owned restaurants, and charming boutiques dotted the town. The Aberdeen National Bank sat in the same place as fifteen-years ago. Heck, Johnson's Pharmacy, a sentinel on the corner of Woodland and Main, was still in its same spot.

"Right on. I knew you thought the cop was hot." Peri's head bobbed just a bit, and a slow smile crossed her face.

Lily frowned. Again, her sister was way off base. "I'm not stopping because he's hot. I'm stopping to report him."

"For what?" Peri's hands shot upward.

"For harassing me."

"He didn't harass you." Peri waved a hand. "He was doing his job."

Tightening her grip on the steering wheel, Lily glared at Peri. "Harassment includes intimidation, and I felt intimidated." Her words weren't an exaggeration, either. Jail intimidated her. Plus, the way he casually suggested the possibility was almost as if he was eager to lock her up. "Besides, I think he violated my civil rights."

"He can violate my rights any day." Peri winked.

Lily rolled her eyes. Peri always got right to the heart of the matter. "Well, good for you. Personally, I never again want to see the egotistical, power-hungry cop."

"I think you've lost your mind." Peri turned away from the window. "Why don't you just forget this stupid complaint?"

"I can't let it go because my civic responsibility is to report him." Lily stopped at the traffic light.

A long, drawn-out sigh escaped from Peri. "Fine. If I can't change your mind, can we at least stop for lunch before you go to jail?"

Lily's stomach lurched. Before, she had almost convinced herself the officer's threat was just an intimidation tactic. Now, with Peri echoing her thoughts...Her fingers tightened their grip on the steering wheel. "You don't really think I can be arrested, do you?"

Peri gazed out the window. "Aberdeen's a small town. What do you think?"

Lily scanned the area. Peri was right. This town was a place where every resident probably knew each other. The odds they would believe the words of a visitor had to be slim to none.

Maybe she should ignore the whole thing. Only a part of her, a large part of her, refused to forget the humiliation at his hands. If doing her civic responsibility resulted in jail, then so be it. She'd be darned, though, if she'd do jail time on an empty stomach. "Sure. Why not. Where do you want to eat?"

"How about Burger, Burger, Burger?"

If Lily ranked places to eat, Burger, Burger, Burger wouldn't make the top-ten list. Or the top twenty. Heck, she doubted she'd put the restaurant on her top one-hundred list. However, in a town the size of Aberdeen, choices were few and far between. As they waited for the light to change, she scanned the shops and restaurants.

She spotted the police station right away. It was just down the street, right next to Karla's Kitchen. Lily figured Karla's Kitchen was a better option than Burger, Burger, Burger. However, the restaurant's proximity to the station was too close for Lily's peace of mind. Did she really want a showdown in the local café with the very cop she intended to report? Not hardly. "Eating all this fat better not make me sick."

"Are you kidding me? We're talking fine American food here. Getting sick is just not possible." Peri rubbed her hands together.

Burger, Burger, Burger might serve All-American food, but the chain in Aberdeen was filthy. The scuffed burnt orange linoleum floors were sticky. The condiment counter, smothered in ketchup and mustard, resembled a Jackson Pollock painting. The soda station was a toxic wasteland of discarded napkins and straw wrappers, saturated in a kaleidoscope of spilled liquids. If she wasn't careful, her white shorts were destined for ruination.

Keeping a safe distance between herself and the counter, Lily placed her order. "I better not get food poisoning, either." She snatched the grease-laden bag of food from the cashier. She could live without the humiliation of making a compliant while bent at the waist with stomach cramps and diarrhea. "We'll eat in the car. I don't want to touch anything in here." She started for the exit.

"Fine by me." Peri grabbed a greasy, limp French fry from her bag.

Lily ate her chicken sandwich in record time during the short drive to the police station. She didn't hurry through her grilled chicken sandwich because it was delicious. Rather, she ate it quickly because she was afraid the officer would spot her eating and driving. With her luck, he'd probably arrest her for reckless driving or endangering others.

Along Pecan Avenue sat a row of brick buildings of varying heights with parking spaces angling in toward the sidewalk. Only one lonely spot was available and that one spot just happened to sit right in front of the police station.

Munching on a French fry slathered in ketchup, Lily considered the tall, imposing, red brick station. A large plate glass window filled most of the front. To the left sat a half dozen steps leading to the main doors. Except for the old man behind the window, the place appeared deserted. Her stomach churned. She suspected the sick feeling had little to do with the lunch she ate and more about reporting of the officer.

Ignoring the quivering of her stomach, Lily tossed the empty sandwich wrapper into the bag, and grabbed her purse. A frown creased her face at the wrinkled receipts, crumpled tissues, debit and credit cards, and a ton of lip glosses discarded within the cluttered depths.

Everything except her wallet with her license and registration. Now, because of her forgetfulness, she was forced to do something she would rather not.

"Are you primping for your officer?" A line of grease slid down Peri's chin.

Lily curled her lip in disgust as she dropped the visor. She ignored the barb and opened the tube of lip gloss. "First off, he's not *my* officer."

"Really?" Peri chewed her burger. "I'm all for hot sexy officers."

She finished glossing her lips. "The lip gloss is to appear respectable."

"For your officer..." Peri mocked.

Rolling her eyes, Lily snapped shut the visor. "I believe you should project a professional appearance when you file a complaint about a public official." *Jeez, didn't Peri know anything?* "Are you coming or not?"

Peri flicked a quick glance to the station window and frowned. "I think I'll wait here."

"Suit yourself." Hiding her disappointment, Lily grabbed the door handle. She never expected a ton of help from Peri, but two people with the same complaint was better than one.

"If I were you, I'd flirt with the old man." Peri nodded in the direction of the building.

Lily glanced toward the window. "What's wrong with you? I'm not here to hit on him. I'm here to demand justice." She took a deep breath to steel her nerves before stepping from her car. She pointed a warning finger. "Do *not* make a mess."

Peri's gaze slid over Lily. "Yeah, okay but you might..."

Lily slammed the door shut before Peri mentioned

flirting again. She marched up the steps of the station. At the top, she took a breath before opening the door and stepping inside the building.

The police station was dim and cool inside. Faded beige paint covered the walls, and the floors were an industrial gray. A bench sat against one wall, and a large bulletin board covered with wanted posters hung on another.

The old man sitting behind a desk, stared at a magazine. The nameplate on the desk read Officer Abe Drummond.

He didn't pause in his reading when she stepped into the room. Spotting the bell on the counter, Lily rang it.

Abe jumped a foot in the air. A scowl scarred his face. "What do you want?"

His manner was as abrupt and rude as the officer who stopped her. His insulting behavior didn't surprise her. After all, what did she expect from small-town police? They probably ran the town similar to the Gestapo. She matched his manner with a brusque glare. "I'm here to report one of your officers."

Sighing, Abe dug out a pad of paper from his drawer. "What's his name?"

"I have no idea." Lily frowned, realizing she'd forgotten his name. Then again, at the time, his name wasn't her first concern. "He didn't tell me."

Abe's scowl deepened. "Can you at least describe him?"

Yeah, she wanted to say. He was beyond hot, with hair the color of midnight, a body women noticed, and enough stubble on his face to make a woman's fingers itch to touch it. She pushed the dangerous thought aside. "I don't know. Maybe six one, black hair…"

She could feel her face heating and heard the way her voice rose just an octave higher in pitch. She hoped Abe didn't notice either. Taking a deep breath to calm her nerves and collect her thoughts, Lily cleared her throat, trying to recall something about the officer other than his attractiveness. Inspiration struck. A smile spread across her face. "He was on a motorcycle. Does that help?"

Abe's eyes widened, and his brows shot upward as he scratched his chin. "A motorcycle, you say? Just outside of town, on Route 87?"

Lily breathed a sigh of relief. "Do you know who I'm talking about?"

"I do." He smirked. "What's your complaint?"

Pleased by the sudden interest in the man's gaze, Lily smiled. The tension in her body eased. She was right to report this officer. Surely, something positive would come from her action. "He harassed me."

Snapping wide his eyes, Abe whistled. "Sexual harassment…has to be a first for him."

She waved her hands, stopping him. "Oh no, not that kind of harassment. Just the plain old regular kind of a harassment."

The frown returned. "Are you sure?"

"Sorry," she returned in a sheepish voice and shrugged.

With another sigh, he grabbed a pencil from his cup. "Go ahead and tell me what he 'did.'"

Stiffening at his use of air quotes, she straightened her shoulders and glared. "He accused me of being drunk." Hearing the door opening behind her, Lily smiled. Peri would vindicate her. She swung an arm toward the door. "Here's my sister. She can verify my—"

The words died on her lips. Her sister wasn't in the doorway, but a man too attractive to be true. Tall, dark, and handsome—the perfect cliché to describe him. She had no idea what eye color hid behind the mirror sunglasses of the irritating officer who stopped her, but *this* officer's eyes were a deep, rich brown similar to the color of wet autumn leaves. Unlike the other officer, *he* didn't have the hard, angry demeanor about him. No, this officer had a welcoming smile and kindness in his eyes. A hint of curiosity lurked within their depths, too.

Self-conscious, she patted her hair, irritated she hadn't taken more time to straighten herself, and all because of Peri's teasing. At least, she put on some lip gloss.

"Can I help you with something?"

His voice was all smooth and sensual, and completely opposite the officer who stopped her. *His* voice had been hard and unyielding. This officer's voice was as a warm as a summer breeze at night, and with his impossibly good looks, Lily thanked the Lord her hand gripped the counter. Otherwise, she just might fall over at the sight of such an impossibly handsome man. "I...ah..." She licked her lips, completely forgetting her reason for being here.

One dark brow cocked upward. "Yes?"

Abe closed his eyes, and his mouth thinned into a frown. A puff of breath erupted from him. "Oh, for God's sakes. She wants to file a complaint, Ben."

Ben's brows rose. Smiling, he turned his attention back to Lily. "Is that right, Abe?" He strolled to the counter, his gaze fixed on her. "Exactly what is this complaint?"

She could drown in the depths of his eyes. She licked her lips and prayed to the Lord she'd keep cool and not do something stupid. Such as bursting into laughter or chattering like a crazy monkey.

What she really wanted was to ignore her attraction and focus on the conversation. However, concentrating was nearly impossible, since all she wanted was to gawk at the gorgeous man. When his head tilted just a bit, she realized he caught her staring. Her face heated up.

"Harassment." Abe shot a frown in her direction. "For falsely accusing her of being drunk."

Lily returned his frown with one of her own. She didn't appreciate the fact he thought she'd made up this story. Well, Ben would hear *her* version of events, which were the *correct* version. "It's true. I mean, I did swerve a tiny bit on the road. As I explained to Officer Drummond, here, I wasn't drunk. I mean, seriously, does anything about me suggest I'm drunk?" She threw her arms wide.

Ben's gaze slid downward, taking in every inch of her body, from the top of her head right down to the tips of her toes, and making plenty of stops in between. Lily could feel her face burning at his careful inspection. She didn't know whether she was flattered or furious at his overt action.

"Nope. Not to me." He turned to Abe. "What do you think, Abe?"

Abe rolled his eyes. "Oh, for God's sake." He picked up his pencil and magazine. "Seeing as you're back from lunch, I'll let you take care of it."

A smile spread across Ben's face as his fingers

circled her elbow. He guided her toward an office off the lobby. "So, Miss…?"

His palm warmed her flesh, causing jolts of electricity to course through her veins. She shoved aside the nervousness bubbling within her. "Evans. Lily Evans."

"Lily Evans. Great. Ben Jordan." He waved a hand toward the worn upholstered chair in front of a scarred wooden desk. "Tell me, what did this officer do?"

Dropping into the proffered seat, she clasped her hands in her lap. By the time she settled, he was already sitting on the edge of the desk, his hooded gaze studying her. She took quick note of his long legs stretched out in front of him, and the way his deep blue shirt strained as he crossed his arms over his chest. She couldn't help wondering if his body was as hard as it appeared.

His smile gave her encouragement. She cleared her throat, ignoring the rolling of her stomach. "He made me take a sobriety test." She waited for the officer's outraged reaction. Instead, he continued to stare, which only increased her nervousness. She swallowed before continuing. "He was rude. Obnoxious, really."

"I see." He tapped one finger on the edge of the desk. "Did he do anything else?"

No matter how hard she tried, she couldn't break her stare. "He told me I couldn't drive in town."

Ben scratched his chin. "Really? I wonder why?"

She watched in fascination the muscles tightening in his biceps. The silence dragged on. Shifting her gaze from his arm, Lily caught him studying her with a soft smile. Her blush deepened. "I forgot my license at home." She gave him an apologetic smile. "But it's not as if I don't have one. I just didn't have one *with* me. I tried to explain. He refused to listen, acting as if I broke the law or something."

"I see your concern." Ben crossed his arms over his chest. "However, I'm sorry to tell you, Miss Evans, you do not have a complaint. Proper protocol was followed. You *did* swerve, and you *didn't* have a license. Any officer would do the same."

Lily tightened her fingers on the armrests. Peri was right. She wouldn't see justice in this town. If she accepted his reason, he would get away with sweeping what she considered a valid concern under the carpet.

She jumped from her chair, causing the back of her knees to catch on the edge of the seat. She thrust forward straight into his outstretched arms. Her palms flattened against his chest, and through the thin fabric of his shirt, she felt his muscles flex, as his fingers curled around her waist.

She caught her breath. Up close, his eyes were even darker. Warmer too. She may have noticed his eyes first. Her mind, though, registered in seconds flat how incredible his body felt against hers. Solid, just as she'd imagined.

Girls dreamt of men like him. That is, until Lily remembered how he'd easily dismissed her case. "My sister warned me about you people." She shoved herself away. "You're all the same. You're just small-town cops bullying innocent people. Well, I won't stand for this behavior. I will report you to the police chief." She started for the door.

"Miss Evans?"

The casual way he spoke her name didn't fool Lily, neither did the hard edge of steel in his voice. She stiffened before facing him. The warmth in his eyes had faded and the once-breathtaking smile disappeared into a scowl. He reminded her of granite, all hard, implacable, and determined. His whole demeanor screamed police officer.

"I'd be careful of your accusations." His stare locked with hers. "Moreover, I'd suggest you don't flip me off, because the next time, I *will* arrest you."

Her stomach dropped, and her knees nearly buckled at his words. Of course! How had she not recognized his voice? Or his frown, for that matter. They were the same as the officer who stopped her. Now, because of her nervousness and his attractiveness, she appeared foolish, not once, but twice in less than an hour.

Lily didn't waste any time leaving the police station. Before he could stop her, she raced past the surprised Abe, out of the building, and into her car. Only after fastening her seatbelt did she remember she hadn't asked for the police chief.

Chapter 3

Lily tried to put the whole encounter from her mind. She wasn't successful. Two days later and the event was still fresh in her thoughts. What made the situation even worse was the fact she'd learned the only topic of conversation in town was her altercation with Ben.

She was beyond embarrassed. If she'd been any other person, she might have jumped into her car and driven back to Buffalo. However, she couldn't for two reasons. One, she didn't have her license, and she remembered only too well Ben's order. And two, and quite possibly more important, she refused to allow him to chase her from town. So, instead of running away, she went running.

Usually, running helped her remove unwanted thoughts. Only, no matter how far she jogged or how hard she tried, the memory of Ben came back to haunt her, which was really quite vexing. Of course, eliminating him from her thoughts was a tiny problem. Her bigger issue was, according to Betty, the owner of the coffee house, when someone caught Ben's attention, he was relentless in his pursuit. One thing Lily knew for certain, she had definitely caught his attention, and not in a good way either. Now, lucky her, she was on the radar of a hot, vindictive cop.

Great. Just great.

Disgusted with the whole thing, Lily dragged herself into the house.

With her usual impeccable timing, Peri burst into the kitchen just as Lily shut the kitchen door. She thrust a skimpy, black dress and a pair of black wedges in Lily's face. "Here, I picked these for you to wear."

Shoving the items aside, Lily headed to the kitchen sink. She grabbed a cup from the cupboard and poured herself a cold glass of water before she answered. "For what?"

Peri whipped out a piece of paper. "For this." She thrust the sheet in Lily's direction.

Lily dismissed the flyer detailing the town's Beer and Brat Festival. She'd read the same sign yesterday when they'd gone to Betty's Cafe for coffee. The fact Peri actually thought she'd go, surprised her. Despite being twins, Peri still had the ability to shock her. "You're kidding, right?"

"I knew you'd say no." Peri plopped into a chair next to the white laminate kitchen table. Her fingers tapped against the table's silver flecked surface. "Please tell me you're not refusing because of yesterday."

Okay, so Peri's comment made Lily sound afraid. However, Peri wasn't the one who had a target on her back. Lily couldn't take any more chances. "Let's just say I'd rather not roll the dice." She set the paper on the counter. "Jail is not my thing."

"Oh please. You don't believe he'd throw you in jail, do you?"

Remembering the look in Ben's gaze caused a kaleidoscope of butterflies to swirl in her stomach…warm, hard, and utterly thrilling. "You didn't see him at the police station. Nothing about him suggested he was kidding."

"Of course, he wasn't." Peri's hands flew upward. "He's supposed to be serious. Trust me though, he has no authority to arrest you. He's highway patrol."

Lily did a double take. "He's what?"

"Highway patrol." Peri leaned back in her chair and smiled. "Ben patrols the highways, not the city streets. He can't do anything unless he stops you again outside of town."

Tapping her fingers on the countertop, Lily debated Peri's words. Was her sister right and he didn't have any authority in town? If this was the case, she played right into his hands, and that possibility was completely unacceptable. Still, doubt nibbled at the back of her mind. "If that's true, why was he at the police station yesterday?"

Peri flitted her hand in the air. "How many highway patrol stations do you think are between here and Albany? I bet the local police station *is* their headquarters."

Peri had a point. Albany was an hour or more away. Plus, he had stopped her near Aberdeen. "I guess that's possible." She picked up the paper and studied it again.

"Listen, even if he's at the festival and he noticed you are driving, he can't do anything about it, because he'll be out of his jurisdiction," Peri added.

An image of Ben flashed through Lily's mind. She could picture his smug smile at her naiveté, knowing he wasn't authorized to restrict her driving in town. How gullible did he think she was? The rest of the women in town might bow to his every command, but not her. She snatched the dress and shoes off the table. Excitement built inside her. "You're right. We'll go."

"And you're driving."

A moment's worth of hesitation filled Lily. Could she risk the cost of a ticket if caught? Of course, what were the odds of her getting stopped again? They were in town now. Not on an open highway. If she followed the speed limit she would be okay. She dismissed her initial doubt. "Fine. I'll drive."

"Now you're talking."

With the outfit and shoes in hand, she hurried into her bedroom. Dressing wasn't easy, considering most of her time was spent either forcing on the dress or keeping the thing in place. Getting on the dress proved the easier of the two. The outfit had a mind of its own. If she yanked on the hem of the skirt, her breasts nearly popped out of the low scooped neckline. When she tugged on the top, the hem rode so high she feared she would be arrested for indecent exposure.

She didn't dare change into something less daring because daring wasn't T-shirts and shorts. Daring was skin-tight black dresses and the mile-high platforms. Peri, on the other hand, loved the exposure a skimpy outfit offered. Case in point was the gold dress she'd shimmied on. If Lily didn't know better, she would have assumed the material was attached to Peri's skin with super glue. The scraps of fabric Peri called a dress exposed more flesh than hid. Comparing shoes, Lily's three-inch wedges were the Pyrenees, and Peri's glittery gold four-inch spikes were Mount Everest. Either way, her feet begged for a flat pair of sandals. "You do realize what a Beer and Brat Festival is, right?"

"Yeah. What's your point?" Peri asked, gliding down the stairs.

Rolling her eyes, Lily strolled into the kitchen. "My point is no one else will be dressed like us."

"Which *is* the whole point. We *want* to be noticed," Peri huffed, following behind.

Peri might enjoy all the spotlight. She did not. Grabbing her keys and money, Lily opened the door. "If you're wrong about me driving, and I am thrown in jail, you're going with me."

A saucy smile slid across Peri's face. She winked. "Great. I've always wanted to get locked up." She followed Lily outside.

The smell of fresh-cut grass and the sweet scent of roses greeted them.

Peri let out a low whistle. With her well-honed radar, she fixed her attention on the yard behind their house. "Well, well, well, what do we have here?"

Lily followed the direction of Peri's gaze. Across the two yards stood one incredible gift from heaven. Tall, broad-shouldered with tanned abs as flat and hard as granite, and arms brawny enough to make any woman swoon. He'd lost his shirt somewhere. Neither woman cared as they ogled him while he mowed his lawn.

"Yum," Peri murmured.

Lily glanced at Peri. Her sister personified a feral cat ready to pounce on her next meal. Shaking her head, she tucked the key beneath the coarse doormat, before standing and brushing the dirt off her palms. "Hey, you don't think he caught where we hid the house key, do you?"

"I sure hope so." Peri hurried down the porch steps. "I'd love for him to break into our house. Preferably when I'm here."

Strolling toward the car, Lily ignored Peri's comment. Opening the door, she noticed a red stain on the driver's seat of her new car. She snapped her head up. "What the heck happened here?"

Peri slipped into the passenger seat. "Remember when you reported Ben? You had ketchup smeared all over your shorts. I tried warning you, but you ignored me."

Great! Here is a perfect example on the importance of checking my clothing before throwing them in the wash. Bad things happen. How embarrassing. She'd confronted him looking like a mess.

Grabbing her seatbelt, Peri shook her head. "Let me tell you the look was bad."

Not appreciating her astute observation, Lily glowered and dropped into the driver's seat.

Peri's face suddenly lit. "Hey, wouldn't it be hilarious if he noticed the ketchup on your butt and thought you had your period?"

Lily's stomach plunged. *Hilarious?* If Peri thought ketchup masquerading as a period was amusing, then her sense of humor was warped. No woman wanted a man to know she had her monthly. Especially, if the man was her archenemy, Ben Jordan. He'd probably blame her complaint on PMS, or something just as offensive. He certainly wouldn't blame himself. Men with over-inflated egos never took responsibility. Right on the heels of that horrible thought came another, even more mortifying. She whipped around her head. "You don't think he'll tell the other cops, do you?"

Peri rolled her eyes. "Are you kidding me? He's not twelve. Trust me, he won't talk. Women's periods are not something men *want* to discuss."

Relief washed over Lily. She jammed the key in the ignition and started the engine "You're right. I'm overreacting. Let's just go and enjoy ourselves."

Chapter 4

Lily was not having fun. In fact, if she ranked the worst times in her life, tonight would top the list. The nightmare began the minute they arrived at the festival, and discovered the parking area almost full. The one measly spot was all the way in the back, directly across the street from the police station. A bit too close to Ben for her comfort.

As if things weren't bad enough, Lily realized she had no pockets or purse to put the key. Clutching the keys in her palm, she started for the tents. "I guess I'll just hold them."

Peri caught her arm. "Don't be silly. You can't carry the keys all night. What if you drop them inside the tent? You could be trampled picking them up." She pointed toward the ground. "Just hide them under that rock. You won't lose them there."

The rock Peri indicated, was just behind her front driver tire, hidden by a clump of tire-squashed grass. "I don't know…"

"Seriously, look around." Peri fanned out a hand. "Who will know?"

Her sister had a point. No one paid them a bit of attention. Plus, carrying the keys would be annoying. Before she could change her mind, she tucked the key under the rock.

As they cut across the field, the smell of burning

charcoal, sizzling brats, and cigarette smoke filled the air. Several large, white tarps with tall steel poles roped together making an oversized tent sat near the side of the City Hall building and occupied a wide portion of the open park.

Lily searched the area. Apprehension churned in her stomach. Everyone, absolutely *everyone,* at the festival had dressed in the very outfit she longed to wear—shorts, T-shirt, and flip-flops. She could feel the livid glances of the women they passed, and even dirtier leers from the men. Peri loved every minute. She, not even a little.

The tent was packed with people. Fighting their way through the crush, they finally found a tiny pocket beside two women. Lily hadn't planned on eavesdropping on their conversation. Ignoring them was impossible, though. Not only did they speak in loud tones, but their gossip was just too scintillating to ignore. When the women mentioned rent-a-cops, alarms rang in her thoughts. She followed their gaze in the direction of their appreciative stare. Her stomach lurched in recognition.

Ben stood just a scant crowd away, surrounded by a group of people. A few were men. Most were women. Big surprise. From her short time in town, Lily heard his name bubbling on the lips of the single women. A few of the married ones, too.

A low fire burned in the pit of her stomach. Harassing her was bad enough, but discovering her nemesis—the man who humiliated twice—wasn't an actual cop, but instead he was a rent-a-cop the town hired for the summer, was too much. Now, she was incensed.

Lily had no doubt who the women were discussing. They certainly weren't comparing notes on the tall blond man by Ben's side. The very same man she and Peri spotted two hours earlier behind their house, mowing his lawn. He could *never* be considered a cop. A surfer? Maybe. A model? Definitely. A cop, though? Never. Not with those mischievous blue eyes, and a smile worthy of melting a woman's heart.

The man standing in front of Ben couldn't be the one they discussed, either. He was too ordinary, too round, and too dull to be confused with a cop. Even a rent-a-cop.

Obviously, their admiring glances were directed on Ben. He wore his power like a second skin as he stood with his back against the chain link fence, his gaze skipping from the many women surrounding him before dismissing them. He made it apparent he was too powerful to deal with the riff-raff.

Something snapped inside her. Lily didn't know whether it was because of his cavalier attitude toward the women, his oversized ego, or even her need to right a wrong. Whatever the reason, she was determined he'd know she wouldn't be bullied.

Shoving her way through the crowds, she didn't stop until she faced him. Moving her gaze past his massive chest, his powerful shoulders, the squared chin with a dusting of stubble, to the dark, fathomless eyes and still, he didn't notice her. Lily ignored her quaking legs in the three-inch platforms, praying she appeared braver than she felt.

The blond-haired man standing beside Ben whistled softly.

Ben straightened, his gaze fixed on her, as he

stepped from the temporary fence. Disentangling his arm from the grip of the beautiful cinnamon-haired woman, he ran his gaze the length of Lily, from the top of her head, straight to the tips of her toes, resting on several stops in between.

Her body hummed to life with the intensity of his gaze. Heat raced up her neck. How dare he intimidate her. Did the obnoxious man think she'd fall at his feet in gratitude because he bestowed a glance in her direction? Well, he would soon learn she wasn't the type of woman to fall at *any* man's feet. She lifted her chin.

His gaze landed on her pink glossed lips for a second. His lips curled into a slow smile.

Lily's pulse raced as his scorching gaze met hers, causing last night's hot, steamy dream to flash through her memory. Why was the man so darn handsome?

"Can I help you with something, sweetheart?" He drew out the question in a long, slow drawl.

Stiffening, Lily shot him a hot glare. Did he have a ton of women at his disposal that he couldn't keep track of them, so he used such an insulting word? "First off, I'm not your *sweetheart*." She fisted her hands at her side. "I'm the woman you stopped for speeding. The one you forced to take a sobriety test. And *you*..."

She drew out the moment. A feeling of satisfaction rose. She tasted the words on her tongue. They were full and rich, and oh, so delicious. She wanted to savor the moment a second longer before she dropped the bomb. When his brow rose, Lily didn't wait any longer. "*You* are nothing more than a rent-a-cop."

Her announcement achieved the reaction she'd intended. Unfortunately, the gasp didn't rumble from

Ben as she expected, but from the crowd surrounding them.

The balding man's face flushed a deep crimson red.

Only the blond-haired man chuckled at Lily's announcement.

Ben straightened and stepped from the fence. He crossed his arms over his chest and stared downward. "What did you just call me?"

His stony gaze locked with hers. Lily's determination faltered, and the desire to flee consumed her. She ignored the urge. "I said, you're just a rent-a-cop. You harass the common people like you're all-powerful. When, in fact, you have no power at all." Satisfied she'd completed her goal, Lily turned to leave.

Peri stood behind her. A smile, as broad as Ben's shoulders, split her face. "Lily, Ben's not a rent-a-cop."

"Of course, he is." Even as Lily spoke the words, warning bells sounded in her head. She ignored them, knowing she was right. "I heard those women. Their gazes were glued on him when they mentioned rent-a-cops."

Shaking her head, Peri pointed to the bald man with the bright red face. "No, *he* was the one who held their attention."

He gave her a sheepish wave. Lily swung her gaze to Ben. He thrust out his hand, and a smile reminiscent of victory slid across his face. A knot formed in her stomach.

"A pleasure to see you again, Miss Evans," he drawled. "I'm Ben Jordan. The Police Chief."

From the amusement thick in his voice, Lily knew tonight was officially her worst night ever.

Chapter 5

The bluest eyes Ben had ever encountered met his gaze. Snapping blue eyes, he qualified, taking in every nuance of her body. From the top of her shimmery blonde hair tousled in disarray, to lips shiny with gloss, down her body filled with curves in all the right places. Only two possible words described Lily Evans— beautiful and sexy. They were the top two qualities he admired most in a woman. "Do you want to see my badge?"

A smile creased his face. She dropped her gaze. A rosy pink flush covered her cheeks at the sight of the badge clipped to his belt, right next to his holstered gun. Being called a rent-a-cop was a blow to his ego. He'd worked long and hard for the title of the Police Chief. Being new to town, she wouldn't know this information. He decided he'd be the bigger person and let the slight go. He did expect her to admit her mistake, though. Or apologize at the very least.

Neither came. Instead, to his amazement, she disappeared into the crowd. He wasn't about to let her escape. He started after her when the woman almost identical to Lily stopped him. Her twin. The flirt from the other day. She smiled, with eyes nearly the same color as Lily's.

"If you're going after Lily. Please tell her I'll find my way home."

He didn't have a chance to ask her plans. Her attention had already shifted to Dax. Ben had no doubt her tactics would be far more successful with Dax than himself.

Now her sister…

Elbowing his way through the crowd, Ben caught her just as a drunk grabbed her arm. He roughly shoved the man aside then turning to Lily, he glared. "Going somewhere?"

Lily spun, her eyes wide. Her mouth opened for a second before snapping shut. Instead of answering, she turned.

Her audacity stunned him. She'd dismissed him a second time in as many minutes. Lesser men lacked the courage to do the same. He wouldn't allow her to escape a third time. He blocked her retreat. "Not so fast. Tell me, how did you arrive at the festival?"

Silence hung heavy between them. Their gazes locked in a defiant challenge. He could see her debating whether to reply or not. Ben refused to allow her to leave until he obtained his answers.

After a moment, an explosion of air burst from her. She threw her hands in the air. "Fine. We walked. Now if you don't mind, I want to leave." She turned.

He didn't know what shocked him more. The fact she'd walked to the festival, or that she thought he'd let her walk home in the skimpiest dress he had the pleasure of seeing on a night filled with drunks. Lily Evans might not know the dangers lurking in the night, but Ben did. "Sweetheart, I'm not letting you go anywhere dressed as you are."

Two bright red spots colored Lily's cheeks. "What's wrong with my dress?"

Her words caught him by surprise. He figured she'd protest his order, not his comment about her dress. Clearly, she didn't understand her effect on men. He did, though, and he wasn't about to let her come to harm. His job was to keep everyone safe, including infuriating, insulting, sexy women like the one arguing with him right now. "Absolutely nothing." He took hold of her elbow. The action earned him a hot glare. Ben didn't care. He drew her along beside him. "I'm not the only man who thinks it, either, and I'm not about to let you tempt them."

"Hey, just because you're the police chief doesn't mean you can tell me what I can do."

Had he not been so furious, he might have found her anger humorous. "I disagree."

"Don't lump me in with the rest of the women here," Lily ground out. "I won't fall at your feet and bend to your wishes. I'd rather slit my wrist with a butter knife and sit in a hot tub of water."

Ben laughed. Her apparent aversion was a first. A dozen or more women stood inside the tent, begging for half the attention he gave Lily, and she behaved as if he was a pariah. "You're being a bit dramatic, don't you think?"

"Maybe." Lily shrugged. "But far preferable than the alternative."

"Then you'll be relieved to know, the only thing I intend is to take you home. To *your* home," he added for clarification.

Her mouth opened and closed, as heat colored her face.

Clearly, she expected a different response. She wasn't far off in her thinking. Tempted though he was to charm her into his bed, he dismissed the idea, escorting her out into the cloudy night. Walking side by side, he guided her through the row of cars toward his vehicle. He glanced down. Her head was lowered and she chewed her lip. He stopped. "Is something wrong?"

"Officer Jordan, if you'd just let me go. I can walk home…"

"Ben."

Her brow furrowed. "What?"

"You can call me Ben." He stopped beside his truck and rested his hand on the handle. Sliding his gaze across the area, he caught sight of an all-too-familiar red sports car. Fire burned through his veins. Tightening his grip on the door handle, he turned in her direction. "You walked here?"

"Yup. All the way." She folded together her hands. "I'm not allowed to drive, remember?"

She rewarded him with a smile, so innocent it could belong on a face of a baby. A muscle flexed in his cheek. "Yes. I do remember. I just wondered if you did." He lifted her. In less than a second, Ben registered the softness of her body and the sensual, floral scent caressing her skin. A second later, her shoulder clipped his nose. As a burst of light exploded behind his eyes he nearly dropped her. Instead, he tightened his grip as he carefully set her on the running board, before clutching his nose.

"Oh my gosh. I'm sorry." Lily gently touched his cheek with her finger. "Are you okay?"

He glared before checking his nose for blood. He was surprised he didn't find any. A bag of rocks slamming into his nose would be softer than her shoulder. "I don't think you broke my nose."

"You have only yourself to blame if it is."

Ben gritted his teeth. "Excuse me?"

"Well, how was I to know you would grab me? You can't expect me not to react." Lily tugged at the hem of her skirt.

Irritation at her criticism warred with the disappointment at the loss of toned thighs disappearing from view. He was done playing games. He pointed a finger across the lot. "Is that your car?"

"Of course not." Lily lifted her chin. "I told you I walked here."

The muscle in Ben's cheek flexed again. "Are you sticking with that story?"

"What story?"

Sincerity stared back. He didn't buy her act for a minute. He lifted her off the running board. Taking hold of her hand, he towed her across the parking lot, not stopping until they stood behind the car. He pointed to the license plate. In bold letters, the plate read *All Mine.* "Do you still believe this car isn't yours?"

"Okay, fine. It's my car." Lily threw her hands upward. "You're gonna arrest me now, aren't you?"

"I should. I won't, though." He pinched his mouth together. He'd lost count the number of women who thought they could sway his decision with a bat of their lashes or seductive smile. She might be cute. However, he wasn't interested in her or cutting her a break. He thrust out his palm. "I will take your keys, though."

"I don't have them."

Again, she batted her eyelashes. Her attempt at flirting wouldn't work. Instead, he let his gaze wander over every inch of her body-clinging outfit, enjoying the enticing image she made. No keys tucked beneath her dress competed for attention with the rest of her assets. Her sister didn't have them, either. If possible, her attire was skimpier and tighter than Lily's. "Sweetheart, I know the car didn't drive here by itself."

Lily snapped her brows downward. "I told you not to call me sweetheart." She pinched her lips together for just a moment before finally exhaling a deep breath. "Fine. They're underneath the rock."

Jerking back his head, Ben clenched his jaw and flattened his lips into a thin line. Only those who wanted their car stolen, or the clinically insane, left their keys hidden beneath a rock. Seeing as Lily seemed rather fond of her vehicle, he concluded she was insane. For a split second, he considered leaving the keys under the rock, just to teach her a lesson. He didn't, though, knowing the amount of paperwork needed if her car was stolen. He refused to subject his men to extra work because of her carelessness.

A sigh of exasperation escaped him as he lifted the rock Lily pointed to. Sure enough, lying on top the dirt sat the car key. Grabbing the key, Ben stood. He ignored her outstretched palm, dropping the key in his pocket. He started toward his vehicle. An outraged gasp sounded.

"Hey, those are mine."

Ben stopped beside the black truck, giving Lily time to catch up. Ignoring her demand, he picked her up, carefully keeping his nose from her shoulder, before dropping her onto the front passenger seat. "Now, they're mine." He slammed the door before she could challenge him.

A look of deep contemplation was on her face when he climbed into the driver's seat. He could just imagine what flimsy excuse she'd created.

She faced him. "You should know, I had an excellent reason for driving."

He wanted to laugh. The woman didn't have a poker face. "Oh?" The silence stretched for just a moment before her eyes sparkled, and a breathtaking smile split her face.

"We drove because of our outfits. You know…less chance of anything bad happening."

He burst into laughter. He'd give her credit. She certainly enjoyed keeping a man on his toes. "Yet, you intended to walk home *alone* at night in it?"

"Okay, fine." A sigh rippled from Lily. "I drove because I didn't think you'd be here. If I had known you were the Chief of Police, I wouldn't have run the risk of driving."

"Those words might be the first truthful thing you've told me since we've met." He started the ignition before facing her. "You know, you could have stayed home and not risked getting caught at all."

Staring at her lap, she let out a soft sigh. "I suppose." She peered his way, tilting her head slightly. "So, you'll give back the keys now?"

Ben heard the hopeful note in her voice. "Sorry. For now I'll keep them."

Lily's chin dropped, and her shoulders slumped. "I don't have a choice, do I?"

He couldn't deny the enraged woman sitting in the passenger seat was beautiful, but when had attraction replaced his irritation? Probably sometime between her outright rejection of his authority and when he set her on the running board. She was saucy and sexy. Those qualities were lethal in a woman. He winked. "No, you don't."

Lily slid her gaze away, her heart thumping. She should be irritated. She wasn't, though. She had bigger worries to deal with—namely, this sudden attraction. What the heck was wrong with her? He wasn't her type. She wasn't drawn to annoying, controlling, sexy men. She certainly wasn't fascinated by men who believed they were God's gift to women. Especially when the man had dozens of women vying for his attention. So, why the attraction?

Tapping her fingers on the door handle, Lily contemplated the thought, when another, more worrisome, one popped into her head. The tampons. She inhaled, mortification burning through her. "I don't have my period."

His brows dipped. "Excuse me?"

Lily's face felt as if it would burst into flames. What possessed her to say such a thing? "I just wanted you to know it wasn't—" She licked her lips before starting again. "What I meant was that the stain was ketchup." *She* sounded lame.

"Ketchup?"

His voice sounded tight. Lily turned away, afraid to see his disgust. "Yes. Ketchup." She fidgeted with the seat belt. "Those tampons in my car…I just carry them because…well…just because."

"O-*kay.*"

His slow response must mean he didn't know how to reply. Lily didn't blame him. She sounded like a raving lunatic. "The other day, at the station…I just finished eating. I must have spilled ketchup on my seat and didn't realize it." She stared at the red light on Main Street while they waited for the signal to change.

The music from the tent blasted through the night air. She hurried on before she lost her courage. "Those tampons are just in my car in case I lose track."

"Do you lose track?"

At the amusement in his voice, Lily stiffened. "Not that it's any of your business, but I guess sometimes I do. Doesn't every woman?"

Ben turned toward her, resting an arm on the steering wheel. "I wouldn't know. I've never had a woman discuss it with me."

Lily heard the note of bafflement in his voice. She shifted her attention to her lap. "Oh…"

The light changed. Neither spoke again. She wanted to study him, to see if his face gave away any of his thoughts. Only, she didn't want to give the impression she found him attractive. Lily focused her attention on the passing scenery.

The glow of the full moon lit the night sky. The streets remained empty, devoid of cars cruising their surface. Every available parking spot lining the town square had a vehicle parked in the space. Lily turned, ready to tell him where she lived when she realized they were headed in the opposite direction of her house. Fear rolled down her spine.

Oh Lord, she was about to be abducted. What if she had mistaken his intention, and he really meant to murder her and bury her body in the woods? He'd get away with it, too, because people didn't question the police chief. They did question insane, though, and right now, she would almost bet the town considered her certifiable. "I should warn you I have a black belt in karate." She really didn't but heck, he wouldn't know this fact.

"A black belt?" His brows rose.

She didn't buy his act of confusion for a minute. "Yeah, so don't get any ideas." Just in case he didn't believe her, she threw out her arm in what she imagined was a perfect karate chop, missing his face by a fraction of an inch.

He ducked to avoid getting hit by her sudden movement, causing the vehicle to swerve.

Lily braced her hands against the dashboard, preventing herself from hitting the windshield. The truck bounced over the curb, flying past a fire hydrant before he righted the vehicle.

"What the hell?"

Lily imagined fire burned in the depths of Ben's eyes. Then again, she didn't need to. His words were hot enough to scorch her. "Consider that punch a warning not to try anything, or I'll be forced to hurt you."

"For heaven's sake," he bellowed. "I'm not attacking you. I'm taking you home."

"Oh really?" She didn't believe him for one minute. "How do you know where I live? I haven't told you the address."

"Sweetheart, give me some credit."

At the ridicule in his voice, Lily bristled. First, he mocked her, and now he used his authority to stalk her. She pointed an accusing finger. "That's an abuse of power."

"What the hell does that mean?"

"You used your authority to find out where I live."

He cast a glance in her direction. "I've lived here all my life. I don't need to search the system to find your address." He parked the vehicle in her driveway.

Lily crossed her arms over her chest and stared. "Oh? Then how *do* you know?"

His lips twitched, as he turned off the engine. "Let's just say it's intuition."

Intuition? What the hell did he mean? She didn't know, and right now she didn't care. She intended to put as much distance between herself and him, as soon as possible.

However, once she opened the passenger door and stared at the considerable distance between the seat and the ground, she knew exiting wouldn't be a cinch. Her choices were limited, though. Either wiggle her way out and pray her skirt didn't ride up too high or jump and hope she only sprained an ankle.

Before she had a chance to make her decision, he lifted her to the ground. The crisp air brushing against her skin did nothing to alleviate the heat of his palms on her flesh. Lily blushed straight to the roots of her hair. "Thank you," she murmured.

Ben set her down without replying. He dug into his pocket. "Is your house key on your key ring?"

"They're out back." The way the muscle flexed in his cheek, and how his jaw worked, led Lily to believe he wasn't thrilled with her answer. "They're hidden."

His shoulders stiffened. "Under a rock?"

Lily scowled. Teasing or not, she didn't appreciate his sense of humor. She sent him a withering glance before marching across the driveway and up the porch steps. "We hid them here." She pointed to the doormat.

"A rug is not a hiding spot." Ben snatched the key from beneath the mat and straightened. He unlocked the door, holding it open.

Lily maneuvered around him.

He caught her wrist.

She frowned. "Save your lecture. I'm tired and I just want to go to bed."

His brows shot upward. She wanted to cringe at the heat in her cheeks, knowing how her words must have sounded. "Alone. To sleep," she blurted, rushing into the house.

"Make certain you lock your doors tonight." He dropped the house key in her outstretched hand.

"Hey, wait," Lily called. "What about my car keys?"

Ben patted his pocket. "Sweetheart, they're safer with me."

Lily clenched her teeth. "I am *not* your sweetheart."

"Don't worry. I didn't ask you to be."

His words hung in the air as she shut the door. The sound of his feet pounding against the porch announced his departure. Lily rushed to the side window. Through a tiny slit between the curtains, she caught a glimpse of him as he climbed into his truck. A soft sigh escaped her. He might be obnoxious, but oh boy, what a body.

Chapter 6

Lily sat on the back porch the next morning, a celebrity magazine abandoned on her lap. Against her will, she replayed in her mind the events of last night.

The screen door banging shut startled her. She turned to see Peri drop into the chair across from her. Long, freshly shaved legs stretched out on the edge of the glass table. Dressed in crisp white shorts, an off-the-shoulder, pink-and-white striped top, and her hair in loose curls, Peri obviously had plans. Lily glanced at the magazine, still irritated by her sister's defection last night.

"How did it go with your police chief last night?"

Lily glanced up from the article about someone from Hollywood doing something spectacular to see Peri blowing on her hot pink nails. After staring at the same page ten times, she still didn't know what she'd read, and all because the one person she deemed off limits refused to leave her thoughts. Ben Jordan. "Thanks a bunch for leaving me alone with *him.*"

"You're welcome." Peri sat back in her chair and fanned her hand in the crisp morning air. A wide grin split her face. "Tell me, is Mr. Police Chief as hot as I think he is?"

He's oh so much better. She didn't dare say the words. Peri's mind followed the same thought process as an expert sleuth and she could find a hidden meaning in a boring newspaper article. Lily tossed the magazine on the table. "He's insufferable and bossy." She glared at Peri. "He refused to let me drive home last night."

"Ah, a controlling man. Nice." Peri winked.

"You might be into bossy, controlling men, but I am not." Lily wagged her finger.

"Oh please." Peri rolled her eyes. "Of course, you are. Which is why you and Eric didn't work out. He was too passive."

Passive? Lily could hardly call her last view of Eric passive. Then again, getting caught with his boxers down to his ankles and her roommate's legs in the air, chances are, passive wouldn't be his first response. She didn't bother to mention this fact, though. She already knew Peri's opinion of Eric—which, incidentally, mirrored Lily's view as well.

Lily ignored Peri's comment. "Why are you dressed up?"

Peri let out a loud yawn. She stretched her arms over her head before answering. "I'm going to the lake."

"Really?" Lily glanced at the row of shrubs separating her yard from the hot neighbor behind her house. Her arch-enemy's friend. *Ugh.* "Just how do you intend to get there? I can't take you. Ben kept my car keys."

"I know." Peri yanked her gaze from the house behind theirs. "He told me during the ride home."

Peri's words poured over her like a bucket of ice water. She whipped her gaze to her sister. Ben escorted Peri, the inveterate flirt, home last night? Did he and Peri have plans? She told herself she didn't care. Which was mostly true. "Yeah, well, you can have him." The sharp tattoo of Lily's fingernails against the hard metal armrest broke the silence of the early morning.

"Hey, no need for anger." Peri smiled.

Lily ground her teeth together. "I'm not angry." She shoved aside her irritation. "If you want to be a part of his harem than have at it."

"His harem?"

The laughter in Peri's voice irritated Lily. The rapid tapping on the table started again. "Oh please. The way those women behaved, you'd think he was every woman's dream."

"You *are* jealous."

Stilling her fingers, Lily shot Peri a glance hot enough to start fire. "I am *not* jealous. I just don't want you to get hurt."

"Well, if it makes you feel any better, I'm not going with Ben. I'm going with some people I met last night." Turning toward the neighbor's house, Peri waggled her brows. "Besides, I'm much more interested in his hot friend. Did you know he's a firefighter?"

Lily didn't. Then again, she really didn't care, either. *He* didn't crowd her thoughts. Now his friend…She ripped her attention from the house behind theirs. "Who?"

Rolling her eyes, Peri tilted her chin in the direction of the house. "Dax Moore." She let out a soft sigh. "Even his name is hot. It's like butter on my tongue. Too delicious to ignore. Too smooth to give up." She shifted her attention back to Lily. "Besides, if you ask me, Ben's interested in you."

Lily shrugged. "The only thing he's interested in is throwing me in jail."

"I don't know." Peri blew on her fingernails. "The way he chased you last night makes me think otherwise."

"Oh please. He followed me, because I humiliated him in front of his harem." Lily picked up the magazine again, glancing at the article without reading a word. "Something is fishy about the whole situation."

"Such as…?"

Lily shifted her attention from the magazine. Peri's gaze remained fixed on her manicure. "I can't help wondering why he didn't wear a uniform last night. He's the police chief, for goodness sake."

Peri glanced up from her fingernails. "Maybe he's not expected to wear them."

"Of course, he has to wear them." Lily chucked the magazine on the table again. "How would people know he's a police chief, otherwise?" The argument was logical. After all, if he had worn a uniform, she wouldn't have assumed he was a rent-a-cop, and he certainly hadn't identified himself as the police chief, either.

"Maybe because everyone knows him…"

Lily hated when Peri was right. Jumping from her chair, she headed down the wooden porch steps.

"Hey, where are you going?"

"To the garage." Lily hurried across the grass.

Peri raced to keep up. "Why?"

"I'm mowing the lawn." Lily didn't *want* to mow the lawn. More importantly, she didn't *want* to discuss Ben. However, knowing Peri's persistence for answers, she chose mowing. Lily headed to the side door. She turned the knob. The door was locked. Cupping her palms, she peered through the glass. Dust clung to the inside of the window, blocking her view. Scooting around Peri, she hurried to the front of the garage.

"Are you wearing Mom's shirt?"

Disdain oozed from Peri's voice. Lily shrugged, refusing to allow her sister's scorn to affect her. "I'm doing yard work."

"Suit yourself." Peri lifted one bare shoulder. "You wouldn't catch me dead dressed in a shirt with embroidered flowers on the front. You could pass for an old lady."

"Then it's a good thing you're not wearing the shirt." Lily crouched in front of the garage door. "Help me open the door."

"Are you kidding me?" Peri thrust out her hands, her fingers spread wide. "I just gave myself a manicure. I'm not ruining my nails just so you can mow the lawn."

"Fine. I'll do it myself." Lily dug her fingers beneath the lip of the garage door. Ignoring the gravel biting into her flesh, she struggled to lift the door. The blasted thing did not budge an inch.

"Hey, I bet if you called your police chief, he'd help." Peri watched the struggle between Lily and the door. "Just think, if he did, he might take his shirt off." A sigh escaped Peri. "Can you imagine it?"

Can I? Hell, yeah. In her mind's eye, he stood shirtless and was all hot, hard, and sweaty. Her stomach tumbled. Lily shoved aside the thought. "Oh please," she scoffed, digging her heels into the ground, gripping the bottom edge of the door.

"You can't tell me you didn't notice how sexy he is," Peri chided. "I'm telling you, he's machismo in action."

An image, vivid and sharp, of Ben, rolled through Lily's thoughts. Firm fingers clasped her waist. Her hands flattened against the hard planes of his chest. Her pulse quickened. From his powerful body crowded against hers, to the strength of his touch, to the depth of his eyes—every inch of the man was scared in her memory. Machismo was right. Lily closed her eyes and sighed. "The man does have a fantastic body…"

"You think?"

Jumping back, Lily swiveled. Her stomach sank. Ben stood directly behind her. With hair just a tiny bit damp and a light dusting of stubble on his face, he looked both dangerous and sexy. A deadly combination in her opinion.

Peri shot Lily an *I told you so* glance.

Lily ignored her. Right now, her problem had grown exponentially. Namely, how the heck did a man as large as Ben sneak up on them? "How long have you been here?"

A smile twitched at the corner of his mouth. "Long enough to know you need some help."

"We tried to open the garage…"

Lily frowned.

Peri threw up her hands in the air. "Okay, fine. Lily tried to open the door. It's stuck."

He started for the side door.

Even as she raced to keep up, Lily took a moment to enjoy the pleasant view of his backside. His navy athletic shorts sat low on his hip and each stride showed his powerful thighs. The white T-shirt stretched across his ample shoulders and drew taut on his biceps. Lily sighed. Peri followed suit. Coming or going, Lily couldn't find one thing wrong with his body.

Ben flicked a glance toward Lily. "Do you have the house key?"

"I'll get it." Peri hurried up the porch steps and into the house.

When Lily turned, she noticed him taking in the ugly embroidered shirt and the shorts with the elastic waistband. *Curses.* "These clothes belong to my mother," she blurted, clutching the edge of her shirt. "I'm mowing the lawn," she rushed out before silently criticizing herself. Why did she explain? She didn't care what he thought of her dress, right? A smile ready to charm the pants, or in this case, elastic waist shorts off a woman, crossed his lips. Lily's stomach fluttered.

Then without warning, the screen door slammed shut, breaking the moment.

"Here they are." Peri trotted down the steps, waving the keys in the air.

Plucking them from Peri's outstretched hand, Ben proceeded to the door without another glance in Lily's direction.

Irrational disappointment surged through Lily at his abrupt dismissal. She couldn't explain why, seeing as she expected this behavior in the first place. He had dozens of women vying for his attention. Why he probably threw out women the way most people tossed their trash—quickly, efficiently, and decisively. Disgusted, Lily marched beside him.

"Hey, do you think your friend is home?" Peri slid a glance in Ben's direction, her eyes as wide as the smile on her face.

His arm brushed against Lily's. Tingles of fire raced down her skin. She jumped away, her face burning. She slid a glance in his direction. If he noticed her reaction, he didn't say anything. Heck, he didn't even spare her a glance.

Ben turned to Peri. "Who? Dax?"

"That's him," Peri replied in a chipper voice.

He slid the key into the lock. "Sorry. He's working today." Throwing open the door, he flipped on the inside light and waited for the women to enter.

"Well shoot. I had hoped I'd see him at the lake," Peri muttered, following Lily inside. She stopped and waved a hand in front of her face. "Wow, what a mess."

Clouds of dust twisted and swirled in the sunlight streaming through the window. Lily stared at the scene. Dirt crowded every conceivable surface, and plenty of surfaces were here to litter. A multitude of boxes, filled with junk, sat scattered throughout the room. A counter, oil stained and scarred from years of abuse from all sorts of tools, ran the length of the wall. Dust, more boxes, and an impossible number of coffee cans filled with rusty nails, screws, and who knew what else, covered the counter. Unwanted rugs, chairs, lawn furniture, lamps, piles of old clothing, rakes, tree trimmers, shovels, and a wheelbarrow completed the mess.

They followed the narrow trail he made to the lawnmower near the front of the garage.

Yanking the overhead cord, Ben drew open the door.

Lily watched with rapt fascination the muscles in his arms and back ripple. Bright light streaming through the garage door windows highlighted his attributes. Her soft sigh echoed Peri's.

"Be still my heart," Peri murmured.

Lily couldn't agree more. Thankfully, he didn't

hear Peri's comment or their sighs. Or if he had, he didn't show it.

Ben brushed the dust off his hands. "There you go, ladies."

Peri scrunched her face. "Eww. Ick. Check out all these dead bugs. They're on top of everything." She glanced at Ben. "You might want to help Lily with the lawn mower. She hates dead bugs."

Heat rushed up Lily's neck. How dare Peri mention her aversion. Sure, she hated bugs, but just because she did, didn't mean she wanted him to know. She glared at Peri. Her sister's attention was already diverted by a car pulling into the driveway.

"Oh good, my ride is here." Raising her hands upward and keeping a careful distance from the dirt and grease, Peri eased out of the garage and hurried to the beat-up car.

One of Ben's brows cocked upward. He shot a half wave in the direction of the driver.

Two women sat in the front seat. They returned his wave with a half-hearted one of their own, before throwing the car in reverse and backing out of the driveway.

Within seconds, Lily and Ben were alone. She turned to see his dark eyes studying her. Licking her lips, she blurted out her first thought. "Hating bugs is normal."

Ben, kneeling to inspect the lawnmower, glanced her way. "I know. My sister hates them, too."

She whipped her head around. "You have a sister?"

His glance flicked toward the departing car. He nodded, rolling the lawnmower from the garage. "She's a few years younger than me."

"I suppose you boss her, too?" Lily wanted to crawl into a hole and hide. What possessed her to say such a thing?

Ben, tinkering with something on the lawnmower, stopped and eyed her. A smile curled on his lips.

"I'm sure she thought I did."

Lily didn't doubt it. "No wonder you're such a respected police chief. You love to give orders."

Standing, Ben wrinkled his brow. "How do you know I'm respected?"

Warmth rushed through her at the inadvertent admission. She'd all but admitted she'd noticed the adoration in the women's gazes and the whispered reverence of his name on the men's lips. She searched for a reasonable excuse. None presented itself. Suddenly he was there, leaning into her and catching her by surprise. She jumped back, bumping into the long shelf lining the wall.

A can of screws tipped over.

Reaching out, he snaked his arms around her. "Is everything okay?"

Heat burned her face at the realization he hadn't grabbed for her. He wanted the gas can on the shelf behind her. Stifling a groan, she stared at a point just to the left of his head and cleared her throat. "Yes, fine."

"You need gas," he told her.

Clasping together her hands, Lily pressed them against her chest and smiled. "I can have my car keys then?"

Ben laughed. "No."

Lily settled her hands on her hips. "If you're not here to return my keys, why are you here? Shouldn't you be busy with your harem?"

Stiffening, he widened his eyes. "My what?"

"Oh please," Lily sniffed. "I spotted those women fawning over you last night."

"A harem? Interesting. I never considered my friends as part of a harem."

Friends? Yeah right. Only a player considered a multitude of women fawning over him 'friends.' "They made fools of themselves just to gain your attention."

"Maybe they sought someone else's attention?" Ben dug into his pocket and drew out a set of keys.

Lily rolled her eyes. "If you hurry, you can catch up with them." She tilted her head in the direction the car disappeared. "I'm sure they'd love you to torment them."

"I doubt *they'd* want me with them." He rubbed his hands together. "Besides, I'd rather torment you."

He did an excellent job. His very presence unnerved her. Lily willed her stomach to stop the odd roller-coaster thing and for her equilibrium to return. Both ignored her.

"Come on." Ben lifted the red metal can. "I'll take you to get gas."

Lily shook her head. "I'd rather not. I mean, I'm a mess."

He started for the car before stopping and studying her. A smile twitched on his lips "You're right. You are." He turned away, and opening the trunk, he set the can inside. "I'll go for you."

After his vehicle backed out of her driveway, Lily hurried into the house. She ripped off her mother's ugly clothing, dropping them in a pile on the floor. Grabbing a pair of yoga pants, she quickly slipped into them. An image of herself in the mirror stared back. Streaks of dirt covered her face, and wisps of hair broke free from her ponytail. Her actions were silly. She didn't care. Being caught dressed resembling a hag once in front of him was bad enough. Twice was not an option.

She took the quickest shower of her life. Afterward, she spied a bottle of body mist on the counter. She hovered her hand over the container for just a second before grabbing it and spraying the light floral scent on her warm flesh, all the while she ignored her inner voice chastising her silliness. Wearing perfume had nothing to do with impressing him. She just wanted to smell nice.

Grabbing her blow dryer, Lily took her time styling her hair. A loud grinding noise sounded through the open window. Flicking off the blow dryer, she hurried across the room and peered through the crack of the curtain.

With his shirt clinging to his sweat-covered body, Ben muscled the lawnmower through the thick grass. A sigh of pure pleasure hissed from her.

Peri hadn't been wrong. His chest was spectacular. The rest of his body wasn't horrible, either. She now understood the whole attraction to wet t-shirt contests.

The abrupt silence startled her from her reverie. She jerked her attention back. Ben rolled the lawnmower into the garage. Fearful of being caught, she rushed into the bathroom, threw her hair into a ponytail then dashed into the kitchen just as his footsteps sounded on the wooden porch steps.

Lily opened and closed the cupboards doors in a lame attempt to appear relaxed. However, the image of him mowing and the look he gave her just before he left for gas kept replaying in her thoughts.

At his knock, she stilled her racing heart. Throwing open the door, she focused her attention on his face, and not on the up-close view of his sweat moistened shirt. Lily waved him inside and hurried to the fridge. Ripping open the door, she dove inside and grabbed the first thing her hand touched. "Do you want a drink?"

Ben arched a brow. "Of straight vodka?"

Lily groaned at the large, clear glass bottle she held. *What the hell?* "I thought I grabbed a bottle of water. I didn't know my parents kept vodka in here." She returned the bottle to the shelf. "Seriously, I rarely drink, and I *never* get drunk." Even as she grabbed a different carafe, she knew her words sounded flimsy. "How about some iced tea instead?"

His lips twitched. "With or without the vodka?"

The tension in Lily's body eased. She curled her lips into a smile. "You decide."

He smiled. "I'll go without."

Her heart fluttered, and her cheeks burned. "I feel as if I owe you for mowing the lawn."

"Consider it a favor." He took a long drink of the tea before setting the half-empty glass on the counter. "Come on. I'll take you to your car."

She blinked. "I can drive?"

Ben shrugged. "It will be impounded otherwise. We need to go now, though."

"Oh, big plans for tonight?" The question popped out before she could stop herself.

"Not really." He dug his keys from his pockets. "Come on, let's go. I don't want to keep Ellen waiting."

Lily's heart dropped at the casual way he mentioned his date. *Ellen.* For some reason, she decided she hated the name.

Chapter 7

Bright sunlight blanketed the sky on Sunday morning. A sense of desperation filled Lily. She spent half the night dreaming of Ben with Ellen. The other half, she spent cursing her stupidity.

Frustrated she couldn't control her misbehaving thoughts, Lily went for a run. However, no matter how far she ran, images of him followed. By the time she neared the center of town, the hope of removing him from her thoughts faded. Spotting the tall, gray brick building with the bright red, wooden door, and the tall steeple sitting on the grassy knoll, on the corner of woodland and main, she forgot all her worries.

All Saints Church.

Her prayers were answered. If she attended Mass, she wouldn't think about Ben or his date. Inspired, Lily raced home to tidy-up. By the time she finished dressing, she had just minutes before Mass began. She debated whether to drive. If she walked, she'd be late. The last thing she wanted was to arrive at church after Mass began, which meant she needed to drive.

By the time she arrived, only one available parking space remained. The spot was a heaven-sent gift. Parking her car alongside the curb fronting the building, Lily shut off the ignition and bolted from her car. She hopped the curb, darted past the sign she had no time to read, and up the massive, concrete steps with the last stragglers. Dashing past the startled priest and his entourage, she rushed inside just as the organist began playing.

Finding a seat proved harder than finding a parking spot. She spotted one halfway down the aisle toward the center of the pew. An elderly man guarded the entrance of the row. She pointed to the open spot.

Scowling, he refused to budge one inch.

The organist cranked the volume. The doors were thrown open, and the priest with his attendants began their ascent up the aisle. Wanting to avoid attention, Lily waved an impatient finger toward the vacant seat.

Like a statue, the elderly gentleman stared straight ahead, his body rigid.

A quick glance revealed the priest gliding up the aisle, his confused gaze locked on her. Lily frowned. Climbing over the surly man wasn't her idea of fun. However, being run over by a priest wasn't high on her list, either. With few options, Lily did the only thing she could. She flung her legs over the man and proceeded into the pew, all the while glancing apologetically at the elderly woman.

The woman glared, but she shifted her knees enough for Lily to pass.

The only welcoming face belonged to the gray-haired woman sitting beside the vacant spot. She patted Lily's hand, introducing herself as Alma Batchelder.

Lily tried to focus on Mass. Her mind, on the other hand, refused to pay attention. She scanned the room—from Jesus impaled upon the large wooden crucifix positioned behind the altar, to each beautifully carved and painted Stations of the Cross interspersed between the glowing stained-glass windows, to the woman sitting two rows ahead and across the aisle.

She wore a large brimmed, lilac hat, with a bright pink bird perched in the center of a plume of purple feathers.

Shifting her focus, Lily gasped. Across the room sat the one person she hoped to avoid. Her heart pounded, and a knot formed in her stomach.

Ben.

Of all the rotten luck. Two churches in town and she picked the one *he* attended.

A slight shifting of bodies revealed a tall, slim woman dressed in a stylish, copper-colored dress. Long chestnut color hair fanned across her back, and when she tilted her head toward him, a soft smile creased her face. A feeling Lily didn't recognize settled in the pit of her stomach. Was she Ellen?

A nudge in her side drew her attention from Ben.

Alma fanned her hands toward the aisle.

A silent signal for her to attend communion. What if he spotted her as she made her way up the aisle? What would he do? What would *she* do?

A line of people stood behind her, waiting to exit the pew. Similar to Alma, they waved impatient hands.

With her stomach twisting, Lily searched the church. Everyone, absolutely *everyone,* lined up for communion. She took a deep breath to calm her racing thoughts. She'd stand out more if she stayed back than if she remained.

She didn't have a choice. On shaking legs, Lily stepped from the pew. Ducking her head and drawing her hair forward, she made her way to the altar. Inspiration struck halfway up the red-carpeted path. Instead of returning to her seat, she'd keep right on going down the side aisle and out of the church to freedom before Ben caught her driving.

Her plan was perfect. Lily started past the seat.

Alma caught her arm. "Mass isn't over yet," she whispered, waving Lily back into the pew.

"I have—"

Alma shook her head. "Father has to bless us. You want his blessing, don't you?"

What could she say? That she didn't need his blessing? Hardly. With Ben only a few pews away, she needed all the blessings she could obtain.

A line of people formed behind them. Everyone stared with their brows raised in expectation waiting for Lily and Alma to enter their pew.

She shot another peek in his direction.

He sat, facing forward.

With slumped shoulders and her head bowed, Lily crept back into the pew, praying he didn't look back. While everyone prayed for peace, Lily prayed for an escape. After the final blessing, she made a beeline straight for the exit. Unfortunately, the rest of the congregants did the same. By the time she neared the doors, a wall of people blocked her get-away. She stared at the backs of two women. Side by side, they resembled an impenetrable barricade. Refusing to be deterred, Lily squeezed past.

"No budging," one of the women snapped.

"I'm not budging. I'm just trying…" Lily grunted, wiggling her way between the two women.

In unison, the two women pinched the tiny opening shut, squishing Lily in the process.

"We know exactly what you're doing. You're trying to get them donuts first," the other woman charged. "Well guess what? You're gonna wait in line the same as the rest of us."

"No, you don't understand." Wiggling an arm over the shoulders of the women, Lily pointed toward the exit. "I just need to leav—"

A hand shoved her from behind. She fell forward, right into the backs of the women.

One of the women spun and glared. "I *said* no budging."

The hum of fervent chatter disappeared, replaced by a dense cloud of unease. Lily scanned the faces surrounding her.

Everyone glared back.

She knew, just *knew*, a riot was imminent and all because of a few donuts. A trickle of sweat rolled down her spine. She didn't know what she feared more—her possible beating from the angry crowd, or Ben spotting her driving. If she could just escape...

Lily glanced over her shoulder. A wall of people surrounded her. She peered through the cracks, searching for the one man she didn't want to spot her. She couldn't see him.

Spotting a slight break in the crowd, she didn't waste a second. Ignoring the outraged grumblings, Lily shoved her way through the gap. Breaking free from the crush, she bolted from the church.

Her exhilaration didn't last long. When she climbed into her car, she noticed a piece of paper stuck under her windshield wiper. Gritting her teeth, Lily snatched the paper off the glass.

"Got a ticket?"

The paper she held was forgotten. Ben, handsome in the black suit and matching dress shirt, stood at the top of the steps. She glared at the man who had been a thorn in her side from the minute she arrived into town. *Great. A ticket. Just what I need.* She waved the slip of paper. "You ticketed me on purpose, didn't you?"

Laughing, he trotted down the steps. "How could I when I was in church?" Nodding toward the sign, he gave her a pointed look. "You parked in a no parking zone."

A signed posted not more than two feet from the edge of the curb and right in front of the passenger door of her car stared back. The same sign she hurried past without reading.

"Perhaps you need glasses, as well as a license."

Lily narrowed her eyes. "I do *not* need glasses," she shot back, stuffing the ticket in her purse. "Or a license. I told you I have one."

He cocked his brow. "Perhaps you could show it to me?"

Goodness, the man is persistent. A huff burst from Lily. She flung her arms upward. "Okay, fine. I don't have my license, but you allowed me to drive yesterday."

His face hardened into a glare. "Yesterday, I permitted you to drive so your car wouldn't be impounded." Ben crossed his arms over his chest. "I never gave you permission to continue driving, and you know it."

"There you are." A voice called from the top of the steps.

They started at the sound.

The woman sitting beside Ben in church strolled down the steps. Lily's heart dropped. She was beautiful with long, luscious lashes framing deep brown eyes, the color of newly turned earth after a summer shower. Nearly as tall as Ben, she held herself with an air of sophistication and determination. As perfect as she was, it was only natural she'd attract his attention.

"Oh. Hi." She stopped beside him. She took in the scene between Lily and Ben, her brow furrowing.

Guilt filled Lily, imaging what the woman thought. She slid a sidelong glance in Ben's direction, expecting him to show some sign of affection toward the woman. Instead, he scowled.

"Ellen, I need a minute with Lily. She and I are having a brief discussion on laws."

A soft, lilting laugh bubbled from Ellen.

"Laws or your rules, Ben?"

Lily liked Ellen, especially since she wasn't the least bit swayed by his attractiveness or his powerful air. Then again, she was with him, which didn't say much about her taste in men.

His face darkened. "They're called laws for a reason, Ellen." He turned back to Lily. "And I expect them to be followed."

Ellen rolled her eyes. "What *law* did Lily break?"

Finally, someone who sympathized with her plight. Ellen might be his girlfriend, but she was on Lily's side. She tilted her chin in the direction of Ben. "He's just upset because he didn't make his 'rules' clear."

"They're not my rules," he ground out. "I didn't make them up. The state did."

Lily sniffed. "Fine. You know I have a license, though. You're just being difficult." She swept a hand toward the offending object. "You can't expect me to know I broke the law when I didn't see the thing."

"No one else had a problem noticing the sign."

Ellen frowned. "You're so stubborn." She turned to Lily and smiled. "He's incredibly stubborn. Always has been."

"*Ellen.*" Ben glared at Ellen.

A sigh rippled from Ellen. "Okay, but I think Lily is right. The sign is too small. She shouldn't receive a ticket. You're the police chief. You can rip it up for her."

His glare floated between the two women. Growling, he thrust out his palm. "Give me the ticket."

Lily didn't wait for him to change his mind. She dug into her purse until her fingers found the crumpled paper. Giving him her most pleasant smile, she handed him the piece of paper.

Scowling, he stuffed the ticket in his coat pocket. "Don't push it."

"See? Ripping up the ticket didn't hurt a bit, did it?" Ellen patted his arm, smiling. "Now, I really need to go."

Lily gave Ellen credit for smiling despite the fierce scowl on Ben's face.

"What about breakfast?" He rested his fisted hands against his hips.

"Change of plans. I'm hanging out with Maybelline today." Ellen placed a kiss on his cheek. She turned and shook Lily's hand. "A pleasure meeting you."

Digging into his pants pocket, Ben drew out some keys and tossed them to Ellen. "Here. Take my truck. It's parked at the station."

Ellen grabbed the keys in mid-air. "How will you get home?"

He shifted his attention to Lily. "I'll be fine."

"Suit yourself." Starting across the street, she waved to Lily. "See you later."

"You're jaywalking," he called to Ellen.

She cast a glance over her shoulder, smiling. "I know."

Shaking his head, Ben returned his attention to Lily. "Give me your keys."

Lily clenched the keys in her hand. "Why?"

"To drive you home."

Her stomach leapt as she clutched her fist with the keys against her chest. She didn't want him in her car or to spend another minute with him, for that matter. "That's not necessary. I'm capable of driving myself."

Gritting his teeth, he thrust out his hand.

Lily knew he wouldn't back down. She sighed and climbed out of the driver's seat. Walking around the car, she slapped the keys in his palm. "Fine. You can drive me. However, once we're at my place, I demand you return them."

Ben arched his brow, his lips thinning before opening the passenger door. "Is that right?"

Clearly, he wasn't thrilled with her order. If the way he slammed the door shut was any indication. Or maybe he blamed her for the near revolt. Either way, Lily wouldn't cower. Tapping her foot on the floorboard, she watched him make his way to the driver's side.

As soon as he was settled in the driver's seat, Lily crossed her arms and glared. "I think you should know, what happened in church wasn't my fault. In fact, if anyone is at fault, it's you."

His head snapped up, his hand hovering above his seatbelt. "Excuse me?"

"You didn't do your job."

His brows pinched together. "And that job is…?"

"The one where you protect people and keep them safe." *Really?* Did he need her to explain his job, too?

"Who did I not keep safe? You, or the people anxious to go downstairs to the Donut and Coffee Hour?"

A smile twitched on his lips, and his eyes sparkled. Lily rolled her eyes at the amusement on his face. *Seriously?* "Me. In there. By that mob—" She pointed a finger toward the church.

He burst out laughing. "You mean when you started a fight?"

Lily gasped. He had seen her. "That was *me* leaving. They nearly killed me. Over a donut, Ben. A *donut.*"

The corners of his eyes crinkled upward. "Now, you're exaggerating."

"Am I? You didn't see their angry stares." Frowning, Lily crossed her arms over her chest again. "I'll tell you what, if a fire had started, we'd have died, and you'd be at fault."

His eyebrows spiked. "Oh? Do you mind telling me why?"

Lily sighed. "You're the police chief. You can't tell me you didn't notice the crowds and not see the fire hazard."

Ben inserted the key in the ignition. "I'm the police chief not the fire chief. I don't determine fire safety or maximum capacity. Mack does."

"Oh." Her cheeks burned. What possessed her to say such a ridiculous thing? She probably sounded stupid, too. "You think I'm crazy…"

He gave her a once-over. "I wouldn't say crazy."

Just as quickly, Lily forgot her irritation with the look of appreciation she saw lurking in his eyes and the sexy tone in his voice. A thrill shot through her. Fearful she'd burst into laughter, Lily turned away. She spotted Ellen darting through the park. The nervousness disappeared replaced by anger.

Five minutes was all the time he needed to forget his girlfriend. She was right. He *was* a player. Lily inched closer to the passenger door.

He shot her a quick glance. "What's wrong?"

"You." Lily jabbed a finger in his direction. "Ellen is beautiful, and you don't care."

Ben started the car. "I never noticed."

"You wouldn't." Lily tilted her chin just slightly upward. "You're too busy noticing things you shouldn't."

He glanced in the rearview mirror before he did a U-turn on Woodland. "Which is?" He stopped at the traffic light.

The man was far too cocky. Lily gritted her teeth. "Other women." She faced him. "Don't you think Ellen might care?"

"No."

What kind of relationship did they have that Ellen would allow such behavior? "I think you're wrong."

He rolled his eyes. "What a surprise."

A puff of air burst from Lily. "Well, excuse me. I guess Ellen *never* annoys you."

"Ellen annoys me all the time."

Lily arched her brows. "She does?"

Ben shrugged. The light changed, and he continued on Woodland Avenue. "Since she moved to Albany, things are better, though."

Ellen lived in Albany? Well, no wonder he wasn't faithful. What did Ellen expect? Women noticed men like him. "Doesn't the separation make your relationship difficult?"

"If you ask me the distance makes our relationship perfect. She can't irritate me there." Ben slowed the vehicle before turning onto Timber Avenue.

Okay, now he was just the worst boyfriend in the world. Thankfully, he wasn't *her* boyfriend. One heartless man was enough to last her a lifetime. "She is fine with you being a womanizer?"

"A what?" Ben pulled into her driveway.

Lily didn't buy his act of outrage. Lifting her chin, she met his glare head-on. "A womanizer. As in a man who cheats on his girlfriend."

"You think Ellen's my girlfriend?" He slipped the vehicle into Park.

Lily gave him credit. He certainly was adept at lying with a straight face. She wasn't fooled, though. "I'm not blind. You were together at church." Lily bolted from the vehicle and dashed forward.

Ben blocked her at the front of the vehicle. "For God's sake, Lily, Ellen's not my girlfriend. She's my sister."

Stopping, Lily spun. His sister? The image of Ellen standing beside him flashed through her thoughts. Both were tall and attractive, with dark hair and eyes that matched. Well, shoot. Now, she sounded ignorant. "Oh, I guess I just assumed…"

A smile split his face. "I'm glad to see you're jealous."

A shocked gasp erupted from Lily. "I'm *not*

jealous."

"Oh really?"

Lily stiffened. Did he assume she was the same as the rest of the women in town? That she'd fall in love with him the minute he gave her even the slightest bit of attention? Well, he was about to learn a lesson. "Here's a news flash, Chief Jordan. Not every woman thinks the sun rises and sets on your shoulders."

She spun on her heels, marched across the yard and up the steps of her front porch. She glanced once over her shoulder, shot him a hot glare, before unlocking the door and storming inside.

Chapter 8

Ben studied the agitated sway of Lily's hips as she stomped across the yard. He couldn't stop himself from laughing. She certainly riled easily. Maybe too easy. She did amuse him, though. The memory of her last withering glare only added to his pleasure. His amusement increased when she slammed the front door, then swiftly changed to surprise when he heard the click of the lock.

Another first. He couldn't name a single person in town who'd consider barring him from their house. Certainly, not a woman. Of course, Lily didn't behave similar to most women. *She* didn't seek his attention. At least, not the way most women did. Yet, despite her best efforts, she'd caught his interest.

With those baby blue eyes and silky blonde hair, Lily would be hard to ignore. With those curves, impossible. Given enough time, Ben would notice her. He knew, without a doubt, Lily could charm a weaker man to his knees. Thankfully, he wasn't a weak man. He did enjoy a challenge, though, and she presented a one he couldn't, *wouldn't*, resist.

He tossed her keys in the air, catching them again. Walking to her car, he opened the passenger door and flipped the glove box latch. Without hesitating, he pitched the keys inside the cluttered compartment. They slid to the bottom, hidden amongst papers and tampons.

Satisfied, he clicked the glove box shut.

Lily didn't realize she'd forgotten her keys. Ben knew eventually she'd remember. When she did, she'd demand he return them. He'd be *disappointed* if she didn't. A smile crossed his face. He could just imagine their next skirmish. Thrusting aside a branch, he strode through the opening of the shrubs separating Dax's yard from Lily's.

He headed up the steps to the house's side door and knocked before letting himself inside. Dax's place could never be confused with immaculate. He was, after all, an inveterate bachelor. However, after one glance at the kitchen, immaculate was the only word to describe the room.

Dax hadn't mentioned his mother coming for a visit, which meant the cleanliness must involve a different woman. This fact didn't surprise Ben. Dax liked women. At least, in passing.

Strolling through the kitchen, Ben noted a sink empty of dirty dishes, the white countertop free of crumbs, and the mail stacked atop the folded newspaper. The dining room showed the same care. Brown-and-green plaid placemats perfectly arranged upon the gleaming surface of the cherry table. Four chairs in front of four place settings. In the living room, not a speck of dust marred the surface of the furniture. Neither a pillow sat out of place, nor a dirty cup or plate sat neglected on the coffee table.

Music, barely audible, played on the radio upstairs. Dax's off-tune voice sang along. Returning to the kitchen, Ben poured himself a cup of coffee. Footsteps sounded on the stairwell just a second before Dax stepped into the kitchen.

He choked on his sip of coffee. "What the hell?" Stunned, he set his cup on the counter and stared at the man he considered more of a brother than a friend. He knew Dax as well as he knew himself, but seeing Dax's attire right now, Ben wasn't certain he knew him at all.

Dax was the epitome of a fireman. He benched two-fifty, raced dirt bikes, worked on his classic car, and played a mean game of ice hockey. He drew women like bees to flowers. He wasn't a man who carried a bucket of cleaning supplies, wore yellow gloves, or had a red-and-white checked apron tied around his waist. Until today.

"What are you doing here?" Dax set the cleaning supplies in his pantry.

"What am *I* doing here? What the hell are you doing? You're dressed like Alice from *The Brady Bunch*." He watched Dax drop his yellow gloves in the bucket. "If you didn't have a beard, I'd be worried."

Dax rubbed the scruff on his chin. "Yeah. The ladies enjoy it. The thing sure itches." He drew the apron over his head and hung it on a hook in the pantry before shutting the door. "I hate cleaning the house. If I were married, my wife would take care of this job."

Ben knew without a doubt Dax would never consider marriage. His life was too perfect right now. "But you'd need to give up your bachelor status."

"Not gonna happen, my friend. I might enjoy a clean house, but I'm not crazy enough to tie myself down for one." Dax grabbed a mug from the cupboard. "Too many beautiful women to sample." He poured coffee into the mug. "Speaking of women...how's it going with the new woman in town?"

Before answering, Ben sipped his coffee. "You

mean Lily Evans."

A smile twitched on Dax's lips. "I heard you two didn't exactly hit it off."

Dax's comment wasn't a surprise. Gossip was the town's specialty. Especially if the gossip involved a beautiful woman. Ben set down the cup before resting his palms against the counter. He curled his fingers around the edge as he replayed his most recent interaction with Lily. "To say the least."

"A woman who doesn't appreciate your authority." Dax smiled. "The idea must drive you nuts."

He ignored Dax's outrageous comment. "I caught her driving…again." A frown creased his face. "She denied it. Then she dared to rope in Ellen to defend her."

"Ellen? I didn't know she's home."

He shrugged, frowning. "She came in yesterday. She's leaving tomorrow. Thank God. I've had enough trouble dealing with one irrational woman. I don't need two."

"Oh, come on." Dax leaned against the counter. "I've seen Lily Evans. I can think of worse torture than her."

Ben arched a brow. "She accused me of having a harem."

Dax choked on his coffee. "A harem? She does know you're the chief of police, right, and you're running for mayor?"

"I haven't made a decision yet." He set his cup on the counter.

Mike Landry, the current mayor in town, announced he wouldn't run for a third term. The city council asked Ben if he would consider accepting the position. He hadn't decided whether to relinquish his role as police chief for mayor. Given the positives in each position, he needed time to consider the possibility.

He discarded his coffee. Right now, he needed something a bit stronger than caffeine. He opened the fridge, grabbed two beers, and handed one to Dax. "She thought Ellen was my girlfriend."

Lifting his brows, Dax smiled. "Your Lily sounds fun."

The psst of the beer cap coming loose mingled with Dax's laughter.

Ben scowled. "Hardly." He took a long swig. "Trust me. Lily is nothing but trouble."

"A beautiful woman challenging you every day?" Dax clamped a hand on Ben's shoulder. "I almost envy you."

"Envy me?" He snorted, setting his bottle on the counter. "You'd change your mind if you dealt with her."

Dax grinned. "Not true. If I was in your position, we'd have our problems solved by now, and we'd have progressed to far more exciting business involving far less clothing."

An image of Lily in her skimpy dress flashed through his memory. He imagined her without it and decided he liked the image even better. He didn't share his thoughts with Dax, though. Instead, he finished his beer before moving from the counter. "Will you give me a ride home?"

Nodding, Dax grabbed his keys from the counter. "Interested in watching a baseball game at Papa's?" He opened the door, giving Ben a sidelong glance.

"Nothing like sports to help you find the answer to your problems."

Ben snorted. "Trust me. Lily isn't a problem I can't handle."

Chapter 9

The minute Ben stepped into the station his day took a decided turn in the wrong direction.

Abe sat behind his desk, his usual plastic cup of coffee in one hand and a pencil twirling in the other, concentrating on the word puzzle he held.

The desk across from him sat empty.

A sinking feeling settled in his stomach. "Where's Heather?"

Abe's attention remained glued to his word puzzle, but a frown tugged at the corners of his mouth. "She's done gone and had that baby."

He couldn't blame Abe for being irritated. Happiness didn't exactly fill him, either. With Heather gone, extra work would accumulate in the office, nothing of which Abe would complete.

People often wondered why he kept Abe. He often pondered the same thing. Abe exemplified the definition of cantankerous, entitled, and lazy. A hard day's work for him meant completing a book of word puzzles. Whereas, Heather was dependable, enthusiastic, and energetic. She handled nearly as many duties as Ben, with a quarter of the complaints as Abe. In truth, if Abe left, the police station wouldn't miss a beat. With Heather gone, though, he didn't know how they'd make it through the day. "That's wonderful." He tried to sound excited. The effort cost him more than he expected.

"Doesn't sound wonderful to me." Abe thrust a stack of messages toward Ben. "I've been your girl Monday all morning, and frankly, I'm tired of it. I told you to hire someone before she left us."

"Yeah, well next time I'll remind Heather to have her baby closer to the due date and not a month early." He flicked through the messages. One was from the Donut and Coffee Committee, which he expected. One from Derrick Thompson, a city council member. Not completely unexpected. Two from his mother. No surprise. One from Ellen. He crumpled her message, tossing the wad of paper into the trash. He wasn't interested in a conversation with her.

Abe flung his pencil on the desk. The pencil rolled across the desk and stopped, resting against the base of the paper cup. "I just bet you expect me to do both jobs now?"

Ben glanced up from his messages. "I'll help."

Abe rapped the curled magazine against the edge of the desk. "Oh, I know what that means. It means Abe do this. Abe do that. Abe, what did you do with the papers? Abe, where's my coffee?"

He rolled his eyes. "First off, I never asked Heather to get my coffee, and secondly, what the hell are you rambling on about?"

"I'm just saying you won't be much help. You're busy being the Police Chief. Now with you running for mayor—"

Ben held up a hand. "Considering it."

Abe waved off his words. "Oh, you know you'll be elected. Now, because of your and Heather's selfish decisions, I'm stuck working harder."

Ben snorted. "I'd just be happy if I *saw* you working."

Abe's mouth dropped open. "What the hell does that comment mean?"

"You're sitting here with a word puzzle, drinking coffee, and eating a donut." Scooping up his messages, Ben flicked a glance toward Abe. "If you ask me, you don't exactly appear overtaxed."

"I'm mentally preparing for the day." Abe reached for his pencil. "With Heather gone, more planning will be required."

"Well, while you're mentally preparing, let me know when Mitch arrives."

"Isn't this just perfect." Abe snapped open the magazine. "First, Heather has the baby, and now, I have to deal with Mitch Bird. The union's not gonna be happy when they hear about this situation."

"I would think they'd expect you to do your job." Ben bit back the sharp retort that had settled on the tip of his tongue. He doubted Abe would appreciate hearing he could easily be replaced by someone who could do his *and* Heather's job.

"I just bet he'll complain about that lady you stopped," Abe called after him. "I heard she caused a ruckus in church yesterday. Makes me wish I were a church-going fool like the rest of you."

Stopping beside his office door, Ben turned. "I thought you're an avowed atheist."

"Agnostic." Looking up from the booklet, Abe waved his pencil. "I'm hedging my bets here. I'm getting up in years. No sense getting caught unaware."

Ben arched his brow. "Being agnostic helps?" He opened his office door.

"Doesn't hurt," Abe called out.

Dropping the messages on his desk, Ben shrugged off his suit coat, draping it on the back of his chair. Hell, he needed a cup of coffee. He didn't bother checking the coffee pot, knowing Abe hadn't made any coffee or even purchased a pound. Abe had stated on too many occasions he preferred coffee made by professionals and not the slop the men made at the station. Tasted better, he said.

Ben regretted not stopping at Betty's Café. Karla's Kitchen was an option, but in his current mood, dealing with Karla's not-so-subtle innuendoes involved too much effort.

Instead of the hassle of making coffee, he spent the first part of the morning working on paperwork. By ten, Mitch and Suzette Bird hadn't arrived. Ben decided he'd waited long enough. Grabbing his coat, he strolled into the lobby. Abe, still in the same position from earlier, sat with his coffee in one hand and a pencil in the other, staring at his word puzzle.

Strolling across the lobby, Ben thrust open the station door. "I'm heading out."

Straightening, Abe yanked his gaze and stopped twirling the pencil. "What? Where are you going?"

"To Betty's for coffee. I'll be right back."

"You can't leave." Abe hurled the magazine across the desk. "What if the Birds come?"

"If they come, just send them to the cafe." He stepped out of the station and made the short walk to the station. He timed his arrival perfectly. The morning rush was over. The mid-day rush hadn't begun.

A few retired men huddled in the corner discussing the upcoming fishing tournament. A couple of older women sat at a table, sharing a pastry and gossiping. Four stay-at-home moms chatted, their forgotten children busy running and laughing, much to the older folks' annoyance.

Most paused in their discussion, their gazes pinned on him. He greeted each on his way to the counter, returning the smiles of the young mothers. He'd attended school with a number of them, and most he considered friends. A few he'd slept with, and those he'd left on good terms.

"Well, well, well, look who survived the weekend." Chuckling, Betty handed him a cup of coffee. "From the gossip I've heard, sounds as if you have your hands full."

Ben wasn't under any illusion. His private life was as much a topic of conversation as his public life. "I'm certain most of those stories are exaggerated."

Betty snorted. "I'm just as certain they're not. Remember, I was at church yesterday *and* at the festival on Friday."

The bell over the entrance sounded.

Turning, he spied his mother strolling into the café. At five-foot-eleven with soft brown hair, deep brown eyes, and skin unlined by age, people noticed Claire. Not only was she attractive, but she was a force to be reckoned with. When she decided on something, she always accomplished her goal. Right now, her goal was to see her children married. Claire didn't hide her wish, either. At least once a month, she made a point of mentioning her desire. He learned years ago to tune out anything marriage related.

"Ben." Smiling, Claire reached out and gripped Ben's arm. "I had hoped to see you today."

"Hello, Mother." He bent and placed a perfunctory kiss on her cheek. He wasn't surprised she found him. Knowing her, she probably gave up calling and resorted to sleuthing in her quest for answers, because the one thing Claire Ellen Jordan excelled at was information acquisition.

She patted his arm, smiling. "I heard Heather had the baby. Isn't that news exciting?"

He handed a few dollars to Betty. "Yes, wonderful."

Crossing her arms over her chest, Claire frowned. "You don't sound excited. We're talking about a baby. You should be happy. I heard they named her Gloria. Isn't that name just beautiful? I could just imagine a Gloria for a grandchild."

Her none-to-subtle tactic of marriage and grandchildren amused him. Especially since neither of her children was married yet, nor even dating seriously. He, however, refused to fall into his mother's trap. "Did you need anything else?"

She huffed. "Ellen told me you ripped up a ticket yesterday for the new girl in town."

He drew his mouth into a frown. The sparkle in her eyes and the smile pasted on her face gave away her intention. "I did." Ben didn't bother adding any further information. She already had more than she needed.

"But why?"

"Seemed appropriate." Ben shrugged, ignoring the silent exchange of glances shared between his mother and Betty. He made a mental note to warn his sister about her big mouth.

"You've never destroyed a ticket before." Claire rolled her hand outward.

"*Mom,*" he ground out.

"Okay, fine." Claire sighed again. "Have you spoken to Mitch yet?"

Another exchange of glances. He held his laughter at their thinly veiled attempt for information. Claire believed she was sneaky. She had a long way to go before she'd trap him. "Not yet, but I'm sure I'll have the pleasure before the day is done."

"Meeting with Mitch doesn't sound pleasurable to me." Betty frowned.

"Why is he's complaining, anyway?" Claire demanded. "That young woman seemed pleasant. She's cute, too."

He could think of a dozen reasons, none of which he planned on mentioning. His mother would glom onto his explanations, twisting them until she found some tiny scrap of information indicating his attraction. He didn't need the hassle. "I'm sure the whole situation is just a misunderstanding. I'll explain to Mitch about Lily—"

"Lily?" Claire clasped her hands. "Such a lovely name, don't you think?"

Ben burst out laughing. She just played her hand. He wasn't ready to fold. Bending, he planted another kiss on her cheek. "Nice try, Mom, but save your matchmaking for Ellen." He stepped from the café and spotted Mitch and Suzette Bird immediately. They hurried toward him like a heat-seeking missile. He had never seen Mitch in such a tither. His wispy gray hair stood on end. His brown checked shirt was wrinkled and his once-pristine black dress shoes, scuffed. The fire in Mitch's eyes gave the bright sunlight a run for its money.

He steeled his patience. Dealing with his mother was one thing. Dealing with the Birds was a whole different matter. Claire might be formidable, but the Birds were merciless. As the originators of the Donut and Coffee Hour, they expected everyone to follow their decisions, no matter what.

"There you are." Mitch rushed forward. "I demand something be done about yesterday."

Ben blew on his coffee. "What about yesterday?"

"Oh please." Suzette rolled her eyes. "You observed the ruckus that woman caused escaping church. She ruined our event, and we want something done."

He couldn't imagine what they thought he should do. He cocked his brow. "What do you suggest?"

"Arrest her," Mitch snapped.

"For what?" Ben exploded.

"Public nuisance, disorderly conduct, and disturbing the peace." Mitch ticked off the list of offenses on his fingers.

"Not to mention protesting at a religious service." Suzette sniffed.

Ben gagged on his sip of hot coffee. "That last one's not even a law."

"Well, all I know is that you're the police chief." Mitch curled his hands into a fist, resting them against his hips and straightening his shoulders. "And soon-to-be mayor. You're the law here and have the power to lock her up."

For the umpteenth time, Ben wondered how the hell he became embroiled in such ridiculous disputes. "I think arresting her is a bit extreme," he told them. "I was there, and she didn't do any of the items you suggested."

"We knew you'd think such a thing." Suzette waved her hand. "Everyone believes you're interested in her, but your job is to protect the citizens of this town, which includes the Donut and Coffee Committee."

Ben purposely kept his demeanor calm, but anger burned inside him. He turned to Suzette. "I take my job seriously. I protect everyone, including the Donut and Coffee Committee *and* Lily Evans. Who I associate with, whether men *or* women, is no one's business."

Mitch raised his hands. "No need for anger, Ben. We're doing what is in the best interest of the DnC…and the church." He dropped his hands to his side. "Mass should be peaceful and loving. Nothing is loving or peaceful when the Westermans are riled."

"After that *woman* escaped, they didn't come to the basement." Glaring, Suzette dropped her hands against her hips. "Their contribution alone is worth twenty dollars in donut purchases. Yesterday…Nothing."

"With the crowds larger than usual, we thought we'd sell out in record time." Mitch's hands rolled outward. "We soon realized most of the people didn't attend for donuts and coffee. They came to see *The Nuisance*. When she didn't show, they left. We had dozens of donuts left, and no one to buy them."

For some reason, he didn't appreciate hearing them call Lily a nuisance. "Her name is Lily Evans."

Suzette shrugged. "All we're asking is for you to suggest she reconsider church on Sunday."

Somehow, he kept his frustration under control. Mitch and Suzette didn't make his job easy, being two of the most determined people he'd ever met. "As far as

I can tell, Lily's done nothing wrong. Talk to Father Frank. He might have a solution."

Crossing her hands over her chest, Suzette stomped her foot and tilted her head slightly to the side. "Frank? Really? He's not gonna refuse a possible parishioner. His whole job is to encourage people to attend, not chase them away."

"Come on, Ben. You're likable. You could order the nuisan…"

Ben gritted his teeth and fisted his hand.

Mitch's face turned bright red. He glanced in Suzette's direction.

Her lips pinched together into a tight frown. With a sideways glance at Mitch, she nodded toward Ben.

Slumping his shoulders, Mitch dropped his gaze. "Well…we just thought you could talk to Miss Evans and suggest she forget about attending church. God would forgive her. I'm sure he wouldn't want Mass ruined for the rest of us."

Suzette bobbed her head. "I think I read in the bible you shouldn't attend church if you plan on causing a disruption. Lily Evans, without a doubt, is a disruption."

Ben tightened his grip on his cup. Lily Evans might cause him trouble, but he'd be damned if he'd let the Birds paint her in such a negative light. She was new here and couldn't be expected to know how these two worked. He sighed. "You need to give her another chance." He dismissed the conversation and started up the steps.

"If you don't help us, you'll leave us no other choice…"

Suzette's words stopped him. Ben turned slowly.

"What did you just say?"

Suzette and Mitch stood at the bottom. With a sharp jab in Mitch's back, Suzette nudged him forward.

Stuffing his hands into his pockets, Mitch cleared his throat. "Suzette just meant we'll deal with the situation ourselves."

Normally, he didn't cave to threats. However, this warning wasn't directed toward him, but Lily. He couldn't allow the Birds to bully her. "I'll deal with the situation." He ripped open the station door, knowing without a doubt, his day had just gone from bad to worse.

Chapter 10

Lily woke on Monday irritated. She blamed her peevish attitude on Ben Jordan. Here, she had gone to bed the night before intending to dismiss the events of the day, only to spend the night dreaming of the blasted man.

Frustrated, she grabbed a book off her nightstand, poured herself a cup of coffee, and stepped outside to enjoy light reading. Thin wisps of gray clouds dotted the watery blue sky. Moisture, thick and heavy, hung in the warm morning air. She plopped into a chair and opened her book.

Within moments, the romance novel consumed her attention. By the time she'd read a third of the book, she was no longer swept away. The hero ended up being a scoundrel intent on tormenting the heroine. The heroine didn't make her circumstances easy. She was consistently in trouble, forcing the rascal to bail her out. The whole story resembled her situation with Ben just little too closely. Slamming shut the book, Lily closed her eyes and threw her head against the back of the chair, willing him from her thoughts.

His parting words from the day before haunted her. He thought *she* was *jealous*. She wasn't *jealous*. In fact, she was so far from jealous, she boarded on uncaring. She just didn't appreciate being lumped with the rest of his women. Her standards were higher. Namely, the next time she wanted a boyfriend, *he* would chase after her, not the other way around.

Besides, she didn't *want* Ben for a boyfriend. They had nothing in common. They were oil and water. Night and day. Black and white.

Lily wanted someone reliable, charming, and trustworthy. Someone understanding, caring, and faithful. She wanted someone who made her heart thunder and her stomach tumble. Someone who incited emotions she didn't think existed.

The only thing he wanted was every single woman in town fawning after him. Lily knew her assessment was unfair. After all, what did she really know of him other than women loved him, and he always appeared when she least expected him? Now, because of yesterday and her stupid misunderstanding, he was in possession of her keys, and the people on the Donut and Coffee Committee would hang her.

Lily sighed. Until she reclaimed her keys, she was stuck with him. Getting murdered by the Donut and Coffee Committee seemed a bit extreme, though. Somehow, she needed to correct her mistake.

Inspiration suddenly struck. Lily snapped open her eyes, and her blood raced through her veins. She jumped from her chair and dashed into the kitchen. Pacing the length, she weighed every nuance of her plan. If she helped the Donut and Coffee Committee on Sunday, they'd change their mind about killing her.

Peri, pajama-clad with sleep-tousled hair, shuffled into the kitchen and headed toward the fridge.

"I'm helping the Donut and Coffee Committee on Sunday." Lily studied Peri.

Bleary-eyed, Peri rested her head on the edge of

the open door. "What did you say?"

She expected a bit more enthusiasm from her sister. Not out-right joy. Peri would *never* exhibit that, but at least some understanding. Lily fanned a hand. "I'm volunteering with the Donut and Coffee Committee."

Closing her eyes and breathing deeply, Peri shut the refrigerator door. "That idea is the stupidest thing I've ever heard."

Lily fisted her hands on the table. "No, it's not."

Sighing, Peri reopened the fridge and grabbed a bottle of water. "Please explain *why* you want to help?"

Lily folded her fingers together. "Well, for one thing, the rumors will stop."

"No, they won't." Peri cracked open the bottle. "You forget we're in a small town. People thrive on gossip. Causing a riot in church is probably the most excitement this town has seen…since…well, since you accused Ben of being a rent-a-cop."

"I *nearly* caused a riot." Lily shifted her gaze to the placemat. Biting her lip, she ran her thumb along the edge of the mat. Why did people forget this mitigating fact? "Besides, I couldn't think of a better plan."

"Why don't you just forget these old people and focus your attention on Ben?"

"Don't be silly. I'm not interested in Ben." Lily dug a nail into a seam of thread. The memory of Ben mowing her lawn flashed through her thoughts. She dismissed the image. So he did her yard work. Nothing unusual about that. Only no matter how hard she tried, she couldn't recall one-time Eric doing anything for her unbidden, including mowing.

Rolling her eyes, Peri took a long swallow of water. "You're the only woman in town who isn't."

The muscles in Lily's neck tensed. She ignored the burst of irritation. Frowning, she watched Peri start from the kitchen. "Hey, where are you going?"

"Back to bed."

Wrinkling her brow, Lily glanced at the clock. "It's nearly eleven."

"Which means it is still bedtime." Peri yawned, leaving the kitchen.

Peri's lack of excitement wasn't a surprise. Between the two, Lily was the one with P.R. problems. Now, if only she could convince the town she hadn't intended to start a riot.

Bursting with pent-up energy and nervousness, Lily dressed in her workout clothing. On her arrival in Aberdeen, she spotted the gym but had yet to visit. Today, she would check out this place. Before leaving the house, she grabbed some money, a towel, phone, earbuds, and a bottle of water. Opening the door, she yelled up the stairs, letting Peri know her plans.

Hot, muggy air hit her face, mingling with the smell of roses and fresh-cut grass. Off in the far distance, soft gray clouds filled the sky. The sound of clippers caught her attention. Her neighbor was busy snipping the pink rose bush in her front yard. For a moment, Lily thought she'd escape without her neighbor seeing her.

The screen door slammed shut.

The woman's gaze shifted upward from the rose bushes.

So much for her escape. Politeness demanded she introduce herself. Lily trotted down her porch steps, wondering if her mother had ever mentioned the neighbor's name. If she had, Lily must have forgotten.

Years had passed since she'd come here for the summer. Since then, new owners replaced the old ones. Forcing a smile, Lily passed beneath the tall maple tree. Despite the wide, arching branches casting shadows against the thick carpet of grass, humidity still hung heavy in the air.

Straightening, the woman shoved back the wide-brimmed straw hat, and tucked her clippers into her apron pocket, before removing her gloves. "I'm Claire." She thrust a hand in Lily's direction. "And you must be Lily."

Claire stood at least three inches taller than Lily. Her eyes were warm brown, her chestnut colored hair didn't have a hint of gray, and her skin was smooth. A basket filled with dried branches, dead rosebuds, and weathered leaves sat beside her feet. Lily smiled and nodded.

Slipping on her gloves, Claire picked up her clippers and snipped a dead rose off the bush. "How are you enjoying your time here?"

Lily stifled her laughter. Between the police chief and his threat of jail time and the parishioners' intent on her death, fun was not how she'd describe her trip. "My vacation could be better," Lily mumbled, watching Claire drop the dead rose in the basket.

Chuckling, Claire snagged another branch. "Things have been difficult for you, haven't they? I'm sure the situation will improve."

Lily didn't see how until she corrected her mistake at church and her license arrived so she could finally collect her keys. "Maybe."

"You don't believe so?" Claire snipped another rose from the shrub and dropped the withered bud into the basket.

Claire's voice dripped with sincerity and interest. A desperate need filled Lily. She wanted, no...*needed,* to discuss her problem with someone. Her mother wasn't here to listen or offer advice, and having a serious conversation with Peri was pointless. She knew only too well her sister's opinion on both issues, and they did not suit Lily. She studied Claire. Kind eyes stared back. She didn't need any more urging. "I'm sure you've heard the rumors..."

Another soft chuckle rumbled from Claire. "Well, you know how rumors can be. A drop of truth surrounded by plenty of exaggeration."

Claire gave Lily the perfect opening. From the minute Ben stopped her for speeding then subsequently confiscated her car keys, Lily spilled every mortifying detail. By the time she finished, a huge burden lifted from her shoulders. "I think I've solved my problem with the church, though."

"Oh?" Claire resumed clipping her roses.

"I'm helping them on Sunday."

"Really?" Claire snapped her attention off the roses and onto Lily. "Why?"

Lily shrugged. "I almost ruined their event. I thought helping would show my regret."

The nippers poised in Claire's hands hovered over a wilted rose. "And Ben? What will you do about him?"

Claire asked the million-dollar question. If only Lily had the answer. She sighed. "I'm not sure what. Until he returns my keys, I'm at his mercy."

Claire searched Lily's face. "Sounds like you're not interested in him?"

Lily snapped her attention off the rose she held.

"Good heavens, no. He has too many girlfriends, and I just left a boyfriend who could never have enough."

"I see." Claire shoved aside a branch before snipping a dead blossom.

Lily circled the shrub. "Besides, Ben's not my type. He's too bossy."

Whipping her gaze upward, Claire arched a brow. "You think?"

Lily continued pacing, plucking a rose from the bush. She ignored the sharp sting of a thorn. "He's always ordering me around. Plus, he's controlling."

Claire stilled, her hand hovering over a rose. "Really? I don't believe I've ever heard anyone say such a thing."

"He took my car keys. I'd call that controlling." Lily tore off a velvety pink petal from the rose she held. A cloying sweetness perfumed the air. The petal slipped from her fingers and floated to the ground. "The only thing I can do is just avoid him until my license arrives."

Sweeping her gaze across the crushed grass, Claire frowned at the severed petal lying upon the ground. "Avoiding him won't be easy."

"I know Aberdeen's a small town." Lily sighed. "However, with all the women chasing him, he won't miss me." She gave Claire a reassuring smile, dropping the decimated rose. "Well, I enjoyed meeting you."

Since her unfortunate meeting with Ben, a feeling of happiness filled her. She'd solved both her problems. She would just avoid him, and hopefully, he'd forget her.

For the first time in weeks, the trek to town was enjoyable. By the time she reached the gym, she was actually looking forward to the rest of her vacation.

Smiling, Lily pulled open the door and stepped into the dim room. A long bank of windows separated the lobby from the workout area. One window filled nearly the whole wall, giving an ample view of the fitness area. Another held a row of vending machines, all selling healthy snacks and drinks. Opposite the vending machines sat a long counter with a door positioned directly behind. Stuck on the door was a silver strip of duct tape. The word *office* was written in thick, bold letters across the front. Beside the door sat an empty stool.

She leaned against the counter and waited. When no front desk clerk returned, she decided to pay after her workout. She barely opened the weight room doors when a loud voice sounded. Lily turned.

A young man with frizzy red hair and gauges the size of small dinner plates in his earlobes, stood in the doorway, glaring. He pointed an accusing finger. "You're sneaking in without paying."

"No, I'm not." Lily hurried back. "I waited. No one came so I decided I'd pay when I left."

Frizzy Red squinted for just a second before his eyes widened and his mouth dropped open. His finger drooped just a bit. "Hey, aren't you Chief Jordan's girlfriend?"

"Is there a problem here?"

Lily's stomach lurched. She whipped around her head. Of all the rotten luck. Pinching her brows together, she settled a hand against her hip. "What are you doing here?"

"Your girlfriend is a thief." Frizzy Red jabbed a finger in Lily's direction.

Lily gasped. "I am not!"

Turning back to Ben, Frizzy Red continued as if she hadn't spoken. "I just caught her sneaking inside."

Ben put up a hand stopping Red. "I'll take care of the problem." He returned his attention to Lily. "So, my little lawbreaker, what's your excuse today?"

She stiffened. How dare Ben assume she lied. However, as provoking as that question was nothing compared to her annoyance with him finding her. She glared. "Did Claire tell you I was here?"

He furrowed his brow. "No. I haven't seen her today."

Lily crossed her arms over her chest. "Peri told you, didn't she?" She vowed if he confirmed her suspicion, she'd have a polite discussion with Peri about sisterly loyalty.

A smile twitched on his lips. "No."

Lily didn't know whether he spoke the truth or not. She narrowed her eyes. "How come you're not working?"

Ben smirked. "Who says I'm not, sweetheart?"

Heat burned Lily's cheeks. She shot a nervous glance in Frizzy Red's direction before turning to Ben. "Would you stop calling me sweetheart?"

He smiled. "No."

Frizzy Red fixed his attention on them.

His apparent interest confirmed Lily's fear. As soon as they left, he'd shared this conversation with the town. Just what she needed, more blather for the locals. Well, Ben might not care but she certainly did. Turning, Lily marched to the gym door.

"Hey, your girlfriend didn't pay," Frizzy Red shouted.

Stiffening, Lily wheeled about, her opinion of his comment on the tip of her tongue. Clamping her mouth shut, she stormed back to the counter. She caught Ben's smirk. Narrowing her eyes, she slapped down the money. Lifting her chin, she spun and strode into the gym. Killing the police chief was a definite no-no. She absolutely, positively, would *not* go to jail over *him*.

Climbing on the first treadmill, Lily shed her T-shirt, preferring to run in her sports bra and shorts. Jamming earbuds into her ears, she blasted her music and focused on running.

Within minutes, she caught herself peeking in the lobby, spotting Ben and Frizzy Red in deep discussion. *Are they discussing me?* Her stomach tumbled. She immediately dismissed the thought. *Why do I care anyway?* She continued to stare while trying to read their lips.

Ben glanced her way.

She yelped and squeezed her eyes shut. Taking a deep breath, Lily blocked Ben from her thoughts. She forced herself to envision running outside, surrounded by beautiful pine trees. Her plan didn't work. Instead of picturing the mountainous country road, she fought against images of Ben with his rock-hard flesh, his ripped stomach, and his muscular thighs flashing through her thoughts.

Lily licked her lips. She started for the water, her hand brushing against warm flesh. She snapped open her eyes.

Ben stood with his arms resting on the handrails, watching.

Stumbling, she pitched forward before lurching backward.

He caught her in his arms.

Slamming a hand against the Stop button, Lily adopted an appearance of nonchalance despite being aware of Ben's scrutiny. She stepped off the treadmill and bent to retrieve the shirt she'd dumped on the floor. Taking deep, gulping breaths, she shrugged the t-shirt over her head, hoping he'd take the hint and leave. When her head popped through the neck opening, he was still there. She frowned. "I thought you left."

"Does my presence bother you?" He tucked a strand of her hair behind her ear.

His fingers brushed against her flesh. Lily's heart thumped. *Hell yeah.* Maybe if he were a town or two away, she wouldn't be bothered. Seeing as she'd taken a vow for him never to know her real opinion, she'd just keep her thoughts to herself. She did have pride, after all, and the last thing he needed was an ego-stroke. "No." She lifted her chin. "I just don't appreciate the gossip."

Another smile flitted across his face. "In a place this size, we're bound to be seen together on occasion." he cupped her elbow.

Warm electricity shot through her veins. "What are you doing?"

"It's raining." He tilted his head toward the front. "I thought I'd give you a ride home."

Lily glanced out the broad expanse of window. Sure enough, rain poured from the dark sky. Her lousy luck in action, again. "I'm not made of sugar. I'm sure I won't melt."

He swept his gaze over her, a smile flickering across his lips.

A warm, soft heat suffused her body which in no

way was caused by running. His thumb drifted across her arm, causing her flesh to pebble. She bit her tongue, stopping the sigh from escaping.

"Maybe, but with the lightning, walking is unsafe."

Proving the truth of Ben's words, a flash of white light illuminated the darkness before disappearing, leaving everything gloomy again. Lily pinched her lips tight. She had two choices—either risk death by a lightning zap or endure more gossip. She decided gossip was only slightly less painful than electrocution. Sighing, Lily grabbed her water bottle and towel from the treadmill. "Fine. You can drive me home."

Without saying another word, Ben smiled and pressed his palm against her back to usher her out of the gym.

A burst of electricity raced down Lily's spine. Her muscles tightened, and her knees weakened. Suddenly, electrocution by a bolt of lightning didn't seem so bad.

Chapter 11

"It's official," Peri announced the next morning.

Lily whipped around her head. She'd been so consumed remembering yesterday's ride home with Ben she didn't hear her sister step outside onto the back porch. "What's official?"

"We're going out tonight." Peri plopped into the chair across from Lily's.

"Excuse me?"

Stretching her legs and resting her heels against the porch railing, Peri peered across the yards to Dax's house. "We're going with Maybelline."

"Who?"

"Maybelline. Remember?" Peri waved a hand. "The other day I went with her to the beach. She's fun."

Lily understood only too well what 'fun' Peri meant—a lot of trouble and possible police intervention. "Thank you, but I think I'll pass."

"You can't pass." Peri shook her head. "Tonight is Ladies Night. We're talking a bar full of hot men."

A picture of Ben flashed through Lily's thoughts. She purposely ignored the image. Even if he was there, he wouldn't notice her. He'd be too busy searching for his next conquest. *Typical man.* "Seeing as I'm not searching for hot men, I'll just stay home."

"Well, duh. You have Ben." Peri stretched her arms over head. "Not all of us are as lucky."

"I do not *have* him." Lily fisted her hand in her lap. "I'm not even interested in him."

She didn't consider this statement a lie. Since meeting Ben, she'd only thought of him occasionally—*if* occasionally meant all the time.

"Really?" Peri snorted. "Then prove you're not by going with us tonight."

Jerking back, Lily frowned. *Really? Peri now resorts to peer pressure?* "Why would I do that?"

Peri rocked her foot back and forth on the railing. "Because going would show you're not a couple, as well as stop the gossip."

She really, really, *really* hated when Peri was logical *and* right. Raking fingers through her hair, Lily blew out a breath. "Fine. I'll go, but I have rules."

"What a surprise."

Lily ignored the sarcasm in Peri's voice. "First off, no picking up men for me—hot or otherwise."

Peri wrinkled her nose. "Sounds boring. That rule won't apply to me."

"Obviously," Lily replied drolly. "Also, no drinking."

"For goodness sake, we're going to a bar." Peri's arms shot upward. "You must have at least *one* drink."

Lily considered Peri's words. "Okay. One drink. No more."

"Fine." Glaring, Peri hopped up from her chair. "Anything else, Miss Boring and Predictable?"

Lily stiffened at Peri's choice of words and frowned. "Actually, I do have one more rule. No dancing."

Peri chuckled. "I don't think you can call what you do dancing, but fine, no dancing for *you*." She ripped open the screen door then stopped. Turning, she scowled. "Just for the record, you're a real buzz-kill."

The screen door slammed shut. Lily stared at the neighbor's house. *What if I see Ben tonight? What if he is with another woman?* Her stomach plunged. She dismissed the thought. She didn't care if Ben was out tonight, and she certainly didn't care if he was with another woman.

She was almost positive she didn't. Of course, if she didn't care, why was she suddenly both excited and anxious to see him again?

****

Loud thumping of music competed with the excited buzz of voices waiting to enter Martinis. Standing near the end of the line, Lily looked beyond Peri's shoulders to the entrance of the dingy bar. A tall, bulky man, blocked the opening as if he were a general, only letting people enter as others left.

Lily gritted her teeth, not thrilled she was stuck outside a bar she didn't want to enter, dressed in an outfit so tight the fabric pinched. Of course, the odds of Peri accepting her leaving were slightly less than zero. Still, the thought of exchanging the too-tight dress and over-the-top heels for bare feet and a pair of comfy shorts and an oversized T-shirt sounded delicious. She flattened one hand against the gray stucco wall while the other slipped off one of her four-inch, pink patent-leather stilettos. She rubbed her aching foot, a soft sigh of pleasure escaping in the process.

Peri glanced her way. "What are you doing?"

Lily stilled her hand. "My feet hurt."

"How can they hurt? We just arrived."

"Yeah, after walking a mile in four-inch spikes."

Not to mention spending the next few hours standing in the same heels before repeating the journey home. The pain in her feet intensified. "I should have worn my—" Movement in front of the police station caught her attention.

The glow of the streetlight rained down on Ben. He wasn't alone. A woman leaned into him, pressing her body against his. He was on a date—which meant he wouldn't be here tonight. A let-down feeling flowed through her. She shrugged off the sensation. At least she wouldn't spend the night watching women vie for his attention.

"Isn't that Ben with a woman?" Peri asked.

Lily snapped her attention back. Staring sightlessly at the entrance of the bar, she slid her aching foot back into the shoe, ignoring the odd tightness in her chest. "Sure appears so."

"I guess he's upping the ante."

The hard edge in Peri's voice matched the challenging countenance on her face. Lily ignored both. Her sister might be competitive. She was not. "Ante? Please. The game he's playing, I'm not interested in winning." She marched into Martinis.

****

Stepping from the board room at City Hall, Ben rubbed his eyes. Damn, he was tired. The council meeting had gone on too long. The length of the meeting didn't surprise him. The board discussed everything ad nauseam. Tonight was no exception.

By the time he left, night had blanketed the city. The overhead glow of lights shimmered on the black pavement. The thump and drone of loud music blared from the open doors of Martinis. Ladies Night. His men

103

would be busy dealing with the drunks.

Karla strolled his way.

He stifled a groan. He wasn't in the mood to deal with her not-too-subtle innuendo. Karla Sweet was every man's dream—from her shirts a size too small to the skirts an inch too short. She had the face of an angel and the talents of a sinner, and she made no secret her quest for him.

The cloying smell of patchouli wafted up. "Karla." He greeted her with a stiff smile.

"How was your meeting with the Council?"

She practically purred the question. Ben knew exactly the answers Karla sought. Right now, though, he didn't care to share them with anyone, and most assuredly not with her. "We have meetings every week, Karla." Her hand, manicured to perfection, stroked his arm. She stepped closer, her silk shirt brushing against his chest. Her seductive smile left no doubt of her intention.

"Do you want to come to my house to…discuss your situation?"

Ben drew away her hand. Disbelief, followed by disappointment, and finally, fury, settled on her face. He chose to ignore her act. "You'll need to excuse me, Karla. I have some work I need to finish." He disappeared into the police station, leaving her fuming beneath the street light.

Vinnie, the night duty officer, sat with his feet propped on the desk, a magazine held in one hand. Country music blasted from the radio.

The minute he stepped inside Vinnie shifted his attention from the magazine. The smile of pure enjoyment caused muscles in Ben's cheek to flex.

"I see Karla cornered you." Vinnie dropped the magazine onto the desk. "My guess is she's lining herself up to be the future's mayor's wife. Am I right?"

"Are you asking me if I've decided to run for mayor or if I've asked Karla to marry me?"

Chuckling, Vinnie dropped his feet to the floor. "Oh, I know you wouldn't marry Karla," he stated without hesitation. "Too much history between you two."

Vinnie was right. He shared decades of history with Karla. Some of their past was good, most was bad, but all was sexual.

Leaning back in his chair, Vinnie stacked his hands behind his head. "I'm old, not deaf. I hear the whispers."

What the hell? Does no one talk about anything else? "You can't always believe what you hear."

Grinning, Vinnie studied him crossing the room. "That's true, but the way I see things, Miss Evans is the first woman who hasn't shown you any interest."

Ben stopped at his office door. "And?"

Shrugging, Vinnie smiled. "I know you. In my opinion, she's caught your attention."

"Oh, she definitely caught my attention," Ben snapped, clenching the doorknob. "However, marriage isn't a road I intend to follow."

Vinnie snorted. "Who mentioned anything about marriage?"

A low expletive rumbled from Ben. He threw open the door and stepped inside. "No one." He slammed the door shut.

Dropping into his chair, Ben rubbed his tired eyes before shifting his attention to the stack of papers piled on his desk. He dismissed Vinnie's comment and focused on work. He planned on finishing a third of the stack before leaving for the night. A picture of Lily juxtaposed against an image of Karla floated through his thoughts.

The comparison was comical. Karla oozed sex and innuendo. She didn't hide her desire or her intentions. She *loved* attention—all attention, any attention. For her, the only bad press was no press at all.

Lily, on the other hand, was innocent and provocative bound together. She was the girl next door. Constancy and commitment surrounded her like a second skin. She made no secret of her hate of gossip and attention. Married to the mayor, attention and gossip would be her life.

Tossing his pen on the desk, Ben drove his fingers through his hair. What the hell? He couldn't remember the last time a woman occupied his thoughts longer than it took to seduce her into his bed. He wasn't Vinnie, or Abe, and assuredly not his father. Marriage and Ben were two opposing forces.

Dismissing his thoughts, he shook his head. He didn't desire commitment, and even if he did, marriage to Lily was impossible, for more reasons than he had time to itemize. He should have taken Karla up on her offer. If he had, he'd be experiencing something a hell of a lot more pleasurable than brooding about marriage and Lily.

A knock sounded on the door, breaking the direction of his annoying thoughts. "Come in," he barked.

Vinnie opened the door. "Aaron called about a situation at Martinis."

"Send one of the men." He picked up one of the reports. Abe used yellow legal paper and a pencil, again. He stilled the urge to crumple the paper.

"Aaron asked for you." Vinnie flashed a smile. "He mentioned something about Maybelline."

Ben closed his eyes and gritted his teeth. What the hell was his cousin up to? He forced back his chair and stood. So much for his quiet night.

Martinis was a short walk from the station. However, at the last minute, Ben drove. This way, he could go home afterward. The reports could wait until morning.

Parking his vehicle in the emergency zone in the front of Martinis, he climbed out and started toward the bar.

Gabe, one of the two bouncers Martinis retained, stood near the entrance.

Ben nodded in greeting before strolling into the bar. The name Martinis evoked images of velvet jackets, smoky rooms, and big band music. The bar had none of those trappings. Instead of burgundy carpets on the floors or walls papered in gold, outdated wood paneling and scuffed gray tiles filled the space. The expected sleek mahogany furniture was absent, replaced with laminated tables marred with scars the size of quarters and mismatched chairs of dubious quality. The smooth stylings of swing or jazz music didn't pump from amplifiers. But rather, rock music blasted through crackling speakers in a room smelling of stale beer.

He wasn't surprised by the number of people packed into the bar. In a town this size, people had few places to go to let off steam. Martinis was their release.

He spotted the problem immediately. Aaron confirmed his suspicion with a nod in the direction of the dance floor. Men crowded the area, their attention fixed on one person, each seeking her notice. Hell, even Conor, the lead singer, bent low enough to gape as he sang. The muscle in Ben's cheek flexed.

Lily appeared oblivious to their attention. He was not. Scanning the area, he searched for Peri or Maybelline but found neither. Swinging back his attention to the dance floor, he studied Lily. He thought she might be dancing. He couldn't be positive. He'd never seen anyone kick their legs with such random abandon or undulate their body in such a disjointed way. The men surrounding her didn't seem to care. Her dancing wasn't what held their attention. At least, not the kind a person did in a bar.

Ben shoved his way through the crowd, ignoring their protests.

She tripped walking off the dance floor.

He caught her in his arms. Bleary blue eyes stared back.

"Well, look who's here. The handsome Chief of Police. Why are you here?"

Her words came out in a soft, slurred purr. She was drunk. Ben held her by the waist until she steadied herself. He didn't mind in the least, finding he liked holding her in his arms. "Time to go home." He curled his fingers into the soft flesh of her waist.

Perfectly glossed lips pouted. "I don't want to go home. I want to dance with you."

Her tongue flicked across her far-too-sexy lips. Desire burned through him. He doubted she understood the temptation of the subtle invitation. "Maybe another time, sweetheart." He brushed a strand of hair from her face. "Where's your table?"

Lily waved a hand toward a table a few feet from the dance floor.

He helped her over. "Is your purse here?" He searched the area for something resembling a purse.

When she didn't answer, he spotted her picking up a half-empty glass of watery looking pink liquid.

She started to take a sip from the straw.

Removing the drink from her grip, he set the glass on the table. "I don't think you need any more."

Wobbling slightly, she frowned.

He spotted the purse on the floor and bent to retrieve it. "Come on." He reached for her, only to see her plop into the chair and slip off a pair of unbelievably, sexy hot-pink heels. "What are you doing?"

A lopsided grin split her face. She held the shoes outward. "Will you carry these?"

Sighing, he stretched out his hand. Hooking his fingers into the straps, he clasped Lily's hand, helping her to stand. Two steps later, she stopped him again. The muscle flexed in his cheek. "What now?"

"I can't go home with you. I'm going home with…"

Fury flared inside him. He glared at the men. Whoever the hell planned on going home with her needed to rethink his idea. The only person she'd leave with tonight was him, and tomorrow, they'd have a conversation about her reckless behavior. "The hell you are."

Maybelline stopped in front of them. "Oh good, you arrived."

Drenched in sweat and a barely-there dress, Peri followed. "I hope you're here for Lily, because I don't think she can make the walk home on her own, and I'm not ready to go."

The tension in his shoulders eased. "What about you?"

Peri smiled and fluffed the side of her hair. "Oh, don't worry. I'll find a way."

Neither Peri nor Maybelline appeared drunk. However, he considered them his responsibility, which meant he'd make certain they arrived home safely. "When you're ready to leave, call me."

A pout formed on Peri's lips. "But—"

He gave her a stern look. "Call me."

Peri blew out a breath. "Fine. We'll call you."

She flounced away then stopped. Lifting her chin, she glowered. "You two are perfect together." She huffed. "You both know how to ruin a wonderful time."

Dismissing her comment and angry glare, Ben escorted Lily through the crowded bar. Several men cast speculative glances in their direction. He returned their stares with a scowl. He wasn't jealous. He was irritated, though. How could he protect her when she put herself into dangerous situations? He tightened his grip on her side, slinging open the door, he steered her outside.

Conor rested against the wall, smoking a cigarette. He swept his gaze over Lily, taking in every inch of her.

Wedged against Ben's side, Lily fixed her gaze on the sidewalk oblivious to Conor's inspection.

Ben, however, noticed and gritted his teeth.

Conor flicked his cigarette to the ground, crushing

the butt with the heel of his boot. When he was finished, he looked up.

Capturing Conor's gaze, Ben glared.

Heat rushed to Conor's cheeks, and he quickly shifted his gaze away.

"Look." Lily tugged on Ben's hand. "The singer. I want to say hello."

Forcing his gaze from Conor, Ben glanced downward. Lily stared up at him, her gaze bleary. He softened his frown. "No."

Lily bobbed her head. "Why not?"

Ben hid his smile at the drunken confusion in Lily's glazed eyes. "Because he's busy." He ushered her toward his truck.

Smiling, Lily threw a glance over her shoulder. "He bought me a drink. Isn't he polite?"

Hell no, Ben wanted to say. Instead, he swallowed back barely-contained ire. "I'll thank him for you." Luminous blue eyes stared back.

"You will?"

Ben nodded, realizing he could drown in their depths. He ignored the outlandish thought. "First thing tomorrow."

She tilted back her head.

The smile she gave him was breath-taking. His irritation softened just a bit. He guided her toward his truck, stopping once he reached the passenger door. Reaching for the doorknob, he noticed Lily chewing on her lower lip. "Is everything okay?"

Shifting slightly back, Lily dropped her gaze. "Shouldn't you be with your girlfriend?"

A small burst of annoyance erupted inside him. Ben rolled his eyes. The woman was obsessed with his imagined girlfriends. "And that girlfriend is…?"

"The one I spotted you with tonight."

Frowning, he opened the passenger door. "Lily, I was at work."

Lily shook her head. "Earlier, you were with a woman."

Jerking back, Ben blinked. "Karla? She's just a friend."

Wrinkling her brow, Lily searched his face. "Oh…"

He watched her contemplate his words. Within seconds, her face lit with excitement, similar to a little girl on Christmas morning. Her enthusiasm made him smile.

"Did I tell you my plan?"

Ben smiled. The woman's conversation bounced from one idea to the next like a ping-pong ball. "What plan?" He helped her into the seat.

"With the church people." Lily dug her fingers into the seatbelt. "They hate me."

Sympathy tugged on Ben's heart. He could only imagine how difficult things must be to acclimate to such an insular town. He tucked a strand of hair behind her ear. "Yeah, they do."

She snapped her gaze upward. "Hey, that's mean."

He didn't bother to point out she mentioned the fact in the first place. "What's your plan?"

"I've decided to make the donuts on Sunday."

She made her suggestion sound reasonable. Ben softened his smile. "Lily, they don't make donuts."

"Then I'll just make the coffee."

He reached for the seatbelt. The soft touch of fingers brushing against his cheek startled him. Stilling, he turned. Her sultry blue eyes held a depth of longing he hadn't expected.

She inched closer.

Their lips were a breath apart. Ben recognized her offer. For a fleeting second, he considered shoving aside his conscience. Reason returned. By tomorrow, Lily will have forgotten the whole night. He wouldn't, though, and he'd hate himself for taking advantage of the situation.

Gently, he cupped her hand, removing her touch from his cheek, before snapping the seatbelt in place. He slammed shut the door, stopping himself from doing anything foolish.

By the time they reached her house, Lily was asleep.

The ink black sky shimmered with stars, and a dog barked, breaking the silence.

Ben opened her door. Her head lolled to one side, the collar of her shirt dipped past her shoulder, exposing her white lacy bra and the gentle swell of her breast. He gritted his teeth, determined to ignore the desire burning inside.

He grabbed her shoes first, dangling them from his fingers before scooping Lily from the seat. Ben cradled her in his arms.

Lily snuggled deeper into his chest.

His shirt muffled her sigh. Ben looked down. Her eyes remained closed, and a contented smile rested on her lips. The sound of gravel crunched beneath his booted feet. He crossed the driveway and climbed the wooden steps of the back porch. Whether sober or drunk, Lily was a complication he hadn't expected. She looked helpless. A tightness settled inside him.

Her eyelids fluttered open, and she stared upward.

Groggy confusion filled her gaze. He gave her a soft smile. "You fell asleep."

Lily widened her eyes. "I did?"

Ben slowly set her on the ground. Her body skimmed over his, causing the desire he desperately wanted to avoid, come alive. He clutched her waist, waiting for her to steady.

Tilting back her head, she searched his face.

Seeing a quick flick of her tongue across her lips, Ben gave up the battle he knew he'd lost. He brushed his lips against hers.

The crash of a metal garbage can in someone's yard broke the moment.

Jerking away, Lily swept her gaze across the yard. "What was that noise?"

Ben shuddered, ignoring the heat burning through him. What the hell? Why did he feel sixteen again, experiencing his first kiss? A not-so-satisfying kiss, either. Clearing his throat, he shrugged. "Probably a raccoon." He held out his hand. "Where's your key?"

Turning, she lifted a small clay pot set atop the porch railing.

The container held dried dirt and little else. The key hid beneath, gleaming innocently in the porch light. Any reaction to the kiss evaporated. He snapped his gaze to Lily. Worry lurked in her eyes.

"I'm not Peri." The words rushed from her lips, and her cheeks turned bright pink.

He had no idea why she'd think he'd forget. The difference between the two women was obvious. Plucking the key from the railing, he stepped forward and opened the door. "I never thought otherwise."

Strolling inside, Lily grabbed the door knob.

Ben started to follow.

She threw shut the door.

Luckily, he was sober. Otherwise, a closed door would be separating them right now. He struck a palm against the door, preventing her from locking him out. "Lily, I just want to check the hou—" All the color drained from Lily's face. He frowned. "Are you okay?"

"I think I'm sick."

She kept her promise.

Ben looked down at his soiled shirt then back to the woman clutching his arm. Complication? Definitely. Was she worth it? Now, Ben wasn't so sure.

Chapter 12

Lily woke with a splitting headache and a churning stomach. She sat upright. Her stomach lurched. Flopping back against the pillow, she pressed a shaking hand to her forehead. What the hell happened last night?

Images of a night filled with too much dancing and even more drinking rushed through her thoughts. She closed her eyes and groaned. Hadn't she explicitly told Peri she would do neither?

Then again, Peri hadn't forced her to dance, and she certainly hadn't bought her all the drinks. No, that honor went to…

She snapped open her eyes. *Oh God! Ben was there.*

Images of them dancing together curled through her. She frowned and raked her fingers through her hair. How was that possible? He'd been on a date. *Wasn't he?*

Of course, he had been. She'd seen him with a woman. The only reason her mind had him in the bar was because she'd seen him prior.

Sitting, she sighed. Relieved to have resolved her dilemma, Lily kicked off the covers and swung her legs over the bed. With a moan, she dressed in a loose nightshirt and plodded to the kitchen. Grit filled her eyes like sandpaper, and her mouth seemed stuffed with cotton balls. What she needed was a cup of strong coffee.

After searching every cupboard, she didn't find a single bean. Giving up any hope for hot coffee, Lily slammed shut the cupboard door. Closing her eyes, she clutched her head and groaned.

Taking a deep breath to calm the queasiness, she stepped outside. Fresh air would help eliminate her headache and clear her mind. Dropping into a lounge chair, she closed her eyes and rested her head against the back of the cushion.

Footsteps sounded on the gravel driveway.

Snapping open her eyes, she whipped around her head.

Ben strode up the wooden porch steps.

She jumped from the chair and flushed, realizing she wore nothing more than a nightshirt. Curling her fingers into the edge of the shirt and drawing the fabric downward, she wished more than anything she'd worn something more...concealing.

Ben held out a paper cup. "I thought you could use some coffee today."

The sight of steam wafting from the lid's opening nearly caused Lily to swoon. Reluctantly, she released her grip on the nightshirt, ignoring the fact he'd caught her less-than-perfect appearance, and today, perfect was so far away she couldn't even see it over the horizon. "Thanks." She accepted the cup. Taking a sip, she sighed in delight. The coffee tasted just the way she preferred—hot, creamy, and sweetened with the exact amount of sugar. "How did you know how I like my coffee?"

****

He shrugged. "I didn't. Betty did." Ben glanced at the houses lining Lily's backyard. At this time of the morning, the Smiths would be at work, and the Waverlys were nearsighted and close to eighty. Hell, he'd bet they couldn't even *see* her backyard. Gritting his teeth, he ignored the burst of irritation.

Spying Dax's yard, Ben tightened his grip on the paper cup. Dax wasn't anywhere close to eighty, and he sure as hell wasn't nearsighted. He might not hit on Lily, but he wasn't a monk either. He could spot a beautiful woman in the dark. By nine in the morning, she would be on his radar. Dressed in nothing more than a skimpy T-shirt, she would be impossible for him to resist.

Turning back, he took a moment to enjoy the curves of her body and her long, toned legs peeking from beneath the hem of the entirely-too-short nightshirt. Incredible didn't begin to describe the sight. Hot might be a better word—or maybe, downright-mouth-watering-torture. "You should wear clothing when you're outside."

Lily blushed, tugging the hem. "I'm in my backyard. No one can see me."

He arched a brow upward and pointed across the yard. "Do you see those houses?"

Frowning, Lily set her cup on the table. "Of course. I'm not blind, you know."

He met her glare with one of his own. "Trust me, the people in the houses aren't either." He kept his annoyance in check. "I guarantee they can see you."

Lily rolled her eyes. "I'm certain they have other interests more appealing than staring at me."

Ben couldn't imagine what interest would be more

entertaining. Actually, he could envision something better. Although, he doubted she'd appreciate his thoughts. He set his cup on the railing before stopping in front of her. "How are you feeling today?"

Lily grimaced. "I'm fine."

He stilled his laughter. Her face was chalk white, her lips seamed together, and her hair a tangled mess. In no way did he believe she was 'fine.' Taking pity, he caressed her cheek with a thumb. "Really? You look like hell."

A gasp ripped from her. "Did you just insult me?"

Her outrage caused him to laugh. "Just pointing out the obvious. After last night…"

She stepped backward. "What about last night?"

He smiled. "You were a little worse for wear."

Narrowing her eyes, she dropped her hands to her hips. "How do you know?"

Shrugging, Ben picked up his cup of coffee and took a sip. "Let's just say, my finger is on the pulse of everything in town."

Lily pinched her lips together. "It's called gossip, Ben."

Chuckling, he brushed a strand of hair from her forehead. "Not gossip, sweetheart, but fact."

"Stop calling me sweetheart." Lily batted his hand. "You need to leave."

"Why?" He stepped close enough to feel her heat.

Tilting back her head, she met his stare.

For a moment, he wondered if she remembered the brief kiss they'd shared in nearly the exact spot where they stood right now, or if she'd forgotten that fact, too. He sure as hell hadn't. Most of last night he spent replaying the events and wondering what might have happened if she hadn't been drunk or gotten sick.

A lawnmower rumbling in the near distance broke the moment. Lily shifted her attention to the backyard. She turned back and frowned. "I told you before. We already have enough gossip. We don't need any more."

Ben gathered her against him. "After last night, I don't think you can stop people from talking."

Leaning back, she smoothed her hands against his chest. "What do you mean?"

He caught a glimpse of uncertainty in the depth of her eyes, and the way she bit her lower lip confirmed his original thought. She didn't remember last evening. He smiled. "How do you think you came home last night?"

She shrugged. "I walked home with Peri."

Laughter burst out.

Pinching together her brows, she frowned. "What's so amusing?"

Ben rested his chin on the top of her head. "Lily, you couldn't even walk out the door of Martinis."

She snapped her attention upward. "How would you know? You were on a date."

Tightening his grip on her waist, he smiled. "No, I wasn't."

She searched his face for just a moment before she shoved her palms flat against his chest and broke free. Dropping her hands to her hips, she glared. "What happened? One woman not enough for you? You had to go to Martinis to find more?"

Ben snorted. Between rescuing her and working, he barely had time for sleep, let alone another woman. Not that he'd even considered the prospect. Since meeting Lily, the thought of another woman hadn't crossed his mind. "Sweetheart, I wasn't at Martinis to pick up women. I was there to pick up *you*."

Lily jabbed a finger into her chest. "Me?"

The look of confusion and discomfort on her face caused Ben a moment of enjoyment. He blew on his coffee, waiting for her to put the pieces of puzzles together.

"You mean, you picked me up because I was—" Licking her lips, she cleared her throat. "What I meant was that you offered to bring me home?"

Ben laughed. "Something like that."

Lily narrowed her eyes. "You left, though, right? I mean after you dropped me off."

"After a bit." Ben shrugged.

She furrowed her brows. "You helped me into the house?"

"Amongst other things." Ben smiled, confident he could see the wheels turning inside her head.

Lily widened her eyes. "Are you saying...?" Her gaze searched his. "I mean, we couldn't have...I'd remember if we had...I mean, I should remember if we...shouldn't I?"

He cocked a brow. So, she didn't remember. Any other time, Ben would be offended. After all, as far as he knew, she was the first woman who didn't remember kissing him. "Maybe I can help you remember." He captured her lips in a hot, searing kiss far better than last night's and exceeded anything he imagined was possible. He drew her tighter against him.

She stiffened for just a moment before her lips softened and her arms circled his neck, pulling him downward and deepening the kiss.

He took his time savoring the moment, resting his

Jules Hahn

hands on her lower back with his thumbs making lazy circles, itching to move lower.

Suddenly, she jolted and broke free.

Ben dropped his hands. Desire burned through him. He raked his fingers through his hair and took a deep breath before turning to Lily. Her face was flushed, and a worried look had settled in her eyes.

"We can't kiss." Rushing across the porch, Lily ripped open the screen door. She turned back to face him. "Never again, Ben. Do you hear me?"

Enjoying her look of outrage, he winked. "Yeah. You mentioned the same thing last night, too."

She stormed into the house and slammed shut the door. A low chuckle rumbled from Ben's chest. He couldn't remember the last time he actually enjoyed a battle of wits with a woman. Anticipation filled him. He eagerly awaited their next skirmish.

Chapter 13

Claire recognized a problem when she spotted one. Or rather, when she heard one. Heck, with all the yelling coming from Lily's porch, Claire figured half the neighborhood heard their argument.

She waited until the growl of Ben's truck engine announced his departure before she made her move. She forced herself to count to fifty, though, just to make sure Lily didn't return. The house remained silent. Claire took a deep breath before darting from the rose bush she crouched behind. She dashed across the yards to Minnie's place, bursting into the house without knocking.

Hank jumped a foot in his chair. "What the heck are you doing?"

"Just here to visit Minnie." Claire breezed past Hank stretched out in the chair. "Cute boxers."

"Good grief, woman. You're not supposed to notice." Glowering, Hank snagged the crocheted olive green and burnt orange afghan from the back of the chair and tossed the blanket across his lap.

She didn't see how she couldn't. Blue boxers with yellow ducks on them had a way of standing out. The ducks didn't surprise Claire. Everyone in town knew Minnie's obsessions with them, but *really?* Ducks on underwear seemed a bit excessive. Dismissing the issue, she burst into the kitchen.

Minnie, standing at the sink washing dishes, spun. She clutched a dripping hand to her chest. "Claire! You nearly scared the life from me."

Claire shut the kitchen door. "We need to talk." Settling into a kitchen chair, she clenched her hands. "I think Ben and Llly broke up."

Widening her eyes, Minnie pressed a hand to her mouth. "But that can't be."

Claire shook her head. "It's true."

Sighing, Minnie dried her hands on a dish towel. "Okay, tell me what happened?"

"Well, I just left my garage when I heard them arguing." Claire dragged her chair closer. "Lily told Ben it wouldn't happen again."

Minnie tilted her head to the side. "What wouldn't happen?"

Claire leaned forward. "She didn't say. She just flew inside the house and slammed the door right in Ben's face."

With a gasp, Minnie dropped into a chair. "What did he do?"

Claire shrugged. "Nothing. He just left."

Minnie sat back and clutched together her hands. "Oh my, that's bad." She sighed. "I just don't believe it. All women love him."

"Maybe she's jealous?" Claire suggested.

"I'd be jealous if another woman loved Hank."

Claire rolled her eyes. Minnie had lost her mind. "I don't think you need to worry."

Frowning, Minnie tapped her fingers on the laminate surface. "Maybe not now. Back in the day, though, Hank was an attractive man. I'm sure he could have any woman he wanted."

Claire was equally sure Minnie had forgotten the Hank of the past. He wasn't far from the Hank of the present, and she doubted much of a change would happen to the Hank of the future, either. "Focus, Minnie. We're not here to discuss Hank. We're talking about Lily and Ben. What are we going to do?"

Lifting one shoulder, Minnie waved a hand. "Maybe it was just a silly fight and they'll make up later, after they've had time to cool down."

Claire slapped a hand on the table.

Minnie yelped.

Flying from her chair, Claire tugged Minnie out the back door. No need to have Hank come in to overhear her plan.

"Have you lost your mind, Claire Jordan? What the heck are you doing dragging me around? I'm not a rag doll." Minnie hissed.

Claire yanked her down the porch steps. "Shsh!" She peered over the shrubs to Lily's house. The yard remained quiet. She towed Minnie behind the garage.

Minnie swiped a hand over her arms. "I think you shoved me through a spider web. Do you see one crawling on me? You know how allergic I am to spiders." She thrust out her arms.

Claire shoved them away. "Minnie, we don't have time for your silly worries. We have a tragic situation, here."

"That's what I'm saying. Imagine the tragedy if I'm bitten. The last time I broke out in huge bumps."

"For goodness sake, Minnie. Everyone breaks out after a spider bite. I meant Ben and Lily, not your trumped-up allergies."

Minnie sniffed. "What's the plan?"

Claire clasped her hands to her chest. "We need to show Lily she needs him."

"Claire Ellen Sheffield Jordan, just what exactly are you planning?" Minnie narrowed her gaze.

Claire smiled. "My idea is simple. We'll just scare the hell out of her."

Satisfied she'd found the perfect solution, Claire outlined the plan. Afterward, she practically floated home, giddy with happiness.

Now, hours later, Claire debated the wisdom of her plans. She knew her idea wasn't the noblest, but heck, desperate times called for desperate measures. She wanted Ben to find his perfect mate, and she knew love wouldn't happen with any of the women he'd dated in town. The Karlas of the world thrived on mischief, and they most definitely didn't meet her standards for a daughter-in-law.

Of course, Jenny Pickler was better than Karla Sweet. Jenny also thought she was better than everyone else. Jenny wasn't Claire's choice for a daughter-in-law, and not just because of her issue with Jenny's parents, Lyle and Gracie Pickler.

Nearly forty years had passed since Gracie stole Lyle Pickler from her in high school, and in Claire's opinion, another forty years would need to go by before she'd even consider forgiving Gracie. Being sixteen and new in town had been hard enough for Claire. Gracie Jean hadn't helped her acclimation. When Gracie announced to everyone that Claire had zero chances of capturing Lyle Pickler because she was an outsider, she'd stepped over the line.

Claire supposed she should be thankful for Gracie's viciousness. Otherwise, she might have missed out on falling in love with Robert. However, she wasn't in a forgiving mood. Just because the situation had worked out for Claire didn't mean she'd forgotten.

Lily Evans was perfect, though. She was down to earth, and she didn't swoon at Ben's feet or fall for his charm, which in Claire's view, was her best quality.

Despite the fight today, she didn't believe for a minute Ben or Lily were finished. Goodness knows, enough sparks flew between them to set the whole Adirondacks on fire. Claire believed her sacred duty was to help them see they were perfect together.

More importantly, Claire wanted grandbabies. Heck, all her girlfriends had grandbabies. Francine had two, with a third on the way. Elma had six and with four kids of her own, who knew how many more grandchildren she'd have. Betty had three grandbabies, and she was gay. Of course, she decided she was gay only a few years ago. Still, she was gay with grandbabies, and here Claire was with two grown children and no grandbabies. The whole thing was shameful…just shameful. Claire, however, intended to rectify that matter, and quickly.

Usually, a mother would hold out hope for her daughter to marry first. Claire didn't expect Ellen to settle down any time soon, though. At least, not with her current boyfriend, Grant. Despite Ellen's opinion of him, Claire just couldn't tolerate him.

Her only option was Ben. She just needed to help Lily see he was a perfect match. She wasn't the only one who held this opinion. Everyone in town thought the same. He had everything going for him—handsome, athletic, respected, and in a few months, he'd be mayor. He hadn't agreed yet, but Claire knew he would, and when he did, he'd need the right woman to help him lead the town into the future.

Claire peeked out the side window. Dark clouds scuttled across the night sky, momentarily obliterating the glow of the moonlight. Glancing toward Lily's, Claire chewed her lip. *Am I doing the right thing? What if I make things worse?*

An image of Ben with Lily flashed through Claire's thoughts. She saw the way he watched her, the way his gaze softened and an easy smile curled on his lips. Lily was more than a fling. Ben didn't waste his time chasing after women—not when another waited in the wings.

A sense of lightness filled Claire. *I'm right. My plan is right. I know it straight down to my toes.*

Claire glanced toward the mantel. The red glow of the clock showed the time creeping closer to the appointed hour. While she waited, she wore a path in her living room carpet, wondering whether her plans were all for naught. Earlier, she had overheard Peri inviting Lily to a party at the lake. Claire prayed Peri hadn't ruined her carefully made plans.

Finally, the moment arrived. She hurried up the stairs and into the bedroom. Scooping the clothing she'd laid out earlier off the bed, she dashed into the bathroom.

Claire dressed in her darkest outfit, which was a pair of black sweats and a black long-sleeved sweatshirt. When she finished, she knotted a black silk scarf around her head. The scarf, a Christmas gift from Ben, was a sentimental touch. Her white sneakers were a real concern, though. They would stand out like a full moon on a dark night. Her other option was a pair of black heels. She discarded the idea. *No need to break my neck in the process of scaring Lily.*

When she spied Peri leaving the house alone, Claire rushed to the phone and called Minnie. "The plan is on." She slammed down the phone before Minnie made up some ridiculous excuse to avoid the plan.

The time finally arrived for Operation Love Machine. With one hand on the wall and the other on the handrail, Claire made her way down the dark stairs. Carefully, she worked her way through the house with only a few minor bumps and bruises.

Opening her door, Claire poked her head outside. Night descended, enveloping the neighborhood in a black velvet cloak. The high-pitched howl of Barney, Mrs. Jones' beagle, broke the silence. She tiptoed from her house, careful to make no sound other than the soft click of the door closing.

"I'm here," Minnie called out in a loud whisper.

Claire stifled a yelp. In the soft light of the cloud-covered moon, Minnie was barely visible. She clutched a hand against her chest. "Dear Lord. You scared me."

"You didn't see me because of my makeup. I bought the paint today at the Hunter's Hut."

A repulsive smell washed over Claire. She waved a hand in front of her face. "Good God, you stink. What is that odor?"

"Deer urine mixed with some camo makeup." Minnie giggled. "The gunk might stink, but we needed something dark to hide our faces and this stuff works. Here's some for you."

Before Claire could say no, Minnie swiped a wad of the foul black goop across her cheek.

"Just rub the paint over your face," Minnie told

her.

Claire didn't have an option seeing as the foul-smelling ointment was stuck to her skin. She rubbed in the gunk, while Minnie chattered on and on. Grabbing the can from her, Claire dipped her finger in the mess and added more. When in Rome…

"Claire, check out my hair. You can't see my grays, can you?"

Claire strained to see Minnie in the darkness. "I can't see anything."

"I know!" Minnie clapped. "I bought a stocking cap today to cover my hair. I figured, this winter, Hank could wear the hat to cover his head. And just look at my feet. You can't see my shoes, either."

Wiping her hands on her pants, Claire searched for Minnie's white shoes. Dang if they weren't invisible. "What did you do?" She tucked the can into the sleeve of her sweatshirt.

"I slipped a pair of Hank's black tube socks over them."

Claire admitted Minnie's disguise was clever. "I wish I thought of the socks."

"Yeah. I could see you coming from your house because of those shoes." She paused for a moment. "Hey, you want me to dash home and grab you a pair of Hank's socks? We have plenty."

"We don't have the time. Ben leaves work by eleven-thirty."

"You're certain he's working?"

Claire nodded. "He'll leave when Vinnie arrives."

The kitchen light flicked on.

Grabbing Minnie, Claire flattened herself against the side of Lily's house. She clamped a finger against her lips, silently watching the window. Holding her breath, she waited to see what happened.

The light remained on for a second before shutting off.

"Whoa, talk about close." Minnie heaved a sigh. "Now what?"

"We scare her." Claire tiptoed to the porch steps and pointed to the garbage cans. "Bang on those cans."

Nodding, Minnie hit one of the cans, making a soft ping.

"Louder," Claire urged.

Minnie banged harder. The can tipped, knocking the garbage can beside it. A loud crash of metal slamming against metal echoed in the still night.

"There you go." Claire fanned her hand. "Hit the can again. I'll bang on the door."

While Minnie gave the cans a swift kick with her sock-covered foot, Claire rattled the knob. Loud, obnoxious noise filled the area. With her heart pounding, Claire peered through the window in the kitchen door. The house remained silent.

"Do you think she's awake?" Minnie asked.

"She was just in the kitchen." Claire couldn't help the tinge of exasperation in her voice. Sometimes Minnie asked the darnedest questions.

"Maybe Peri turned on the light," Minnie suggested.

Claire shook her head. "Peri left earlier with Maybelline." She nudged her chin toward the cans only to realize Minnie couldn't see her. "Kick them some more. I'll work on the doorknob."

She rattled the handle for so long her arms hurt and still she heard no screaming sirens racing toward Lily's house.

"How long do you want me to kick these things? I think my toes are black and blue," Minnie grumbled.

Claire pointed toward the driveway. "Check and see if anyone is coming."

Minnie inched her way to the edge of the porch and peered around the corner of the house. She whipped her attention back to Claire. "A car is out front."

Claire waved her hands. "Well? Who's here?"

Swiveling, Minnie peeked again. The glow of the street light in front of Lily's house illuminated the area. She let out a gasp. "It's Ben."

Springing forward, Claire darted toward the steps.

"I don't want to be sent up the river." Minnie jumped back and into Claire.

Stumbling, Claire slammed into the trash cans. The loud clatter of metal against metal sounded loud in the night. She whipped around and glared. "Oh, for goodness sake, we won't go to jail." Tugging on Minnie's shirt, Claire towed her down the steps.

The kitchen lights flicked on.

For a second, Claire thought her heart stopped beating. She released Minnie's shirt and hurried across the grass. She didn't know what she'd do if Ben spotted her. How would she explain why she was dressed in pure black, smelling like a latrine? The worry was enough to propel her through the grass. Dashing across the yard, she eyed a small break in the shrubs.

A soft shriek sounded behind her just a scant second before a body landed against her back, propelling her forward. She crashed onto the hard dirt with a thud, nearly jamming out an eye with one of her rose branches. Gasping for breath, she looked over her shoulder to see Minnie flattened atop her. "Get off *me,*" she said through gritted teeth.

Minnie rolled away.

Wiggling beneath the bushes, Claire peered across Lily's yard.

Minnie followed suit.

The glow of a flashlight fanned over the grass.

"Here he comes," Claire whispered. Holding her breath, she prayed Ben didn't spot her.

The bright light skimmed the bushes, pausing for a second on where Claire hid.

Sucking in a breath, Claire stayed deathly still until the flashlight shifted. When Lily opened the back door, and Ben stepped inside, the tension in her shoulders eased. "Do you think we were successful?"

"I sure hope so." Minnie wrinkled her nose. "I have a plastic bowl stuck to my foot."

In the moonlight, Minnie's foot was easy to spot, especially with an empty plastic butter tub wedged on her sock-covered sneaker.

Claire burst into laughter. "Are you saying you ran across the yards with that container stuck to your shoe?"

Minnie kicked the dish off her foot. "I was so worried he'd spot us, I just took off."

"Oh my gosh, we've never done anything this crazy." Claire giggled.

"Yeah, what a hoot." Minnie chuckled. "I hope your plan worked."

Claire nodded. "I'm certain it did."

Chapter 14

Sleep refused to come to Lily. For two long hours, she tossed and turned. In the end, her only accomplishment was tangling herself in the blankets, and all because of Ben's kiss. If he had just kept his lips to himself, she'd be snuggled under her crisp, cool sheets, dreaming of...

She scrubbed her fingers through her hair and groaned. *Who am I kidding?* Her dreams weren't filled with soft, cottony sheep jumping over wooden fences. Instead, Mr. Tall-Dark-and-Handsome held the starring role.

Gritting her teeth, Lily kicked off the blankets and strolled into the kitchen to grab a glass of water. She finished her drink and set the glass into the sink before stumbling into the bedroom. Plopping down in the bed, she clutched the sheets to her chin, determined to fall asleep.

Images of Ben swirled through her thoughts. Lily drummed her fingers on the sheets. *Okay, so I find him attractive. No big deal. What woman wouldn't?* A confident man was a sure aphrodisiac for any woman. Given the fact she hadn't had sex in months, dreaming of sex with him was only natural. She wasn't an angel. Sex thoughts happened—which just happened to be especially true since her arrival. Add the fact all her previous assumptions were wrong and well...the thoughts had become more frequent. Still, that realization didn't mean she *liked* him.

Does it?

A soft noise sounded outside her window. The sound was hardly audible—Barely a ping of metallic. The noise was loud enough to cause the hairs on her arms to stand on end and her heart to skip a beat.

Lily bolted upright. Clutching the sheets, she strained to identify the noise. Clearly, the sound hadn't come from Peri. Eleven at night was far too early for her to come home. Heck, she'd be lucky if her sister stumbled in before eleven *a.m.*

Another loud crash sounded. Lily scrambled out of bed. With her heart pounding, she raced to the window, her steps muffled by the soft, plush carpet. She leaned against the wall, willing herself to remain still.

She strained to listen. The night remained silent. A sigh escaped her. She started for her bed, when voices sounded again, soft and indistinct. She stilled, and every muscle in her body tensed, ready to flee.

Muffled footsteps sounded on the porch.

A scream burned in her throat. Lily clasped her hand against her mouth, stifling the cry.

When the kitchen doorknob rattled, instinct kicked in. She spied her closet. Tossed inside lay loads of dangerous weapons with pointy spikes which caused bunions and hammertoes. Right now, she'd be happy if she poked out an eye or two. Racing to the closet, Lily grabbed the first thing her hand touched—a pink, four-inch stiletto heel.

Grabbing her cell phone off the nightstand, Lily bolted from her room, dashed through the kitchen, and straight into the darkened living room. She stilled her shaking hands while she dialed nine-one-one. In her fright, she forgot her address.

Apparently, the officer didn't care. In a cheery voice, he dismissed her lack of memory, assuring her he knew exactly where she lived. Lily frowned. *Is he happy because the town has few emergencies?* If so, she wished he was cheerful at another person's expense.

One amazing thing resulted from the phone call. All thoughts of Ben disappeared. Although, Lily vowed once she resolved her problem, he'd know her opinion of his personnel taking her call lightly.

Hurrying to the window next to the front door, Lily thrust aside the brown velvet curtain and peered down both ends of the street. No police cars with red lights flashing raced toward her house. No loud sirens alerted the neighbors of the danger. She debated running to Claire's house. However, considering how old Claire seemed, Lily figured she'd gone to bed hours ago.

A few moments later, and after countless times of peeking out the window, Lily spotted a car in front of her house. Recognizing Ben's vehicle, she sighed. He would take care of the burglars.

Walking to the front of his vehicle, Ben scanned the yard.

He wore the same clothing as earlier. Only now, he had added a dark brown sports coat over his once wrinkle-free shirt. A frown creased her brow. *Something isn't right.* A quick glimpse and she had her answer.

He didn't have a gun. Lily shook her head and swept her gaze over him again. *Yup. Definitely no gun. How the heck does he expect to take care of a burglar without a gun? Doesn't he realize he risks death? Well, shoot.* She didn't want him to die. *Talk about creating gossip.* The police chief getting murdered while protecting her would guarantee *every* person's hatred.

Opening the door, Lily popped her head out the crack. In the glow of the street light, she spotted Ben heading toward the driveway. "Ben," she hissed.

Stopping dead in his tracks, he snapped his attention to the front door.

She waved her shoe. "They're out back." She opened the door farther. "Come this way."

He widened his eyes for just a second before narrowing them. "Did you just invite me inside?"

Lily flinched. *Jeez, his voice is loud enough to wake the neighborhood.* "You don't need to yell."

He gritted his teeth. "Lily, get inside."

Clenching the door jamb, Lily glared. "If your plan is to scare them away, you're doing an excellent job."

The muscle flexed in Ben's cheek. *"Lily..."*

He growled her name. Lily dropped her hands from the edge of the door and huffed. "Fine," she muttered. "You take care of the outside. I'll cover the inside. I have this shoe to help me." To prove her point, she waved the pointy, pink lethal weapon.

His face turned to granite.

Lily frowned. He had a bunch of nerve being angry. All she wanted was to help. Well, if he thought she'd allow him to behave in such a rude manner, he'd better think again. Now, she had *two* topics to discuss with him—his lack of manners *and* his lack of preparation for his job.

He grumbled something about her mental abilities.

She slammed the door, adding his rude comment to the list as well. Assuming he was alive for her to explain anything.

Rushing into the kitchen, she shoved aside the yellow-and-white checked curtains and peered out the side window.

Ben clung to the shadows of the driveway on his way to the backyard.

He certainly took his time. Did he think this visit was a social call? Did the man have no sense of danger? She tapped the shoe against the glass and pointed to the back porch.

He snapped his gaze to Lily.

A shiver raced down her spine. His typically placid face was nowhere close to calm. Heat burned in his eyes, and his jaw clenched with enough force she was certain he'd crack a tooth. This look was his *I-mean-business* face. For once, she was grateful he didn't direct his anger toward her.

Thinking to help him locate the intruders, Lily flipped the light switch.

He shot another glare in her direction before disappearing around the corner of the house.

Lily hurried over to the kitchen window. She started for the curtain then stopped. The thought of seeing him kill someone—or worse, him getting killed—caused her to drop the curtain. Straining to hear through the walls, she gripped the shoe so tightly her knuckles turned white.

She didn't want to attack the bandits. She would, though, if she needed to. Holding still, Lily listened for gunshots, or grunts and yells, or feet scuffling in the grass. Silence filled the darkness.

The seconds stretched into one long, interminable minute. Just when Lily thought her nerves would snap, heavy footsteps sounded on the wooden planks outside. With a shaking hand, she gripped the edge of the curtains and peeked out.

Ben strolled across the porch.

All the tension that had built in her shoulders disappeared. Closing her eyes, Lily sighed and said a prayer of thanksgiving before ripping open the door.

He shoved past her and into the house.

Glancing behind Ben, Lily searched for the intruder, but she didn't see one. Ben was all alone. *What the heck is happening? Did he leave them on the porch?* She turned to peek outside, only he yanked her back.

The door slammed shut with a resounding thud.

Lily turned and glared.

Blocking the door, Ben fisted his hands on his hips and braced his legs.

A scowl marred his handsome face, causing a lesser person to quake in their shoes. Thankfully, she wasn't a lesser person. She patted his chest. "Don't be upset you let them escape."

Ben blinked. "*I* let them escape?

Lily snatched back her hand. "You don't need to yell. If you had just listened to me—"

"Listen to you?"

She frowned. For a police chief, he certainly had trouble keeping track of their conversation. Lily nodded. "I gave you a perfectly suitable idea, and you ignored my suggestion." She fisted her hands on her hips. "Why didn't you listen and come through the house? You would have caught them if you had."

His eye twitched once and again.

No doubt a delayed reaction to the events of the

evening. Lily really couldn't blame him. He put himself in remarkable danger, and all because he ignored her.

"*Would* have?" he growled.

Lily glared. "Yes, *would* have," she shot back. "Although, I don't know what you'd do with them if you had caught them. You don't have a gun or handcuffs, and where is your backup?"

"A gun…"

A sigh burst from Lily. "Yes, a gun. You do know what one is, don't you?" Tapping one foot against the floor, she crossed both arms over her chest. The shoe got in the way. She gave up and dropped her hands against her hips instead.

His gaze followed the shoe. The tick in his eye intensified. Another one started on his cheek.

She refused to let his anger deter her. "All cops carry a gun. You should know that detail. You're the police chief, for goodness sake." Just to make certain he understood what he'd done wrong, she ticked off his many mistakes. "How did you expect to catch them? With your glare? You might frighten them, but glaring won't stop them. What if they had a weapon? What would you have done? What would *I* have done?"

Lily didn't wait to hear his response. She had plenty to say, whether he wanted to hear her opinion or not. Didn't he understand she was worried about him and all she wanted was to keep him safe? "And what about handcuffs? I don't see any. Please explain how you planned on restraining them. By duct taping them to the porch?" She studied him, scowling. "You don't even have duct tape. And where is your backup? As the police chief, you should know you need two items—a gun and back-up." Lily threw her arms upward.

Ben took a step toward her. "Are you finished?"

Lily frowned. His voice was calm, yet his stance remained rigid. *No doubt he is upset hearing of his errors.* She didn't blame him. The list was extensive. "I suppose, and I'm sorry to be the one to mention what you did wrong." She opened the door. "Now, seeing as the intruders are gone, I want to go back to sleep."

Instead, he shut the door.

Shaking her head, she sighed. "Honest to goodness, you really are ornery. Fine, if you don't want to use the back door then go out the front."

"Why the hell did you open the door?"

Lily flinched. She didn't think she'd hear clearly for the next week. "I had to for you to leave." Realization dawned. "Oh wait. Is your irritation about etiquette? Because, if you're upset I didn't let you open the door, I apologize. I didn't realize you were such a stickler for propriety. I promise I won't make the same mistake again."

The tick returned.

Now what made him angry?

"Not now." He crossed his arms over his chest. "Before!"

"Oh that." Lily shrugged. "I heard you come up the steps, so I opened the door."

The muscle flexed in his jaw, and his eyes narrowed to tiny slits. "No, you *saw* me coming because you turned on the light."

"I wanted to help," Lily insisted. "You didn't have a gun..."

Shoving open his coat, he dropped his hands to his hips.

Lily spotted the gun clipped to his belt, right next

to his shiny badge. "Are you telling me you had a gun this whole time?" She shook her head. "You know, you really shouldn't keep your weapon a secret."

Ben gritted his teeth. *I don't want to kill her. Honest to God, I don't.* Surely, though, she was the only woman in the world who drove him crazy and stirred his desire simultaneously. "Help me? How the hell did you plan on helping me?"

"I had this shoe." Lily waved the make-shift weapon in the air.

He plucked the shoe from her hand. The same one she'd worn the other night. He decided he'd enjoyed them better on her feet. "A shoe is not a weapon, Lily."

"I know that," Lily retorted, frowning. "But it's all I had."

Ben gritted his teeth. He didn't know why he expected a logical answer. Since the day they'd met, logic and Lily were two words which did not go together. Tonight was no exception.

The metal can he found outside her bedroom window lay heavy in his coat pocket, a reminder of her danger. He dug his fingers into his hips. The action took effort, considering he'd rather shake some sense into her. "Where's your phone?"

Lily narrowed her eyes. "Why?"

He opened his mouth. No words escaped. He couldn't believe she'd dared to question his motives. He locked his unwavering stare on her. Clearly, Lily didn't understand he wouldn't quit until he achieved his objectives.

After a second or two, Lily blew out an exasperated breath and dropped the phone in his outstretched hand. "Honestly, you act like I'm the one in the wrong here."

He ignored her comment, adding his phone number to the others in her contact list. "You'll call me in the future if you have any problems."

Lily accepted the phone from his outstretched hand. She stared down at it for a moment. "I can't call you every time I need you." She let out a sigh. "Think of your men. If I call you, they'll think you don't trust them."

Ben snorted. The minute he'd stepped into the kitchen and spied her attire, plenty of images crowded his thoughts. All required little clothing and a hell of a lot less talking. Like hell he wanted his men to have the same thoughts.

Running his gaze the length of her body, he stopped to linger in all the right places. He took in her sleep-tousled hair and the tiny T-shirt she wore. The fabric ended a few scant inches below her hips, giving him ample view of a curvaceous body and long legs. A low fire burned deep within him. Whether from desire or anger, he wasn't sure. Ben reluctantly tore his attention from her long legs. "Sweetheart, when it comes to you, I don't care if my men think I don't trust them."

He dismissed the topic. Now wasn't the time to explain his expectations. Tightening his jaw, he gripped the back of a chair, drawing the seat toward her. "Have a seat."

"Why?"

He couldn't recall the last time someone questioned him. Maybe his mother. Certainly no one else and never a woman.

Until Lily…

Ben took a deep breath. His irritation didn't alleviate. "Because I want to have a brief discussion about safety."

She crossed her arms over her chest. "Will I participate in this discussion?"

He doubted she was aware her nightshirt had inched upward. He noticed smooth, toned thighs peeking from beneath the hem. Desire, hot and intense, shot through him. He forced his attention from the enticing sight. "No. You'll listen."

Lily frowned. "You assured me this was a discussion."

"This is a discussion." He waved again to the chair. "I'll discuss. You'll listen."

"Doesn't sound like one to me." Despite her complaint, she sat and tapped her fingers against the tabletop. Wrinkles as deep as the Grand Canyon furrowed her brow.

He didn't care. Her irritation paled compared to his worry. Crossing his arms, he gave her an unflinching stare known to make even the hardest criminals nervous. "Let's start with the lights…"

"I already explained I turned them on because I wanted to help you."

Ben took a deep breath, holding his anger in check. Barely. "You frightened them away."

Lily threw her arms upward. "Then why are you upset? We wanted to scare them."

He gritted his teeth. The woman had the innate ability to send him over the edge and back. "No. *I* wanted to catch them. Thankfully the problem was only raccoons. If an intruder had been here—"

"Raccoons? You're yelling because of raccoons?"

Jumping from her chair, Lily opened her mouth to say something then just as suddenly clamped her mouth shut. She stared for a moment or two before she narrowed her eyes and pointed a finger. "You planned this whole charade, didn't you?"

Snapping back his head, he blinked. "What?"

"Of course!" Lily scrubbed her fingers through her hair. "The whole thing makes perfect sense."

He wished her logic made sense to him. "That's ridiculous."

Lily pinched her lips together and took a deep breath. "I called the station tonight. When I told the officer where I lived, he laughed." She stopped pacing, fisted her hands against her hips, and pivoted in his direction. "Now, I know why. You wanted to scare me."

"I what?" He roared and crossed his arms over his chest.

"I bet you think if you rescue me, I'll just throw myself into your arms. Well, think again."

Ben wasn't sure when he'd lost control of the discussion. He figured his power slipped somewhere between noticing her wearing a barely-there T-shirt and when her shirt inched upward and his mind when into sexual overdrive. He leaned against the counter and watched her pace.

Her every movement was filled with a sensuality no other woman possessed. He gave up any hope of focusing on their conversation. His mind had other ideas. Namely, inappropriate thoughts he knew he shouldn't have, and yet, he didn't stop them either.

"That's the reason why you want me to call you instead of the station. Isn't it?"

The question drew him back to their discussion. He was finished with this ridiculous conversation. Other, more exciting, pursuits occupied his thoughts from the minute he stepped into the kitchen. Ben caught her in his arms. He itched to trail his fingers beneath her nightdress, longing to stroke her soft, smooth skin. Instead, he settled his hands on her lower back. "Do you know what my men think when they see a beautiful woman dressed in only a nightshirt?"

Lily pinched together her brows and frowned. "They're professionals."

Her voice was soft and husky, her bright blue gaze darkening just slightly. He would almost bet she was as affected by his nearness as he was hers. "You're right. They are professionals." Ben ran his hands down her back, stopping just shy of the hem of her nightshirt. "They're men, too, though."

She wrinkled her brow. "So?"

The woman was far too innocent for her own well-being. Clearly, he'd need to show her effect on men. He planned to give her a quick kiss—just a brief lesson into the minds of men. The minute his lips touched hers, he forgot the lesson. He wrapped his fingers into her hair, gently drawing back her head. With his teeth, he tugged on her lower lip.

Her tongue met his, and a hot, lightning rod of desire burst inside him. He released his grip on her hair, and sliding his hands downward to rest against her lower back, he drew her closer. He savored the feeling of her skin against his palms and knew how much better she would feel with less clothing separating them.

Ben waged a battle. If they continued, they'd be doing more than kissing. As much as he liked the idea, he knew they needed to stop. When they had sex, and they *would* have sex, he wanted the interlude to be mutual with no lingering misunderstandings. Tearing away his mouth, he stepped back. He needed to leave before they did something they'd regret. Ripping open the back door, he threw a glance in Lily's direction. "That, sweetheart, is what men think."

Chapter 15

"What the hell happened here last night?"

Peri's voice caused Lily to bolt out of a deep sleep. She thrust the tangle of curls from her face. On the tip of Peri's finger dangled Lily's pink stiletto. The same one she had thrown in frustration. She had missed Ben and hit the wall instead.

Now, eight hours later, and following one incredibly hot dream, the reason she'd thrown the shoe in the first place returned with a vengeance. The memory of his hard body against hers, his calloused fingers grazing her soft skin, and the unbelievably hot kiss…delicious heat curled in the pit of her stomach.

Groaning, Lily dismissed the dream *and* last night from her thoughts. She snatched the shoe from Peri, tossing the offending item onto the bed. "I have nothing to explain."

Peri pointed an accusing finger. "You had a party last night, didn't you?"

Lily kicked off the blankets. Oh, a party had occurred, all right. A party of two, and it hadn't ended well. She mentioned none of this information. "No." Shoving aside Peri, Lily hurried into the kitchen. "Just another uneventful night."

Peri chased. "Uneventful nights do not result in shoes thrown around the house. And what about the backyard? The yard looks like dozen people paraded through the grass."

Lily glanced out the kitchen window. The yard was a trampled mess. Combing her fingers through her hair, she decided to give Peri a simple explanation. "I thought intruders were outside, so I called the cops."

Two bright blue eyes, similar to her own, narrowed.

"The cops or Ben?"

"I called the *cops,*" Lily insisted. "They sent Ben."

"Oh really? Now, the story is getting interesting." Peri dropped into a chair and propped her elbows on the table. Resting her head in the palms on her hand, she smiled. "What did you two do?"

"We didn't *do* anything." Unless one incredible kiss counted then something definitely happened. Lily opened the cupboard door. "The whole thing ended up being nothing, so he left."

Grabbing the can of coffee from the shelf, Lily ripped off the lid. The canister was empty. She groaned softly. No coffee fairy arrived during the night to restock the cupboard, and she sure as hell refused to wait for Ben to appear bearing two steaming cups. Slamming shut the cupboard door, Lily headed toward the bedroom to change. "Get dressed. We're getting coffee, and then I'm stopping at the post office."

Peri stood. "Great. We'll go to the game afterward."

Lily stopped in front of her bedroom door. "What game?"

"The one I told you about the other day." Peri rubbed her hands together. "Just imagine hot men in shorts and T-shirts..." A smile curled on Peri's lips.

Lily rolled her eyes. She wasn't exactly interested

in a game. On the other hand, staying home guaranteed she'd spend the day replaying last night's kiss with Ben. She definitely didn't relish that idea. "Fine. I'll go."

They left the house less than a half hour later. An unbelievable achievement because on most days after Peri spent the night out, her preparation time was usually twice the length.

"Check out that trash can. You'd think someone beat the hell out of the thing."

She glanced in the direction of Peri's gaze. Her sister was right. The trash can did resemble a punching bag in a losing battle. Lily knelt and tucked the house keys under the mat. "I didn't realize how strong raccoons are." Standing, she brushed the dirt from her hands and started down the steps.

"Did you say raccoons?" Peri followed.

"Yes." Lily passed her car and frowned. Once Ben returned her keys, he'd be out of her life forever—which meant, her crazy dreams would disappear, and all their recent kissing would stop. Regret settled in the pit of her stomach. Lily dismissed the silly feeling.

"I hate those animals."

Lily turned in time to see Peri visibly shudder. "You're kidding, right?"

"I don't think so." Peri scrunched her face. "Those creatures are disgusting. They have creepy, human-like hands, and those dark eyes follow your every movement. Don't forget those masks, either. Anyone who's out to rob a bank or hurt someone covers their face—which just proves they're dangerous. Let me assure you, nothing is cute about those creatures."

"You're not serious, are you?" Lily turned onto the

sidewalk.

Peri raced to keep pace. "I'll have you know, I have what they call agrizoophobia," she huffed, breathless.

Lily shifted her attention from the passing houses. "What the heck is agrizoophobia?"

"The fear of wild animals."

Laughter burst from Lily. "Since when do you have a fear of animals?"

"Not animals," Peri qualified with a wave of her hand. "*Wild* animals."

She made the statement as if the two were different. Lily rolled her eyes. "Fine. When did you become afraid of *wild* animals?"

Scowling, Peri shrugged. "For a while. Dr. Norton told me this affliction is common among people living in cities."

"Who's Dr. Norton?" Lily scanned the traffic for any familiar, and most definitely *unwanted,* cars— namely Ben's. Thankfully, she needn't have worried. The only car on the street belonged to the postman.

"My psychologist," Peri replied. "Don't you pay any attention to me?"

Lily thought she had. Apparently, she missed this part of the conversation. Not that Lily could argue with Peri's comment. If anyone in their family needed a psychologist, Peri fitted the description. "Do you fear all wild animals or just a few?"

Again, Peri shrugged. "Mostly raccoons."

"What about rabbits? Are you afraid of them?"

"How can anyone fear rabbits? They're cute and harmless, and at Easter, they deliver chocolate."

"And birds?" Lily asked, turning onto Woodland

Avenue.

A row of houses, all with well-groomed yards and bright, cheerful flowerbeds, lined the street. Wicker chairs with colorful pillows decorating the seats sat upon the porch, and flower-filled baskets dangled from a rainbow of macramé hanging from the beams.

The last house, a bright, yellow two-story building, had a historic gold plaque tacked next to the door. The sign was as weathered as the house. Another large wooden sign with painted gold lettering reading THE ABERDEEN HISTORICAL SOCIETY sat perched in the grass. A parking lot lay between the Historical Society and the tall, brick building housing the Aberdeen Public Library, which guarded the corner of Main and Woodland.

"Birds aren't animals," Peri scoffed as they passed in front of the library.

Lily stopped and stared. "They sure as hell aren't minerals or plants. Didn't you learn a thing in Mr. Anderson's science class?"

Peri shot Lily a saucy look, a flirtatious smile upon her face.

Lily rolled her eyes.

"I was too busy flirting with Tommy Johnson." Peri fluffed her hair.

Ah...Tommy Johnson. The class flirt of Amherst High. The boy every girl loved, who to this day, resisted settling down. He was Amherst's version of Ben.

"Right." Lily kept her focus straight-ahead, refusing to allow her attention to drift toward the police station.

"Anyway, you know what I mean. They don't

attack people."

Lily waved a hand. "Really? Have you ever noticed a bird?"

Peri scowled. "Of course, I have. I mean when they stay still long enough for me to study them."

"You've noticed their beaks and sharp claws?"

"Yeah."

"You realize they use claws and beaks to attack people, right?"

The color drained from Peri's face.

She suddenly thrust her arms upward. "Great, now I need to add birds to my fear list."

Enjoying her sister's reaction, Lily hid her smile. Teasing Peri helped remove thoughts of Ben. When Lily arrived at the café, only Betty and two other women were inside. One had gray hair wound tight with pin-curls, and thick Coke-bottle glasses perched on the tip of her nose. She read a paper inches from her face. Next to her gold sequined purse sat a cup of coffee.

Another woman sat across the room, scribbling in her notepad. She stopped her writing and fixed her attention on them.

"Look who's here." Betty leaned forward and rested her forearms on the counter. "Aberdeen's newest residents. What can I make for you ladies?"

Lily placed her usual order. Peri's drink, on the other hand, was a creative cocktail of espresso, lightly steamed milk, caramel, chocolate, and who knows what else. Left in Peri's hands, something basic became an intricate mess.

Betty poured milk into a metal carafe. "What are you girls up to today?"

"We're going to the game," Peri told her.

"*After* the Post Office." Lily leaned a hip against the counter and waited.

"Right, the Post Office." Peri turned, and tilting her chin slightly, nudged Lily in the side. "Is she blind?"

"Peri," Lily groaned. *Why does my sister have such little tact?*

"What?" Peri's attention swung between the two women. "I just wondered…I mean, check out how she's reading the paper."

Betty nodded toward the woman under discussion. "Oh, that's Emily Waverly." She handed Lily her coffee. "She's reading the latest edition of *The Aberdeen Almanac*."

Wrinkling her nose, Peri pursed her lips. "*Really*? People actually read the newspaper?"

Everyone in the family knew Peri read for necessity, and for her, necessity meant either a fashion magazine or a tabloid paper. Anything else she considered a waste of time—like a good romance or historical novel, Lily's favorites.

"I'd call the article more of a gossip column. Rose writes the paper." Handing Peri her drink, Betty nodded to the woman with the notebook. "Most people enjoy the stories. One or two readers don't always appreciate Rose's way with words. They're the ones with the best stories." She smiled and winked. "If you know what I mean."

Peri nudged Lily. "Let's go and meet her."

"No time." Lily paid for the coffee then grabbed Peri's hand and tugged her from the café before Peri said anything further. Because she never knew when Peri would say or do something embarrassing.

"I've never met anyone famous before," Peri complained.

Lily didn't bother to explain the difference between small-town famous and Hollywood famous. Peri wouldn't care. To her, famous was famous.

The post office was next. The place not only looked ancient but smelled old, too. Tarnished bronze post office boxes lined one wall. The other had the ubiquitous wanted posters scattered amongst pictures for postage stamps and prices of parcel mail.

An old man, who was tall as a reed and as skinny as one, too, stood behind the counter. A few trailing wisps of hair dotted a head covered with liver spots. With weathered skin and hollowed-out cheekbones, he reminded Lily of a person from a century earlier.

Watery blue eyes swung in their direction. "How can I help you lovely ladies?"

His voice wavered, and he sounded as if he'd smoked a carton of cigarettes before breakfast. Lily rested her hands against the counter. "I'm here to see if I received a package."

Peri frowned. "To see if *we* received a package."

"Our mother mailed the box last week." Lily smiled.

"What's your name?"

"Evans. Lily Evans."

"And Peri Evans." Peri leaned against the counter.

The gentleman scratched his forehead. "Now, why does your name sound familiar?" He again shifted his glance between the two women. "Where did you say you lived?"

Lily gave him the house number.

He snapped his fingers. "You're my neighbor. I'm

Raymond Waverly."

"Are you related to Emily?" Lily furrowed her brow.

Mr. Waverly nodded. "Yup. Been married nearly sixty years."

Lily widened her eyes. "Are you telling me you live in the house behind mine?"

Mr. Waverly shrugged. "Really behind Claire's, but the corners of our yards are adjacent, which makes us neighbors."

Lily glanced in Peri's direction to see her reaction, but she was too busy studying her nails to pay any attention to this newest bit of information. Huffing a sigh, she turned back to Mr. Waverly and leaned in. "So, you can see into my backyard any time you want?"

"Not really. Got cataracts. The missus, too." He brushed a hand across the counter. "I'll go see if I have something here for you."

Lily waited until Mr. Waverly disappeared into the backroom before facing her sister. She fisted her hands "I don't believe it."

"I can. We live in the worst neighborhood." Peri dropped her hands on the counter. "The word hip bypassed our street fifty years ago. If Dax didn't live behind us, I'd turn around and head right back to Buffalo."

"I don't mean the neighborhood. I'm talking about Ben lying."

Closing her eyes, Peri sighed. "What?"

"He told me the people behind our house could see us, and they can't."

"That fact doesn't mean he lied." Peri thrust out an arm. "Just because the Waverlys can't see us doesn't mean the others are blind. You know, you need to learn to trust again."

Narrowing her eyes, Lily lifted her chin. "I trust people."

"Really?" Peri scoffed. "Then why do you think he's lying?"

Shuffling feet drew Lily's attention. She turned to see Mr. Waverly returning, carrying a large, brown-paper-wrapped box.

"I think this package is yours." He took a deep breath before heaving the packet on the counter then wiped his brow. "Do you see your name on the label?"

Lily breathed a sigh of relief. Now she wouldn't need to prove her point, because honestly, she didn't know if she could. She turned her attention to the package, scanned the label then looked up and smiled. "I sure do." Ripping open the box, she found her wallet buried beneath piles of crumpled newspapers, notes from their mother, and Peri's purse.

"My purse." Peri reached inside the box and snatched the bag.

The purse hit Lily in the forehead. Scowling at Peri's carelessness, she flipped open her wallet. Tucked safely in the protective plastic sleeve sat her license. She clutched the license to her chest. Finally, she could drive. Grabbing hold of Peri's hand, she fairly jerked her out the door and across the sidewalk toward the police station. "Now, Ben will return my keys, and we can start driving again."

"I can drive?"

Lily snorted. The last time Peri drove, she ended up in an accident. Peri being involved in a crash wasn't unusual. Plowing through the closed garage door was.

Peri blamed the door opener for the crash. However, if that was the case, why had she kept on driving when the door remained closed? "What I meant is *I'll* drive, and you'll ride."

Peri waved a hand. "Sure, you cause one minor accident, and no one forgets."

Glancing over her shoulder, Lily gave Peri a quick look.

Sighing, Peri followed. "Okay, more than one."

Lily started for the police station.

Peri grasped Lily's arm. "Hey, you said we could go to the game."

Breaking free from Peri's grip, Lily started up the steps. "And we will, just as soon as I get back my keys."

"But we'll be late. Let's skip the station. We can come back after."

"No." Lily stopped at the door. "Besides, it's just a game. How much will we miss?"

Peri scowled. "Ah...only the men stretching—that's the best part."

Laughing, Lily drew open the door to the police station. "I think you'll be okay."

A young officer, someone who couldn't be much older than herself, sat behind the counter. Lily smiled and hurried over. "I'm here for my keys."

A frown crossed his face. "Excuse me?"

"My keys. Ben..." Blushing at the familiar use of his name, Lily cleared her throat and flipped open her wallet. "I mean, Chief Jordan asked me to bring my license here." She flashed her driver's license. "Can I have my keys now?"

The officer flicked a glance at her outstretched

hand and shrugged. "Sorry. We don't have them."

Lily gritted her teeth. *The officer could at least show some interest in my dilemma.* "Are you sure? I was told to come here with my license."

"We're not lost and found. We're a police station. Police do not keep people's keys."

"Maybe the police don't." She hadn't expected such difficulty getting her keys returned. Lily tapped her fingers on the counter. "But Ben does."

The officer shrugged. "Then discuss your problem with him."

Her hopes failing, Lily dropped her shoulders. "Can't you call him?"

The officer shook his head. "Nope. Not allowed."

Not allowed? He is the Police Chief. "Isn't he on duty twenty-four/seven?"

Turning, the officer grabbed a paper. "He's involved in a police/fire matter."

Her stomach tightened. "I hope the situation is not serious."

The officer glanced up. "Oh, it's definitely urgent." He shifted his attention back to the article.

Their dismissal was obvious. Frowning, Lily stomped to the door and stormed out, furious she still didn't possess her keys. The next time she saw Ben, she'd make certain he heard her opinion of his employees, *and* she'd get her keys—no matter what.

During her walk to the game, Lily tried not to show her worry. Of course, whatever Ben dealt with was dire. He was the police chief, for goodness sake. He probably faced danger every day. She could just imagine the constant worry she'd endure married to him.

Her stomach leapt.

Now, where did that crazy thought come from?

She couldn't marry Ben. The idea was beyond ridiculous. She just got out of a relationship—one that she thought was good, only to find out, her boyfriend cheated. Why would she enter another now, and take the chance of getting hurt again? Especially since, she was reasonably sure Ben didn't want a relationship or even anything close to a commitment. Besides, she didn't live in Aberdeen. She lived in Buffalo, and after summer was over, she'd have to go back and find a job. Shaking her head, Lily dismissed the absurd notion.

The baseball field sat between Aberdeen High School and John Witherspoon Elementary. Stadium-style bleachers ran along each baseline. Lily searched the bleachers for a vacant seat. "Can you believe this crowd?"

"I can't believe we're late." Peri scowled, her focus fixed on the baseball field. "I told you we should have skipped that stupid police station."

"It's just a game." Lily followed Peri toward the side of the backstop.

Peri huffed. "Easy for you to say. You have Ben."

"I don't *have* him." Heat burned Lily's cheeks. She shifted her gaze to the ground, studiously avoiding Peri's probing gaze.

"You're not fooling anyone, you know. You notice him. He notices you. Whenever you're together, you two generate enough electricity to light up Aberdeen." Peri stopped walking and smirked. "If you want my opinion, I think you two should just have sex and satisfy your craving."

Lily's stomach thumped at the thought. She

swallowed and licked her lips. Avoiding Peri's keen gaze, Lily leaned in. "Trust me. I don't want to have sex with Ben."

Peri widened her eyes. "Yeah? Well then, you're the only woman in town who doesn't, and that fact, sweet sister, includes me." Peri started for the chain link fence.

Gasping, Lily raced after Peri. "What did you say?"

Peri dragged her gaze from the players huddled in the dugout. "Don't act surprised. The man's hot."

"I thought you didn't want a commitment?" Imagining Peri with Ben unsettled Lily more than she cared to admit.

"Oh, I don't." Peri fanned a hand. "I do have an imagination, though, and picturing sex with Ben is not too shabby." She patted Lily's wrist. "Don't worry, though, I wouldn't go after your boyfriend."

Lily's heart fluttered. She ignored the sensation. Stopping behind the cluster of women surrounding the dugout, she shrugged, dismissing Peri's outrageous comment. Sure, she and Ben shared one heck of a kiss, and yes, recently she'd spent more time dreaming of him than she cared to admit. She'd even acknowledge imagining sex with Ben. However, *wondering* about sex did not mean she *wanted* to have sex. Besides, sex and Ben were two items on her taboo list. Because then she'd do exactly as he expected—fall into his arms— which would make her the same as the rest of his women.

Once he returned her key, she could put an exclamation point on their relationship. Other than the occasional conversation, they wouldn't need to see each

161

other. First, though, she needed her keys.

"Hey, I see Ben."

Lily whirled to see Peri gripping the fence, her face pressed against the chain links. Wedging her way between the women, she immediately noticed him. Even if she hadn't spotted the words "Chief" written on the back of his jersey, she would still recognize his broad shoulders and muscular arms. "He *lied*."

Peri jerked her gaze away from the dugout. "Who? Ben?"

Men clustered inside the dugout. Lily ignored them, focusing her attention on the one man who absorbed her every waking moment since she'd driven into town. "Not Ben. The officer at the station. He mentioned an emergency."

"To be fair, he didn't say an emergency. He said Ben was involved in a police matter." Peri patted her hair. "Seeing as the players are a part of the Aberdeen police-fire department, I assume he's supposed to be here."

Sucking in a breath, Lily whipped her attention to Peri. "Are you telling me, you knew this game involved the police/fire team?"

Peri shrugged. "Sure. You didn't?"

Of course, she hadn't. Would she have worn a plain, white T-shirt and ugly blue shorts, if she had? And her hair. Jeez, a ponytail? Really? Was she so lazy she couldn't spend a few extra minutes styling her hair? Good God, her make-up. She barely put on mascara and lip gloss... Frowning, Lily turned back to the dugout. Incredible was the only word to describe Ben, dressed in a chest-defining, gray T-shirt.

He tugged on batting gloves, causing the muscles

to flex in his arms, before grabbing the baseball bat resting against the bench and starting for home plate.

Just like the rest of the women in the crowd, Lily stared mesmerized.

A collective sigh erupted from the women.

Lily almost did the same.

He chatted with the umpire for a moment, a smile creasing his face, before knocking the bat against his cleats and tugging on his gloves again.

Anticipation rumbled through the crowd.

Lily scanned the faces surrounding her and frowned at the admiration in the women's eyes.

The crack of a bat sounded.

She turned in time to see him running the bases.

"Oh, my gosh." Peri grabbed Lily's arm. "He hit a home run."

"I missed it." Lily watched Ben run the bases before sliding across home plate and easily beating the incoming throw.

Standing, he dusted the dirt from his pants before shaking the hands of the umpire and catcher. Heading toward the dugout, he scanned the crowd.

His gaze found hers. Last night and the unbelievable, unforgettable kiss they shared flashed through her memory. Her stomach tumbled.

Women shouted his name, vying for his attention.

He ignored them. His smile made her wonder if he remembered last night, too. With a nervous flutter of her hand, she fussed with her hair.

The memory of Peri's words sat juxtaposed against last night's all-too-steamy dream. Her heart raced, and she stood rooted to the ground, paralyzed by the dark promise in his eyes. He kept right on coming, not stopping until he stood directly in front of her. His slow, sensual smile made her forget everything except him.

"Lily…"

A warm heat suffused her body at the soft, sexy tone in his voice. She licked her lips, searching her memory for what she meant to tell him. She couldn't remember, so she blurted the first words to come to mind. "We can't have sex." Closing her eyes, she blew out a soft breath. *What made me say such a thing?* She opened her eyes.

Cocking his brow, Ben's lips curled into a smile.

Peri leaned against Lily. "Smooth."

Lily's heart thumped. *Great.* Now, how will she get out of this debacle?

Chapter 16

A collective gasp rippled through the crowd. Lily wanted to crawl into a hole and hide. Seeing nothing even close to resembling one, she did the next best thing. With her head held high and her ego low, she broke through the wall of women. Snickers of laughter and whispered comments followed her. She needed to escape before she was forced to explain her comment. "Come on, Peri."

Storming across the grass, she darted through the crowds. The crunch of gravel sounded behind her just seconds before someone caught her elbow. She spun, expecting to see Peri.

Ben stood a foot away.

Her heart plunged straight to her stomach.

Resting both hands on his hips, he tilted his head to the side and arched a brow. "Going somewhere?"

Laughter filled his voice, and amusement sparkled in his eyes. She lifted her chin, refusing to allow her humiliation to show. "I'm leaving with Peri."

Ben scanned the parking lot before turning back. "Peri is leaving with Maybelline."

Sure enough, she spotted Peri climbing into Maybelline's old car. *So much for sisterly love.* Lily pinched her lips and straightened her shoulders. "Fine. I'll just go home by myself."

"Hold on." He gripped her elbow. "I want to know

what you meant by your comment."

Heat crawled up her neck. His persistence was the reason she hurried away. "I'd rather not have this discussion."

He held her gaze. "I'd rather we did."

Ben's unwavering glare spoke of authority and submission—her submission. She fought a losing battle. Knowing his tenacity, she knew eventually she'd relent and unfurl the white surrender flag. She yanked her arm from his grip and crossed them over her chest. "You're not letting me leave, are you?"

A soft smile flickered across his lips, and his eyes sparkled.

Lily pinched together her lips. The man certainly enjoyed her irritation.

"No."

A childlike urge to stamp her foot filled Lily. *The man is beyond infuriating.* She threw wide her arms. "Fine. I said those words because I had a sunstroke."

Ben glanced upward before pinning his gaze on her. One brow spiked. "Really?"

Lily hated lying. She hated liars. However, admitting the truth made her so much more vulnerable, and the last thing she wanted was to be vulnerable. Especially after catching Eric cheating. She lifted her chin and met his challenging stare. "Yup. In fact, I think I'm having one right now." To prove her point, she swiped a hand across her brow.

The muscle flexed in his cheek. "No, you're not."

His calm insistence really annoyed her. Lily drew her lips together and narrowed her eyes. "Oh, so now you're a doctor? Do you want to feel my head? I'm sweating."

He glared. "People don't sweat during a sunstroke."

Lily didn't know whether this fact was true or not. Whatever the case, she refused to admit the real reason for her words—which was how she thought about sex with him—a lot. She licked her lips. "Maybe I'm different, and I sweat during a sunstroke."

Ben rolled his eyes. "The temperature is barely eighty today."

Keeping her face impassive, Lily shrugged. "I'm almost certain a person can have a sunstroke even if the temperature is only eighty outside."

She stepped forward.

Ben caught her arm.

Lily turned and frowned.

The muscles in Ben's neck throbbed. "For God's sake, the sun isn't shining. How the hell do you have a sunstroke when the sky is threatening rain?"

Lily glanced upward. Thick, gray clouds filled the sky. *Dang!* She pinched together her lips. "Okay, fine. I didn't have a sunstroke. Now, if you don't mind, I want to leave." She couldn't go far, considering he held her with an ironclad grip.

"Lily…"

His words came out in a strangled growl. Scowling, Lily yanked her hand free. "Are you interrogating me? Because if you are, you need to read me my rights."

The twitch in his eye returned. "How about we consider this conversation a personal matter?"

The man had lost his mind. She practically announced in front of the whole town she wanted to sleep with him, and he called the matter personal?

However, she knew just how stubborn he could be. He'd keep pestering until he obtained his answers—which meant she'd need to tell the truth.

Sighing, she waved a hand. "Fine. If you must know, Peri made a suggestion—a completely inaccurate suggestion, I might add about us having sex, and well…her words must have stuck in my head." A warm glint settled deep within his eyes, causing a tingling feeling to spread in her belly. Lily refused to acknowledge the sensation.

He brushed a strand of hair off her shoulder.

A shiver raced down her spine. So much for her plan of remaining impervious.

"And you never think of us having sex."

At his slow, sensual words, she couldn't keep her imagination from kicking into overdrive and with them, all the fantasies she'd determinedly tamped down each day flashed through her thoughts. She shoved them aside and shifted her gaze to the ground. "No."

"Really?" He arched his brows. "Because sex with you is all I think about."

Despite the brisk temperature and the sky filled with thunderclouds, Lily noticed a warm feeling spread through her. The heady promise in his voice didn't help. Her throat tightened. "You have?"

Nodding, he brushed a thumb against the side of her jaw.

Her stomach tumbled, and all she could think about was how his hands would feel caressing her body. *What the hell?* She wasn't supposed to think such thoughts. She stepped back and licked her lips. "I want to—"

He swept his gaze downward, inch by inch over her body, then back to meet her gaze. "Me, too."

His voice was deep and husky. Oh lord...her resistance slipped, and the wall she'd carefully built slowly became nothing more than a teetering pile of willpower. Lily lifted her chin and ignored her thundering heart. "I meant I need to leave. Besides, from what I've been told, you're too busy for me."

"I was busy." He took hold of her arm and guided her through the crowds.

He held onto her elbow as if it was a matter of life or death. She raced to keep pace. "I hate to tell you, Ben, baseball isn't a police matter."

"Maybe not, but I am the team captain."

"Then you should be at the game. Not here." She assumed he'd leave. When he didn't, she pointed toward the field. "Don't you understand? You need to return. Otherwise, you'll be abandoning your team."

Ben burst into laughter and dropped an arm over her shoulders. "Lily, we're talking about a baseball game, not a ship."

Lily pursed her lips. "I know, which means your responsibility is to stay."

He shook his head before again guiding her toward his vehicle. "The game's over."

Did he think she was stupid? She just watched him play. She tilted her head to the side. "You were just at bat."

Stopping, Ben looked down. "I had a walk-off."

Lily drew together her brows. "A what?"

Ben exhaled. "A walk-off home run."

She guessed his sigh was guy code for the game being over. "Did your team win?"

Closing his eyes, he rolled his head from side to side. "Yes, we won."

She smiled, ready to congratulate him until she spotted his truck. Or rather, where he parked the vehicle. She dug her heels into the gravel, forcing him to stop.

He arched his brows. "Is something wrong?"

Lily jabbed a finger toward the vehicle. "You parked in a playground? How could you? You've taken the kids' sandbox. How the heck did you expect them to play?"

"You're exaggerating." Ben swung his arm wide. "I'm thirty feet from the playground."

Tapping her foot on the gravel, she glared. "You should have to park with the rest of us."

"Look around, Lily. What do you see?"

A grassy expanse separated the playground from the parking lot. Somewhere near the middle sat his vehicle. Swarms of people strolled past, casting conspicuous glances their way. Lily pasted on a smile for their benefit, before turning. She lowered her voice. "I see cars and trucks parked in an area reserved for vehicles." She pointed to his truck. "When I look there, I see someone who thinks he can do whatever he wants, including parking in the playground."

Ben swept wide his arm. "You can see as well as I can, the parking lot is a mess. George Newcomb has blocked both Betsy Waters and Emil Jackson. I'm the Chief of Police. If an emergency happens, I need to leave quickly. I can't take the chance of getting trapped in the parking mess."

She flipped out one palm. "I thought you were off work."

"As the police chief, I'm always on the clock." He clutched her hand again and led her to his vehicle.

Cars flew past as she attempted to keep pace with his long stride. She tugged on his hand.

He stopped and, cocking a brow upward, waited.

She returned his look of impatience with a scowl.

Ben sighed. "What now?"

She pinched together her brows. "You lied to me."

"Excuse me?" Jerking back, Ben glared.

Straightening her shoulders, Lily nodded. "You told me the neighbors could see me in my nightshirt. That statement is not true, and do you know why?" She didn't wait for his response. "Because they're blind, and don't tell me otherwise. I spoke to Mr. Waverly today, and he told me he has cataracts and couldn't even read my name on the package. He asked *me* to read the label."

"You're right." Ben fanned a hand. "Raymond can't see into your yard. His son, Shawn, can, though."

She didn't know whether to believe him or not. She narrowed her eyes. "How old is his son?"

"Fifty." Ben opened the passenger door.

"*Fifty?*" Lily laughed. "My dad's fifty, and he wouldn't notice."

He rested an arm against the door frame, the corners of his eyes crinkling. "I should hope not. Trust me, though, Shawn's not your father."

"Ben, I really think I need to walk home. *Alone.*" She turned.

Clasping her hand, Ben helped her into his vehicle and winked. "I know you do, sweetheart."

Heat invaded her body at the warmth in his gaze. Lily licked her lips, watching him walk around the front of the truck. Her mind told her to open the passenger door and leave. Somehow, she couldn't get her hands to follow her brain's directions. Then, once he climbed into the truck and she caught a glimpse of his muscular thigh flexing as he shifted the clutch, she completely forgot her concerns. She couldn't keep her thoughts from flying into sexual overdrive.

She told herself to drag her gaze away. Yet, no matter the effort, she couldn't fight looking at his powerful legs and sinewy arms. The memory, strong and visceral, of his body against hers, burned through her. With each passing mile, Lily felt her willpower waning, and her desire intensifying.

What she needed was some distance between him and her imagination. The minute he parked in her driveway, she unbuckled her seatbelt and flung open the door. "Thanks for escorting me home. I'll see you later…" She leaped from the vehicle. Slamming shut the door, she hurried across the driveway, heedless to the soft raindrops falling. She prayed he would take the hint and leave.

He met her on the porch.

She narrowed her eyes. *The man is so darned difficult.* Bending, she blew water from her face and lifted the doormat. "You were supposed to leave."

He caught her hand. The key, slick with rain, lay in a pool of water. Heat lit his eyes and his mouth thinned into a frown. He ripped his gaze from the key. "I told you not to put them there."

Wondering how to explain the hiding spot, Lily chewed her lower lip. "Not true. You told me not to put them under the flower pot."

He flashed a glare in her direction before snatching the key from the puddle. Standing, he fixed his gaze at the door, his brows dipping. "What happened to the doorknob?"

Lily exhaled. The immediate crisis was averted. She glanced toward the door. Dings and scratches marred the surface. She leaned forward to study the lock. Dents covered the knob. *Were they there yesterday?* She couldn't remember. "I don't know."

Frowning, Ben swung his gaze toward her. "I didn't notice the damage last night. Did you?"

Lily remembered plenty of the events. None had anything to do with the lock, and all with the man opening her door right now. However, she planned to keep her thoughts and feelings under wraps. "No." Glaring, she brushed past him and stepped into the house, intending to close the door, only he followed her inside.

He shut the door.

"Ben—"

He walked toward her bedroom.

Her protest died on her lips. She raced after him. Droplets of water fell from her hair. Lily swiped the moisture off her face. "Hey, what do you think you're doing?"

"Checking your house." Throwing open the bedroom door, he glanced inside, before turning back to Lily. He frowned. "Your window's open."

She remembered exactly why she opened the window. Heat burned in her cheeks. "Last night was…ah…hot." His frown disappeared, replaced by a seductive smile that sent a thrill straight to Lily's toes.

"You're right. It was." He brushed a thumb down the side of her cheek before turning and leaving her standing in the middle of the room.

She hurried into the kitchen, but Ben had already

disappeared into the living room. She didn't dare follow him, not with the heat of his touch still burning her cheek, and the way his words sent a thrill through her. No, she was better off remaining right here, trying to calm her racing heart.

Resting her elbows against the kitchen counter, Lily stared at the lazy rivulets of water streaming down the window. *What now?* He certainly couldn't stay. Her emotions were balanced on a precipice. Left alone with him, who knew what she'd do.

A few minutes later, he returned.

Her stomach lurched. *Yup, I'm definitely on a precipice and now dangerously close to jumping.* She handed him a towel to wipe the water from his face. His wet shirt clung to his muscular chest, reminding her of the time he mowed her lawn. Frankly, in her opinion, the view was terrific either time.

She caught his hot stare and blushed, realizing her shirt was just as wet and revealing. She threw her arms across her chest, breaking the moment.

Chuckling, he drew her into his arms. "Everything's okay."

"I never thought otherwise." She refused to notice the warmth of his body against hers or the way his hands roamed over her flesh, enticing her.

He brushed a brief kiss over her mouth.

The sensation coursing through her made her forget everything except the havoc his kiss wreaked.

He abruptly stepped away. "I'll be right back." He left the house and shut the door.

What the heck just happened? Determined to put aside her ridiculous thoughts of sex and Ben, she walked into the bedroom and took a long shower.

Seeing as she thought of him only once or twice the whole time, she was successful. Her self-congratulations lasted only until she stepped into the kitchen and noticed him working on the doorknob. Then her no-thinking-of-sex-with-Ben plan flew right out the window. "What are you doing here?"

****

"I told you I—" He shifted his attention from the door. Desire, hot and intense, burst inside him. He took in Lily wearing tight yoga pants and a white tank top. Little was left to his imagination, and the few scraps missing, he easily filled in the blanks. The woman had a singular determination to torment him—first with the wet T-shirt, and now dressed in something almost as provocative. If he didn't know better, he'd think her actions were intentional.

He glanced toward the door. With concerted effort on his part, he finished tightening the screws. "I told you I'd be back." When he finished, he set the screwdriver on the counter next to the keys before striding purposely toward her. He felt her toes brush against the tip of his shoes and watched her tongue glide over her lips. Burning hunger exploded within him. Logic told him to wait. His body had a different opinion. He curled his fingers into her waist, trapping her against him.

Arching her brow, she stared back.

Last night he spent in acute pain replaying the events of the evening. Today wasn't any better. He'd known the minute she arrived, leaving his concentration on the field in tatters. She attracted him like no other woman. He pulled her against him and gave up the battle he didn't want to win.

She met his lips halfway.

He swept his tongue inside her mouth and inched his hands beneath the edge of her tank.

A low moan rumbled from her.

His willpower crumbled even further. The buzz of his cell phone broke the moment.

Lily pulled away, ending the kiss.

He groaned. *This call better be important.*

"We shouldn't be kissing," she whispered, pressing two fingers against her lips.

He ignored the persistent caller, searching her crimson face instead. "Why not?"

Lily wound her fingers together. "Because nothing positive can come from us kissing."

Ben felt warm heat curl through him, and his mind went into overdrive thinking of all the wonderful things they could share. Clearly, he'd need to persuade her. "Not true. I can think of plenty of positive activities we'd both enjoy."

The ringing continued.

Glancing at his phone, he frowned. *At times, being a police chief is a hassle.* He sighed. "Here are three keys." He nodded toward the counter. "One for you, one for Peri, and a spare." He narrowed his gaze. "And don't hide it under the mat or the flower pot."

She snapped her gaze upward. "I already explained—"

Ben pointed a finger. "Inside."

"Peri won't be happy."

"Peri's a big girl. She needs to become responsible." He rested his chin on the top of her head and settled both hands on her hips. Sighing again, he wished he'd forgotten his cell phone in the vehicle. "I need to go."

"Where are you going?"

"To work." He brushed his mouth against hers.

Her fingers curled into his shirt, and a soft sigh eased past her lips.

Lifting his head, Den smoothed a thumb over her lower lip. "See you tomorrow, sweetheart."

Lily's stomach tumbled. She turned to tell him no, to not bother. Only, he was gone before she had a chance. She closed her eyes and dropped back her head. Scrubbing her fingers through her hair, she wondered how she'd get out of this mess.

Chapter 17

Lily woke Sunday ready to conquer the world, including the Donut and Coffee Committee. She just wished she had her car keys when the conquering began. However, by the time he finished kissing her yesterday, keys were the last thing on her mind.

She spent most of her night tossing and turning, wishing she could forget his kiss and the emotions they evoked. Hours after Peri returned home, Lily finally fell asleep. By the time she woke, she was irritable, desperate, and frustrated.

A bad mood wouldn't stop her today, though. Because today she would assist the Donut and Coffee Committee. She didn't have time to focus on him or his amazing kisses. If she wanted to impress them, she'd need all her wits.

However, she had just one problem. Just like the real Ben, the Ben in her thoughts refused to be ignored. While getting ready, she vacillated between remembering his kiss and wondering whether he'd attend church. She was reasonably sure he wouldn't attend. After all, he'd probably gone last week because Ellen was in town. She couldn't imagine him enduring Mass two weeks in a row.

But just in case…With two outfits to choose from, one of which she'd worn last week, the choice was simple. She tugged the unworn, two-piece dress off the hanger and quickly dressed.

Finished with her outfit, she examined herself in the mirror. The pearls circling her neck and dangling from her ears complemented the white lace blouse and skirt she wore. The white-and-silver, low-heeled sandals were perfect for standing while she helped the committee. Her hair, wrapped in a clip, was neat and sophisticated. She was sure the Donut and Coffee Committee would approve. Taking a deep breath, she stepped into the living room.

"Where are you going dressed up?" Peri asked, coming down the stairs.

"Church." She smoothed a hand over the front of her dress. "Do you want to go?"

Peri burst into laughter. "Church? You're kidding, right?"

Lily hid her disappointment. Having Peri by her side would help her relax and ease her tension. She stared in the mirror and adjusted an earring. "Relax. I just thought I'd ask."

Peri studied Lily. "You're dressed like a bride."

"I am not." Lily turned to the mirror. She dug a soft pink lipstick from her purse.

Peri slid her gaze over Lily. "You're dressed in white lace, your hair's done up, and you're wearing pearls. Brides dress the same exact way."

Frowning, she drew off the lipstick cap. "First off, I'm wearing a summer dress. Not a *wedding* dress." She peered in the mirror.

Peri's reflection stared back.

Lily carefully smoothed the lipstick over her lips. "Second, I wore my other outfit last week."

Resting her arms against the back of the couch, she

studied Lily. "You could wear one of mine."

Pausing, Lily held the lipstick in mid-air. She could just imagine the Donut and Coffee Committee's opinion if they spotted her in one of Peri's super-tight, super-indecent dresses. She finished applying the color. "I'll pass." She snapped on the top, before dropping the tube into her purse. "By the way, thanks for leaving without me yesterday."

"You're welcome." Peri winked. "Hey, did you see Rose at the game?"

Lily shook her head. Hundreds of people attended yesterday's game. How was she expected to remember one person? Especially since one man occupied her thoughts for most of the day. She smoothed a hand over her hair. "Who?"

Peri nodded toward the kitchen. "Rose Smith. Remember? From Betty's? The gossip blogger?"

Worrisome thoughts churned through Lily. Namely, what had Rose seen, or *worse,* heard? Her stomach clenched. Licking her lips, she fought to keep her face impassive. "Are you sure?"

Leaning against the couch, Peri clasped her hands together. "I don't think she paid any attention to the game, though. Not after the scene you two made."

Again, her stomach tumbled. *Okay, this information is terrible—the worst, really.* "You don't think she'd write about us, do you?"

Peri smiled. "I think the question is, why wouldn't she?"

Panic shot through Lily. She immediately dismissed the crazy emotion. "I'm sure she has better topics to write about than us."

"That's what you think." Peri straightened and

walked over.

Lily rolled her eyes without responding to Peri's outlandish suggestion. She started for the door. "I need to leave."

"What time will you be home?"

"I don't know." Lily stopped beside the door. "I'm helping the Donut Committee today."

Peri snorted. "Do you remember your first restaurant job? The one where you were assigned to the salad bar?"

Of course, she remembered. She had spilled a whole canister of pickled beets all over her science teacher, who just happened to be wearing a white linen dress. Then again, she had been sixteen and on her first job. She was older now and wouldn't again make the same mistake. "Mrs. James forgave me. Besides, this time is different. We're talking donuts here, not pickled beets."

"Don't forget about the coffee." Peri wagged a finger. "Coffee not only stains but burns too."

"I think I can handle the pressure today."

Peri shook her head. "Honestly, I don't know why you care. You're on vacation. You don't need to impress them. You need to avoid them."

She ignored her sister's ridiculous comment and opened the door. Glancing toward the driveway, Lily gasped and jumped back, slamming shut the door. She flattened her back against the hardwood.

Peri rushed over. "What's wrong?"

Lily peered through the crack of the curtain. She clutched the window sill, watching him climbing from his truck. "Ben's here."

Peri peered over Lily's shoulder. "Wow. Talk

about hot."

Hot was right. Dressed in a charcoal suit and a crisp white dress shirt, the top button left undone, he held an air of power, sophistication, and command. Her pulse quickened. "Why is he here?"

"My guess is to see you."

Frowning, Lily watched him stroll toward the house. Didn't he ever listen? Didn't he understand? "He shouldn't come here anymore."

Peri whipped around. "What? Why?"

Why did no one understand? She was on *vacation.* "Because I'm here only for the summer."

"Are you asking for a lifetime? No. You just want some excitement." Peri wiggled her shoulders, fanning her hands outward. "If you ask me, Ben looks exciting."

Oh, she knew only too well the kind of 'excitement' he provided. Images, one after another, jumped through her thoughts.

He reached the bottom steps.

Lily stilled her shaking hands and opened the front door.

Gazing at her, Ben started up the porch steps.

For the barest of seconds, Lily thought his steps faltered. Only, his countenance held such a quality of self-assurance and determination, she figured she'd imagined the action.

At the second step from the top, he stopped and gripped the white porch columns.

Lily's heart thundered. She licked her lips. "What are you doing here?"

"I came for you."

Desire stretched taut in her body. She could think of a thousand places she wanted him to take her, and all led right back to Peri's suggestion. "Where are you taking me?"

His arms flexed and his fingers tightened on the porch railing. He leaned forward so that his face was inches away. He smiled. "For now, church."

His warm breath brushed against her flesh. Heat curled in the pit of her stomach. Again, he ran his gaze over her body, and his smile slowly disappeared. When his gaze met hers, his eyes were dark and serious Lily smoothed a hand down the front of her dress. "What's the matter? Is my dress wrong? Peri claims I'm dressed like a bride. I'm not, you know." She heard the panic in her high-pitched tone. Clearing her throat, she gathered her thoughts. She didn't want him to think…well, she didn't want to look foolish. "I just don't want anyone to stare."

His steady hand circled her, drawing her toward him. "As long as they know you're with me, they can stare all they want."

She strolled by his side, conscious of the heat of his arm brushing against her side. "Don't you see? We don't want people to stare."

"Oh?"

The corner of his eyes crinkled upward, and a flicker of a smile curled on his lips. Her heart tumbled. She really needed to gather her thoughts. Reacting to his smile just wouldn't do. "We don't need Aberdeen's gossip columnist to write about us."

He winked. "Sweetheart, we're allowed to be seen together."

His fingers brushed against her skin, and the memory of his kiss hit her full force. Heat filled her, and the alarm bells in her head screamed 'warning!

dangerous territory ahead'—an area she desperately needed to avoid. "I'll just go by myself." She dug inside her purse, found her license and registration, and flashed both for him to inspect. "Or you can give me my keys."

"Sorry." He laughed. "You're coming with me."

She didn't have a choice and wanted to stamp her foot. Ben held her keys hostage. Unless she stayed home and forgot about helping the Donut and Coffee Committee, she must accept his offer. She wasn't happy, though. How the heck did he expect her to listen to Mass with him sitting beside her? More important, how could she help the Donut and Coffee Committee, if he remained by her side? "Fine," she grumbled. "However, when we arrive, we go our separate ways."

His answer was to drop his arm over her shoulder.

She frowned.

Again, he winked.

The man was beyond difficult. She wouldn't let his obstinacy stop her, though. She planned to leave him the minute they arrived at the church. Only, when the time came, she found herself trapped and tugged against his grip.

Peering down, he arched a brow.

"I need to go," she whispered. "Remember?" She expected him to release her. Instead, he tightened his grip just slightly, drawing her closer to his side. Lily sighed and scanned the area.

People strolling past slid their gazes between them. Some smiled. Others had looks of wide-eyed disbelief.

Ben greeted everyone.

She leaned toward him. "We're causing a scene."

He rolled his eyes. "No, we're not."

She scowled. He acted too blasé for her peace of mind. Lily forced a smile and pretended holding hands with Ben was completely natural.

"I need to speak with Avery." Ben tugged Lily across the lot.

Lily slowed her pace.

Turning, Ben tilted his head to the side. "What's wrong?"

"I don't want to." She meant it too. *What is he thinking? He can't introduce me to his friends. Why, who knows what conclusion they'll come to.*

Ben stopped and directed his full attention on her. "Why not?"

Gripping his hand, Lily leaned closer. "Because, they'll think…things."

Ben rolled his eyes upward then back. "They won't. Now come on." He pulled her across the lot.

Lily feigned nonchalance, but the action was harder than she expected. She was well aware of the passing people's stares fixed on her and Ben. She supposed this wasn't her problem but his. She figured she'd let Ben introduce her, and then she'd make her escape. Only her plan failed, because not only did she meet Avery Jacobs, but soon after Mr. Nelson, Tony and Marie Ranger, and a dozen other people stopped by to chat.

With each person, Lily was forced to make polite small talk while hiding her embarrassment.

Resting his palm on the small of her back, he guided her up the steps of the church.

An older woman stood on the top step, watching them approach.

"Lily, have you met Mrs. Peabody?" Ben smiled

and nudged her forward. "Joan, this is Lily Evans."

Mrs. Peabody clasped her hand in greeting while beaming at Ben. "I'm certain your mother is pleased."

When Mrs. Peabody left, Lily turned to Ben. "Will your mother be happy because you're here?"

"No." He laughed.

She frowned. "Oh?"

Ben sighed. "She probably envisions me getting married."

Her stomach tumbled. She ignored her reaction. Of course, his mother wanted him to marry. What mother didn't? Staring straight ahead, she started walking. "And you're not interested."

He shrugged, curling his fingers around her waist. "Before now, I never gave marriage a thought."

She wasn't surprised. The man led a charmed life with women chasing after him, left and right. A tight, gnawing feeling settled in the pit of Lily's stomach. Ignoring the sensation, Lily shrugged. "You wouldn't. You're not the type to settle down."

A smile teased the corners of his mouth. "Oh? What does the 'settling down type' look like?"

She rolled her eyes. For such a smart man, he certainly could be obtuse. "Well, for one, he doesn't date a bunch of women. He sticks with one."

Opening the church door, Ben fastened his gaze on her. "I'm with one woman now."

Despite the thrill his words caused inside her, Lily knew they meant nothing. She was only a conquest—nothing more, nothing less. "I don't count." She breezed past him and stepped inside the cool vestibule. "Now, if you don't mind, I'll go find a seat."

He snagged her arm.

His grip was gentle, but his gaze was determined…and completely compelling. She could hardly rip her arm away. With all the people in the vestibule, they were bound to notice, and then he'd be embarrassed. Lily exhaled. "I'm not gonna run away, you know."

He winked. "I know." Clasping Lily's elbow, Ben guided her up the aisle.

All gazes swiveled in their direction, and the buzz of conversations faded to a soft whisper, and then complete silence. The only sound in the church was the faint rap of her sandals against the worn, red carpet stretching from the entrance to the altar.

Dropping her gaze to the carpet, she was well aware of the heated glares the women shot in her direction. They probably wanted to murder her, which was ironic because they were in church. She wanted to tell them not to worry. She was here only for the summer. He would lose interest before she left, and if not, he would the second her taillights disappeared from his view. That truth annoyed her almost as much as the women glaring.

"What's wrong?" he asked.

They stopped next to a pew near the front of the church. The organ cued a song, and suddenly, the sound of papers shuffling in the stifling air filled the church.

She returned her attention. "Just thinking about the end of summer."

"We still have some weeks left." He waved her into the pew.

Claire, her neighbor, sat in the same pew next to the aisle. Shimmying past, Lily offered an apology before sitting in the empty space next to her. She frowned when he seated himself on the other side, dropping an arm over her shoulder. Hoping he'd take the hint, she glared.

He squeezed her shoulder, drawing her closer. The heat of his thigh warmed her leg and caused her stomach to flip-flop. She tried to inch away, but with his arm anchored on her shoulder, she couldn't put enough distance between them. Her only other course would be to remove his arm. However, she knew that attempt would be futile. Better to just ignore him and focus on Mass, which would be a lot easier if she wasn't acutely aware of Ben beside her.

Mass was torture. Lily hardly heard a word the priest spoke. She barely noticed the tapestry hanging behind the altar, or even the colorful glow of light shining through the stained-glass windows.

A whole new issue consumed her. Namely, sneaking away so she could help the Donut and Coffee Committee. She spent most of the service devising an escape.

A solution presented itself just before the end of communion. Instead of returning to the pew, she'd continue walking until she was out of the church and into the basement, where she could escape from Ben, and correct her mistake.

Chapter 18

Stepping inside the vestibule, Lily sighed in relief. She raced across the room toward the heavy, wooden door. The matted, red carpet lining the room muffled her footsteps. Now, all she needed to do was go downstairs, and she could complete her objective. Reaching for the knob, Lily opened the door.

A hand slammed into the wood, forcing the panel shut.

She jumped and turned. Her heart plunged to her stomach. *Great!* Ben caught her in the act of escaping. Glaring, she pointed a finger. "You left church early." She cringed, knowing he caught her doing the exact same thing.

He cocked a brow. "You did, too."

He would point out that fact. She glanced toward the closed vestibule doors. The low hum of music filled the area. Lily turned to Ben, and curling her lip, she lifted her chin and lowered her voice. "Yes. However, I have an actual reason."

Ben laughed. "Sweetheart, helping the Donut and Coffee Committee isn't a reason."

How the heck did he find out about my idea? "At least I have one. What's yours?"

"You."

She frowned. "Did Peri tell you my plan?" Amusement lit his eyes. Lily pinched her lips together and gritted her teeth. The man was forever laughing at her.

He held her gaze. "You told me."

She fisted her hands. In all their conversations, not one involved the Donut and Coffee Committee. "I don't remember telling you."

Ben shrugged. "Maybe because you were drunk."

Of all the situations for him to remember, he had to remember this one. She shook her head. "No, I wasn't."

"Sure, you were, sweetheart." He leaned toward her. "Want to know what else we discussed?"

Unease settled in the pit of her stomach. She lifted her chin in false bravado. "Not especially."

A battle of sorts ensued. Lily tugged on the handle while Ben rested a hand against the door. She gritted her teeth and again yanked on the door. Her efforts were pointless. She wanted to stamp her foot in frustration. He didn't understand her situation. "I need to help."

Tilting back his head, he closed his eyes and gritted his teeth.

She watched the muscles work in his throat.

A second later, he huffed a long, annoyed sigh. He raked fingers through his hair and opened his eyes. "You don't understand what you're getting into."

She appreciated his misplaced concern. However, she refused to be swayed. "Don't worry. I'll be fine."

A muscle flexed in his cheek. After an endless moment, he shook his head and yanked open the basement door.

Lily hurried down the stairs before he changed his mind. His footsteps sounded behind her. Humid air met her near the bottom steps. Second thoughts nipped her heels. What if they didn't like her? What if she ruined their event like Peri warned? She could run up the stairs this minute, and only Ben would be the wiser. She wouldn't, though, because she wasn't a coward. Stopping on the bottom rung, she took a deep breath. He settled his hands on her shoulders—calm and comforting. She turned.

He gave her shoulders a gentle squeeze. "You can change your mind."

She patted his hand. A warm feeling settled inside her, grateful for his concern. However, she refused to back out now. "I promise you everything will work out."

The basement was a large rectangular room with scuffed white floors and walls painted a soft yellow. Throughout the area were rows of long, white plastic banquet tables with matching folding chairs on both sides. Across from the stairs stood a door she assumed led into the kitchen. Next to the door was a pass-thru with a long stainless-steel counter where a dozen boxes of donuts were stacked atop the surface. Bright fluorescent lights lit the area.

Threading his fingers through hers, Ben led Lily farther into the kitchen.

Three people stood grouped near the far counter, their gazes swinging in her direction.

Fear, nervousness, and uncertainty filled her. She inched closer to him, thankful he was with her.

Ben settled an arm on Lily's shoulder. "Mitch, Suzette, Fern, this is Lily Evans." He glanced at each, holding Mitch's gaze the longest. "She'd like to help today."

Fern rushed forward. Smiling, she shook Lily's

hand. "It's a pleasure to meet you "

With her short, curly hair, and wide-rimmed glasses, she reminded Lily of a grandmother. Warm, welcoming, and eager to please.

The other two, Mitch and Suzette Bird, wore matching scowls. Both ignored her proffered hand. Her smile faltered. Dropping an arm to her side, she cleared her throat. "If you don't mind, I'm here to help." The smile Mitch gave her didn't quite extend to his eyes.

His eyes narrowed and his brows shot downward. "Great. The door's that way." He motioned toward the door.

She gave Ben a questioning glance, but he didn't notice. He was too busy glaring at Mitch with a look somewhere between resolute determination and outright anger. Lily turned to Mitch. "Did you need me to fetch something?"

Fern hurried over. "Don't mind Mitch." She patted Lily's hand. "We'd love your help. With Janine out, we are down to three people. Any extra hand is needed to make our social hour go without a hitch. Don't you agree, Mitch?"

Mitch shifted his attention from Lily to Ben then back. He pinched his mouth into a tight frown. "Can you make coffee?"

She wrinkled her brow. *Now, what kind of question is that? Does Mitch think I've never made coffee before?* "Sure."

Turning toward Fern, Mitch waved a hand. "Show her what needs to be done." He glared at Lily before marching toward the stairs.

Giving Lily's shoulders a gentle squeeze first, Ben followed Mitch. "Do you have a minute?"

Ben hadn't made a request. Resolve filled his hard gaze, and she knew only one answer was acceptable.

Mitch's shoulders slumped, and his chin dropped slightly. He shot one more glance in her direction before nodding and heading toward the stairs.

Taking hold of Lily's hand, Fern drew her toward a long counter. "Now, about that coffee…"

Mitch's reaction to Ben wasn't a surprise to Lily. In the few weeks she'd been here, she understood why people accepted his authority. He exuded strength and dominance—qualities people sought in a leader.

"…and this one is already made. You won't need to worry about that pot. Are you listening?"

Lily snapped back her attention. Occupied with her thoughts, she forgot to focus on Fern's instructions. "What? Oh yes."

"Now, you'll need to make lemonade, too." Fern studied her. "Do you have any questions?"

Yeah, dozens. Namely, what she missed while wondering about Mitch's reaction to Ben's order. She didn't ask, though. Instead, she scanned the expansive counter. A ginormous canister of powdered drink mix sat beside two decorative glass urns, presumably for the lemonade. "Nope. I'm good."

Fern smiled. "I'm certain you'll be a big help."

The heavy thud of footsteps followed by a burst of organ music sounded overhead.

Glancing toward the ceiling, Fern thrust a can of coffee into Lily's surprised arms. "Oh goodness, I hear Georgina cueing the organ. You finish here. I'll help Suzette."

Lily scanned the counter. As promised, one silver urn held coffee. The other, water. A large, metal basket

193

sat empty, waiting for coffee grounds. A scoop not much larger than a tablespoon sat inside the coffee can. She frowned. She couldn't use the tiny scoop, not if she wanted to complete her task before the end of the event.

Setting aside the spoon, she dug through the drawers until she found a measuring cup. She ladled out three heaping cups of coffee, dumping them in the basket. They barely covered the bottom of the plastic container. She decided to add a few more scoops.

While the second urn brewed, she made lemonade. The instructions were for a gallon of lemonade, not for a batch large enough to fill the urn. Logically, she figured she'd need the whole canister of powder to make an adequate amount.

Suzette clapped her hands, drawing Lily's attention.

"Hurry. The basement will be filled with hungry, thirsty people in about two minutes."

Panicked, Lily dismissed the instructions, filled the decanter with water, and dumped in the contents of the can. She grabbed a large ladle, and stirred swiftly.

Mitch and Ben entered the kitchen.

Each carried several stacks of large, rectangular boxes.

Setting the boxes on the serving counter, Mitch straightened and hurried away.

Worried that she'd caused a riff, she glanced in Ben's direction.

He winked, setting his stack next to Mitch's.

"Is everything okay between you and Mitch?"

"Yes." He encircled her waist with his arms.

She pulled back slightly, but Ben tightened his hold, drawing her against him. She wanted to question him. He kissed her instead.

Voices sounded behind them.

Lily jumped. Pressing a hand to her cheek, she snuck a peek around the room. "You're not supposed to kiss me."

Grinning, he rubbed his hand down the length of her back. "But I enjoy kissing you."

Her stomach tumbled. "Aren't you afraid you'll ruin your chances of finding a wife?" Lily immediately regretted her words. Now, she just sounded jealous.

He chuckled. "Shouldn't I be the one who's worried?"

He dared to wink then, before sauntering away. She studied him. For a man wishing marriage, he certainly wasn't concerned about being seen with her.

Lily shook off the kiss. She couldn't worry about whom he would marry or why his kiss had been brief. She had the Donut and Coffee Committee to impress. A few boxes of donuts sat on the far end of the counter. She hefted the stack in her arms.

The kitchen door swung open.

The boxes began to tilt sideways. She quickly righted them, before setting them down.

Fern bustled into the kitchen. "We certainly are busy."

A quick peek through the pass-thru into the gathering area showed a steady stream of laughing and chattering people filing into the basement. A line had formed in front of the refreshment table. Between the hot, steaming urns of coffee sat plastic cups, stir sticks, sugar packets, and creamer. The transparent coffee indicator was a deep, rich brown. She smiled, satisfied with her completed task.

Sneaking a furtive glance across the room, she spotted Ben, leaning against the far wall, surrounded by a group of women.

They simpered and giggled, touching their hair—all in an attempt to garner his attention.

He spoke to an older gentleman without once glancing in their direction.

A feeling she couldn't define filled her. Contentment? Pleasure? Satisfaction? She didn't know, and right now, she didn't care to define the emotion.

"Oh my, are we crowded today."

Lily slid her gaze around the crowded area. People glanced in her direction. She noticed the smile pasted on their faces and the enthusiastic laughter emanating from them. Her stomach twisted. She turned to Fern. "Is today a special occasion?"

Smiling, Fern rested a palm against the stainless-steel counter. "You could say that."

Suzette stepped out of the kitchen and stood beside Fern. Suzette tilted her head slightly to the side. "Ben's never escorted a woman here after church...certainly not as a couple."

The women's faces held expectant looks. Heat burned Lily's cheeks. She picked up the boxes of donuts and hurried into the main room.

Both women followed.

Needing to be busy, she placed the stack next to the others. "Oh, we're not a couple." She wished he was near to hear their comments. Maybe he'd understand what she'd been explaining.

Suzette shifted her gaze to Fern before turning back to Lily. "He's at your house all the time, though."

One of the silver platters was nearly empty. Lily

grabbed the tongs and set more donuts on the plate. She was positive she heard derision in Suzette's voice. They didn't understand her dilemma. She sighed. "He's the police chief. I can't say no to him, now can I?"

Fern's mouth dropped open. "You can't?"

Suzette's mouth twisted into a frown.

Great. Now, they probably thought she'd fallen under his spell with one glance of his smoldering looks. Well, she wouldn't let them believe such a thing. "Don't get me wrong. I don't give in easily."

Suzette's eyes widened. "You don't?"

Fern nodded.

Lily could see they were impressed with her independence. Their approval eased her worry. Maybe now they'd accept her. Smiling, she added donuts to the other platter.

Wyatt Westerman reached for one.

Quickly picking up the tray, Lily pasted a tight smile and offered him a donut.

His face turned bright red, but he didn't say a word. He just took the donut and marched off.

Setting aside the platter, she turned to the women. "Well, Ben's extremely persistent. Sometimes giving in to his demands is easier."

Suzette's mouth dropped open, and her face changed to three shades of red complementing Fern's suddenly chalk-white face.

"Are you feeling okay?" For a moment Lily wondered whether to fetch Ben or not.

Both women scurried away without answering.

Turning to watch them, she came face to chest with Ben. "What are you doing here?"

Ben grabbed her shoulders, and ran his hands down

197

her arms. "I wanted to check on you."

The teasing glimmer in his eyes made Lily uncomfortable. She dropped her hands to her hips and narrowed her eyes. "Okay, just how much did you hear?"

A slow, lazy smile spread across Ben's face. "Enough to know they think we're having sex."

"Don't be silly." Ignoring the way her stomach lurched, she quickly busied herself with arranging the donuts on the platters. "Besides, if they do, you only have yourself to blame. I warned you. You can't kiss me all the time and not have people talk."

"They don't think we are having sex because we kissed." He drew her into his arms. "Your comments took care of that problem."

Nothing she discussed with the women even hinted they'd had sex. She rolled her eyes. "That's ridiculous."

He shrugged. "I need to go to the office for a bit. Will you be okay here by yourself, or do you want me to take you home?"

"I'll be fine." Lily expected him to leave. Instead, he gave her another kiss, right in front of everyone in the hall.

"I'll return to pick you up."

Heat burned her face and her lips tingled. Licking her lips, she quickly scrutinized the area. Did the room suddenly seem just a tiny bit quieter? She turned, intending to tell him not to bother, but he'd already disappeared. Lily shook her head, uncertain whether she should be upset because he ignored her orders, or thankful he did. Only one thing she knew for sure, kissing wouldn't help the gossip.

Chapter 19

Several hours later, Ben signed the last document, clipped together the stack of papers before placing them in the file folder. Setting the file atop the rest on his desk, he stood and stretched. The memory of Mitch's furious glare flashed through his thoughts. Frowning, he grabbed his keys off the edge of his desk, suddenly anxious to see Lily. He was worried for her and wanted to be with her. If this fact surprised most people, it downright shocked him. Since when had he ever wanted to spend longer than a few days with any woman? He could count on one hand, and that number was precisely one. Lily.

Smiling, he remembered her no-kissing order. He knew the reason for her rule, which was the very same reason he chose to ignore the demand. The fact was, she liked kissing him as much as he enjoyed kissing her.

He might be a realist, but he was also determined. Lily's presence began as a problem. Hell, she still posed a challenge. However, she was a challenge he refused to let escape.

By the time he arrived, the parking lot was empty. He parked the truck and looked around for a reason for the deserted area and found none. He scratched his chin. When was the last time the Donut and Coffee Hour ended before noon? He couldn't remember. Sunday provided a prime opportunity for the town to chatter. Turning off the engine, Ben opened the door and stepped out. Heck, none of the residents needed to wait for Sunday to exchange tidbits. Any time was perfect for them.

However, the Donut and Coffee Hour held a unique appeal. Sunday gave them license to compare notes, and they had plenty to discuss, most of which included his relationship with Lily.

The echo of his shoes sounded in the silent church. He headed to the basement and stared at the empty hall. A few hushed voices drew his gaze. He stepped into the kitchen. Trays filled with donuts littered the counters. Stacked off to the side sat a half dozen or more boxes of donuts. Two coffee urns stood next to the sink. One was empty. Thick, black liquid oozed from the other. A few plastic cups littered the table. Only Mitch, Suzette, and Fern remained. All three swung their attention in his direction.

Mitch made a beeline straight toward Ben. "Again, your girlfriend ruined our Donut and Coffee Hour."

Fern hurried to stand next to Mitch. "I wouldn't say ruin." She shrugged. "Although, we might have a few lawsuits leveled against us."

All color drained from Mitch's face. "Oh heavens, I never thought…" He swung his gaze to Ben. "What are we gonna do?"

Ben ignored Mitch's comment. He kept his attention focused on Fern. Of the three, she appeared the calmest. "What happened?"

Grabbing an empty cup, Mitch poured a thick goo inside, before thrusting the drink at Ben. "Try this slop and tell me what you think."

Ben stared at the thick liquid and frowned. He

raised a hesitant hand, saw the challenging look in Mitch's eyes, before tasting the sludge. He wanted to chew the thick brew. Instead, he set down the cup. "The coffee is a bit strong."

A squeak pealed from Suzette. "Strong? Crude oil tastes better than that muck." She grabbed a donut from one of the trays, shoving the pastry toward him. "Try this *donut*. Tell me if you think coffee will help *that rock*."

Ben didn't need to dunk the hard donut in the oil to know the effort wouldn't make either more palatable. "Okay, the coffee tastes bad, and the donuts are hard. I don't think you can place the entire blame on Lily. These aren't Dainty's Donuts. You can't expect them to be as delicious."

"Don't blame the baker for your *girlfriend's* mistake." Suzette fisted her hands. "She's the one who put out last week's donuts."

"To be fair." Fern fanned out a hand. "She didn't know the donuts were stale. We should have thrown them out last week."

Suzette ripped her gaze to Fern. "We forgot. Remember the whole scuffle in church? The one *she* created?"

He didn't stay to hear any more. Taking the stairs, two at a time, he shot a wave to Father Frank. Thoughts of Lily and her desire to impress the committee swirled through his mind. He knew she didn't understand Mitch's obsessive need to have a flawless Sunday. How could she know this fact? He certainly hadn't informed her, and Mitch would expect her to be just as obsessive.

I hope she's okay. Climbing into his truck, he did a U-turn on Woodland, and headed in the direction of

Lily's house. He spotted her crossing Main Street.

****

The tall, stately oak trees dappled the sidewalk in shadows. Cars cruised past on Woodland, blowing a soft, summer breeze in Lily's face. She ignored the passing scenery. She was too busy cursing her unfortunate luck. Here, she'd gone to help the Donut and Coffee Committee with pure intentions, and everything blew up.

Okay, she hadn't made the best coffee in town—or maybe even the world. So, the coffee was as thick as tar. Maybe they were right to say her drink tasted vile, but boy, did their comments hurt. After all, how was she to know a sixty-cup urn needed only two cups of ground coffee and not five? *Oh, why did I let my mind get distracted by Ben, instead of listening to Fern's instructions?*

Stomping down the sidewalk, she hugged her arms to her chest. Sure, she'd made a tiny mistake by serving last week's donuts, but did people really need to blatantly mention donuts and hockey pucks in the same sentence, all the while casting accusing glances her way? And why exactly was she the one who was at fault when no one bothered to throw out the stale rocks in the first place? She certainly wasn't a mind-reader.

Crossing Main Street, Lily grumbled her fury to the passing scenery. She glanced up just in time to see Ben's vehicle come to a complete stop.

Perfect. Her humiliation was complete.

Now, he'd want to know why she left the church early, which meant she'd need to admit the horrible truth. She was a terrible cook. If she could, she'd dive into the bushes edging the sidewalk and hide. The idea arrived too late, though. Ben rounded the vehicle and headed her way.

Smoothing a hand over her white dress, she schooled her features into a blank expression. She wasn't certain she was successful with the way her hand shook. *Great, now I will have to admit my mistakes and then he'll see how pitiful I am.* "I thought you were at work."

Ben jumped the curb and stopped in front of her. He clasped her hand and drew her toward him. "I finished early. How come you left? I asked you to wait for me."

Lily buried the side of her face into his broad chest. He smelled wonderful—like a warm blanket on a bleak day. "I didn't know when you planned on returning, and seeing they didn't need me anymore, I decided to walk home."

This statement was almost the truth. She *had* finished early. Well, if she was honest, they demanded she leave…and not too kindly, either. Slinking away seemed a better alternative than death. Besides, Ben shouldn't be forced to choose between saving and killing her.

"I see." He smoothed a hand up her back. "How did your day go?"

He would ask the one question she wanted to avoid. What did he expect her to say? Everything had been perfect. She could say the day had been perfect, if perfect included ruining the coffee and nearly killing people on hockey-puck donuts. "I imagined something a bit different." She sighed, expecting some sympathy.

Instead, he laughed.

Easing back, Lily met his gaze and frowned.

"When they shoot me, you won't be laughing."

His smile deepened. "I'm certain you'll be just fine."

"Oh yeah? Well, I think I've poisoned some people with my coffee, and Wyatt thinks I want to kill him. Not to mention Mrs. Nussbaum nearly broke a tooth on the donuts." Lily pressed her hands against his chest. "Although, to be fair, someone really should have thrown out those stale donuts."

More laughter rumbled from him.

She glared. Her muscles tightened. "What exactly do you find so hilarious about this situation? The fact they might hang me, or the fact I nearly killed half the town?" His arm encompassed her waist, escorting her to his vehicle.

"I don't think you need to worry about either happening."

"Easy for you to say." Lily climbed into the truck and settled herself in the passenger seat. She smoothed a hand over her skirt and sighed. "You're not the one with half the town suspicious of you."

Softening his smile, he placed a kiss on her forehead.

The act was gentle, and Lily knew he meant to comfort her. She didn't feel comforted, though. How could she? She came to this town to forget her problems, not collect more. Yet, the greatest challenge of all sat beside her.

What the heck? When she agreed to this vacation, she never intended to meet a man, let alone be drawn to one. She could hardly blame herself for her attraction. He was a living, breathing cliché right out of a movie script. If tall, dark, and handsome didn't seal the deal, then powerful, dominant, and distracting would. Each day she edged closer to falling into a dangerous abyss—one she wasn't sure she wanted to escape.

During the ride home, she contemplated her options. She could always take Peri's suggestion. The only problem was the fact she didn't do flings. She needed love and commitment, and the simple fact was Ben didn't love her. As for commitment, the only one he made was seduction.

The truth hit in her in the face. Whatever the situation was between them, needed to end today. Before she did something stupid—namely fall in love with him. Because Lily refused to be hurt again.

While Ben parked in her driveway, Lily fidgeted with the seatbelt, contemplating exactly how to explain her dilemma. She'd ease into the discussion, explain her position, and her reasons for the decision. Ben was a practical man. He'd understand. Heck, he'd probably be thrilled.

Ben opened the passenger door and lifted her.

She looked at his soft brown eyes, felt his fingers clutch her waist, and all her intentions flew from her thoughts. "We can't see each other anymore."

For a moment, he held her mid-air, their gazes locking. He tightened his grip slightly before releasing her. "Oh?"

"Really, this decision is for the best." Starting for the house, she slid a glance in his direction.

A slight smile curled on the edge of his lips, and his brow furrowed just a bit.

Lily frowned. *Fine.* If he didn't care, then neither did she. She stopped mid-way up the porch steps and turned to face him. "I mean, all we have is a physical attraction, and let's face it, sex is hardly a way to build a relationship."

He rested one foot on the bottom step, his fingers gripping the porch railing. "Sweetheart, I can't think of a better way to build a relationship." He thrust out his hand. "Your house keys?"

The change in topic surprised Lily. She blinked. *Since when do men open doors for women?* She couldn't think of one time when Eric even hinted at such an action. "Didn't you hear me?"

Ben nodded slowly. "Every word."

"If you're leaving, why do you need my house key?"

He smiled. "Because I want to open the door."

Despite the ease of his tone, Lily could tell by the hard determination in his gaze arguing was fruitless. The man had a singular point of purpose. She twisted her fingers. *Why the heck does my sister have a memory of a gnat? Now because of Peri's chronic forgetfulness, I'm the one who has to deal with Ben's displeasure.* "You promise not to become upset?"

The smile slipped from his face. "No."

His eyes darkened slightly. Lily frowned. The man was beyond unreasonable. She huffed, pointing to the secret spot she and Peri finally settled on. The rusted nail tucked near the tall grass surrounding the porch was the perfect hiding spot. "We hid the key there."

The minute he spotted the hiding place, she knew he was angry. His face turned red, his eyes deepened to nearly pitch black, and the now-familiar tic beat with a life of its own. Heck, irritation didn't begin to describe his appearance. From his rigid shoulders to the vein pulsating in his neck, every inch of his body spoke of anger. Furious might be a better description—or maybe murderous. Yes, murderous was definitely better. She just wished he didn't intend to murder her.

"Under the porch is not a hiding place." Ben fisted both hands on his hips. "That spot is the first place a thief looks."

Crossing her arms, she gave him a fierce glare. "You told me the first place is under the doormat." If possible, his face hardened even further.

Shoving aside the tall grass, he snatched the key from the nail. "For God's sake, the key is not even hidden. You can spot the damn thing without bending," Ben growled. "Why the hell doesn't your sister carry her purse?"

Lily shrugged. She wished she knew the answer to that question, as well. "She rarely carries a purse, but even if she did, she'd probably still forget the key. Peri forgets everything. She's replaced her phone three times this past year." Sighing, she held out a hand. "Here, give me the key. I'll find a better spot."

Ben flicked a glance toward her outstretched palm before heading up the porch steps.

Her heart raced, and her stomach did a flip-flop. She chased after him and threw herself against the door. "We agreed you shouldn't come in."

He unlocked and opened the door. "I never agreed."

Lily stumbled backward. Ben caught her, his arms encircling her waist and, against her directive, his lips capturing her mouth. Her pulse kicked up, and her heart beat against her chest. She gave up her futile effort of resistance. After all, if this kiss was the last they'd share, she might as well enjoy the moment.

His lips caressed hers, and his fingers inched their way beneath the white lace of her shirt to stroke the skin along her waist. As she sank into his arms, a low heat radiated from her belly.

As soon as her fingers shifted to the top button of his shirt, he tore free his mouth. She snapped open her eyes. His gaze was hooded, but a small smile curled on his lips. *A look of victory.* Lily stiffened, and her heart plunged.

Dropping his arms, he stepped away.

The sudden action surprised Lily, and the warmth she felt in his arms just moments ago faded. *Dammit!* She'd been trapped by his seduction. She gritted her teeth and glared. "I won't sleep with you, Ben Jordan."

"Sweetheart, trust me. When the time comes, we won't be doing a lot of sleeping." He dropped the key on the counter and left.

She stood in the open doorway. Fury burned inside her. She spotted a flowerpot sitting on the corner of the railing. Without a second thought, she grabbed the pot and threw it across the porch. The container landed with a thud in the gravel, only a clump of dried dirt and shattered terracotta.

He never once broke his stride.

She fisted her hands. *That man!* She stormed into the house. Slamming the door was her only satisfaction.

Chapter 20

Ben sat at his desk on Monday morning, deep in thought. The contract in his hand was long forgotten. He considered himself a calm and reasonable man, qualities which made him successful as a police chief. These same qualities would help him as a mayor. With Lily, though, calm and reasonable never once entered the equation. She drove him crazy, and that fact was the truth.

Lily stated they could no longer see each other, as if he'd agree to the ridiculous dictate. Didn't she realize he never gave up if he wanted something? And he wanted her.

He spent all morning replaying yesterday's events. From his urge to protect Lily from Mitch's wrath over Sunday's ruined event, to his pride as she slowly ingratiated herself with Fern, and finally his worry over her disappearance, and the subsequent relief at finding her safe were emotions he'd never experienced with a woman. On a practical level, he kept his relationships to a non-committal basis. With Lily, though...

Ben raked fingers through his hair. Without a doubt, he knew, she desired him as much as he wanted her. Hell, yesterday they'd been within moments of sex. He'd left because every prying eye in the surrounding area was trained on her house.

Leaning back in his chair and closing his eyes, he

sighed. He needed to decide what he wanted. Lily wasn't the kind of girl a man trifled with—at least, not a man with any amount of self-respect. He liked to think of himself as that kind of man. One thing he knew for certain, their relationship wasn't finished. Not by a long shot.

His office door opened, and Claire stepped inside.

He dismissed the unread contract in his hand, not the least bit surprised to see her bright and early this morning. After yesterday's event, he would have been surprised if she *didn't* show up. He stood and eased around his desk, pressing a kiss to her warm cheek. "Good morning, Mom. What a surprise."

Dropping into the chair, Claire placed her purse on her lap and studied him for a moment. "Everyone is discussing you and Lily."

Ben wasn't surprised by this news. He shrugged, settling himself on the edge of his desk. "And?"

Claire pinched together her lips. "*And* I want to know what's going on between you two."

Crossing his arms, he frowned. He was a thirty-year-old man. *Why does my mother think she can still pry into my personal life?* "What's between us does not involve you."

"But the gossip…"

Ben laughed. "If you don't like the rumors, don't spread them."

Claire huffed out a breath. "I can see you're not willing to discuss this issue." She studied him, tapping fingers against her purse. "I'm worried about you."

He lifted his brows. "Oh?"

"With Heather out, you're here endless number of hours. Working that hard is bad for your health. You

210

need to hire an assistant."

"I have Abe."

Claire rolled her eyes and waved a hand. "Abe's no help."

He couldn't argue his mother's assessment. Abe and help were not synonymous. He appreciated Claire's concern. However, the fact she mentioned Lily a day after the church incident was too coincidental. "Did you have someone in mind?"

"Actually, I do." Claire flashed a smile. "You should ask Lily. She's a secretary, you know."

Reclaiming his seat, Ben laughed. "Didn't you just warn me about the gossip? Asking her to work here won't help."

Claire pinched together her lips. "You need assistance, though."

Ben heard the plea in his mother's tone and ignored it. Instead, he retrieved the discarded contract. "I'll be fine."

Claire's shoulders slumped, and a sigh rippled from her.

He knew her mother's guilt act only too well. Ben maintained his silence.

Standing, Claire hiked her purse onto a shoulder and frowned. "At least consider my suggestion."

Ben noticed the worry in his mother's eyes. He didn't want to disappoint her. Leaning back in his chair, he dropped a hand to his desk and closed his eyes for just a moment. "Fine. I'll think about it."

Claire gave him a jaunty wave before departing his office.

Ben shook his head. At least he resolved one problem. Again, he picked up the contract and skimmed through the text.

The office door creaked open.

Ben glanced up.

Abe stepped inside. "Got another visitor."

Nathan Walkman, a young reporter from *The Aberdeen Times*, followed Abe. He looked like the typical reporter from days past. His shaggy blonde hair needed a good combing, his shirt was wrinkled, and the glasses perched on his nose were taped together at the bridge. He gripped a battered briefcase in one hand and a notepad in another.

Ben forgot about the interview to discuss the election. If he had his way, he'd reschedule, or better yet, cancel entirely. Unfortunately, neither was an option.

Gripping his notepad, Nate fixed his gaze on the paper. "So, let's start with your decision. When did you make it?"

"I always expected I would." Ben shrugged. "I just didn't think it would happen this quickly."

Scribbling on the pad, Nathan nodded. "I see."

Ben's thoughts drifted, wondering what Lily would think of his election.

"…and the ceremony is…?"

Ben snapped back his attention. "Excuse me?"

Clearing his throat, Nathan blushed. "I just wondered if you've set a date?"

He cursed himself for losing focus. "Of course. It's planned for November fifth, the Saturday after the election." Ben tapped the edge of a pencil on the desk while Nathan wrote the information.

Nathan glanced at the note pad. "So, will you have a large celebration?"

Ben waved a hand. "I suppose. Traditionally, it's expected, although in truth, if I had my way, the event would be small—just family."

"And your mother? Is she happy?" Nathan arched a brow.

What does he think? Ben frowned. *My mother won't be happy with me running for mayor?* "Of course. She's dreamed of me doing this for a while."

Leaning forward in the chair, Nathan looked up from the notepad. "I'm certain you're aware a few people are not happy about this news."

Nathan's comment caught him off-guard. He hadn't heard any dissension in town regarding him running for mayor. Then again, Mike Landry had been mayor since Ben's father died. While Mike might be ready to leave the office and the town wanted someone new, change happened slowly here. "I'm certain they'll accept this decision in time." Lily kept intruding into his thoughts, and all he wanted was to see her and gossip be damned. He drummed his fingers on the desk, waiting for Nathan to finish writing before standing. "I'm sorry. I have another appointment I need to attend."

"Oh, sure." Nathan stopped writing. He flipped the pad shut and tucked the pencil into his pocket. Standing, he offered his right hand. "Thank you, Mr. Jordan, for the interview. For the record, may I be the first to say congratulations."

Clamping a hand on Nathan's shoulder, he steered him from the office. He waited until Nathan left before turning to Abe. "I'm heading out."

Abe whipped his gaze from the word puzzle. "You can't leave. Karla and Jenny have stopped by a dozen times to see you." He tossed his pencil across the desk, hitting the plastic cup of coffee. "They're bound to return."

Ben wasn't overly concerned about Karla, Jenny, or Abe's dilemma. "You can handle both women." Now, if only he could figure out a way to handle Lily, his life might return to normal.

Chapter 21

Lily spent Monday morning debating what to do about the spare key. She knew Ben didn't want her to hide the key, but he didn't understand. Peri losing things wasn't new. She'd spent half her life in search of missing items—wallets, cell phones, keys. Heck, once she'd even lost her car in the mall parking lot.

She should really teach Peri a lesson and not hide the key. Only Lily knew she would be the one punished. Peri would undoubtedly wake her up in the middle of the night, begging to be let in.

Sighing, she pressed her hands against the counter and thought. Obviously, keeping a spare key inside the house wasn't a viable option. If either locked themselves out, the only way in would be with a locksmith or breaking the window. Neither option was acceptable.

Some people might say she purposely avoided the weightier issue of her encounter yesterday with Ben. They'd be right, too. Every time his passionate promise scrolled through her thoughts, she felt her resolution weaken.

She stared out the kitchen window toward the side yard. When she spotted the garage, the answer to one problem presented itself. She might not solve her problem with him, but she could with the key. Snagging the key from the counter, Lily ripped open the kitchen door and stepped outside.

Starting up the porch steps, Peri spotted Lily. She stopped and nodded toward the driveway. "Hey, what happened to the flower pot?"

Shards of terracotta and clumps of old dirt littered the gravel. Lily hurried down the steps, refusing to clue in her sister on yesterday's events. "No idea. Probably just the raccoons."

"Please don't say raccoons. You know how I hate them."

Footsteps crunched on the gravel behind Lily. She turned to see Peri chasing behind. Rolling her eyes, she headed across the yard. "I'm kidding."

"That was mean," Peri snapped. "What are you doing anyway?"

Remembering the insistence in Ben's words and the implacable look in his eyes, Lily scowled. "Ben didn't like our last hiding spot." She glanced at Peri. "You know, if you didn't lose things, I wouldn't have this problem."

Peri snorted. "Yeah, right. Like that's happening." She fanned a hand back toward the house. "What was wrong with our last hiding spot?"

She tightened her grip on the key. "He complained the nail was too visible."

Peri waved a hand. "What did he think? We'd actually crawl under the porch to hide the stupid thing? Does he understand the whole creepiness about bugs and spiders?"

Lily shrugged. "He didn't care." She stopped beside the garage door.

"You see? Just one more reason why men are weird." Peri shook her head. "They don't care about bugs."

Secretly, Lily agreed. "Yeah, well, weird or not, we need to find a better spot." She opened the garage door and flipped on the light. Scanning the cluttered area, Lily reconsidered her idea. She spotted plenty of viable places amongst the discarded debris where a burglar would never find the key. However, she didn't think she or Peri would either. A nail jutted from the window sill. The location wasn't ideal, seeing as anyone could spot it through the window. However, the spot was close to the door and had a clear path. "I figure if we hide the key in here and don't lock the door, we'll satisfy Ben and have the key available." She looked around the area. "How about there?"

"You mean by the window covered with spider webs and dead flies?" Peri shuddered. "I don't think so."

An image of sticky spider webs clinging to fingers popped into Lily's thoughts. Another tremor of revulsion rolled through her. She shook off the feeling. Ben only meant to keep her safe. While she appreciated his concern, couldn't she make this decision on her own? Considering his personality, she supposed he did. Curling her lip in thought, she lifted her gaze and pointed to the ledge above the doorway. "Here?"

"On the ceiling?" Peri exclaimed. "Are you kidding me? I'll never reach the key up there."

"Not the ceiling." Lily jabbed a finger upward. "The ledge *above* the door. All we need is to put the ladder next to the door. Here, help me."

Carefully keeping her body away from the dead bugs littering the surfaces, Lily made her way across the room to the ladder hanging on a pair of hooks.

Peri followed. "Now what?"

Stepping forward, Lily sized up the wooden ladder. She stretched her gaze upward. Ten dusty rungs later, she spotted the top, hanging from a hook. "Well, for starters, we lift it."

Standing next to Lily, Peri thrust her arms upward. "Are you nuts? The last time we lifted something heavy, I broke a nail."

"Only because the garage door was locked." Lily positioned herself on one side, waving to Peri to take the other. "For goodness sake, we're not talking anything difficult here. We just lift the ladder off the hooks. Easy peasy."

"But it looks heavy." Peri stepped forward and clutched the legs.

Lily wrapped her fingers around one of the legs. A little struggle wouldn't deter her. "How heavy can this ladder be? It's wooden. Now, on the count of three…" Gritting her teeth, she bent her knees and thrust upward.

Peri did the same.

The ladder didn't budge.

"Are you trying?" Groaning, Lily tightened her grip on the ladder legs and struggled to push her arms upward.

"You told me wooden ladders were light." Peri grunted, her arms straining against the weight.

"Keep pushing." Gritting her teeth, Lily stared at the top of the ladder. Just an inch more and they'd have the ladder off the hook.

'I can't." Peri moaned.

"Yes, you can," Lily insisted. "Come on."

Suddenly, the ladder shot from the hook.

Peri let out an ear-piercing scream and released her

grip.

Lily stumbled under the weight while Peri waved her arms in the air.

The ladder fell.

Panicked, Lily twisted to the side and lost her grip. The ladder tumbled from her grasp and bounced off her shoulder. She fell backward into a chair. "I landed in a pile of dead bugs," she screeched, flailing her arms and bolting from the chair.

Peri clutched her neck. "I ate a tarantula!"

"Are you kidding me? I *sat* in dead bugs." Lily swiped her hands against the back of her shorts. A quick glance revealed palms covered in cobwebs. Her muscles tightened, and she nearly shrieked. In a frenzy, she shook her hands. "Is that a spider?"

"Oh my God. Oh my God." Bending over, Peri wrapped her arms against her waist and moaned. "I ate a tarantula, and now I'm gonna die."

Ignoring Peri's theatrics, Lily twisted her body to see the back of her shorts and failed. "Do you see any bugs stuck on me?"

"Did you hear me?" Peri croaked. "I ate a *tarantula.* They're poisonous, you know."

"They don't have tarantulas up here." She turned her attention from her shorts. "Besides, eating a tarantula requires chewing. Did you chew?"

Peri gagged. "Seriously, did you really need to say such a thing?"

Lily blew out a breath and prayed for patience. She just wanted to go into the house, change out of her clothing and take a shower—and maybe, if she were lucky, the nightmare would disappear. "Relax. I'm sure all you ate was a house spider." She weaved her way toward the counter filled with tools.

Peri followed. "And *that* answer is better, how?"

Grabbing one of the old, rusty coffee cans on the disgusting shelf, Lily tossed the key into the pile of screws and nuts. She couldn't imagine anyone willingly digging through the repulsive dead bugs in search of a key. She brushed her palms against her ruined shorts. Pain stung her shoulder. Ignoring the ache, she tucked the can near the window sill. "Come on. Let's go, and *don't* lock the door."

She turned to leave, and bumping into Ben's broad chest, she ripped her gaze upward. A multitude of thoughts rushed through her, and every single one included how amazing he looked and how wonderfully perfect his hands felt resting on her waist. "I didn't expect you."

"What are you doing?" He plucked a cobweb from her hair.

"She made me lift the ladder, and now I've eaten a tarantula." Glaring, Peri pointed to the offending object strewn across the dusty chair.

"Oh, for goodness sake, you didn't eat a tarantula." Stepping free from his arms, Lily quickly glanced at her shirt and sighed. *Thank God. No dead bugs are stuck to the fabric.*

Peri turned to Ben. "She refuses to believe I ate a tarantula."

He burst out laughing. "Your sister's right, Peri. We don't have tarantulas in northern New York."

Peri scowled. "I hope you're right. I'd hate to die unnecessarily." She turned then abruptly stopped. "I'm telling you, if I had known about the raccoons and bugs here, we'd be vacationing elsewhere." She stormed out of the garage.

****

Ben waited until Peri left before turning to Lily. "Do you want to tell me why you needed a ladder?"

Lily didn't want to lie. However, if she admitted the truth, he'd yell. Receiving a lecture wasn't on her top ten list today, not with her shoulder hurting, and the key tucked in a place Ben was destined to hate. "I'd rather not." She turned to leave.

He caught her arm.

She batted her eyelashes, feigning innocence. "Did you want something else?"

A growl ripped from him. "*Lily...*"

Narrowing her eyes, Lily dropped her hands to her hips. "Are you always persistent?"

The muscles in Ben's jaw clenched. "When I want something, I am."

The man is stubborn. She huffed a sigh. "Okay, fine. We decided to hide the key above the door."

Ben thinned his lips into a hard frown. "You what?"

Lily didn't appreciate the accusing tone in his voice. "I told you, Peri loses things all the time. I know you don't want us to hide the key by the house, so I thought the garage was our next best solution."

Pinching his lips together, Ben thrust out his hand. "Where's the key?"

Lily considered not telling him. However, the fire in his eyes made her decision easy. Sighing, she pointed to the hiding spot. "There."

Leaning forward, Ben studied the can for just a moment before whipping back his attention. "For God's sake, the damn thing isn't even hidden," he exploded, grabbing the key off the top of the can.

The man never liked her suggestions. She fisted her hand so that her nails dug into her palms and glared. "Fine, then where would *you* suggest I hide it?"

"I can think of a dozen places." He tucked the key in his pocket.

"Hey!" Lily frowned. "What are you doing?"

"Keeping your key."

Lily snapped back her head and raised her brows. "What?"

"I said I'll keep it."

Lily hated this idea. She gritted her teeth. She didn't need supervision, and she *especially* wasn't impressed by the way he tucked the key in his pants, either. His pockets were the same as a black hole. Once inside, the key was gone forever. "I'd rather just keep it myself." She rubbed her shoulder. "Besides, what if we lock ourselves out?"

"You'll call me."

The memory of yesterday's kiss flooded Lily's thoughts. She licked her lips. "I don't think that idea is wise."

Shifting his attention, Ben furrowed his brow. "What's wrong with your shoulder?"

Lily quickly dropped her hand. "Nothing."

He narrowed his eyes.

Lily propped a hand on her hip. "Fine. If you must know, the ladder landed on my shoulder."

Ben grabbed the edge of her shirt.

Her pulse leaped. She took a step backward.

He sighed. "I just want to check and make sure everything is okay."

Gripping the bottom of her shirt as if crazy-glued

to her palms, Lily frowned. "Ben, you're not a doctor. You're the police chief. You attended police school, not medical school."

A smile twitched on his lips. "It's an academy." He released her shirt and clasped her hand. "You're right, though. I'm not a doctor."

She was halfway to his truck before realizing his intention. "Where are you taking me?"

"To the hospital." Ben opened the passenger door.

"What?"

"Lily, be reasonable. Your collarbone might be broken."

"That's impossible." She held her elbow carefully, ignoring the sharp sting slicing through her arm. "If I broke a bone, I'd throw-up."

"That fact isn't always true."

Not always true implied it *might* be true, which meant if she agreed to go to the hospital and her collarbone wasn't broken, she wasted money she didn't have. "I'm sure it's just a minor bruise. By tomorrow, the pain will be gone."

Ben shook his head. "We won't know until we have your shoulder checked."

She considered running straight across the driveway and into her house. However, one substantial obstacle stood in her way. Ben. His look was hard and determined, his stance challenging. Every part of her knew, if she wanted to argue, she better be prepared to lose—which meant, no matter what her opinion, he would take her to the hospital, not to mention the blasted man had her key. "Fine. I'll go, but I am *not* happy." She grumbled just to make her point.

He placed a soft kiss on her forehead. "I know,

sweetheart."

The x-ray took less time than she expected. She should have anticipated immediate attention. She *was* with the Chief of Police, after all. Being on friendly terms with Dr. Kimball, or Charlie, as Ben introduced him, didn't hurt, either. Of course, he was friends with everyone in town.

In the end, her collarbone wasn't broken. She planned on gloating, only the pain meds Charlie gave her put her to sleep before they wheeled her from the examination room.

****

Ben maneuvered the wheelchair from the hospital.

Charlie strode by his side.

Stopping beside his vehicle, Ben turned. "What should I do to help her tonight?"

Charlie shrugged. "Not much. Put ice on the bruise for twenty minutes every one to two hours, and make her comfortable. She'll probably sleep through the night." He paused, shifting his gaze between Ben and Lily. "Are the rumors true?"

Knowing feigning ignorance was pointless, Ben shrugged. "Don't read too much into what you hear."

A whisper of a smile crossed Charlie's face. He clamped a hand on Ben's shoulder. "No need to be defensive. I just know what people think when a man and woman attend church together."

"We went to church. Nothing more." He gently lifted Lily and settled her into the passenger seat.

Driving to Lily's, Ben replayed Charlie's words. He had known the implications of escorting her to Mass, and yet, he'd taken her anyway. Of course, the issue with the Donut and Coffee Committee helped him justify his actions

Was he being honest with himself, or finding an excuse? He didn't know, and right now, he was too tired to care.

He parked his vehicle in her driveway, dismissing the problem. The issue could wait. Right now, she needed him. Cradling her in his arms, he carried her into the house. Once inside, he settled her in bed before going into the kitchen to grab a bag of ice from the freezer. Walking quietly into the bedroom, he carefully placed the icepack then secured it with a soft towel. Satisfied he had made her as comfortable as possible, Ben stretched out beside her. He planned to stay only long enough to make sure she was okay.

Carefully, he gathered her into his arms, while she continued to sleep. Resting his chin on the top of her head, he considered all the possibilities. He fell asleep holding her close.

He woke to a sky tinged milky pink. He glanced at the clock. *Damn. I'm late.* Even later, once he went home to shower and change. He should feel guilty, but somehow, he couldn't quite summon the emotion.

Curled on her side, Lily rested her sore shoulder against his. Carefully, Ben eased away. With a sigh, he climbed from the bed. Stretching his arms over his head, he eased the kinks from his muscles while studying her.

Her dark lashes lay against the creamy skin of her cheek, and her soft rose-colored lips parted just slightly.

From the way she slept, and her relaxed position, he knew she trusted him.

He reminded himself she was only here for the summer, but damn…

Chapter 22

Minnie fumbled her way into the kitchen. The soft glow of the sunrise provided enough light to find the sink without tripping over the chair Hank had not put back into place, *again*. Grabbing a glass from the cupboard with one hand, she nudged the lever on the faucet with her elbow.

As water filled the glass, she glanced out the side window. Minnie blinked, and just to make sure she wasn't in the middle of a dream, she rubbed the sleep from her eyes. "Oh, my goodness…" The glass slipped from her fingers and tumbled into the sink.

Minnie slammed her hand against the faucet, shutting off the water then darted into the living room. Flattening herself against the wall, she hooked a finger in the edge of the curtain, thrusting aside the fabric just enough to peek outside. Excitement swelled inside her.

Dropping the curtain, she raced across the room to the phone. Her foot caught the edge of the stool sitting directly in her path. With her arms flailing, Minnie reached for the receiver. She missed. The phone clattered to the floor.

Scrambling across the carpet, she grabbed the handset and dialed Claire's number. She waited in breathless anticipation for Claire to answer. As soon as she heard Claire's voice, Minnie blurted out her news.

"Are you certain? You've been wrong before."

Claire grumbled. "Remember the Rufus incident?"

Minnie frowned. Sure, she made one stupid mistake, and no one forgot. How the heck was she to know Rufus had taken a fondness to streaking? No one sure had. Heck, when she first spied him dashing through town, she figured he'd dressed in a nude bodysuit. When she called Claire, she only meant to share what she'd witnessed. She certainly hadn't intended for Claire to sprint into the street and investigate. *And* she definitely hadn't expected Rufus to run straight into a stunned Claire's arms.

"I watched him leave, and it's barely five-thirty," Minnie pointed out with a nod. "He wore the same clothing from last night."

Claire's sharp intake of breath crackled across the phone lines. "He did?"

"Yup. I noticed his clothing when he accompanied Lily home last night. He carried her into the house."

Another sharp gasp sounded. Minnie smiled. *That news certainly got Claire's attention.*

"How come you didn't call me last night?" Claire demanded.

"I couldn't. You were at Francine's." Minnie shrugged. "Besides, I didn't know he planned to spend the night."

"I didn't know, either," Claire grumbled, hanging up the phone.

Claire lied about not knowing. The minute Minnie read *The Aberdeen Times* the next morning, she realized Claire withheld vital information. In disgust, she hurled the paper on the table. *She* shared her news with Claire all the time. Miffed, Minnie dialed the phone.

"Hello?"

Claire's voice sounded on the other end. Minnie tightened her grip on the receiver. "Thanks for *sharing* your news with me." She slammed down the phone before Claire could reply.

Between *The Aberdeen Times* and *The Aberdeen Almanac*, word spread quickly. By the time most citizens finished their breakfasts, the gossip was in full swing.

****

Abe gritted his teeth. Nearly six in the morning and Ben still hadn't arrived. He didn't care if Ben showed for work or not. However, since Heather left for vacation, he always arrived first with breakfast for Abe.

Today, however, no steaming cup of coffee or a bag filled with donuts sat amongst the clutter of pens, pencils, and stacks of word puzzles on Abe's desk. He shouldn't expect to have coffee and donuts waiting on his desk every morning. Once Heather returned, he'd be lucky if someone even *made* coffee. Still, he'd come to enjoy the little perks, and that meant coffee and donuts.

Nate, the night duty officer, sat alone in the silent station.

Clearly, Ben hadn't given Abe's needs a lick of consideration. "Where's Ben?" Abe demanded, dropping his lunch pail on his desk.

Nate shrugged, yawning. "Hasn't arrived yet."

"It's past five thirty. He's late." Abe never realized Ben was so selfish.

"You're the one who's expected to be here by five."

Abe shook his head. "I'm only working these hours while Heather is out. Six is the time I start, which

228

means, I'm a half hour early." He dropped into his chair and stared at his empty desk. A forlorn sigh escaped him.

An image of the white bag with a grease stain on the bottom, and the top neatly folded, flashed through Abe's thoughts. Inside, would be warm donuts, fresh from the fryer, covered in white powder with gooey grape goodness nestled in the fluffy dough. His mouth watered, and his stomach rumbled.

Scanning his desk once more, Abe turned to Nate. "If you ask me, he hasn't paid us a lick of attention since he decided to become mayor. He's focusing all his energy on the election and slacking on the one he's paid to do. The union will be mighty interested in my complaint." He tapped the eraser of his pencil on the desk.

"Not certain how you can say such a thing." Nate leaned back in his chair. "Ben's been working eighteen hours a day since Heather left."

"Don't you see? If he had done his job and hired someone to replace Heather while she's on vacation, I wouldn't be stuck with all her work."

"She's not on vacation." Nate pointed a finger. "She's on maternity leave."

Abe gave a dismissive wave. "Maternity leave. Vacation. If you ask me, they're both the same. The fact is, while she's home relaxing, I'm doing her work." With two fingers, he squeezed the bridge of his nose, closed his eyes, and dropped his head against the back of the seat. "These early shifts are killing me."

He debated whether he should call Ben to remind him of the donuts and coffee, or not. In a man's life, a time came when he had certain expectations. Ben couldn't rip them away, thinking people wouldn't notice.

Nate let out another loud yawn. Grabbing his lunch cooler, he stood. "Bryan caught Rufus running down the street. Make certain you tell Ben."

Abe groaned. Why couldn't the blasted man just keep on his clothing? Now, because of Rufus' penchant for nudity, Abe received the pleasure of doing the paperwork, and F.Y.I., little pleasure was involved in the process. The quantity of paperwork alone would take up most of his day. Not to mention, he'd need to call witnesses, contact Bryan for an official statement, and notify Judge Harrington. His already lousy day just worsened. He tossed his pencil on the desk. "You see what I mean? He should be ticketing Rufus. If he had, I wouldn't be stuck sitting at my desk doing all the paperwork."

Shaking his head, Nate opened the door. "Well, at least the phone's been quiet tonight."

Nate jinxed the situation. As soon as he left, the phone started ringing and didn't stop. The constant noise was enough to drive a sane man insane, and plenty of people would argue Abe wasn't even close to sane. He certainly didn't feel sane right now with the endless ringing and no coffee to ease his stress.

He eyed the blaring phone. One caller would disconnect, and another would call. Abe could have answered them. He didn't, though, for two reasons. First, in the event of an actual emergency, the caller needed to dial nine-one-one, not the administrative office. Plus, with his luck, Rufus would call, wanting him to take some notes. Seeing he wasn't much interested in writing the report, he wasn't too concerned about Rufus' comments

Perhaps the most important, though, in his opinion, was the fact answering the phone wasn't in his job description. That job fell on Heather's shoulders. Seeing Heather wasn't here, Abe figured the responsibility transferred to Ben.

Not to mention, answering the phones set a dangerous precedent. If he answered just one call, Ben would send more work his way. Plus, just considering answering the phone was a violation of his union rights, and Abe was committed to following the union contract to the letter. Ben was the one who was in the wrong.

Abe drummed his fingers on the desktop. Wasn't this behavior just like the powerful? They always just take, take, take from the little guy. The more he considered his grievance, the more irritated he became.

He liked Ben and never minded working for him. However, Abe refused to allow the Aberdeen Police to think they could roll over him. Even though he might be getting up in years, he wouldn't be bullied.

In a few short weeks, he planned on attending the next union meeting. The executive board would be fascinated to hear about the happenings here. Opening his desk drawer, Abe found his notepad of grievances. Grabbing a pencil from the cup on his desk, he wrote the date along the top. Next, he wrote *no coffee prepared.*

He considered the complaint. Prepared seemed rather strong, considering the only preparation Ben did was to buy the coffee. Still, a steaming cup of coffee should be sitting in the vacant spot on his desk. Abe scratched out prepared and wrote *available* instead.

He scrawled *abuse of staff,* and beside these words

he wrote, *no donuts*. As a member of the police force, donuts were a necessity. Some might say a God-given right. The fact no donut was in sight proved Ben had violated Abe's rights. For his last grievance, he wrote in big bold letters *DISTURBING THE PEACE*. He added *phone ringing* to prove his point.

He started to add lack of break time, considering he hadn't gotten a minute to work on his word puzzle, before dismissing the thought. He didn't want to press his luck with the union. During the last meeting, they warned him to discuss only viable offenses. He doubted they'd accept word puzzle as a viable complaint.

By five forty-five, he gave up expecting the ringing to stop. By six, he considered shooting the phone just for some peace and quiet. For a moment, he pointed his gun at the phone. He didn't pull the trigger, though, because last month, Ben warned weapons were to be used as a last resort. Even then, Abe needed to think twice before using one. He figured blasting the phone with bullets wasn't on the allowed to shoot list. He swung his gaze between the gun and the phone. Sighing, he set the gun on the counter.

By six thirty, Abe had enough. How could a man think straight with all the non-stop ringing? Even though he wasn't allowed to shoot the phone, he sure as hell could quiet the blasted thing. Without a second thought, Abe slammed his palm against a button, forwarding the phones to dispatch. Except for his stomach rumbling, thanks to Ben, blessed peace filled the office.

Sighing, Abe grabbed his word puzzle. Licking the tip of his pencil, he leaned back in his chair, propped his feet on the top of his desk, and began his first puzzle of the day.

A few minutes after six-thirty, Ben finally strolled into the office.

A full hour and a half past his expected arrival. Abe noticed Ben's empty hands. He slapped his book on the desk. "What? No coffee, and where are my donuts?"

"Sorry," he replied. "I figured you'd have bought some by now."

"How the heck did you expect me to go for coffee and donuts when you're not here, and people are constantly calling?"

Ben glanced at the silent phone. "The phone's not ringing."

"Trust me, I nearly lost my sanity over the racket and shot the damn thing. I didn't, though, because I remembered our conversation from a few weeks ago." Abe regarded Ben crossing the room. "Because you weren't here, I forwarded the phone."

Snorting, Ben stopped next to his office. "Did you ever consider answering the phone yourself?"

"Nope," Abe snapped. "Heather was hired to answer phones."

Ben glared. "Heather's not here, which means the task falls to you."

"Not unless you want to explain the new duty to the union." Abe pointed a pencil in his direction. "I've added three complaints to my list. If you want, I could add disrespect and unhealthy work conditions."

Crossing his arms over his chest, Ben arched a brow. "Is that right?"

"Yes, it is." Abe nodded. "I have a desk filled with paperwork and not a single cup of coffee or donut in sight. If you ask me, these working conditions are unhealthy. Trust me, the union won't be happy to hear you're creating a hostile work environment."

"Hostile?" He flicked a glance at the word puzzle on Abe's desk.

Abe snatched the book off the desk, clutching the ragged pad to his chest. "You heard me. No one gives me any consideration. Frankly, this office is becoming a health hazard."

He shot a glance in Abe's direction. "I'd hate to lose you over unhealthy conditions. If coffee helps you complete some work, then feel free to go, and take the damn phones off forward."

Standing, Abe walked toward the door. "We wouldn't have this problem if you'd just hire someone to replace Heather. I can't be expected to do *all* the work."

Ben snorted. "I'd be happy if you did *some* work."

****

For the umpteenth time, Ben wondered why he accepted Abe's behavior. He made police officers look bad. And yet, a part of Ben respected Abe's age and time on the job. Years ago, Abe had been the star of the force, a real go-getter. But age and disappointment at not being promoted to police chief soured him, making him the cantankerous man he was today. Ben figured, dealing with Abe was a perfect test for becoming a mayor. No one was perfect, and everyone had opinions…including Abe.

Dismissing Abe's outburst, Ben walked into his office. He had enough to do without spending any additional time on Abe's issues. Each day, his list of jobs grew by a dozen or more. Arriving late to work didn't help. Not that he could help that fact. After spending the night at Lily's, he needed to go home to shower and change clothing.

Abe was right, though. He did need help in the office.

He sat at his desk, tapping his pencil against the paper blotter. Finding someone to work in the office would be easy. In fact, he could name several willing candidates, and all were women. He rubbed his forehead. Dealing with them outside the office was bad enough. Forced interaction here would be too much.

An image of Lily popped into his thoughts. He remembered his mother's suggestion. When she'd made the comment, he dismissed the idea. Now, though...Ben smiled, satisfied he'd found the perfect solution, he turned on his computer and began his day.

He was in the midst of compiling a monthly report when his door opened, and Abe stepped inside. The ubiquitous white powder of a sugar donut clung to his lips. A splotch of grape jelly marred his wrinkled police uniform.

"I thought you might enjoy some coffee." Abe set a cup of coffee on Ben's desk. "I brought you the paper, too."

Ben frowned. Paperwork cluttered the area, a stack of messages requiring his attention sat beside his phone, and Abe thought he had time for a break? "Why don't you read the paper? Unless you'd rather complete the budget report." He fanned a hand across the desk.

"Hey, no reason for you to be huffy." Abe snatched back the newspaper. "Besides, I can't. I don't want to be in violation of the union's contract. You'd make me a scab."

Ben gritted his teeth. *Why I deal with Abe's insubordination is beyond me.* He glanced at his computer. Columns and numbers filled the screen—all critical for monthly documentation. Abe wasn't a lot of help, but he was a warm body, which meant, he helped in his own way, leaving Ben to handle the important stuff—like legal issues and state regulations. "You're only a scab if you come to work when the union is on strike. The last I heard, you weren't on strike." He blew on his coffee.

"Not yet." Abe wagged a finger. "If they hear the stress you have me under, they might."

The muscle flexed once in Ben's cheek. "If you don't want more stress, you'll leave me alone, so I can finish the report for City Council."

"Jeez. Relax. No need to take out your problems on me." Abe marched across the room and flung open the door. "I have plenty to do."

"Abe," he called out. "I don't want to be disturbed for any reason. None."

Turning, Abe cocked his brow. "What about a terrorist attack in town?"

Ben ignored the ridiculous comment. The odds of a terrorist attack occurring here rated the same as one of Abe's alien spacecraft landing in the city square, which was zero. "Not under any circumstances."

"The union's not gonna be happy." Abe stormed out, slamming shut the door.

Ben stared at the closed door. An image of Lily skidded into his thoughts. He doubted she'd be happy learning he spent the night. Imagining her reaction when he broke the news, he smiled.

Chapter 23

The ringing of the phone woke Lily. Groaning, she grabbed her cell off the night stand. "Hello."

"Meet me for breakfast."

Scrubbing a hand across her eyes, she winced at the throbbing pain shooting down her arm. She rubbed her bruised shoulder. "Where are you?"

"Karla's."

Karla's sounded like more effort than she cared to make. "I'm not in the mood, Peri." She kicked off the covers. The soft cotton sheet slid across her skin. Frowning, she glanced down. *What the hell?* Why was she wearing only her bra and panties?

"You need to," Peri insisted. "I have something you'll be interested in seeing."

Lily couldn't imagine what information was so crucial for her to make the trek into town. However, knowing Peri, she'd keep pestering Lily until she caved. "Fine." She sighed. "Give me a half-hour. Whatever you tell me better be important."

"Trust me, you'll want to hear my news," Peri assured her.

Lily hung up the phone. Starting toward the bathroom, she caught a glimpse of the pillow next to hers. A distinct dent hollowed out the center. Remembering the events of yesterday, she frowned. Vague, hazy images and words crept through her thoughts. Ben talking to Dr. Charlie, the instructions for her care, Ben telling the doctor…

Lily gasped. Oh, dear lord, she remembered hearing him say to the doctor he would spend the night. Dropping on the edge of the bed, she stared at the dent in the center of the pillow. With shaking hands, she grabbed the pillow and held it against her nose. The spicy scent of his cologne rose upward.

Oh God…

Tossing down the pillow, Lily bolted from the bed. As she dressed, she replayed all the possibilities. Had he spent the night? But if so, why had he left without waking her? And if not, did he just stay with her to make sure she was okay, or had his plan been more nefarious?

With shaking hands, she slipped on her sneakers, wincing at the throbbing pain in her shoulder.

They didn't have sex. She was almost positive. After all, wouldn't she feel different today? Tired, but sated? Not edgy and tense. Then again, how much of last night did she actually remember? After the hospital—nothing.

How the heck could she find out the answer? She couldn't actually walk up to Ben and say, "Hey, just curious, how far did we go last night?" She could just imagine what *his* thoughts would be to that question. Besides, she might not know Ben well, but what she did know showed a man with high integrity. Still, a niggling of doubt swirled inside her.

Taking a deep breath to calm her nerves, Lily finished tying the laces of her shoes. Only one thing she could do. She'd just have to act like nothing happened, and pray that hope was the truth.

Despite her best intentions, she couldn't stop her thoughts from returning to this morning, when she discovered herself nearly naked and smelled Ben's cologne on her pillow. The signs were obvious.

Peri! Hope flared inside Lily. Maybe Peri had been home, and she'd know the answer. She practically ran to the diner. The minute she burst into the restaurant, she spotted her sister.

Sitting in a booth toward the back of the café, Peri read the paper while sipping her coffee.

Lily hurried down the aisle, heedless to the glances she received from the passing patrons. Sliding into the seat across from Peri, she leaned forward. "Did Ben spend the night last night?"

Peri coughed on her sip of coffee. "What?"

Giving the people at the table next to them a quick smile, Lily turned back to Peri and lowered her voice. "I think Ben and I had sex last night."

Peri burst out laughing.

Lily frowned. "What is so amusing?"

Resting her forearms on the table, Peri stifled her laughter. "Trust me, sweet sister, you did *not* have sex with Ben last night."

Slumping her shoulders, Lily ignored the tightness in her chest. Fidgeting with her menu, she studied Peri. "Really? You were home when we returned?"

Peri shook her head. "Nope. When Maybelline and I left Martinis it was late, so I spent the night at her place."

Again? Another night partying with Maybelline? Her sister took the art of vacation to a whole new level. Furrowing her brows, Lily tilted her head to the side and studied her sister. "How can you be sure then?"

Rolling her eyes, Peri flicked a hand in the air. "Seriously? You need to ask?"

Yeah, I seriously do. "Then you explain why I woke up nearly naked."

"Nearly naked is not naked." Peri shrugged. "Besides, you've seen Ben. He's freakin' hot. Basically, a pleasure guarantee. No way did you have sex with him and forget. It's just not possible."

"I don't know." Lily chewed her lip. "The pain med I was given at the hospital knocked me out."

Peri folded her hands on the table. "I don't think enough pain meds exist to forget sex with Ben."

An ache settled in Lily's chest that had nothing to do with her bruised shoulder. She ignored the sensation. After all, she was relieved. *Aren't I?*

"Hey, don't be upset." Peri smoothed a hand over a folded newspaper. "Looks like you'll have plenty of opportunities soon."

Lily's heart thumped hard. "What do you mean?"

Peri thrust the paper across the table. "Apparently Prince Charming, or in this case, Mr. Mayor, is getting married." Her words hung in the air. She smiled. "To you and soon, too. According to the paper, November fifth is the big day."

Snatching the paper, Lily read the article. A burning heat quickly replaced her wordless disbelief. Peri hadn't lied. In bold print, on the front page of the newspaper, announced Ben's marriage…to *her?* Her stomach clenched, and her thoughts spun with a myriad of confusing emotions. Flopping back in the booth, she stared at the incriminating article. The damning words stared back. The heat of anger slowly simmered deep within. "We're not engaged." She yanked her gaze from the page. "We're not even dating, and he never once mentioned becoming the mayor."

The pain in her shoulder was forgotten, replaced by an intense throbbing in her head. Fisting her hands, Lily glanced again at the paper. *What possessed him to tell people we plan to marry?* She tapped her fingers on the table. *Did he spend the night only to confirm his lie to everyone?* She didn't know the answer to these questions, but she meant to find out. Grabbing the bogus article, Lily climbed from the booth.

"Hey! Where are you going?" Peri called out.

Lily glanced over her shoulder. "To demand some answers." During her short march to the police station, she was determined to discover the reason why he lied. Once she had her answers, she'd inform him, in no uncertain terms, of her rules.

She'd need her wits about her, though. She couldn't let his charm or charisma sway her. Keeping her distance was vital—any closer than three feet, she'd be in his arms, and he'd be melting her resistance with his kisses. Lily stomped up the station steps, ripped open the door, and stormed inside.

Abe snapped up his attention. "Hey, you can't just barge into Ben's office." Bolting from his chair, he grabbed a gun off the counter and waved the weapon in the air. "He doesn't want to be disturbed."

Lily stilled. The chill of cold fear raced down her spine. She fixed her gaze on the gun in Abe's hand and swallowed. Seeing his arm falter then lower, she sighed softly. "I'm sure he won't mind a visit from his fiancée." Any other time, Abe's shocked expression might have amused Lily. Right now, though, nothing was funny.

Abe dropped into his chair. He opened his mouth. No words escaped. Clamping his mouth shut, he just stared.

Yanking open the door, Lily was ready for a confrontation. Instead, she fell into Ben's arms at almost the same moment her heart tumbled into her stomach. *Why is the man so attractive? Or smell so sexy, for that matter?*

Her anger over the newspaper faded, replaced with a far greater worry. Namely, the fact a desk, or even three feet, didn't separate them. Heck, not even a scrap of air separated their bodies. "You're not at your desk."

Creases marred his forehead. "I was before you arrived."

Pressing her hands against his chest in a vain attempt to separate them, she frowned. "I don't care about before. I care about now. We need a three-foot buffer between us."

He chuckled, circling her waist with his arms. "Absolutely not."

Why does he always argue with my ideas? Can't he see I want to avoid creating problems? "Why not?"

"Because what I have in mind requires a hell of a lot less distance than three feet."

Her stomach did a weird kind of flip-flop. "Which is exactly the reason why we need three feet separating us. We're not supposed to think about sex." A soft, sexy smile flitted across his lips, and all Lily could think about was the very thing she longed to avoid. She let out a soft sigh. She really needed to get her priorities straight, and right now, those priorities had nothing to do with her body's wants.

"Sweetheart, sex is all I've thought since the day

we met," he told her before pressing a kiss on the side of her neck.

Her pulse raced, and she swore to the good Lord her legs went weak at his words. *Okay. So much for forgetting my wants.* Lily tilted her head to the side to give him better access. She'd just have to make him see reason. She licked her lips and vowed to stay firm. "Well, you need to stop—which is why I propose we have rules."

His lips stopped working their magic.

Lily fought against letting her disappointment show.

Lifting his head, he smiled. "Rules?"

Lily rested her hands against his chest. His heart pounded beneath her fingertips, and she was aware of every inch of his body pressed against hers. Delicious images—of things she wanted, events she wasn't sure of and couldn't remember—floated through her thoughts. She pushed them aside, trying her best to focus on what was the best for both. "Yes. We need to agree not to think about sex, and we absolutely need to forget about last night."

Ben widened his eyes for just a moment before knitting together his brows. "First off, I wouldn't agree to such a ridiculous idea. Secondly, why the hell do we need to forget last night?"

"Sex, Ben. Remember?" Lily curled her fingers into his shirt. "Have you not heard a word I said?"

Laughter burst from him. "Sweetheart, we didn't have sex last night."

A sense of letdown filled Lily. She dismissed the emotion. "Are you sure?"

He narrowed his eyes, and the muscle in his cheek

flexed. "Now you've insulted me."

"Oh…I just thought…I mean, the way I was dressed when I woke…and the pillow…" Heat burned her cheeks, and she couldn't meet his gaze. "I just thought you slept with me."

Ben tilted her head upward. "I did sleep with you."

Okay, now she was confused. *Or maybe* he *is the one confused.* Lily knitted her brows. "In case you didn't know, 'sleeping together' means sex."

Pinching together his lips, Ben scowled. "Not in this case."

Uncertain whether to believe him or not, Lily narrowed her eyes. "Are you telling me, you slept in my bed, and we didn't have sex?"

Ben sighed. "Lily, you were in no condition for anything last night. Your shoulder was a mess, and you were on meds. However, I assure you when we have sex, neither of us will forget the occasion." He rubbed her back. "Are you here because you were worried I took advantage of you?"

His words reminded her of the reason for her visit. She broke free from his grip. Glaring, she hiked her purse onto her good shoulder. "Actually, I'm here to tell you I don't accept your marriage proposal."

Snapping back his head, Ben blinked.

If she didn't know better, she'd guess he was as shocked as she. Only, she knew his reaction was an act. After all, she'd just read the article. No doubt, he hoped she hadn't read the paper. *Jeez, doesn't the man know, even if I didn't, the gossip would reach me sooner rather than later?*

"My what?" Ben yelled.

"Your proposal." Lily walked toward the door then

stopped and faced him "And just so you know, I'm a September bride. Not a November one." She had the satisfaction of slamming the door on his reply. She smiled at the memory of his stunned expression. Now, maybe he understood how having decisions made without his consent felt.

Chapter 24

Lily burst from the station and hurried down the stairs. The warm sunshine added to the heat of embarrassment coursing through her body. She didn't want Ben chasing her. A person could handle only so much humiliation.

Peri stopped her pacing. "What did he say?"

Rushing down the sidewalk, Lily breezed past Peri. She had no destination in mind other than being as far away from the station as possible. "For one thing you're right, we didn't sleep together."

"I told you he's not a man you'd forget sleeping with." Peri followed. "What did he say about the announcement?"

"Nothing." Lily didn't slow her stride. Her stomach twisted, and thoughts, mainly about how incredibly stupid she was rushed through her. "I told him I wasn't a November kind of bride."

Grabbing Lily, Peri frowned. "Why the heck did you say that?"

Embarrassment licked at Lily's stomach. *What the hell possessed me to say such a thing? To Ben, nonetheless.* She closed her eyes and blew out a breath. Raking fingers through her hair, she shrugged. "I don't know."

The unreality of the whole situation amazed her. She glanced at her cell phone. Was the time really only ten in the morning? She marched a few more strides before stopping at the corner of Pecan and Coventry. Across the street was the park. People filled the area, a testament to the beauty of the morning. She spied City Hall, and suddenly the pieces of the puzzle snapped into place. Yanking her attention from the building, she glanced back toward the station. "I don't believe him. He's using me for his election."

Peri scowled. "What?"

Lily ignored the contempt in Peri's voice. Peri might think her idea was crazy, but Lily knew only too well how a man would do whatever he needed to achieve his goals—*especially* a goal-driven man with political ambitions. She slammed a palm against the crosswalk signal. The heat of anger and embarrassment burned low in her belly. "If he's engaged, he'll be a shoo-in to win. Politicians do that kind of stuff all the time. They want to appear reliable. I'm certain the one thing he needs is the appearance of stability. The town doesn't want their mayor chasing after women. They want one who's married."

Peri slid her gaze around the area. "Is something in the air? Are you lightheaded? Altitude sickness, perhaps?"

Lily frowned. "I have no idea what you mean."

"That makes two of us." Scowling, Peri crossed her arms. "Do you realize how ridiculous your theory is?

If she was the one involved, Peri wouldn't think the situation was silly. In fact, Lily would almost bet she'd be downright livid. She tapped a foot on the concrete, replaying the whole incident. "It's not ridiculous."

The light changed to green.

She crossed the street, heading nowhere in particular when she spotted Candi's Candies. The quaint brick building with the pink-and-brown striped awnings and potted pink geraniums lining the front welcomed her. Pastel chalk drawings of decorative chocolates covered the large glass windows, luring passing pedestrians inside.

The door opened, and a woman laden with a brown and pink bag strolled out.

The rich smell of chocolate filled the air. The charming shop smelled delicious. Usually, Lily didn't indulge in unhealthy foods. However, right now, she needed some good old comfort food, and nothing comforted her more than chocolate. She opened the door of the shop. "Do you want to go to Candi's Candies with me?"

Peri clapped her hands. "You had me at candy."

Inside, the store smelled even better. The pink and brown theme continued. Brown bags and boxes with pink polka dots covered every available surface. A multitude of chocolates, every kind imaginable, sat nestled inside a bakery case, begging to be eaten. Candi, the creator of Candi's Candies, offered samples of nearly a dozen of the tasty, petite bites of heaven.

By the time they left, Lily had consumed more chocolate in a few minutes than she had in the past year. Plus, she now owned a decadent box of the house specialty. She sighed. Sweets wouldn't solve her problems. Frowning, she held up the package. "I shouldn't have bought these chocolates."

"Why not? They're delicious." Peri reached for the box and grabbed out a candy. Popping the chocolate into her mouth, she closed her eyes and chewed. When she was finished, she licked the tip of her finger and smiled. "Besides, chocolate is an aphrodisiac."

Rolling her eyes, Lily continued along the walkway. "Don't be ridiculous."

"I'm not." Peri scowled. "Candi showed me an article about how chocolate increases the desire for sex."

Lily laughed. "Oh, come on. Be serious."

Peri stopped and glared. "I *am* serious. I read the whole article, too. It was published in some prestigious scientific journal. Had all sorts of stats and data, and other things I had no clue about." She pointed toward Lily. "Even you can't argue with the experts."

Lily's heart thundered. *What the heck? Peri read a whole article? That thought doesn't bode well.* "Where was I?"

Peri jerked her attention to Lily. "You were over by those stupid books about cooking with chocolate."

A niggling of doubt filled Lily. She immediately dismissed it. Peri might be naïve, but she wasn't. "Yeah. Yeah. I've heard the stories. But you can't tell me you actually believe that nonsense, do you?"

"Well, I guess we'll find out." Peri smiled and winked.

Lily slowed her steps. Her stomach twisted. The gloating sound in Peri's voice couldn't be good. "What do you mean?"

"Look." Peri stopped and shrugged. "You've got a guy who's an erotic turn-on practically begging to have sex, and you just ate a box of chocolates purportedly an aphrodisiac." She rolled a shoulder and lifted her brows. "*You* do the math."

Her heart thumped. *Peri is right.* Lily closed her

eyes and groaned. Even if the article was only partly true, she was in deep trouble. If Ben discovered her candy-eating binge, he'd redouble his efforts. In her already weakened state, she couldn't resist a sustained attack. She'd need a strategy to survive his seduction. "Fine. Then I'll just take a vow of abstinence."

Peri's face twisted.

If the situation wasn't so dire, Lily might have laughed. However, at the moment, the same kind of fear filled her, only for a vastly different reason.

"What? Are you crazy?" Peri flung her arms outward. "You shouldn't be taking stupid vows of abstinence. Your intention should be to get him into your bed."

"Yeah, I don't think so." Lily continued down the walk. She expected to hear some kind of argument from Peri, but only silence surrounded her. She turned.

Stopping in front of a building, Peri stared upward at a sign.

Lily walked back. "What are you doing?"

Peri smiled and pointed. "In here. We've got to check out this place."

Blazoned above the door were the words CLASSY CHASSIS. IT'S ALL ABOUT WHAT'S UNDER THE HOOD. Apparently, the shop specialized in bras, panties, and lingerie, if the scantily dressed mannequins in the window were any indication. She shot Peri a glare. "Have you already forgotten my vow?"

Grabbing hold of the door handle with one hand and Lily's wrist with the other, Peri yanked her inside. "I wish you would. You're crazy to say you don't want sex, and crazier still if you didn't want sex with him. And you'd be downright certifiable if you followed through with your ridiculous plan."

Glancing around the store, Lily sighed. Tasteful colors of gold and black decorated the store. White dressers reminiscent of the French provincial style dotted the room. Folded neatly and tucked inside the open drawers lay bras, panties, and lingerie of every imaginable color and style. Bottles of perfumes, lotions, and creams covered the white linen surfaces. The air smelled of pink peonies and white lilacs.

If Peri was thrilled by Candi's Candies, she was absolutely giddy seeing all the sexy merchandise inside the boutique. Her eyes, as round as plates, had a glazed appearance.

A shiver of dread rolled down Lily's spine. Her sister resembled a rabid dog, both drooling and shaking simultaneously. The words 'calm down,' lay on the tip of Lily's tongue. She caught herself before she blurted out the words.

"I'm not gonna lie. I'm incredibly excited right now." Peri rubbed her hands together, scanning the decadent lingerie. "What are you getting?"

"Me?" Lily pointed to herself. Her voice rose an octave higher. "Nothing. I have all the bras and panties I need."

Laughing, Peri swept her gaze over Lily. "I've seen your bras and panties. Trust me, they belong on a twelve-year-old virgin."

Images of boring white bras and panties filled her thoughts. Lily couldn't argue with the assessment. Her undergarments were old, ugly, and exuded as much sexiness as her stained, ratty robe. "Fine. I'll look. I'm not buying anything, though."

After thirty minutes wandering in the store, she

ended up purchasing three new bras and matching panties, and she lost her sister in the process. *Go figure.* She strolled to the counter where an elegantly dressed woman busily wrote on a piece of paper. Lily cleared her throat.

The sales clerk looked up.

"My sister? Do you know where she is?"

Nodding, the clerk pointed to the dressing room.

Not wishing to spend any more money, Lily decided to wait outside. Passing pedestrians threw her a few curious glances. Quickly folding the edge of the bag, she clutched the package against her chest and crossed her arms over the name embellished across the front. She paced out front, waiting for Peri.

A few minutes later, Peri exited the shop with her arms loaded with three bags stuffed to overflowing. Grinning, she held up one of the bags. "I bought you something." With extreme precision, Peri drew from the bag the white teddy. Holding the edge of the thin satin strap, she displayed the lingerie for inspection. "Well? What do you think?"

Mortified, Lily snatched the lingerie from a surprised Peri's hand and stuffed it into her shopping bag, before hurrying away.

"Hey, be careful." Peri reached Lily's side. "You're gonna rip the lace. That's Ben's job."

Glaring, Lily stopped in front of Papa's Pizza. "I told you I took a vow of abstinence."

"Ugh." Peri scowled. "Don't remind me." Glancing at her watch, she sighed. "I have a bit of time before I meet Maybelline. Let's eat."

Lily blinked. "We just ate breakfast."

"Coffee is not breakfast." Peri grabbed the

restaurant door handle. "Besides, Papa's caters to the firemen. Dax could be here."

Peri is interested in Dax? Lily didn't know how she felt about this fact, especially since Ben and Dax were such good friends. "You do realize he lives right behind our house, right?"

"I know, but the possibility he *might* be here makes seeing him more exciting." She leaned in. "Plus, if he is, he won't think I'm following him." Peri looked over her shoulder. "From my experience, men seem to have a problem with the whole stalking thing."

Lily grabbed Peri's elbow. "What about the police?"

Stepping inside the darkened interior, Peri broke free from Lily's grip. "What about them?"

"Do they come here?" The scent of fresh garlic and yeasty dough filled the air. Lily scanned the area. She didn't see Ben. However, just because he wasn't here didn't mean he wouldn't show up.

Peri shrugged. "I'm not sure. Why?" A slow smile crossed her face. "Oh, wait. I understand. You're hoping to see Ben." She winked. "Excellent call. Make sure he sees the Classy Chassis bag. His interest will be piqued."

Lily's stomach leaped. "I don't want to *pique* his interest," she hissed.

"Don't remind me." Peri rolled her eyes and shook her head. "The whole 'abstinence' thing." She shuddered. "Yuck."

Peri didn't understand. Lily didn't *want* abstinence. She *needed* it for her own protection. However, explaining this fact to Peri would take more effort than she wanted to expend. Instead she waved to a table in the middle of the room. Taking a chair, she sat and browsed the menu. She set aside the menu and looked up. "I think I'll just get a salad and a diet soda."

Peri wrinkled her nose. "You and healthy eating."

A server came over.

Peri smiled. "We'll get a large pizza. I'll have a soda." She glanced at Lily and gagged. "She'll have a diet."

The petite server, a young girl, no more than twenty, if Lily guessed, scribbled on her notepad and hurried away.

Frowning, Lily leaned forward. "I said I wanted a salad."

"Hey, I got you a diet soda." Peri unrolled her napkin. "Besides, we're on vacation. We're supposed to have fun, which means eating all the bad stuff we normally don't allow ourselves."

Within minutes, a group of aged men surrounded their table.

Lily glanced at Peri, wondering what the heck these men wanted.

Peri shrugged.

Smiling, she turned to the men. "Can I help you?"

All of a sudden, the men started their questions.

They wanted to know her plans. When she explained she didn't have any 'plans' for Ben, they refused to believe her. So, she told them she would return to Buffalo. They accused her of stealing him. When she admitted they really weren't engaged, they gasped.

The server brought their drinks and pizza.

Lily looked at the grease pooling on the top of the cheese and pepperoni. Her stomach lurched, but whether from the smell of the spicy meat or the fact she couldn't win in this discussion, she wasn't certain.

More questions came—about sports, of all things. She tightened her grip on the drink, hoping to calm her shaking hands. Why they thought she *knew anything* on the subject eluded her. An older man asked her if she liked red socks. She had no clue why he'd asked such a question.

Peri grabbed a large slice of the pie. Grease slid off the top and dropped onto the plate.

Lily's stomach heaved. Pushing aside her plate, she grabbed her drink and glanced toward Peri to see her reaction.

Shrugging, Peri nibbled on her pizza.

Turning toward the gentleman, Lily smiled. "Sure." She scraped a nail over the condensation clinging to her glass of soda. "I mean, who doesn't like red socks?" She picked up the glass.

The man stiffened and glanced at the group of men. Loud grunts of displeasure erupted, and scowls creased their faces. A few crossed their arms over the chest. Others fisted their hands against their sides. The elderly gentleman leaned downward and growled.

She stilled and carefully set down her glass without taking a sip. A lump formed in her throat, and a heavy pit settled in her stomach. A quick glance toward Peri showed her pushing her chair back, as if she wanted to bolt. Lily didn't blame her sister. Her stomach lurched, and her muscles tightened. She, too, feared they'd hang her.

After digging into her wallet, Lily tossed some bills on the table. Ignoring the remaining pizza, she yanked Peri out of the chair. Grabbing her bag, she towed her sister from the restaurant.

"What's the hurry?" Peri grumbled. "We still have pizza left."

Lily stepped outside. "What the heck just happened? I thought I was dead."

Peri burst into laughter. "Yeah, picking the Red Sox wasn't a career move."

Glancing over her shoulder, Lily peered inside the restaurant's window. A few of the patrons glanced her way, but none appeared interested in following her outside to continue their argument. Feeling the tension leave her shoulders, she sighed. "Well, jeez." She walked away. "I didn't know I was supposed to be a Yankees fan."

Peri fanned a hand. "Everyone knows about the whole Yankees/Red Sox rivalry."

Lily slowed her pace. "Really?"

"Sure. Remember my old boyfriend, Tommy? He used to watch sports all the time. Football. Baseball. Hockey. Ugh. I thought I ignored the whole conversation. What can I say? Some of the information must have stuck." Peri shrugged. "I'll tell you one thing I did learn. Don't stick with one man. Too many nights committed to sports." She smiled. "I'm all for hot, sweaty, athletic men. However, I'd rather see them in person than on the T.V., if you know what I mean."

Lily didn't need the details. Peri wasn't exactly a closed book. She relayed her preferences on a daily basis. Lily frowned. "I wish you'd clued me in. I could have used the information for the whole baseball championship question."

"Hey, I did try to help you. Don't you remember? I showed you my drink?"

Lily flung upward a hand. "How is holding a glass helping me?"

"I gave you a clue that the trophy is called the Stanley Cup." Peri waved a hand. "What did you think? I was saluting you?" She shook her head. "You know you'd be terrible in Charades."

Lily ignored Peri's insult. "Well, you're wrong about the championship for baseball anyway."

Peri glanced toward the park. "Hey, do you want to go with Maybelline and me to the beach?"

A day at the beach sounded terrific. A day at the beach with Peri and Maybelline sounded like trouble. "The last time I partied with you two, I got drunk, and Ben drove me home."

Turning back, Peri smiled. "You're welcome, by the way."

Lily blinked. *What the heck does she mean?* "Why should I thank you? If I recall, that night is how the gossip started."

"No. The gossip was the result of you confronting him at the Beer and Brat Festival."

Lily didn't bother to argue. She didn't accept the offer, either, and turned toward the direction of her home. A tall, leggy, blonde woman with sharp green eyes stepped from a small boutique next to the restaurant. She was beautiful and elegant. The kind of woman you didn't forget.

"You're Lily Evans, right?" The woman offered a hand. "Alexis Armstrong. My aunt, Minnie Wilson, lives next to you." She smiled. "I've been meaning to meet you, but I've been busy. So, you're the one who nabbed Ben?"

Her stomach tumbled. The last thing she needed

was for the woman to think she and Ben were an item. Lily shook her head. "We're not engaged, and I'm only in town until the end of summer."

Alexis snorted. "Yeah, most of the women are hoping you'll leave. At least, you're not Jenny or Karla." She shifted the purse handle on her shoulder. "We'll have lunch sometime. I can tell you all about them." She turned then stopped. "I have a feeling we'll have much in common soon."

Alexis gave her a conspiratorial wink before sauntering away. Lily frowned. *What the heck does she mean by that remark?*

Chapter 25

Lily spent the whole journey home consumed with her growing attraction to Ben. By the time she stepped inside her house, she'd eaten the entire box of chocolates. Worse, she realized she'd fallen in love with him.

She cursed her stupidity. He didn't love her. He certainly wasn't interested in marriage. He wanted her for a night—a weekend, maybe, or the summer, at the most. Not forever, though. He was all about conquest and sex, not marriage or commitment.

A tightness settled inside her chest somewhere close to her heart. Lily ignored the sensation. The feeling must be directly related to the number of chocolates she ate and not because he didn't love her. What she needed was a long run to clear her mind and digest the chocolates.

Entering the kitchen, she tossed the empty box and the lingerie bags on the counter. She changed into her workout clothes and left the house. She ran through the neighborhood, a good five miles. When her legs wobbled, and her breath burned her lungs, she returned home.

After her shower, Lily blew dry her hair, wincing at the stabbing pain in her shoulder. When she was finished, she slipped one of her old sports bras over her head. She remembered the pretty new bras sitting on the kitchen counter. Shrugging on her robe, she opened her bedroom door and skidded to a dead stop.

Opening the back door, Ben stepped into the kitchen. Glancing in her direction, he blinked and his steps faltered. His lips pressed together and his fingers clutched the door knob. He shut the door with a soft click. Locking his gaze with hers, he tossed his keys on the counter.

Her body took immediate notice. She tightened the sash, desperately hoping she gave the impression of being cold. Nothing could be further from the truth. A fire burned low in her belly, shooting straight to the tips of her toes, and all because of the heat burning in his eyes. "What are you doing here?"

"I was worried." He nodded toward the door. "You left the door unlocked." He swept his gaze over her again and a slow, soft, smile curled on his lips.

Lily's blood thrummed, knowing she was one step closer to falling into the abyss she'd been desperately avoiding.

****

Ben commended himself for keeping his emotions in check, but damn, he should have ended his day at work. If he had, the temptation Lily presented wouldn't be tormenting him, right now—especially considering her attire. The big, fluffy robe was as far from sexy as clothing could get, and yet, with the pink polished toes peeking from the oversized, white, cotton cocoon, the low vee in the neckline, and her freshly flushed skin, she was as sexy as hell.

The robe was only part of the problem. His imagination of what hid beneath the pile of fluff nearly drove him to his knees. He itched to run his fingers beneath the cottony depths to discover her treasures, instead he raked his fingers through his hair.

"I must have forgotten after my run."

Her words tore his thoughts from her outfit. "What did you say?"

"I ran."

His frown deepened.

Tilting her head, she wrinkled her brow. "Why are you upset? You know I run every day."

A muscle flexed in his cheek, and his throat ached. He wanted to yell. Instead, he glared. "For God's sake, you were injured yesterday. Have you forgotten this fact?"

"Of course not. And because of you, I'm injured."

"Because of me?" Frowning, he stepped from the counter. "What the hell did I do?"

She flung out a hand. "You told me to hide the key. You know, you really need to do something about your memory. If you plan on being mayor—" She dropped her gaze to the counter. Ripping her gaze upward, she narrowed her eyes. "You put *my* house key on *your* key ring?" She reached for the key.

He snatched the keys before she could snag them. If looks could kill, Ben figured he'd be dead right now. She didn't understand. She compelled him in ways no other woman had. An almost uncontrollable need to keep her safe consumed him, and if that meant he needed to retain her keys, then so be it.

Lily crossed her arms over her chest. "Is my car key on your ring, too?"

He shrugged. "I never had your car keys."

Dropping her hands to her hips, she glared. "You're holding them hostage, aren't you?"

"Sweetheart, I promise you, I don't have your car key." He smiled. "However, I'll tell you where they are on one condition—you become my secretary."

Lily lifted an arm, her palm outward. "Excuse me?"

He knew his suggestion wouldn't be appreciated, however, the way he figured, both would end up getting what they wanted. Shrugging, Ben deepened his smile. "It's simple. You agree to become my secretary, and I'll tell you where your keys are."

"Are you telling me you've known where they are all along?"

Watching Lily's expression change from disbelief to anger, he couldn't help the mixture of amusement and satisfaction that filled him. He decided to prick her temper just a bit more. "I did."

Lily gasped and pointed. "You're blackmailing me?"

He burst out laughing. "I wouldn't say blackmail."

Scowling, she fisted her hands to her hips. "Oh? Then what would you call your demand?"

He leaned against the counter and rested his palms against the surface. "Let's just say an equitable agreement."

They locked stares in a silent contest of wills. He wasn't worried. In the end, he knew he'd win. He wasn't wrong, either.

"Why should I believe you?"

He sighed. "Lily, when have I ever lied to you?"

Crossing her arms, she tapped a foot against the floor. Finally, she swung her arms upward. "Okay, fine, maybe not to me, but you *did* lie to the newspaper."

"When?" He grabbed hold of the lapels of her robe,

dragging her between his legs. He reveled in the feel of her body against his, knowing how much better she'd feel without the fabric separating them.

She scowled. "When you told them about our upcoming 'wedding.'"

Smoothing a strand of hair from her shoulder, he brushed a kiss against her neck. The smell of warm wildflowers wafted upward, filling him with a sense of calm. "I didn't."

She stiffened.

Sighing, Ben straightened. "I did an interview with Nathan for the paper. He asked about the date. I assumed he meant the election and—" Spotting the lacy garment on the counter, he gripped the counter while his knees nearly buckled. He picked up the silky fabric, imagining sliding the garment off Lily's soft flesh. His desire exploded, and he needed every ounce of willpower to control his body's reaction. His hand shook, and his mouth suddenly felt as if a desert invaded it. "Is this lingerie yours?"

Lily's cheeks turned a soft pink. "Yes. Peri bought the lingerie for us…" She snapped her gaze upward.

The pink in her cheeks flushed a deep red.

She cleared her throat. "I meant me."

He didn't think he'd ever heard anything sexier. The lingerie slid from his fingers to pool in a pile of satin and lace. The implication of the teddy was clear. The white gown was made for a honeymoon. A niggling of doubt warred with his desire. He needed to make clear his intentions, and yet—staring at her luminous blue-eye gaze, he couldn't summon the words. *Yup, I definitely should have stayed at work.*

She licked her lips.

Ben didn't need any further invitation. He gave up any thought of his duties, instead he captured her mouth with his. He wanted to go slow. Lily didn't let him, though. Her fingers wove through his hair, drawing down his head to deepen the kiss.

She moaned.

His willpower nearly broke. The woman drove him to distraction. He kissed her neck.

"Damn," she murmured.

Her curse caught him off guard. He drew back. Women didn't curse when he kissed them, including Lily. "Is something wrong?"

"We're not allowed to kiss. Remember the rules?" She grumbled.

She contradicted her own order, brushing her lips against his. A smile tickled his lips. He doubted she was aware of her action. "Those are your rules," he replied before capturing her lower lip between his teeth and gently tugging.

Her fingers curled into his shirt. "I'm serious, Ben. The kissing must stop if we want to eliminate our attraction to each other," she whispered, tilting her head to the side.

Seizing the opportunity, he brushed feather-light kisses against her neck. Her skin, warm and soft, caused sexy images to flash through his thoughts—images he'd envisioned for some time now. "I don't want to get over the attraction."

A soft, shaky moan hissed from her mouth. "I've taken a vow of abstinence."

He wanted to laugh. "Sweetheart, you weren't made for abstinence." He brushed his lips against hers. Ben couldn't wait any longer. "Lily...?" He held his breath, expecting resistance.

He vowed if Lily hesitated, he'd stop, even if the effort killed him. When she leaned on the tip of her toes to place a kiss on his lips, he seized the offer. Scooping her into his arms, he carried her toward the bedroom.

Don't. The words rolled through his thoughts, warning him. If he put her down right now, he could end this whole madness, and no one would be hurt. Only, no matter how much he tried, he couldn't make his body cooperate.

The only sound was the soft click of the door shutting.

Chapter 26

Lily woke up smiling. During the night, she had a revelation. Peri was right. Her vow of abstinence *was* ridiculous. She stretched her arms overhead, enjoying the sensation.

Curling onto her side, she expected to see Ben stretched out beside her. He wasn't. Her heart squeezed tight. Well, he certainly hadn't wasted a minute escaping her house.

She tapped her fingers against the soft, cotton sheets. She didn't know why she cared. After all, hadn't she expected him to leave her soon after they had sex? He'd gotten what he wanted and didn't need to stay any longer. She should be grateful he'd snuck out like a thief in the night. Now, she could enjoy the rest of her summer without him harassing her. Plus, he saved her a bunch of aggravation with his abrupt disappearance. The neighbors wouldn't spot his vehicle parked in her driveway, which would have given them something more to discuss.

Yes, she definitely should be thankful for his desertion. Only, she wasn't, which in her opinion, was a conundrum.

The smell of coffee wafted into the bedroom. Lily frowned. Peri wasn't known for purchasing coffee, let alone making the stuff. However, if her sister went to the effort, Lily wouldn't complain.

When the smell of bacon frying followed the aroma of coffee, she experienced an odd combination of dread and relief. Peri *might* make coffee, but in no way would she cook bacon. In fact, she doubted Peri knew *how* to make bacon.

Lily scrambled upright. Bright sunlight streamed through the filmy curtains. *It is morning, and Ben is still here.* She hyperventilated. Jumping from bed, she raced across the room and grabbed a pair of yoga pants and T-shirt. She dressed quickly before ripping open the bedroom door and dashing into the kitchen.

Ben, dressed in the same jeans from last night and no shirt, stood in front of the stove. Turning, he smiled and set the tongs he used to flip the bacon on the paper towel.

She glared. Okay, her actions didn't make any sense. Only three minutes ago, she was kind-of-halfway-sorta-thankful, in an extremely disgruntled way, that he'd left her house. Now, she was frustrated he stayed? What the hell was wrong with her?

Raking fingers through her hair, Lily glanced out the kitchen window. Sunlight streamed through the panes. Her chest tightened. Mrs. Waverly was in her backyard, hanging laundry on the lines, and Mr. Slater, another neighbor, hedged his shrubs. She raced across the room, grabbed Ben's hand, and dragged him toward the door. "You need to leave."

The smile evaporated from Ben's face. "Excuse me?"

She stopped and studied him. What was she thinking? He couldn't leave half naked. The neighbors would know the truth. Lily quickly switched directions, tugging him into the bedroom. "You need to dress and leave."

He yanked her toward him.

She landed with a thud against his bare chest. Agitation flared. "I'm serious, Ben." Apparently, he didn't care, if the way his lips nuzzled her neck was any indication. His warm breath floated against the sensitive skin of her neck. She tried to remember what had upset her. The only thing she could focus on was how wonderful, how perfect, and how incredibly decadent his lips felt against her skin.

The roar of a lawnmower ripped through the room.

Snapped back to reality, she whipped her attention to the open window. "Someone is mowing."

Ben lifted his head. "So?"

Laughter filled his voice. Lily stiffened. As the police chief, he should understand the implications of being discovered spending the night with her. More importantly, he should know without her having to say the words. "Don't you think, with your truck parked in my driveway, people will know you spent the night here?"

"No." Circling her waist, he settled his palms on her lower back, while resting his chin on top of her head. "Besides, I stopped at Dax's before coming here. I cut through the yards, figuring I'd retrieve my truck later."

All her tension disappeared. She sighed. "People won't know you spent the night."

Dropping his arms and stepping aside, he snickered. "Sweetheart, I'm a thirty-year-old man. I haven't slept over at Dax's since the sixth grade." Turning off the burner, he placed the pan of bacon on the metal trivet. With tongs, he plucked the four strips from the pan and set them on a paper towel, before starting for the bedroom. "You're right, though. I do need to leave. I'm already late for work."

The distinctive clack of hedge clippers through the bedroom window drew her attention. Her heart thudded. Rushing across the room, she shoved aside the curtains. She could just make out Claire's straw hat above the rose bush edging their properties.

Her pulse raced. *The situation just worsened.* Turning, she pointed. "The bedroom window is open. Did you know?"

Ben shrugged. "No. Why would I?"

"You're the police chief. Isn't it a prerequisite for you to be intuitive or something?" She grabbed his shirt from the ground. Stretching on tippy-toes, she stuffed the shirt over his head. "You'll need to leave from the front and go around the block. No one will know you spent the night, and I won't be subjected to any heat."

He snatched his shirt from her grip. "I'm not gonna tiptoe out of here, and you have no 'heat' on you."

Lily frowned. "Don't you understand? Claire's outside. She'll see you leaving my house, and she'd think…she'll know…" Warmth invaded her face.

"Mom won't care." Ben grinned, drawing the shirt over his shoulders.

For the love all that was holy, why did he mention his mother now? Didn't he realize she had enough to worry about with Claire outside and Ben inside her house? She watched him casually button his shirt like he had not a care in the world. "Your mother is not my concern. Claire is."

Pausing while rolling his sleeves, he glanced in her direction. "Right, my mother."

Her knees buckled causing Lily to drop onto the bed. "Are you saying my neighbor is *your* mother? How come you didn't tell me?"

Shrugging, he finished rolling up his sleeves. "I thought you knew." He grabbed his cell phone and wallet from the bedside table, tucking them in his pockets. "What's the big deal?"

She leaped to her feet. "You spent the night here. She'll think we had sex."

Ben smiled and softened his gaze. "Sweetheart, we did have sex."

She hated his calm, reasonable tone, especially when the situation called for panic and urgency. "Your mother doesn't need to *know* this information."

Chuckling, Ben drew her into the kitchen. "We're adults. We did nothing wrong."

He had her halfway to the kitchen door before she realized his intention. She dug her heels into the linoleum floor. The only reward for her effort was to slide, her feet squeaking ever closer to the door. "What do you think you're doing?"

"Going to see Mom."

Lily tried to wiggle free. "Well, have fun."

Stopping, he narrowed his gaze. "You're coming with me."

"I don't think so," she scoffed. "I'm sure your mother is used to you parading around your flings. However, I refuse to be embarrassed."

He glared. "I don't take every woman I sleep with to meet my mother."

****

He didn't bother to add he didn't need to because she knew most, and the few she didn't, he wouldn't have introduced anyway. Figuring the discussion was over, he opened the back door.

With her free hand, Lily grabbed the door frame.

Ben sighed. "You know my mother."

Lily scowled. "You don't understand. She'll judge me."

She worried for nothing. His mother wouldn't care, and even if she did, he wouldn't. He didn't need his mother's approval to live his life. Ignoring Lily's protest, he escorted her outside, closing the door with finality. He ushered her the short distance, pushing through a break in the rose bushes. His mother was just on the other side. Securely holding Lily's hand, he covered the short distance. "Good morning, Mom."

Straightening, Claire shifted her gaze from the rose branch, her gaze drifting between them. "Ben, what are you doing here?"

He settled an arm on Lily's shoulder and hauled her against his side. "I stopped by to see Lily."

Claire dropped the rose cutting into the bucket. "How nice." She glanced at her watch and frowned. "What about work? You told me you have too much to do to take off time."

He studied Lily. Her face was pinched tight as if she'd just eaten a lemon. He gave her shoulder a gentle squeeze, a silent message to not worry. "Actually, she has agreed to work at the station for a bit. She starts on Monday."

Smiling, Claire clapped. "That's wonderful news."

Lily's mouth dropped open for a bare second before snapping shut.

Her abrupt silence didn't fool him. He knew, without a doubt, she'd voice her opinion the minute they were alone. Keeping his arm firmly anchored on her shoulder, he turned to his mother. "We'll see you later."

Grabbing his hand, Lily yanked him away.

He reached out, catching a thorny branch and lifting it before it could scratch her face. She sped across the yards like the hounds of Hades were nipping at her heels, forcing him to keep pace.

At the top step, Lily turned and glared. "Does your mother know you resort to blackmail to exhort what you want?"

He burst into laughter. "My mother will understand." He pressed a quick kiss on her mouth, before stepping onto the porch.

She followed. "My keys. You promised."

Ben smiled, eager to see her reaction to his announcement. "They're in your glove box."

Her brows knitted for just a second before being replaced by a frown.

Enfolding her in his arms before she could argue, he brushed another quick kiss across her mouth. "I have a meeting later and won't return until tonight. Lock your door. I have a key."

Lily widened her eyes. "Tonight?"

He lifted his brows. "Did you have plans?"

She licked her lips. "I thought…" Heat rushed to her face. Spinning on her heels, she ripped open the door. "Oh, never mind."

Watching her disappear into the house, Ben smiled. He didn't know what amused him more—her look of stunned surprise when he told her where the car keys were hidden or the fact he would return.

One thing he knew for certain—if she wasn't

happy he didn't care what the neighbors thought about last night, she definitely wouldn't be thrilled with his intentions for the summer.

He could hardly wait to see her reaction when she found out.

Chapter 27

Claire pretended to snip her roses—her clippers slashing at the velvety petals with abandon. Bright red blossoms, scraps of green leaves, and chips of brown stems fell to the ground in careless disarray. For the first time in her life, she didn't care where she snipped. She was too busy watching the scene unfold. As soon as Lily's door slammed shut, she tossed her clippers to the ground, and breaking through the rose bushes, made a beeline straight across the yards.

She barely reached the edge of Lily's porch when again the door screeched. Stifling a scream, Claire dove to the ground. Like the most intrepid soldier, she crawled to the side of the porch. Crouching against the warm vinyl siding, she tucked her knees beneath her chin, praying to the Lord the arborvitae hid her from their view.

Honest to goodness she felt foolish hiding as if she were a thief. If someone spotted her, she'd be humiliated straight to her core. She'd rather chance humiliation, though, than having Ben catch her dashing over to Minnie's house.

Claire patiently waited, holding her breath while she scanned the area. She noticed movement in the Smiths' upstairs window. Frowning, she watched Rose Smith squish her face against the glass.

The audacity. She never knew her neighbor was a

peeping Tom. She should have figured, seeing as Rose made no secret of her love of gossip, which was the whole reason she wrote her blog. Now she wanted the scoop on Ben and Lily's relationship? *The nerve. Does Rose have no respect for people's privacy?*

Lily's screen door slammed, scaring the hell out of Claire. Scrunching lower, she ignored the pins and needles in her feet. Her past returned to haunt her. Guilt reduced her to the guise of a naughty child caught cowering in a corner, all because she had a son.

Ben acted like she'd asked him to divulge his most personal secrets, unlike a daughter who had the decency to share details with her mother. At least, her friends with daughters assured her of this fact. If she even mentioned the word relationship, *her daughter,* on the other hand, became radio silent.

"Bye, Mom."

Ben's voice drew Claire from her disgusted reverie. She turned to see him waving in her general direction as he strode across the lawn. For a breathless second, she worried he might have spotted her. She immediately dismissed the notion. He believed she was busy with her roses, not wedged between the house and an arborvitae listening to their conversation.

Still…

She didn't want him to spot her running across the yard either. Digging deep within herself, she counted to fifty, *twice* no less, before bolting from the shrub. On shaking legs, she darted across Lily's yard, like she ran the 100-meter dash.

Her foot just touched the edge of the driveway when she heard Lily's screen door open. Claire thrust out her arms and vaulted through the thick greenery, ignoring the scrape and sting of the branches against her skin. She landed with a thud on the other side of the shrub, out of breath and her heart pounding.

Gasping, Claire scrambled across the gravel, keeping her head low. She darted up Minnie's front porch steps. When she neared the top, she threw herself across the porch as swift and perfect as if sliding into second base. She nearly slammed her head against the door in the process. Wiping the sweat from her forehead, she tapped her knuckles against Minnie's door.

"Oh, dear." Minnie clutched a hand to her chest. "I thought you were dead."

"Shsh." Claire yanked the edge of Minnie's dress.

"Claire Jordan, what the hell are you doing?"

"Keep quiet." Claire waved Minnie lower. "I don't want Lily to see you."

Crawling to her knees, Minnie lay on the wooden deck and glared. "Do you mind telling me why we are hiding?"

"Do you see her?"

Frowning, Minnie arched upward and looked around the area. "Who?"

"Lily." Claire waved a thumb over her shoulder. "Do you see her outside?"

"I don't know if she is or not. I'm down here with you."

"Well, go look." Claire scowled.

"Oh, for crying out loud. First, you don't want anyone to see me. Now you do. Will you make up your mind, Claire?"

Claire waved a hand. "Would you just go and look."

Sighing, Minnie stood. "Does Ben know you've lost your mind?"

"Hurry." Claire fanned impatiently toward the bushes. "I don't have all day to lie around here."

Minnie spun, and glaring, pointed a finger toward the bushes. "Did you run through our shrubs? Hank won't be happy. You know how he is."

"Forget the shrubs," Claire hissed.

Minnie fisted her hands to her hips. "How can I forget? The hole is as wide as the St. Lawrence." She pinched her lips and glared. "When Hank asks, you'll be the one to explain how the gaping hole got in those bushes."

"I'll worry about Hank later. Right now, I want to know if she is leaving."

Sighing, Minnie peered through the gap. "She's searching her car." She turned to Claire.

The sound of a vehicle approached. Minnie thrust out her hand, her palm outward. "Wait, Maybelline just arrived."

Claire yanked on the hem of Minnie's skirt. "For goodness sake, why don't you put a bulls-eye on yourself?"

Glaring, Minnie dropped to her knees.

Lifting a hand, Claire peered at the bushes. "Not all the way. You need to tell me what's happening. For goodness sake, though, don't let Maybelline see you."

Minnie shot Claire another glare. "Talk about embarrassing. You better hope Hank doesn't come and investigate. He'll think we both belong in the loony bin."

Waving off her words, Claire pointed in the direction of the house. "What are they doing?"

"They're talking. What the hell do you think they're doing?"

Claire gritted her teeth. "What are they saying? I can't hear with you talking."

"You might if you'd shut up." Minnie sniffed and threw up her hands. Finally, emitting a drawn-out sigh, she crouched and glanced toward Lily's. "They're discussing Ben. I can't hear what they are saying…Oh goodness." She dove onto the floor of the porch. "Maybelline just glanced over."

"What?" Claire shrieked. Lowering her voice, she lifted her head and searched through the opening of the shrub. "Do you think she spotted you?"

Again, Minnie peered through the hole. Closing her eyes, She sighed and turned back. "No. They're gone."

"Thank God." Claire stood.

"I don't know what just happened here." Minnie ripped open the door to her house. "I'm not six anymore, Claire Jordan. You can't expect to boss me whenever you want."

Claire hurried into the living room. "Where's Hank?"

Minnie brushed the dust from her skirt. "He's in the backyard. Why?"

"I have the best secret." Claire waved Minnie closer. "Ben introduced me to Lily."

Straightening, Minnie frowned. "I don't see what the big deal is. You already know her. She's your neighbor, remember?"

Claire rolled her eyes. "He's never introduced a girlfriend to me before."

Minnie curled her lips. "Maybe because you know them all." She shrugged. "Well, except for the few visitors from out of town."

"This time is different." Claire frowned. *Why does everyone question my instinct?* "Ben's engaged to Lily."

Minnie shook her head. "Herb Potter said the article was a mistake."

Claire fanned a hand. "Oh please, think about everything. Ben accompanied her to church. He's *never* taken a woman to church before." She clutched her hands against her chest and sighed. "Lily must be the one."

"You think they'll marry?"

Claire nodded. "Trust me. I have a feeling about these two, and you know I'm never wrong. Remember the feeling I had about Jackson's house burning. I warned him, but he refused to listen. Look what happened. His house burnt to the ground."

"You can't take the whole credit." Minnie waved a hand. "Jackson's house was already on fire when you told him."

Claire wagged a finger. "What about when Sandy capsized his boat on the lake?"

Minnie shrugged. "His boat hit the rocks. The thing was bound to capsize."

Claire tapped her foot against the floor. "Remember, though, I was the one who flagged the Lake Patrol."

"Well, to be honest, the lake patrol was already on their way. You just happened to be in the way of their boats."

Fisting her hands on her hips, Claire scowled. "Didn't I warn Sandy about his failing eyesight, though?"

Minnie rolled her eyes "Claire, everyone knew Sandy's eyesight was bad. Don't you remember how he plowed over the Popcorn Hut just the week before?"

"What's your point?" Claire sniffed.

"I just don't want your hopes to be dashed."

"Don't worry. I'm right about this one." Claire hurried down the steps. Looking over her shoulder, she shot Minnie a warning glance. "Promise you won't say a word to anyone. Including Hank."

"My lips are sealed." Minnie zipped her fingers across her lips.

Whether Minnie uttered a word or not didn't matter. By ten in the morning, Claire learned half the town knew Ben spent the night. By eleven, the rest did.

****

The clock read six in the morning, and Ben was M.I.A. Abe tossed his puzzle book onto the desk. He had gone a full thirty minutes without his coffee and donuts. He always knew the day would come when Ben no longer worried about his employees and focused solely on himself. He just didn't expect the day to arrive so quickly.

Well, Abe had enough. He wouldn't work for such a self-centered boss. He wrote his resignation letter in no time. By seven, the letter was signed. By seven-thirty, Ben still had not arrived. He paced the office then popped his head out the station door, hoping to spot Ben pulling up with no luck. Abe forgot about resigning. Instead, he focused on worrying.

By eight, he was panicked. He picked up the phone and called Ben's cell. The phone went to voice mail.

By nine, he tossed the unpalatable coffee he'd made into the trash and prepared himself to go to Ben's funeral. By nine-thirty, Abe wondered if he'd take to the new Police Chief.

By ten, his day went from worse to atrocious, and all because Samantha James entered the station. With curlers still in her hair and no makeup on her face, she looked worse than Abe ever imagined.

She stepped forward with her arms outstretched.

He dropped his gaze, skipping past her chipped, red nails, to his nirvana—a bag of donuts and a steaming cup of coffee. His mouth watered.

She waggled the offering.

Thrusting out a hand, he snatched the white bag and ripped open the sack. Dipping his hand inside, he grabbed a donut and bit down, enjoying the sweet confection as the sugar melted in his mouth. Glancing upward, his pleasure faded. Her smile could only mean one thing…trouble. She didn't take any time to gloat, either. Abe blamed the sugar high from the donuts for being caught off guard. "What did you say?" Clumps of powdered sugar dropped from Abe's chin, landing with a puff of white on the front of his faded, blue shirt.

"Ben spent the night at Lily's house."

Abe swallowed the lump of donut caught in his throat. "You mean Lily Evans? The woman who accosted me?"

Samantha smiled and leaned forward, propping her hands atop Abe's desk. "Yup. Just think, once they're married, she'll complain all the time. Now, you have a lovely day…" Smiling, she waved and sashayed out of the station.

A lovely day? Not possible, now. He plopped into his desk chair. His appetite disappeared. For the first time in his life, Abe threw out a donut. He didn't drink his coffee either. He couldn't. Remembering Lily's anger toward Ben was enough to cause him to lose his appetite.

Abe considered calling dispatch. What if something foul happened? What if *she* perpetrated the criminal act? The blood in his veins chilled. With shaking hands, he grabbed the phone receiver and dialed the emergency line. Listening to the phone ringing, he recalled Ben's complete disregard for him. Glaring at the desk, he tapped his fingers against the cluttered surface. The lack of coffee, no donuts, the added work, Lily Evans…

A voice sounded on the other end of the line. Abe hung up. Being murdered would serve Ben right. Talk about selfish. He hadn't given Abe's feelings any consideration when he died.

He ripped out his pad and paper. He scribbled the words *abdicating authority*. The union would want to hear about this offense.

Spotting his crumpled resignation letter in the trash, he dug out the creased paper and carefully smoothed the wrinkles. He'd need this paper, too.

Chapter 28

Lily waited a few minutes after Ben's departure before hurrying to the car. She ripped open the passenger door and threw open the glove box. Piles of tampons spilled onto the passenger seat. The roar of a car engine startled her. Whipping her gaze upward, she banged her head against the roof. She rubbed her crown, watching Peri and Maybelline saunter toward her.

Maybelline stared inside the vehicle. "Holy cow, that's a ton of tampons."

"What are you doing?" Peri asked, peering from the driver's side.

Lily returned her focus to the glove box. "Searching for my car keys. Ben said he left them in here." As soon as the words popped from her mouth, she regretted them. Peri had characteristics of a bloodhound. The only way to avoid the whole topic was to divert her sister's attention. "Hey, did you know Claire is Ben's mother?"

Peri shot a glance in Maybelline's direction before turning back and frowning. "Yeah."

Wait. What? Peri knew? Lily frowned. "How come you didn't tell me?"

"We're not talking a big secret here." Shrugging, Peri rested a hand atop the car. "The way you two are together all the time, I figured you discussed the topic once or twice."

Lily figured the topic should have come up once or twice herself—only it never had. She knew why, too. Just like not mentioning Ellen was his sister, Ben didn't feel she needed to know about his family—like any person who wasn't interested in commitment.

Scowling, Lily resumed her search. She spied the keys nestled in the bottom of the glove box beneath a mound of old receipts, a stash of tissues, and dried pens. Ben hadn't lied. She dug them out. "My keys."

Tilting her head to the side, Peri studied Lily. "When did he tell you?"

Shrugging, Lily slammed shut the car door, avoiding her sister's intense stare. "This morning, I guess."

Peri narrowed her gaze. "You guess? You don't know?" She slid a glance toward Maybelline and winked.

Debating the best answer, Lily chewed her lips. Vague was definitely the way to go. "I didn't catch the time."

"Liar." Peri pointed a finger. "We drove by last night and spied Ben's truck at Dax's."

Peri and her habit of snooping bordered on annoying. Heat curled in the pit of Lily's stomach. She huffed. "Maybe he stopped by to see his friend."

"At two in the morning?" Peri scoffed.

Frowning, Lily shrugged. "Sure, why not?"

Peri sighed and rolled her eyes. "Oh, please. Ben wasn't at Dax's last night. We both know the truth."

"You don't know." Heat burned Lily's cheeks. She turned away before Peri could spot the telltale sign and hurried toward the house.

"Let me clue you in on what I *do* know." Peri reached out and nabbed Lily's arm, turning her. "Dax worked last night. Now, are you sticking with your story?"

Lily threw up her arms. "Fine. He spent the night here. Are you happy, now?"

Peri clapped. "Immensely. Especially since I have no idea whether Dax worked last night or not."

Great! Today, Peri decided to be Sherlock Holmes. Glaring, Lily marched up the porch steps. "You lied."

"You say I'm lying. I say I'm digging for the truth," Peri argued. "So, give us the details."

"Absolutely not." Lily opened the screen door and stepped into the house.

Peri stopped abruptly. A dark scowl filled her face. She snatched the box of chocolate off the kitchen counter and waved the container in the air. "You ate all of the chocolates? You couldn't save me one." She tossed aside the box. "Just for that, we want the scoop."

"No, we don't," Maybelline rushed out, taking a step back and waving her hands.

Peri frowned. "Don't be squeamish."

"Eeww, yuck." Maybelline gagged. "He's my cousin. I don't want the details. In fact, I don't want to hear anything about what happened."

"Good." Lily shrugged. Within days of arriving, Peri had informed her of Ben's relationship to Maybelline. "Because I'm not telling either of you."

A stare-down ensued between the sisters.

Peri blinked first. Crossing her arms over her chest, she glared. "At least, tell me you wore the lingerie?" She turned to Maybelline. "You should see what I bought her. A sheer, silky teddy. I'm talking hot-hot-

hot. Très sexy."

Maybelline picked up an item from the table. "Are you talking about this?"

The silky fabric dangled from the tip of her finger. The price tag, spinning in circles, hung from a thin satin ribbon.

Ripping the lingerie from Maybelline's hand, Peri waved the lacy fabric in Lily's face. "I can't believe you didn't wear my gift."

"I'm sorry." She looked down at her hands and grimaced. "Things just happened."

Peri sighed. "I can't say I'm not disappointed. After all, I bought you the lingerie to wear the first time with him." A second later, she clapped. "I know. You can wear the negligee on your honeymoon."

What the heck was wrong with Peri? How could she expect a honeymoon when they weren't engaged? He didn't even love her. Lily stuffed the lingerie into the bag. For all of Peri's insistence on remaining single and unattached, a part of her was a hopeless romantic. Right now, Lily wished Peri would focus the hopeless romantic part on herself. She thrust out the bag, smacking Peri in the chest. "If wearing this lingerie on a honeymoon is important, why don't you take the gown?"

Peri batted aside the package. "Good try. However, I'm not ready for marriage. You, on the other hand, sweet sister, are."

Lily's heart raced. "No, I'm not." She glanced down at her hands, devoid of a commitment declaration. Her stomach tumbled. She glanced up and lifted her chin. "Neither of us is."

When I say the words, I almost believe them.

Chapter 29

Before Lily knew what happened, the weekend she shared with Ben was over, and the day she dreaded arrived.

Bright and early Monday morning, Ben gave her a thorough kiss. Lily pretended to ignore him.

"Rise and shine. Time for you to go to work."

Lily buried her head under the blanket. "I'm sick." She feigned a cough.

He snickered. "I need to go home and change. You're not expected at work until eight."

Her stomach tumbled. She couldn't work for him. The idea was preposterous. Why, she could just image what the townspeople would think. "I'm not coming." She peeked out from beneath the edge of the blanket, fearing his reaction.

Standing beside her bed, Ben rested his hands on his hip. "You promised to help me. I take commitments seriously." He stared down and frowned. "You don't want to disappoint me, do you?"

She pursed her lips. "I might…"

A muscle flexed in Ben's jaw.

She knew that look only too well. Closing her eyes, she emitted a long sigh. "Did you know you're stubborn?" She expected him to argue. When she peeked, he surprised her with a saucy wink.

"I believe we've covered this topic before."

He left before she could dispute his words. She intended to sleep. Her mind had other ideas. For another hour, she tossed, wondering what the heck she'd gotten herself into. Disgusted, she shoved aside the sheets and marched into the bathroom to get ready. She didn't want to be late on her first day. When she was finished, Lily stomped into the kitchen.

Peri finished pouring a cup of coffee before sweeping her gaze over Lily. "Where are you going?"

"I'm not going anywhere." She stormed from the house. She could have driven to work. After being without her keys, driving would be a welcome treat. However, she was far too nervous to get behind a steering wheel. With her luck, she'd hit someone and then she'd be in a heap of trouble. Besides, with the pleasant weather, she figured a brisk walk would help calm her nerves.

Instead of relaxing her, she spent the whole time preoccupied with the problem of Ben. Unfortunately, just like a sliver in a thumb, he refused to leave her thoughts. Maybe if he stayed the playboy she had initially believed, her feelings might be different, but he refused to do even that simple act.

He wasn't a one-night deal, either—or even two, for the matter. Though, she didn't expect him to stay forever. She knew only too well he'd soon become bored and find someone new and different. They all did. Hadn't Eric taught her this lesson? Still, the hurt wouldn't be any less painful when the day arrived, and he did leave.

She debated whether to stop for coffee at Betty's Café. Betty meant well, in the end, though, her curiosity would get the best of her. She'd want the details, and right now, Lily wasn't ready to discuss her relationship with anyone.

Her choices were limited, though. Either suffer through Betty's prying questions or deal with Karla's snide comments. Sighing, she chose Betty's Café. Entering the café, she spotted Betty at the espresso machine.

Looking up, Betty smiled. "I hear the town has a new working girl." Chuckling, she wiped the counter.

Lily ignored the curious stares. "I didn't have a choice," she grumbled before ordering her coffee.

"Oh, don't be upset. You're doing a marvelous thing." Betty started the latte. "Ben needs you."

She knew Betty spoke the truth, and despite the way she was coerced into helping, she knew her assistance would benefit him. "Working for him won't help the rumors." Lily dug through her purse, searching for money.

Finishing making the coffee, Betty winked. "Honey, working for him is the one thing that *will* help the rumors."

Expecting Ben to greet her, she was surprised to see only Abe in the office. He didn't appear to be working either, with his feet propped against the top of his desk and his gaze fixed to a magazine.

He whipped his attention toward her and widened his eyes. "Oh, dear God," Abe moaned. "When Ben told me he hired you, I didn't want to believe him."

She didn't bother to mention she wasn't thrilled either. She glanced around the area, spotting the open door of Ben's office. His desk sat empty. Slumping her shoulders, she sighed. A sharp sting bit her flesh. She yanked her gaze to her hand. Steaming coffee dripped from the edge. Shifting the cup to her free hand, she casually wiped the hot liquid on the side of her jeans. "Where's Ben?"

Abe locked his gaze on the cup of coffee. "Where's my coffee?"

Lily flicked a glance at the cup she held. "Why would I have brought you one?"

Abe stiffened, a scowl flashing across his face. "Bringing me a cup is the least you could have done. When you buy coffee for yourself, you purchase one for everyone. You ever heard of etiquette?"

Apparently, rudeness didn't qualify as etiquette in Abe's book. She set her purse on the empty desk, and smiling, sipped her drink. "In my experience, everyone brings their own drinks."

Abe's eyes widened for a split second before narrowing. Tossing down the magazine, he leaned back in his chair and crossed his arms over his chest. "You know, working in a police station isn't all fun and games."

"I never expected it to be," Lily muttered. Then again, she never expected to be blackmailed either.

"You've got to know how to run a computer." Abe tapped his pencil on the desk calendar. "And not just games, either. You need to have other skills, too."

Lily set the cup of coffee on the desk. "Of course. I was an administrative assistant at my former job."

Abe glared. He threw down his pencil before dropping his feet to the floor and standing. Walking toward her, he pointed to a computer on the empty desk. "Oh yeah? Why don't you show me how to turn on this thing?"

Now, she knew he was crazy. She turned. "Do you

have a password?"

Looking around, Abe curved his lips. "I suppose Heather kept one here someplace." He shifted through a stack of papers and dug through the drawers. Finally, he snatched out a tiny slip of paper. "Here, you go. HEA55217." He tossed the paper toward her.

With a frown, Lily snatched the paper, setting it aside. She pushed a button on the front of the computer tower and another on the monitor, waiting for the start-up menu. When the process was complete, she glanced at the note and entered the code. Finished, she twisted in her chair to face him.

Scratching his head and frowning, Abe pointed toward the computer. "You just press this button…huh." He frowned then stiffened. "Oh yeah, well how fast can you type?"

"I type at a decent speed." Lily shrugged, praying Abe wasn't her supervisor. She'd much rather work under Ben's direction than this cantankerous, old man.

Abe smiled. "So, what are you talking? Maybe twenty or thirty words per minute?"

Lily burst into laughter. "More like ninety words."

His brows shot straight to the top of his forehead, and his mouth dropped downward. *"A minute?"*

"Yeah." She noticed surprise on Abe's face. "Do you want me to show you?"

"No," he mumbled, frowning. "I'll take your word. Now about reports—Ben's crazy for them. Thinks he needs one for every council meeting. He'll probably expect you to do them. Can you?"

Lily lifted a shoulder. "Depends on the kind of report he needs. Does he need spreadsheets or minutes?"

Abe scratched his chin. "Spreadsheets?"

Lily nodded. *What the heck has Ben gotten me into? And what about the lady I'm replacing? What are her duties?* Frowning, she opened the program. "Yeah. You know, like reports with numbers and calculations."

Abe's face turned pink. "Oh, right. Spreadsheets." He shrugged. "The council likes hard numbers on paper that they can scrutinize—arrests, citations issued, and what-not—a bunch of nonsense, if you ask me."

From his scowl, she figured he didn't agree. She turned to the screen and built a spreadsheet, adding some lines and numbers and a graph, as well. "This report is kind of simple. I can make them more complicated. I'll need more time, though. Will this report work?"

Abe rubbed his chin. "I don't know. I write the information on paper and let Ben take care of the rest."

Long-hand? Seriously? Still, she was new and only helping out—under protest, no less. She removed her hand from the keyboard. "I guess I could do the same."

"Yeah, you might want to consider hand-written reports, seeing as he's used to that style." Abe nodded toward the file cabinet. "Can you file?"

"Sure."

"We have special files here." Abe strode to the file cabinet and opened one of the drawers. "We keep all of our cases and reports in here. They're in a particular and scientific order. These files need to be maintained exactly as they are right now."

She strolled over and stared at the clutter. Apparently, particular and scientific meant something different to him. Personally, she thought a tornado had ripped through the cabinet. "Maybe I should leave them for you?"

Abe wagged his finger. "Oh no, you don't. If you're working here, you must do your part. Don't think you can go to Ben to avoid work. Now, can you answer phones?" He pointed to the main desk.

An old-school phone sat on the right corner. On the front were six buttons—five were clear and one was red.

"We're not talking no wimpy phone system." He rested a hand on the receiver. "This phone has three lines. Can you answer three lines?"

Lily glanced downward. "I see five buttons."

Abe waved a hand. "Those two don't work."

She shrugged. "Where I worked before, we had an eight-line phone."

"Are you done?"

Lily jumped and turned.

Ben lounged against the open door of his office, his gaze fixed on them.

Damn. Amazing was only one word to come to mind. Incredible, irresistible, and superb were a few more. If possible, his black suit coat made his eyes darker, and his shoulders broader.

"You're late."

Lily glanced at the clock. She was, by a whole thirty minutes. If she had her way, she would be much later—say, not here at all. "I lost track of time."

Shifting from the door, he strolled toward her. "I see Abe's interviewed you." He smiled. "I hope you met his criteria."

Abe frowned. "Too soon to tell."

Sitting on the edge of a desk, Ben turned to Lily. "I'm not asking for much. Abe has his work, which is mainly doing word puzzles. You'll do the rest."

Searching for the humor, she stared at the two men. A scowl marred Abe's face. Ben's remained resolute. Neither disputed the comment. "And that work is…?"

Ben shifted his gaze, nodding toward the vacant desk. "Just answer the phones, take messages, and help people. You mentioned building reports on the computer. I'll show you what I need, and you can do them. The rest is maintaining the office."

Before she knew what happened, Ben wrapped her in his arms and kissed her right in the middle of the station. Heat burned her cheeks. Glancing at Abe, she noticed worry creasing his face. She turned, ready to admonish Ben for his lack of manners. She was too late. He'd already left the station. She didn't see him for the rest of the day. An acute sense of loneliness filled her. As much as she didn't want to admit it, she actually missed him. Sighing, she sat, cursing her need.

Chapter 30

Lily realized right away why Ben worked eighteen hours a day. The reason sat across from her, busy working on word puzzles. Not once had she seen Abe work. He didn't answer the phone, create one report, or write a single letter. From what she could tell, he had two job duties—word puzzles and gossiping with the endless stream of people coming through the station's door. By mid-afternoon, she had enough. "Do you want me to show you how to build a spreadsheet?"

Abe didn't pull his gaze from his puzzle. "No."

She frowned. "Are you sure? Reports are simple to create, and they will help Ben."

"Not my problem." Abe scribbled in the magazine.

Lily returned her attention to the computer screen. Ben had stuck a note on the side of the monitor requesting a memo to the City Council. She turned to face Abe. "Do you want me to show you how he likes his letters written?"

Abe snapped up his head. "I know how he likes them. Besides, he hired you for that job." He returned his focus to his puzzle.

Lily dropped the argument. Sighing, she stared at the piles of notes on her desk, wondering what to address first. By the time she left for the day, she was exhausted and wanted nothing more than to go home and fall asleep.

However, the minute her head hit the pillow, she couldn't stop her mind from switching into overdrive. She couldn't imagine how Abe worked in an office for years without learning any basic office skills. Why did Ben allow his behavior?

The questions were endless, and she had too few answers. Sleep became impossible. Instead, she paced the living room while searching for a solution to help Abe help Ben.

Consumed with finding an answer to her dilemma, she looked up and stilled.

Ben leaned against the living room door jamb.

His gaze was soft and warm. Her heart thumped. "I thought you'd be home earlier."

Shrugging, he shifted from the door. "City Council meeting." He drew her into his arms, brushing his mouth against hers and curling his fingers beneath her nightshirt. "Where's Peri?"

Desire raced through Lily. "She's with Maybelline for the night."

With measured steps, he advanced, forcing her to walk backward toward the bedroom. A smile creased his face. "Good to know."

Lily stopped in her doorway and pressed a hand against his chest. "Wait, are you hungry?"

"Famished." He led her into the bedroom, shutting the door after him.

By the time she woke the next morning, Ben had left. She sighed. She'd need to wait until later to discuss her concern. Today, however, her goal was to reason with Abe about the office. Maybe, when he realized she only wanted to help Ben, he would want to learn.

At nine, she stepped into the station.

Abe glanced over and frowned. "Where's my coffee?"

Lily stifled a groan. With all her attention focused on her problems, she completely forgot the discussion from her first day in the office. "I figured you'd get your own like most people do."

Snapping his brows downward, he waved a hand over his desk. "Do you see one?"

Frowning, Lily pointed a finger. "You have a cup on your desk."

"Oh, I see what you're doing." Abe crossed his arms over his chest. "You want me to get fired, don't you?"

Lily recoiled. "Why would you think such a thing?"

"Because you want me to leave." Abe wagged a finger. "Then when Ben arrives, he'll fire me for abandoning my job."

Lily wrinkled her brow. "Aren't you in a union?"

Abe threw his pencil. "Are you saying I refuse to work because I'm union?"

Stepping back, Lily lifted her hands. "I'm saying Ben couldn't fire you because you are union."

"Oh sure, now you think you know everything." Abe dropped his feet to the floor, creating a resounding thud. Leaning forward, he pressed his palms on his thighs and glared. "Let me tell you something. If he wants to fire me, he will."

Sitting at her desk, she grabbed a note stuck to the side of her computer. She gave up understanding Abe. No matter what she told him, he didn't believe her. She spent the rest of the morning working while he gossiped with the locals or mumbled words while solving a puzzle.

His constant murmur drove her to distraction. She had a pile of work, and no help. She pounded on her key pad, filling numbers on the chart. After a while, she couldn't take his mumbling any longer. He worked on the same puzzle since they called a truce, and still, he was nowhere close to being done. Without thinking, Lily blurted the answer.

Abe's head shot up. "What did you say?"

Lily sighed. "I said, 'crocus.'"

Scowling, he scratched his chin. "What about crocuses?"

"Not crocuses." She pointed her pen at the paper he held. "Crocus is the answer."

Abe shot a quick glance at his book before snapping up his gaze. "Now you're doing my work?" He grabbed the yellow notepad from the desk and scribbled something on the sheet.

Clamping shut her mouth at the sight of the all too familiar pad, Lily refused to say another word. She'd rather cut out her tongue with a dull butter knife than help the man. By the time she arrived home, she was again exhausted and on edge. She flopped on the couch, intending to put aside the worries of Abe.

The sound of someone in the kitchen woke her. She sat up and looked around. Bright sunlight streamed through the bedroom windows. Scrambling from the bed, Lily wrapped herself in a robe and stepped into the kitchen.

Finishing a sip of coffee, Ben set down the cup and flipped a page of the newspaper he read.

The scene was a bit too domestic for her peace of mind. "I didn't hear you come in last night."

Glancing up, he arched a brow.

Despite needing a shave, he was still the hottest man she'd ever seen.

He folded the paper before placing it on the table. Three steps later, he wrapped his arms around her and kissed her. "I know. I helped you into the bedroom."

Lily widened her eyes. "You did? I don't remember."

"You were dead to the world." He brushed his mouth against hers. "I'm heading home to change before work."

"Oh." She hoped her disappointment didn't show. Of course, he had responsibilities. She did, too.

He set his cup in the sink. "I should just store some clothing here."

"What?" Lily stepped back and flung out her hands. "You can't."

His forehead wrinkled. "Why not?"

She tapped a foot. "Because people will notice."

He laughed, drawing her against his chest. "Sweetheart, I hate to break the news, but they already have."

Dropping her chin, she sighed. She might not agree with him living here but certainly enjoyed his hugs. He kissed her, causing her to forget everything except how perfect his mouth felt against hers.

He broke free. "I'll be gone for the day, and I have a meeting tonight with the mayor."

Storming into her bedroom, Lily flopped on the bed. She didn't know how to feel about his comment. She did know, though, him living in her house could only cause more gossip.

What she needed was a reasonable argument to

explain why he had to move out. She might have found one, too, if she hadn't fallen asleep. She woke up to streams of sunlight. Jumping from the bed, she bolted into the bathroom. She was an hour past the start of work, which meant she'd just done one more thing to irritate Abe.

She took the swiftest shower of her life. When finished, she grabbed a shirt and yanked it over her head before drawing on a pair of pants. Forgoing a fancy hairstyle, she gathered her hair into a simple ponytail and rushed through her makeup routine. In fewer than fifteen minutes, she was out the door. She raced into the station twenty minutes later, breathless, carrying two cups of coffee.

Frowning, Abe tossed aside his paper. "Well, look who decided to come to work."

"Sorry, I'm late." Lily handed him the cup. "Here, I bought coffee for you."

Abe glanced at the coffee then back to Lily.

Pushing the cup farther toward him, she gave him an eager smile.

Pursing his lips, Abe gingerly accepted the drink and took a sip.

She didn't know what response she expected. Him spitting the mouthful of coffee into the trash was definitely not what she'd imagined. Staring down in the can, she dropped her mouth.

"What the hell did you buy me?"

Lily shifted her attention from the trash. "A mocha latte."

"Well, the stuff tastes like garbage." Abe dropped the cup into the garbage. "Is the coffee your way of killing me? Because if that's your intent, this coffee will accomplish your objective."

Ungrateful. She dropped her shoulders and wiped the smile from her face. "I didn't know what you liked—"

Abe fixed his gaze downward while scribbling something on the pad of paper.

Swiveling in her chair, she grabbed her coffee. Tapping one finger on the arm rest, she lifted a brow. "What are you doing? A report?"

He glanced up. "You could say that."

"For Ben?"

Abe finished writing then tossed the pad on the desk. "No. For the union."

"So, you're doing work for the union?" Getting answers from him was like pulling teeth on a squirming child—nearly impossible.

"No. I'm a part of the union. I don't do their work."

"I haven't seen you do any work." The words slipped out before she could stop them.

Abe pinched his brows downward. "Oh yeah?" He eyed her while scratching his pen across the surface, mumbling "Harassment."

Lily gripped tighter her cup. *Two can play that game.* "Hey, can a person get fired in the police department?"

Tossing down his notebook, he looked over. "Why? You looking to?"

A look of hope filled his gaze. Lily offered him a sweet smile, while sipping her coffee. "Not me. You."

Abe sat back and frowned. "Are you in Congress?"

Snatching a taped note stuck to her computer, Lily glanced over her shoulder toward Abe. "No."

Crossing his arms over his chest, he smiled. "Are you God?"

Lily shifted slightly and frowned. "What?"

Abe grabbed his puzzle book. "If you're not God or Congress, then you can't fire someone in public service." He waved a pencil. "Trust me on this one."

She didn't hear another word for the rest of the day. Every once in a while, she'd glance from her stack of work to see him finishing one puzzle before starting the next. Apparently, his words were the truth, because since starting, she hadn't seen him answer one phone call, create a single report, or file a piece of paper.

He dismissed her comments about work, scorned her attempts at conversation, and ignored her offers of help. She supposed the reason Ben kept him had something to do with Abe's age and years on the job. Abe certainly stated often enough how he'd worked for the department for thirty years, and if the council hadn't been against him, he'd be chief now.

When she arrived home, she tossed her purse on the table, then sat, propping her chin on a hand.

Peri stepped into the kitchen. "What's wrong?"

Lily looked up. "It's Abe. He does nothing to help Ben, and when I try to explain what has to be done, he ignores my advice."

"Why do you care?" Peri waved a hand. "He's not your problem. He's Ben's."

She refused to accept Peri's explanation. She just needed to find something Abe excelled at and show him the solution. Once he realized his abilities, he'd want to help in the office.

Since she'd solved her dilemma, Lily took a long shower. Just as she finished getting dressed, the kitchen door screeched open. Heavy footsteps followed. She marched across the bedroom, threw open the door, and stopped dead in her tracks. The arrival of Ben didn't surprise her. The sight of what he held was a different matter, altogether. "Why do you have your luggage?"

He set the case on the floor before hauling her against him. "Remember? We discussed this topic earlier."

The smell of his spicy cologne filled her nostrils. Licking her lips, she shook her head. "I remember saying you shouldn't live here."

Ben bent to nuzzle her neck. "How about we think of us as having a sleepover?"

A shiver of desire tingled through her. Lily wrapped her arms around his shoulders, reveling in the feeling of his strength beneath her fingertips. "We're too old for a sleepover."

"If you ask me, we're a perfect age." He winked.

A scant second later, he claimed her lips in a thorough, toe-curling kiss.

The next morning, Lily sat at the kitchen table, contemplating her problem with Abe when her other problem strode into the kitchen. Solving the riddle of Abe proved distressing enough. Now, she had the problem of Ben living here. Life was unfair.

Tapping her fingers on the table, she watched him stride across the room to the coffee maker.

After pouring his coffee, he turned and walked to the table. "What's the matter?"

"Nothing," she mumbled, even though the statement was far from the truth. A lot of "matter" had occurred, and none made her happy.

Ben placed a kiss on her forehead. "Thank you for

helping me."

Lily curled her lip and frowned.

Straightening, Ben dropped his hands to his hips. "You're coming to work today."

His comment wasn't a question. She tapped her fingers on the table, locking her gaze with his. *To argue or not?* She fisted a hand on the table and gritted her teeth. "I guess I don't have a choice."

He winked. "You're right. You don't."

His breath fanned over her face, his mouth inches away. Lily's heart fluttered before finally melting. She supposed Ben living at her house wasn't the worst thing. Her growing attachment was a different matter. She didn't know how to solve the issue. On her way to work, she stopped at the café.

Turning from the espresso machine, Betty smiled. "How are things going with Ben?"

"They're terrible." Lily sighed.

Betty blinked. "You must be the first woman to ever say those words."

More importantly, she might be the first woman stupid enough to fall in love with the man, too. She refused to admit her dilemma, though. The way word traveled in town, her problem would be on the newspaper's front page by lunchtime. "I need to get coffee for me and Abe."

"Sure thing." Betty turned away and poured coffee into two paper cups. She dumped four heaping scoops of sugar into Abe's coffee.

Dropping a ten-dollar bill on the counter, Lily frowned. "I thought he liked plain coffee."

"Abe? Naw. He likes his coffee extra sweet."

"I bought him a mocha latte," Lily protested,

remembering Abe's reaction.

Shrugging, Betty scooped up the money and dropped it into the cash register. "Probably not enough sugar."

When she stepped into the station, she heard constant ringing from the phone.

Abe studied a word puzzle, never once lifting his attention from the pages.

Neither action surprised her. "The phone's ringing."

Abe's gaze remained fixed on the page. "Not my job to answer phones."

"I wish I knew what your job was," she mumbled, racing to catch the call. She missed by seconds.

"What was that?"

Sure, he hears that complaint. "I just don't understand what your duties are around here."

Abe snapped down his brows. "Those are between me and Ben."

Lily bit back a retort. Setting the two cups and her purse on the counter, she turned and stared. Abe again focused on his non-work work. Pinching her lips together, she picked up a cup and held it out. "I don't know why, but I brought you coffee—"

He put up a hand. "No, thank you."

She willed herself not to throw the cup. Instead, she mustered the sweetest voice possible. "I purchased the kind you prefer, extra sweet and creamy. I had Betty make your drink."

Eyeing her over the edge of his paper, Abe let out a sigh. He hesitated before accepting the cup. "I don't know if I can believe you."

Just another wonderful day working with Abe.

Sighing, she sat at her desk and began the day. Three hours later, she was buried knee deep in a report Ben asked her to create.

Abe stood. "I have a doctor's appointment."

Lily snapped her attention from the computer.

Abe jabbed a knobby finger into the stack of newspapers and word puzzle books littering his desk. "Don't touch anything on my desk."

Gritting her teeth and clenching her fists, Lily refused to comment. However, the minute the door closed, a wide smile split her face. He told her not to touch the paperwork on his desk. He never mentioned the file cabinet. Setting aside her work, Lily rushed over to the files, eager to organize the chaos. She imagined she'd have the disarray neatened in no time.

An hour later, she was no closer to straightening the mess. Initially, she figured she'd find logic to the files. However, nothing in the cabinet made sense. She expected to see the files in some sort of alphabetical order—which was ridiculous, considering the files weren't labeled correctly. Heck, some weren't even labeled. She spent the next half hour laboring over each, meticulously organizing them and making labels.

A bellow erupted.

Lily's heart skipped a beat. She snapped her attention to see Abe, red-faced with fire shooting from his eyes, standing next to his desk.

"What the hell is going on here?" Abe tossed down his lunch pail, scattering a stack of newspapers and puzzle books.

"I was just—"

"Did you ever think I have these files perfectly arranged?" Abe threw up his arms. "Now, I need to go in and figure out a whole new system."

Lily fanned her hands over the files. "No, you don't. They're in alphabetical order."

Abe yanked the notepad from the drawer. "I'm *not* happy."

She slumped in her chair—tired and dusty. Abe didn't say another word to her the rest of the day. To the rest of the stream of visitors, he said plenty and cast several heated glances her way.

By the end of her day, she went home feeling defeated.

Peri sat at the kitchen table, munching on potato chips. She scooped some dip on her chip. "So, how was work?"

Lily gritted her teeth at the smug tone in Peri's voice. She flung her purse on the counter and grabbed a bottle of water out of the fridge. "That Abe drives me nuts. Do you realize all he does is gossip? People come in all day with no police business. They just stop by for a gabfest, and Abe is more than willing to oblige."

Peri swallowed her mouthful, wiping a hand across her lips. "I don't know why you waste your energy on that grumpy, old man. Who cares how the office runs or if he knows anything? He won't be your problem after the summer, anyway."

Maybe not, but what about Ben? Lily leaned against the fridge and cracked open her water. "He is Ben's, though."

"Not when Ben becomes mayor." Peri shrugged.

She paused in drinking the water. "*If* he becomes mayor."

On Thursday, Lily didn't want to go to work. She cornered Ben just as he opened the door to leave. "I'm done. I can't fight with Abe anymore."

"So, then, don't."

Lily fisted her hands. "You don't understand. The man is beyond cantankerous."

Ben arched a brow. "I understand more than you think. Besides, I've dealt with him for five years. I'm certain you can handle him for a few weeks." He left the house.

Lily stared at the closed door. *For a few weeks, but not forever...*

Her heart clenched. So, he didn't plan on a permanent future. She should be relieved by his words. Instead, she felt...stung. Closing her eyes, she raked her fingers through her hair. *Get over the hurt. Aren't his words exactly what I expected?* She pushed aside her pain and entered the bathroom.

Her concern with Abe disappeared, only because she had a whole new set of worries to replace them. They were spread out all over the place, too. Since when did she have a man's shaving case in her bathroom? Or men's suits hanging in her closet or shoes lining the floor? Or, for that matter, a man's belt slung over the back of the chair and men's jeans folded in her dresser. What about his watch sitting right next to a pile of change on the bureau and his cologne she loved? She plopped on the bed and raked her fingers through her hair.

What am I doing? I don't have men living with me in such a short time.

And what about him? What the heck is he thinking? Doesn't he realize the ramifications? Or the fact my heart is involved?

He obviously didn't care about any of these

concerns. For him, their relationship was just a momentary fling. Lily jumped from the bed and rushed to the closet. Shoving the offending suits out of her way, she dug deep into the back and ripped a shirt off the hanger, before yanking the fabric over her head. Leaving the house, she slammed the front door, frustrated by the whole situation.

On her way to work, Lily stopped at the café. She desperately needed coffee. Otherwise, she'd skip the place and the gossip.

A wide smile split Betty's face. "Heard you have a new roommate."

The cheerful tone in Betty's voice irritated Lily. *Does everyone know Ben moved in? And why the heck do they care?* She gritted her teeth. "Not by choice."

Glancing over her shoulder, Betty scooped ground coffee into a filter. "Honey, you might be the first woman successful enough to nab him."

Her relationship with Ben was short-term, at best. An ache, piercing and sharp, sliced through her chest. Ignoring the pain, she kept her voice controlled. "I'm only here for the summer."

Betty's eyes widened. "With you two together, I thought things had changed."

Lily averted her gaze. "Nothing's changed." She paid for the coffees, left the café, and headed to Dainty's Donuts.

If Abe believed he'd defeat her, he was wrong. She possessed the golden ticket. Coffee hadn't won him over. She was positive, though, the fresh, hot donuts in the paper bag would. When she arrived, Lily didn't expect a warm greeting. The wide-eyed look with his mouth agape, though, was uncalled-for.

"You're dressed like an old lady," Abe barked.

The choking sound in Ben's office drew her attention.

A second later, he appeared in the doorway.

His gaze swept over her and on his face was a mixture of shock and laughter. She stilled.

"What the hell are you wearing?"

Lily peeked downward and stifled a groan. Of all the items to grab this morning, why her mother's clothing? She frowned. "What's wrong with my shirt? Don't you enjoy cats?"

Ben shrugged. "Not especially, and definitely not embroidered on a shirt."

"Yeah, well, I don't have room in the closet for my outfits." She turned to Abe and frowned. "And you're rude to say I look old, especially since I've purchased your coffee."

Swiveling, he turned to Ben. Pinching his mouth into a tight scowl, he glared. "Did you tell her to make this purchase? Is this your way of killing me?"

Ben rolled his eyes. "Oh, for God's sake, neither of us plan to kill you...yet." He turned to Lily and winked.

Lily dismissed the whole shirt thing. She had a different fight to pick with Ben. She set the coffee cup and bag on the desk then drew him close. "The town is talking about our..." She slid a glance in Abe's direction. She couldn't tell if he paid attention to their conversation or not. His attention was fixed on the bag of donuts. Not willing to take a chance, she leaned closer. "About our sleeping arrangements."

Ben snatched her into his arms. "So?"

"What did you say about Ben living with you?"

Turning, Lily frowned, unwilling to give him even

one tiny bit of information regarding their living arrangements. She wiggled from Ben's grip and lifted the bag of donuts, effectively diverting Abe's attention.

He reached upward.

She held the donuts out of his reach. "You need to accept my conditions to receive them."

Abe's mouth dropped open. "Are you holding them donuts captive?"

"I am." Glancing over, she smiled and waggled the bag. "Now, do you want the donuts or not?"

Ben sat on the edge of Lily's desk with his arms crossed over his chest and his face set. "Those are Dainty's Donuts." He tilted his chin toward the white paper bag. "If I were you, I'd find out what she wants."

Tapping his fingers against the desk, Abe glared. "Okay. What kind of ransom are you expecting?"

"I want you to help around the office."

Abe narrowed his eyes. "What do you mean by 'help?'"

Lily waved a hand toward the phone. "Well, for starters, I'd like you to handle the phone calls. I don't know all the answers. You do." She glanced at the stack of notes piled on her desk. "And letters. You need to write letters. I have some form letters already created, so basically you'll just have to make a few changes to fit the response."

Ben remained silent the whole time.

Feeling his gaze, she felt her skin warm. She shot him a quick glance. His face remained unyielding. She returned her attention to Abe. "Well?"

His shoulders slumped. "I'll answer the phone and help with the letters." He frowned and thrust out a finger. "But you're doing the reports."

311

Lily was more than willing to accept his counter-offer. Smiling, she held out the bag. *The victory isn't much, but it is a start.*

Ben caught her wrist before Abe could grasp it. "You tell me if he doesn't keep his end of the bargain." He released her hand, flicking a narrowed glance in Abe's direction.

Abe shot Ben a glance, snatching the bag. "The union won't be pleased hearing this complaint."

She ripped her gaze toward Ben to see his reaction, but he'd already walked into his office.

Abe growled.

She turned. "Now, what's wrong?"

"What the hell are these?" Abe held out the bag. "These aren't the right donuts. I don't see any powdered sugar and not one drop of grape jelly."

She gritted her teeth. *The man is beyond ungrateful.* "Dainty's didn't have any. I bought what I could."

Abe tossed the donut bag in the trash. "Deal's off."

Glancing at the mounds of work on her desk, Lily sighed. *What the heck did I get myself into?*

****

The sound of Ben in the kitchen woke Lily. She groaned. She couldn't handle another day with Abe. Jumping from the bed, she grabbed her bathrobe, intending to catch Ben before he left. She ripped open the bedroom door and stormed out of the room. "I'm not working today."

Ben finished pouring coffee in his cup, carefully returning the pot to the warmer. He turned, and bracing his legs apart, crossed his arms over his chest. "Why not?"

"It's Abe." She tightened the sash on her robe and stepped farther into the room. "He's driving me nuts. Do you realize as soon as he found out I didn't buy the right donuts he refused to keep his deal? He went right back to doing word puzzles and gossiping. Honestly, I don't understand why you allow this behavior."

Screwing on the top of his travel mug, he glanced her way. "I realize Abe does all those things. I could write him up, ruin his career, fire him even, but I won't."

"So, you'd rather let him get away with these actions? It's not right."

Ben turned and leaned back, setting his mug on the counter. "Listen, I understand your concern, but you need to understand Abe's worked for the department for nearly thirty years. Up until a year ago or so, he'd led a career of distinction. Things happened, and Abe changed." He shrugged. "I won't ruin a lifetime of efforts for situations beyond his control."

Lily threw up her arms. "But you're the police chief. You should do something about his lack of effort."

Raking his fingers through his hair, Ben sighed. "And I have, but he's in a protected class and with unions, the process is even trickier. I have contracts and conditions I have to abide by. Abe's a longtime employee with tenure. To terminate an employee requires reams of documentation and a lot of arbitration. The previous chief didn't report issues. For me to gather enough now would be pointless. Besides, in a year he'll have his time in, and he'll retire. Until then, you and I will handle the load." He pushed away from the counter and picked up his mug. Walking over, he brushed his lips against hers, before running a hand down her hair. "I'll see you at the office."

Lily threaded together her fingers. She had no idea what happened to change Abe, but she trusted Ben's decision. She turned and watched him walk to the door. "I think I should warn you, if I kill Abe, his death will be on your shoulders."

Chuckling, he pulled open the door and stepped outside.

Conceding defeat, Lily frowned at his departing back. Her threat might be empty. However, just because she wouldn't kill Abe didn't mean the idea wouldn't be in her thoughts.

Frustrated and resigned to her fate, she strode into her bedroom and ripped open the closet doors. A solid navy suit she'd never seen hung on the rod, blocking her view of her clothing. She slammed shut the closet door. "What the hell are they? Gremlins multiplying during the night."

She moved to the dresser, digging through the drawers until she found a pair of capris she'd borrowed from Peri. She yanked them out and shook out the wrinkles. Next, she chose a black and white lightweight sweater to wear with the pants. When she finished dressing, she hurried out of the house, praying today Abe might be more agreeable.

She made her usual stop to Betty's, and then Dainty's afterward. Today, she made sure they had Abe's donuts. Lily smiled. "Any chance you could dust those donuts with arsenic?"

Giving her a weak smile, Mary Margaret folded the top of the bag. "I'm not allowed to use arsenic."

Sighing, she accepted the white paper bag from

Mary Margaret's outstretched hand. "That's too bad." She marched across the park with the bag of donuts in one hand and the tray of coffee in the other. Too many other thoughts occupied her mind to worry about needless matters such as pleasant weather and cheerful hellos. Ripping open the door to the station, Lily stormed across the lobby and slid the donuts and coffee across Abe's desk. "Here you go. White powdered donuts with grape jelly, and no arsenic in sight."

Abe arched his brows. "What? No conditions today?"

Lily shrugged. "What's the point?"

Smiling, Abe accepted the bag. "Good. Because I have a ton of work here."

She swept her gaze across Abe's desk. *What work?* Her area was a cluttered mess of crumpled papers, pens all over the place, piles of messages she needed to act on, and reams of data ready to be compiled into reports.

On the other hand, *his* desk was a picture of fastidious organization. A chipped coffee mug filled with pencils, the pointed side down, sat near the top of the desk. The coffee mug read *When I retire, I'm not working.* Lily didn't know what would be different, seeing as the only work he did was his puzzles. Two pens, one blue, one black, lay next to the pencil cup. A yellow pad sat beside the pens.

Next to the pad sat Abe's favorite office equipment—his stapler. He wielded this weapon like nobody's business—mostly in the process of killing a bug. Still, he was impressive. His ever-present stack of word puzzles completed the scene.

Not a piece of paper was out of place. Not a discarded staple marred the surface. Not a crumpled note cluttered the area.

If she were to describe each desk, she'd say one was a place of work, the other an area of leisure. Anyone could determine which desk belonged to whom. That realization was the last straw.

She stormed across the room to the dusty, ancient typewriter sitting unused in the corner.

Abe glanced up from his word puzzle.

She lifted the typewriter over her head.

He opened his mouth and jumped from his chair just in time to avoid getting crushed. His donuts weren't as lucky. Grape jelly and white powder splattered everywhere.

"What the hell? You ruined my donuts."

Lily spied an old, unused phone sitting on the file cabinet she'd arranged yesterday. She darted across the room and grabbed the phone, flinging it across the room. The phone slammed against the brick wall, scattering bits of plastic everywhere.

She felt better. *Much* better. Brushing off her hands, she peered in Abe's direction then almost burst out laughing. His expression vacillated between the desire to murder her and crying over the loss of his donuts. She figured he might be considering both options.

He collapsed into his chair. "What the hell is wrong with you?"

His voice was high-pitched and shaky, and his eyes were filled with fear. Lily didn't care. She glared. "Me? *Me? What is wrong with me?"* Her words tumbled out—fast and hot. "You need to learn some office skills." She fisted her hands. "Do you know why? Because I won't be here forever."

Crossing his arms over his chest, he lifted his chin. "Not my problem."

"Don't you get it? Heather won't return until sometime in the fall." She rested her hands against his desk and stared him straight in the eyes. "You need to help with the work duties. If I wasn't here, Ben would do all the work. Plus, as the election gets closer, he'll need more of your help."

Shrugging, Abe fixed his gaze on the glob of grape jelly clinging to the edge of the desk. In one swift movement, he swiped a finger across the sticky mess. "Sounds like his problem, not mine—not that he will win."

Lily's heart slammed against her chest. "What did you say?"

Abe held a finger coated in grape jelly above his lips. His cheeks turned pink. Quickly, he jammed his finger into his mouth, removing the evidence. "Don't you know anything? With you in the picture, no one will elect him—especially, since you two are living together."

The implications of Abe's words spun through her thoughts. Hadn't she warned Ben? Now, because of his stubbornness, he would lose the election.

Her head throbbed and all the feelings she tamped down bubbled to the surface—anger toward Ben for his stubbornness, irritation at the town gossiping about something private, and most importantly, frustration with her weakness.

She needed to escape—right now—fast, so she could have a minute to think and figure out things. Spinning, she bumped into Ben's broad chest.

He circled her waist with his arms. "Where are you

going?"

She shot a glare in Abe's direction before focusing on Ben. "Home."

Ben scanned the room, stopping for a second on the smashed typewriter before moving to Abe's desk with the grape jelly and powdered sugar dusting the surface, and then finally to the broken phone. He turned to Lily. "Do you want to explain why the typewriter is in bits on the floor and why your pants have a big black stain on the front?"

She glanced downward. Peri's white capris were ruined. Spinning, she faced Abe. "Are you happy now?"

"Hey, I'm not the one who pitched the fit and dropped the typewriter, smashing the thing to smithereens—on *my* donuts, no less." Glaring, he pointed a finger toward Lily. "She nearly killed me."

Brushing a hand against her ruined pants, Lily frowned at Ben. "I warned you this morning."

Digging out his notepad, Abe scrawled across the pages. "Hiring of potential murderers." He looked up at Ben and waved his pen. "The union won't be happy with this news."

Enough. She spun on her heels and marched toward the exit.

"Hey, where do you think you're going?" Abe called out.

Lily ripped open the station doors. "Out."

"You can't leave. Quitting time isn't for hours yet."

Lily rounded on Abe. "You wanna bet?" Uncaring of Abe's or Ben's response, she stormed out of the station.

Chapter 31

Silence descended on the station after Lily's furious departure. Turning toward his office, Ben glanced in Abe's direction. Red-faced and tight-lipped, for once Abe was speechless.

Ben stepped into his office, intending to focus on the contracts, reports, and complaints stacked on his desk. He wasn't successful, though. Through the walls, he could hear Abe voicing his opinion of hiring deranged people to work for the police. He whole-heartedly agreed. No one could ever argue Abe's sanity.

When Ben figured he'd given Lily enough time, he grabbed his coat and walked out of his office. A full hour had passed, and the room still appeared as if a tornado had blown through. In amazement, Ben watched Abe whistling some jaunty tune while sweeping up the mess of broken plastic and scattered paper.

Maybe, after all these years, Abe is in the wrong line of work. Ben needed to give the idea some consideration, but first he wanted to see Lily.

Turning, Abe stopped sweeping. "Where are you going?"

Ben shrugged on his suit coat. "To Lily's."

Abe tossed the broom. It clattered against the edge of the desk. "You've got to be kidding."

Ignoring him, Ben departed the station. During the

drive, he kept turning over the events of today. Lily was under pressure, what with the gossip and all.

Except for his years in college, he'd lived his whole life in Aberdeen. He accepted the chatter as part of living in a small town. Lily wouldn't be used to the constant rumors, though.

He understood her dilemma. She expected him to leave. Truthfully, in the beginning, he'd had the exact same plan. Yet, somewhere along the way circumstances changed and became more complicated, more serious…more important.

Ben parked his truck under the oak tree in her driveway and climbed out. After shutting the door, he started toward the house. Movement on the road caught his attention. Turning, he spotted Lily completing her run. His breath caught in his throat, and his heart squeezed tight. She might be sweating, red-faced, and out of breath, but to him, she looked downright gorgeous.

All the tension in his muscles eased. His worry was ridiculous. After all, she still had a few weeks left of vacation, enough time for him to figure out his plans. Still, a part of him feared she changed her mind, and then what would he do?

Stopping in front of him, Lily looked up. "Why aren't you working?"

Worry wreathed her face, and her voice trembled. He wanted to pull her close and comfort her. Knowing she needed to make the decision on her own, he remained still, giving her a fleeting smile instead. "You mentioned quitting time."

Her brows pinched down. "You're not funny, Ben."

Sighing, he leaned against his truck and crossed both arms over his chest. "Do you want to tell me why you're upset?"

Her cheeks turned pink, and she shifted her gaze downward. "This whole situation is a mess."

His heart ached at the forlorn tone in her voice. "I know, sweetheart."

Her blue-eyed gaze shifted directions, probing his. Silently, she smoothed a hand against his chest.

With one finger, she played with a button on his shirt. "Abe's the most difficult man in the world. He doesn't want to learn anything. All he does is word puzzles, and if he's not doing them, he's gossiping while drawing a salary."

Ben wrapped his fingers around hers. His palm easily spanned her small hand. A protective emotion— pure and visceral—filled him. He wanted to keep her safe and shield her from life's worries. "The town is small. People thrive on gossip."

Silence filled the air separating them.

He watched, waiting to see her reaction.

Slowly, she drew her gaze upward, searching his face. "Abe said you're gonna lose because of me."

She didn't understand the dynamics of the election or of the town. Wanting to assure her everything would be fine, he gathered her in his arms. "I won't."

Taking a deep breath, she leaned back. "You need to move out."

Hooking a finger under her jaw, he tilted her chin upward. "Do you want me to leave?" Holding his breath, he waited for her response.

Closing her eyes, she exhaled and shook her head. "No."

The tension in Ben's muscles eased. He hadn't realized he feared her answer until she responded. He lessened his grip. "Why don't you let me worry about the election?"

Lily bit her lip. "Don't you see? You won't be elected because you're not married. The 'engagement' is a lie—a sham. Once the town finds out, you'll lose."

Ben didn't care about the election. If the choice was between the election or her, the answer was obvious. He didn't need to be mayor. But he did need Lily. "Then we'll marry." The words slipped out before he could stop them. He surprised himself. Not only by the statement he never expected to make, but the fact the idea didn't horrify him as in the past.

Her mouth dropped open, and her eyes widened just a fraction of an inch before narrowing. "What did you say?"

Ben shrugged. "I said we'll get married." He kept his voice calm and assured, knowing she would listen for any inflection contradicting his intention.

Lily broke free and pointed. "You don't want to be married. You just want to win the election." She spun about and marched to the house, slamming shut the kitchen door.

Ben watched her leave, wondering what he said to give her such an impression.

****

Within minutes, Peri burst into the kitchen. "What the hell are you doing? I'm napping."

"I'm venting." All sorts of thoughts, crazy and tumultuous, rushed through Lily, each competing with the next, and all revolved around Ben toying with her emotions.

Peri yawned. "Can you go vent somewhere else, then."

Lily glared. "What are you doing here anyway? I thought you had plans with Maybelline?"

Peri stepped farther into the kitchen. "She dropped me off a while ago. We're going out later." She strolled toward the fridge. "Shouldn't you be working?"

"I quit." Lily dropped into the kitchen chair.

Peri's hand stilled on the door handle. Slowly, she turned. "What did you just say?"

"I said I quit."

Shaking her head, Peri sighed. "Why?"

"Because Ben asked me to marry him."

Peri shut the fridge door. She hurried to the kitchen table and dropped into a chair. Resting an elbow on the placemat, she propped her chin on her curled hand. "And?"

Eagerness lit Peri's gaze. Lily rolled her eyes. "I told him no."

Eyes wide, Peri thrust out her arms. "What? *Why*?"

"Because the proposal was fake." Sadness filled her. Bolting from the chair, Lily paced the kitchen. "He doesn't want to marry. He wants to become mayor."

"Do you realize how many women would kill to have a fake proposal from him?"

Pointing to her chest, she glared. "Do I look crazy to you?"

Ripping open the fridge door, Peri grabbed a bottle of water. "Right now, you do."

Lily stomped to the bedroom. Pausing, she turned. "I'm telling you, Ben is the most stubborn person I've ever met."

"He's not the most stubborn person *I've* met." Peri

stormed from the kitchen.

Later that night, Lily begged and pleaded with him to see reason.

Ben fisted hands to his hips. "Did you lie?"

His gaze held hers, challenging. Her stomach fluttered. She couldn't lie to him. She looked down at her hands. "No."

He pulled her close, resting his head atop hers. "Then I don't see what the problem is."

She had only herself to blame. If she'd just kept her mouth shut and hadn't admitted she enjoyed him staying here, she wouldn't have this dilemma.

Here was a perfect example of why honesty was bad. Very bad. In fact, being honest was so horrible, she soon realized Ben intended to take permanent residence.

Just when she didn't think the situation could become any worse, he trotted her about town. On Friday night, they went to Aberdeeni's for dinner. While there, Ben introduced her to Marco, the owner. Sipping a glass of wine, she listened as they discussed Ben's plans as mayor.

On Saturday, he took her to his baseball game.

Dax rode with them and shared antics of their childhood.

Afterward, they stopped at Papa's Pizza, where the team congregated. The affection Ben's teammates shared showed in their camaraderie. Each tried to out-best the other as to who was the most valuable player on the team.

Lily enjoyed their easy banter. What surprised her most, though, was how quickly she was accepted as part of Ben's life. More importantly, not one person suggested he wanted to eliminate her because of her lack of sports knowledge.

On Sunday, he escorted her to church, and then to the Donut and Coffee hour afterward, much to Lily's annoyance. She tried to dissuade him, knowing only too well how Mitch and Suzette wouldn't appreciate her presence. In the end, she needn't have worried. They welcomed her, all be it, begrudgingly. Once they realized she hadn't come to help, they smiled and expressed their pleasure to see her. She figured the twenty Ben dropped in their offering basket might have encouraged their enthusiasm.

While Ben introduced her to some of the members of City Council, he kept an arm anchored on her shoulder. Each heaped praise on him, assuring her the town needed him as their mayor, to which his face turned just a bit red.

They ended their day with dinner at his mother's. Claire mixed her praise of Ben with plenty of embarrassing stories of his youth while coaxing Lily into sharing a bit of her life in Buffalo. After dinner, they went home, where he showed her just how much he enjoyed spending time with her.

Lily didn't know what to make of the weekend. She did know all the gallivanting with Ben wouldn't help the gossip. Although, seeing as she no longer worked for him, she wouldn't hear the chatter on Monday.

She woke Monday morning and stepped into the kitchen.

Ben stood at the kitchen sink, pouring coffee into his travel mug. Turning, he smiled. "Good Morning." Setting down the mug and the pot, he reached for her and brushed his lips against hers. "I'll see you at the station."

Lily jerked back, and stepping from his arms, grabbed a cup from the cupboard. "I told you I quit." She poured herself a cup of coffee. "You really need to have your memory checked."

Ben thinned his mouth into a frown. "My memory is perfect, and I don't accept your resignation."

"What?" Lily spun. Coffee dripped on her hand. She slammed the cup on the table and wiped the liquid on the bathrobe. "Why not?"

"I told you before, I'm a man of commitment. Therefore, I expect the same from everyone, including you." He smoothed a kiss across her lips.

She glared.

He laughed. "Don't be late for work." He pulled open the door and stepped outside.

Pinching tight her lips, Lily stared at the closed door. Arguing with a closed door wasn't nearly as effective. She flopped in a chair, debating whether to disobey him. In the end, she stood and marched across the room. The fact was, he needed help. He needed *her*.

Chapter 32

Abe peered over the top of a sheet of paper. "You returned."

Strolling across the lobby, Lily was aware of his gaze. Ignoring his stare, she dropped her purse on the desk.

Setting aside the paper, Abe leaned back in his chair. "I thought you quit."

"Me, too." She handed him a cup of coffee and a white paper bag. *What makes me want to please him? To be accepted? Or, do I appease him to make life easier for Ben, or myself?*

Abe glanced toward the items. "Are these a peace offering?"

Maybe both. "Sure." Lily shrugged. "Why not?"

He reached for the bag then stopped and shot her a frown. "Do I have reason to be concerned?"

Does he seriously think I'd poison him? The question nearly slipped from her mouth. She stopped herself. "They're fine. Seriously."

Abe scowled, but he dug one donut out of the bag and studied it for a moment, before taking a bite. "I see you remembered what I liked."

Crumbles of white powder and chunks of donuts tumbled from his mouth. Lily ignored the disgusting look and walked toward her desk. "What are you reading?" The paper wasn't a report, seeing as he avoided them as if they were the plague. His sly smile was a real concern, too.

Abe waved the sheet of paper. "I just printed it. It's *The Aberdeen Almanac*." He bit into his donut. More white powder dusted his chin and shirt. "Boy, Rose sure has a way with words." Taking another large bite, he shoved the printed paper toward her.

Skimming the page, Lily gasped, her heart beat rapidly. The details of her relationship with Ben were printed in black, block type. She pulled her gaze from the intrusive words. "Where did she get this information?"

Abe shrugged. "Don't know why she wouldn't, seeing as she's your neighbor."

Her stomach flopped. Blinking, she jerked back. "What did you say?"

Abe swallowed the bite of donut. "She's lives right next door to Dax. Don't you know any of your neighbors?"

Lily snagged the offensive article and marched into Ben's office.

Ben sat at his desk, reading a stack of papers. He looked up. "Good morning again."

Dismissing the look of victory in his eyes, Lily thrust the paper toward him. "Did you know Rose Smith lives behind our house?"

His brow rose.

The look of victory in his eyes turned to amusement. Lily closed her eyes and exhaled. "I meant *my* house."

Dropping the report, Ben stood and edged around the desk. He stopped in front of her and smiled. "Yes, I know where Rose lives. Everyone does. Her home isn't exactly a secret."

Everyone knows, except me. Lily rested her hands on her hips. "Well? How will you stop her gossiping about us?"

He shrugged. "I can't control what people say." He nudged aside her hands and gripped her waist, drawing her close. "If I did, I wouldn't have any time for my actual job, which is keeping the residents of the town safe."

Lily fisted her hands against his chest. "We should be allowed a scrap of privacy."

"You're right, sweetheart." Ben rested his chin on her head. "And at some point, we will but not right now."

She heaved a drawn-out sigh. Flattening her palms, she smoothed the wrinkles from the front of his shirt. "So, we have no choice but to accept it?"

Ben laced together his fingers behind her back. "Eventually, people will lose interest."

The gossip continued. Rose shared every tiny detail she discovered in her blog, and every place Lily stopped, people lowered their voices while their gaze followed her. The whole situation drove her crazy.

On Wednesday, she arrived at work in a foul mood. She spent a good portion of her evening prior, reading the past articles. Seeing Abe reading the newest edition didn't help matters. "When will people stop caring?"

Abe took a big bite of donut and a sip of coffee. Setting down his cup, he leaned back and smiled. "You probably won't be pleased with this news."

Lily dropped into the chair. "What now?"

He took another sip of coffee, before snapping open his paper napkin and dabbing the white powder dusting his lips.

Desperately searching for inner peace, Lily gritted her teeth.

Finally, he crumpled the napkin and tossed the dirty mess in the trash. "Ben has an opponent now."

"An opponent?" Lily's stomach tumbled. "For the election?"

Nodding, Abe sipped his coffee. "Jackson Curtis."

Lily searched her memory but without success. "Who's Jackson Curtis?"

"He owns the Aberdeen Feed. He's real popular, plus he's been married to Betsy for nearly thirty years."

Grabbing the paper from Abe's desk, she marched into Ben's office and thrust the sheet toward him. "Did you read the latest gossip?"

Ben rocked back in the chair and stacked his hands behind his head. "No. Anything interesting?"

She fisted her hands. *What the heck? He behaves like I want pleasant conversation.* "Did you know Jackson Curtis is running for mayor?"

Ben shrugged. "So?"

He took the news just a bit too casually for Lily's peace of mind. "You do understand who Jackson Curtis is, right?" She dropped her hands to her hips. "He's a businessman, gets along with everyone, and he's been married to the same woman for like…ever."

Leaning forward, Ben propped his elbows on the desk and steepled his fingers. "You think because of those reasons he's a guaranteed win?"

Lily jammed her fists downward. "You need to take this stuff seriously."

"Lily—"

"I know." Lily thrust her arms upward. "Trust

you." She marched from his office and spent the rest of her shift wondering how to get out of this mess.

Later in the afternoon, Ben stepped out from his office. He stopped at her desk. "I've got a meeting. I won't be back for a while."

Lily watched him leave. *What I need is to get out of town and clear my mind.* As soon as her shift ended, she hurried outside.

Maybelline and Peri waited out front.

Peri turned. "Hey, want to go shopping?"

Hiking her purse on her shoulder, Lily smiled. "You read my mind."

Maybelline dug her keys from her purse. "We can go to the mall in Albany. I'll drive."

"Not until we eat. I'm dying for a double-double," Peri said.

"Fine. I'll get my car, and we'll go to Burger, Burger, Burger drive-thru." Maybelline nodded across the street. "My car is parked over there."

Lily wasn't hungry, but she was so upset, she ordered a grilled chicken sandwich, hoping food, conversation, and shopping would help take her mind off her problems.

Chapter 33

Four hours later, Maybelline pulled into Lily's driveway.

A cramp ripped through Lily. Another soon followed, and her stomach tightened. Flinging open the door, she jumped out. Another cramp gripped her abdomen. Dropping her shopping bags, she clutched her stomach. "Oh *no*."

Peri hurried around the front of the car and stared at her sister. "What's wrong?"

As wave after wave of cramps washed over Lily, she stumbled up the steps. Sweat broke out on her forehead. To calm her stomach, she inhaled a deep breath. The fresh air didn't help. "I'm sick."

"Sick?" Peri blocked Lily's words with her hands. "Stay away."

"Is everything okay?" Claire pointed to the hole in the shrub. "I just left Minnie's when I heard you and Peri." She swept her gaze over Lily's bent form. "Are you sick?"

"I'm fine," Lily lied, smoothing a hand down her front, hoping to soothe her stomach. "Just tired, and feeling a little nauseous."

"Oh dear." Claire clasped her fingers together. "Can I help you with anything?"

Lily didn't want Claire to worry. More importantly, she didn't want Claire to tell Ben. "Oh, no. I'm fine."

Another wave of cramps rolled through her abdomen. She took a deep breath. "I'll feel better once I rest. I'm just exhausted." If she stood outside much longer, she worried she might vomit on Claire's scuffed white sneakers and ruin the lie. Darting up the porch steps, Lily gave a half-hearted wave to Claire.

Peri followed. "You know what's gonna happen now, don't you? We're gonna have a bundle of joy on our hands." She slammed shut the screen door.

Lily reached the bathroom in time to vomit. She vomited three more times before her stomach settled. Stumbling into the bedroom, she flopped on the bed, threw an arm over her head, and moaned.

Peri stepped into the room. "Why so grumpy?"

Groaning, Lily curled into a tight ball. "Thanks for saying I'm grumpy."

Peri chuckled. "Hey, I've seen you sick. You're not a picnic."

Cracking open one eye, Lily glared. "Well, thanks to you, I think I have food poisoning..."

Plopping down on the bed, Peri pressed a hand against the sheets. "Really? How?"

Again, her tummy churned. Lily gritted her teeth and inhaled. "How do you think? Burger, Burger, Burger. I told you eating there would make someone sick." She moaned and clutched her stomach. "Ben needs to close that restaurant."

"What?" Peri thrust out her arms. "He can't, can he?"

The bed rocked causing Lily's stomach to churn. Closing her eyes, she licked the moisture from her upper lip. She didn't have time for this conversation. Couldn't her sister see she was sick? "He's the Chief of

Police. Part of his job description is public safety *and* health."

"I told you not to eat chicken." Peri shook her head. "I'm telling you, eating healthy is terrible for a person. If you'd just eaten those greasy burgers—"

Lily's belly lurched. Whimpering, she drew the sheet upward with shaking hands. "Don't."

Peri heaved a sigh. "Fine. I'll go into town and find you something." Opening the door, she stopped and glared. "I just hope I don't get sick. I've got big plans for July Fourth."

Curling onto her side, Lily tucked her knees to her chin. "I just hope I'm alive by then." She spent the rest of the afternoon in acute pain. Hours later, she fell asleep, exhausted and weak. The next morning, the incessant ringing of the phone woke her. Whether Ben spent the night or not, she had no idea. She just prayed he hadn't noticed anything unpleasant. "Hello?" She croaked.

"Where are you? Today is July Fourth. We need you here," Abe grumbled through the phone line. "Don't tell me you're taking a day off."

She shoved a tangled mass of hair from her eyes. "I'm sick, Abe."

Abe let out a sharp breath.

She could just imagine the scowl creasing his face. At the moment, she didn't care if her absence made him happy or not.

"Oh, I see your plan. You think because you're marrying Ben, you don't need to come to work. Well, let me tell you, this department needs you."

The phone went silent. Sighing, she dropped the cell phone on the table. Right now, all she wanted was more sleep. By dusk, she felt semi-alive and agreed to attend the festival at the city park with Peri. Despite her exhaustion, she wanted to support Ben.

The area was busier than Lily expected. Carnival rides with flashing lights and barkers calling out their games filled the area. Residents swarmed them, each juggling the crowds attempting to reach the front. A multitude of stands selling a variety of different foods circled the area, each with lines ten people deep. Despite the heat of the evening, everyone seemed to be enjoying the area judging from the excitement filling the air.

The heady smell of fried foods and sugar-laden treats made her stomach heave. Hoping to calm her nausea, Lily sipped a soda.

Peri slurped on a dripping, strawberry ice cream cone. Pink cream trickled down the sides, plopping in a sticky mess on her hand. She tilted the cone and licked the trail of melted sugar.

Lily's stomach twisted. She averted her gaze, and sipping the fizzy soda, spotted Maybelline walking toward her. Nudging Peri in the side, she shifted her head.

Peri looked over then back. "Do you want to go to Martinis with us?"

Her stomach heaved. She closed her eyes and blew out a breath. The idea of having a drink was enough to make her want to vomit. "No, I told Ben I'd meet him here."

Peri slid her tongue around the slushy cone. "Suit yourself." She waved and met up with Maybelline.

Wandering through the park, Lily enjoyed the soft sparkling lights illuminating the area and the sounds of happy laughter mingling with carnival music. Passing by groups of people, Lily pasted a smile on her face, hoping to make them believe she felt fine.

They returned her greeting.

Sally Maple approached. "I heard the news."

Turning, Lily hugged her arms over her chest and smiled. "About Ben and the election?"

Sally waved a hand. "Goodness no." She leaned in and patted Lily's stomach. "About your sickness. So, how are you feeling?"

Surprised by Sally's bold action, Lily stepped back. "I'm just exhausted."

Sally nodded. "Oh, I know exactly how you feel."

Lily widened her eyes. *So, Sally experienced the same from Burger, Burger, Burger?* "Really?"

"Oh, my yes." Sally held up her fingers. "Three times. All were ghastly. Vomited for months."

For months? I can barely handle twenty-four hours. She empathized with Sally. Since her bout with food poisoning, she didn't wish this misery on anyone. "I should have expected this situation to happen."

"It's a happy circumstance, right?"

Lily didn't consider vomiting for twenty-four hours a happy circumstance. On the other hand, she'd survived the Burger, Burger, Burger food poisoning incident. "Well, I guess my condition could be worse."

"Trust me, things will get better." Sally hugged her.

Frowning, Lily watched Sally brush past a couple, casting a glance over her shoulder. *Why the concern?* A soft breeze kicked up, tossing hair into her face. Brushing her fingers through the tangled strands, she turned and watched the crowds.

"You must be excited."

Lily yanked her gaze back to see Rose Smith standing in front of her, a look of anticipation lit her eyes. *Excited? Hardly.* She forced a smile. "Thank you, I am."

Rose grabbed Lily's hand. "I'm sure Ben is thrilled, too."

Seeing as he'd worked non-stop for the past few days, Lily didn't know how he could be—and if he *was* excited by her food-poisoning, she'd discuss with him more than just the closure of the restaurant. "Oh, he doesn't know." She extracted her hand from Rose's grip. "I plan to tell him later, though, and I'll expect action."

"He will." Rose waved a hand. "Ben's an honorable man."

He is, but still... Lily rubbed a hand across her stomach. "Well, I certainly hope so. I don't want this situation to happen to anyone else."

Rose's mouth dropped open, and her eyes widened.

Lily flinched, wondering what caused such a reaction. Only, Rose ambled away before she could ask.

A few feet away, Rose stopped to talk to Joan Peabody. Leaning in, Rose cupped a hand to Joan's ear. Both women turned in her direction for a brief second.

Dismissing their odd behavior, Lily found a vacant bench. Sighing, she sat, thankful for a minute alone and just watched the activity.

People milled about, happily enjoying the pleasant evening. Colorful lights flashed from the rides, beating time to the music thrumming from the loud speakers dotting the park. The swell of excitement was palpable in the air.

The smell of fried food and sugary sweets turned Lily's stomach. She closed her eyes and took a deep breath, hoping to stop the rush of sickness.

"You look like you could use a long nap."

Opening her eyes, Lily watched Father Frank take the empty space next to her. "A nap does sound wonderful."

Frank patted her wrist. "I imagine you'll feel tired for a while."

Never in her life had she experienced so much concern for her health—and from virtual strangers, too. The feeling was—nice. Lily smiled. "I just wish the whole thing hadn't happened."

Frank frowned. "Oh, I'm sure you don't mean those words."

I'm pretty certain I do. Who wants food poisoning? Taking a deep breath, Lily waved a hand over her stomach. "I just meant I hadn't planned on this complication."

Sighing, Frank shook his head. "Everything will turn out okay. Ben certainly will do the right thing. I'll make certain he does."

Sitting straighter, Lily shifted her attention. "I didn't mean to cause Ben trouble."

Frank patted her leg. "Don't worry. I'll take care of everything." He stood and smiled. "Now, I expect to see you both in my office, promptly at nine tomorrow. We have much to discuss."

Heat burned Lily's cheek. *He knows Ben's living at my house.* She stared at her hands. "We'll be there, Father." When he left, she closed her eyes and rested her head against the back of the bench, wondering how much trouble she'd gotten Ben into.

"Do you want to go home?"

Lily snapped open her eyes. Ben stood in front of her, a look of concern in his eyes. Furrowing her brow, she surveyed the area. "What about work?"

Ben placed a gentle kiss on her forehead. "My men know where to find me."

Her muscles tensed. *I'm already in trouble with Father Frank. What about the rest of the town?* "But the fireworks. You'll miss them."

Winking, Ben held out his hand. "How about we make some of our own?"

She looked up and saw warmth deep in his eyes. Heat suffused her. *Time to take some of Peri's advice and not worry—besides, I'm leaving soon, anyway.* Smiling, she gripped his proffered hand. "I'm ready whenever you are."

He dropped his arm over her shoulder, squeezing gently. "Then let's go."

She just hoped, when the time came, she could fix her broken heart.

Chapter 34

Lily woke the next morning to bright sunlight streaming through the bedroom windows. Rolling to her side, she cracked open one eye. The bedside clock read nine. They were late. She shot upright in the bed, searching for Ben. He wasn't in the room.

The clink of dishes in the kitchen sounded through the closed bedroom door. Scrambling out of bed, she threw on an outfit and darted into the kitchen. "You need to get dressed. We're late." She hurried toward the bedroom.

Catching her by the shoulders, Ben drew her against him.

She landed with a thud against his chest.

Wrapping his arms around her waist and bending down, Ben nuzzled her neck. "Late for what?"

His warm breath brushed against her flesh. Tingles raced down her spine. Biting her lips, she did her best to ignore the havoc his kisses created. She leaned back and tilted her head to the side. "Last night, I saw Father Frank. He asked for us to meet. Only, I forgot to tell you."

The kissing stopped. He straightened and turned her. "What?"

She pulled back. "I think it's because you're living here."

Ben chuckled. "Don't be ridiculous."

Pressing a hand against his chest, she scowled. "I'm serious. He's a priest. Of course, he wouldn't approve."

Ben leaned back and stared down. "Frank wouldn't involve himself in our relationship."

Lily dropped her hands to her hips. "Well, what other reason could he have?"

Sighing, he clutched her hand and drew her to the table. Gently, he pressed her into the chair and knelt. "Lily, we need to talk."

She arched a brow. His eyes were lined in worry, and his face stretched taut. Reaching out, she pressed a hand on his shoulder. "Ben, what is wrong?"

"I hadn't planned on telling you, because I figured the gossip would die." He licked his lips. "But, it hasn't."

She snapped back her head and pressed a hand to her mouth. "Oh no. Is he concerned you'll lose the election because of me?" She jumped from the chair and began to pace. "I knew it." She threw a glance over her shoulder. "I warned you people wouldn't be happy."

He stood and caught her wrist. "Frank doesn't care whether we live together or not. Neither do the others."

She drew together her brow and fanned out a hand. "What, then?"

He pulled her against him and wrapped his arms around her waist. "Everyone thinks you're pregnant."

Lily stiffened, and a soft buzzing drowned out all the questions swirling through her head. She stepped back, and crossing her arms over her chest, dropped into the chair. *What the heck? Sure, I've been sick. Still, why will anyone jump to such a conclusion...unless...*

341

She gasped. "I bet Peri told everyone I'm pregnant."

Ben leaned against the counter. "Why would she say such a thing?"

Jumping up from the chair, she rushed forward and dug her fingers into the soft cotton of his shirt. "Don't you understand? Her whole goal since I arrived has been to get us together." She debated the best way to kill her sister—quick and painless or slow and agonizing. Either way, Peri would pay for her big mouth.

Chuckling, Ben drew her closer and rubbed his hands down her tense back. "Don't tell me, she's worried about my election, too?"

Lily pulled back. "Why are you laughing? She has some crazy idea we're in love…"

Ben stilled his hands. "And, of course, we're not?"

She opened her mouth. No sound came out. His eyes narrowed and his hands tightened on her sides. He looked furious. Of course, he would be. The last thing he wanted was love—and definitely not marriage or children.

And she…well, she wanted all of those things. A lump in her throat threatened to choke her. She swallowed back the pain. *What is wrong with me? Why do I keep falling for men who don't want to be serious?* Humiliated to the core, she dropped her hands and wiggled free. He caught her before she could move away.

"*Lily*…" He sighed.

Fixing her gaze on the house behind hers, Lily pressed fingers to her mouth. "Oh no." She whirled. "I bet Rose is the one."

Ben gazed toward the yard then back. "What?"

Lily pinched tight her lips. "Don't you see? She sees you living here and writes about us. Now, with Peri telling people I'm pregnant…" She fanned a hand. "You're the police chief. You need to make Rose stop."

Ben heaved a sigh. "No."

Shoving her hands against her hips, Lily frowned. "Why not?"

He gritted his teeth and glared. "Because it's her First Amendment right."

Lily threw up her arms. "But, she's discussing us."

"For God's sake, so is everyone else. If I arrested her for gossiping, I'd need to arrest the whole town." Ben raked fingers through his hair. "Aberdeen's jail isn't big enough to hold everyone."

Just my luck, I came to the one town with a jail too small and a police chief who refuses to address the matter.

She broke free and stepped back. "Well, you just better hope the talk stops." Storming toward the bedroom, she shoved open the door then pivoted. "Because, I'm a woman on edge, and there's no telling what I might do." She stepped inside and slammed shut the door.

Chapter 35

Lily didn't get the opportunity to confront her sister. Peri's note on the counter, unseen until later in the day, stated she was at the lake for the day. Lily figured her sister was lucky. Maybe by tomorrow, her anger would abate, and she could calmly and rationally discover exactly what Peri told people.

Only on Monday morning, she was still furious. Plus, with Peri still out, she didn't get any answers to her questions. Her day got progressively worse. People streamed into the station seeking her out.

Since starting to work for Ben, people stopped by every day, all day, just to gossip with Abe. On Monday, though, they directed the questions to her—which meant she spent the morning discussing the whole wedding/non-pregnancy gossip. Despite her honesty, no one believed her. They couldn't imagine any woman who wouldn't want to marry Ben.

She couldn't imagine not wanting to marry him, either. Maybe if Ben was here to explain, they'd see the truth. Only, he was busy in a meeting with the City Council.

By the afternoon, she gave up on the truth, not because she wanted to lie, but because she didn't want to ruin his chances in the election. Everyone so thrilled, stating he was a sure winner.

As she walked home, gnawing guilt filled her. *Why*

didn't I just say I was too busy to discuss the matter? Why didn't I insist on the truth? I'm so stupid. I've made a mess of everything. Worried and annoyed, she stepped into the kitchen.

Peri stood at the counter. Her face was burnt from a weekend in the sun, and her hair was a tangled mess of blonde curls. She turned. "What's up?"

Blasé? Really? Lily stormed across the room. "What the heck did you tell people about my sickness?"

Barely glancing in Lily's direction, Peri ripped open the fridge. "What do you mean?"

Fisting her hands, Lily slammed them against her hips. "You told everyone I was pregnant."

Peri shut the fridge door and straightened. "No, I didn't."

Lily flung up her arms. "Then tell me how come the whole town thinks I'm pregnant?"

"I don't know." Peri cracked open the bottle. "I told them you were sick—which was the truth."

Arching her brow, she waved a hand. "Did you tell them I had food poisoning because of Burger, Burger, Burger?"

"And have Ben close the place? I don't think so." Peri lifted the bottle and took a big gulp. "Besides, why are you complaining? Marrying Ben and having his baby is far more exciting than food poisoning."

Lily flung up her arms. "I'm *not pregnant*."

The kitchen door opened.

Ben strolled into the house.

She pointed a finger. "You really need to do something about Burger, Burger, Burger. Because of them, everyone believes I'm pregnant." She bit her lip. *Why didn't I try harder to force people to hear the truth?*

Peri's eyes widened, and her mouth gaped. "Wait." Holding up a hand, she turned to Ben. "You can't close them, can you?"

He leaned against the counter and crossed his arms over his chest. "No."

Lily threw her arms out to the side. "Why not? You're part of Public Safety."

Ben shrugged. "But, not part of Public Health."

A rush of air escaped Peri. "Excellent. I don't know what I'd do if you closed them." Sighing, she started toward the living room. "I love that place."

Tuesday wasn't any better. Lily stopped for coffee on her way to work. The minute she entered the café, the only thing the people wanted to discuss was the wedding and the baby. Everyone seemed pleased with the news.

Worried about the misinformation flying about town, including her own, she left the cafe, disheartened.

Jenny Pickler darted from the bank. Scowling, she pointed. "You purposely became pregnant just to trap Ben."

The accusation was like a slap in Lily's face. She stepped backward and glared. "I didn't 'trap' him."

Jenny fluffed her hair and straightened her shoulders. "Oh please, he wouldn't get married, otherwise. He doesn't fall in love, and he's not the kind to commit—especially to a woman not from Aberdeen. He tried once with a woman from New York City and failed. Why do you think you're different?"

Lily stiffened. *Ben was in a relationship with a woman from out of town? When? What happened? Had they failed because of the distance, or because she wasn't from here?* She clutched her drink. *But, we're different—I'm here.* A little voice called out a warning. *For the moment. What happens when summer ends?* Her heart plummeted. *I can't worry about leaving. Right now, Ben needs me.* Licking her lips, she shoved past Jenny, refusing to react to the hurtful words. "I need to go. Ben's waiting."

Jenny seized hold of Lily's arm. "I could have helped him in the office. With my family's support, he was guaranteed to win."

"He didn't ask you, Jenny." She shrugged free. "He asked me." Fury shook Lily. She should have worked harder to make people believe the truth. Only she hadn't. Staring ahead, she forced her feet forward toward the station. Her mind swirled with thoughts, all bewildering and overwhelming.

Why had she lied?

A little voice inside suggested maybe a part of her wanted the engagement to be a reality. Of course, the idea was crazy. Ben had absolutely no desire for marriage. So, then why hadn't she just fessed up? Lily pulled open the station doors.

Abe narrowed his eyes. "What? No donuts?"

Setting her purse on the table, Lily glanced at Abe. He sat at his desk, a puzzle book in one hand and a frown on his face. *How can one person be so totally and completely self-absorbed?* Scowling, she held out the cup. "Sorry. I've been too busy dealing with the rumors."

Glowering, Abe snatched the cup. "Oh sure, as soon as you're engaged to Ben, you pick up his bad habits." He set the cup on the desk and plucked a notepad from his drawer. "Not certain I can be your child's godfather now. I might not be as gracious as I should be."

Godfather? What the heck? Abe was the last person she'd select. "Where's Ben?" She was surprised at how calm her voice sounded.

Abe's attention remained focused on the pad where he scribbled something. "In his office."

Marching across the room, Lily threw open the door and stormed inside. She pointed to the open doorway. "Abe's planning on being the godfather of our child."

Looking up, Ben discarded the paper. "Excuse me?"

She stopped in front of the desk, leaned forward, and pressed her palms against the surface. "He's planning to be the baby's godfather."

Ben studied her. "You realize you're not pregnant, right?"

She relaxed her grip, and the tension eased in her shoulders. *What's wrong with me? Of course, I'm not pregnant. The gossip has upset me to the point I don't even realize my own words. How embarrassing.* She cleared her throat and ignored her burning cheeks. "I just thought you needed to know what Abe is thinking."

A whisper of a smile flitted across Ben's lips and his eyes sparkled. Lily frowned. Clearly, he didn't understand the import of her words. If he did, he wouldn't act so calm *or* amused.

He rested his elbows on the desk. "Sweetheart, I can assure you, Abe will not be the godfather."

A rush of air burst from her. "Thank goodness." Chewing the edge of her lip, she tapped her fingers on the top of the desk and debated whether to tell him the whole truth. The way talk ran through town, he'd probably hear before she left the station. Straightening her shoulders, she took a deep breath. "I ran into Jenny today."

Ben arched a brow. "Oh?"

The memory of their altercation twisted her stomach into knots. Lily licked her lips and nodded. "She accused me of getting pregnant to trap you." She frowned. "What kind of person does she think I am?"

The smile evaporated from Ben's face. He burst upward. The chair careened backward, crashing into the credenza behind the desk. The loud bang broke the silence. Striding around the desk, he fastened his gaze on Lily. "Are you saying you could be pregnant?"

Lily shook her head. "No. I'm saying if I *were* pregnant, I'd raise the baby on my own."

He dropped his hands on her shoulders and pulled his mouth into a deep scowl. "Excuse me?"

Lily jolted at the sparks shooting from his gaze and the firmness of his grip. "What is the matter?"

Ben held her stare. "What the hell? Are you saying you wouldn't tell me?" He crossed his arms over his chest.

Lily snapped back her head. *How dare he take that tone! Doesn't he realize I am doing him a favor, relieving him of a burden he hadn't asked for and probably doesn't want?* She curled her lip. *Fine. If the truth is that important...* She waved a hand. "Of course, if you're that insistent, then yes, I'd tell you. I just wouldn't expect you to help."

He stiffened. His dark eyes burned and his lips seamed into a thin line. She had never seen him so furious, including the great raccoon incident. She met his glare with one of her own. "Why are you upset? I'd think you'd be relieved. Most men would be grateful."

The tick returned to his eyes, the muscle flexed in his cheek, and the fabric of his shirt tightened on his biceps.

She checked her last thought. *Now* was the angriest she'd ever seen Ben.

"I'm not most men," he growled.

Lily sighed. "Okay, fine, but I'm not pregnant, remember?"

"But, it could happen."

Her stomach lurched. Any bravado she had disappeared. "What?"

He blew out a breath and raked his fingers through his hair. "Are you on birth control?"

Of course, she wasn't. She hadn't planned on having sex during her vacation. When she left Buffalo, birth control wasn't a concern. Enjoying her summer was, though, and right now, she was so far from enjoyment she couldn't even imagine the feeling. "Well, no." Heat burned her cheeks. She shifted her attention to her hands. "You're taking care of it."

Pressing a finger to her chin, Ben tilted up her head. "Sweetheart, condoms are not foolproof."

His gaze was gentle and his words were intended to soothe. Only neither comforted her. She'd been so busy denying the pregnancy, she never considered the possibility. She couldn't be, though…could she? She stiffened. *Of course not.* She pulled back and frowned. "Well, you don't need to worry, because I'm not pregnant, and I don't plan on getting pregnant in the near future, either."

Ben smoothed a piece of hair from her face.

"You'd tell me, though, right? Because you realize, as the father I have the right to know?"

She searched his face, wondering what the heck he expected her to say. His expression gave away nothing. Finally, she blew out a breath. *He is right. He deserved to know.* "Of course. I already told you I would." She pressed a hand against his chest. His muscles flexed then relaxed. She frowned. "Are you happy, now?"

He smiled. "Immensely."

Lily's stomach tumbled. *Why does he look so pleased?*

****

On Wednesday, instead of a greeting from Abe, she noticed his giddy smile. Her stomach lurched. Lily narrowed her gaze.

He slid *The Aberdeen Times* across the desk.

She dropped her gaze and scanned the front page. She stiffened and the muscles in her neck tightened. In bold letters was the announcement of her pregnancy. The article went into more detail, discussing possible plans for the ceremony and reception.

Quotes from people wishing a future of happiness to the bride and groom filled the paper. Included in the article was speculation on whether the baby would be a boy or a girl. The town was eighty-twenty that they'd have a boy. If she didn't know better, she would think she was engaged to the Prince of England. Lily flopped into the chair. "This news is terrible."

Abe reached across the desk and patted her shoulders. "I'm still the godfather, right?"

On Thursday, Abe waved *The Aberdeen Almanac.* "Boy, another fantastic story."

Ripping the paper from Abe's hands, Lily read the

article. Everything, including her telling the town she and Ben were truly excited, was detailed in black and white. Her pulse thundered and her hands shook. She cursed her stupidity for opening her mouth in the first place. Crumpling the paper, she tossed it in the trash.

"Hey!" Abe slammed down his cup. Coffee sloshed over the sides, marring the pristine surface of his desk. "That paper belongs to me. You didn't have the right to destroy it."

Ignoring him, she marched into Ben's office. "We have a problem."

He glanced from the computer. "Don't tell me. Abe wants to go with us on the honeymoon?"

"Ha. Ha. Very funny." Lily fisted her hands on her hips. "Every minor detail is in the paper. How will we get out of this mess?" *Why am I the only one concerned? Why doesn't he take this situation more seriously? Why isn't he worried about the election?*

Ben moved around the desk and pulled Lily against him. "Sweetheart, for now, we do nothing."

On Friday, she stumbled into the kitchen.

Ben sat at the table, reading the newspaper.

She shoved a strand of disheveled hair from her eyes and studied him. Dressed casually in a pair of jeans and a soft-yellow, collared shirt was an unusual choice for him on a workday. She walked to the counter and grabbed a cup from the cupboard. "Where are you going?"

Ben dropped the paper and stood. "Albany." He glanced at his watch. "I wanted to see you before I left."

She picked up the pot and poured coffee into her cup. "Do you have a meeting there?"

Walking over, he wrapped his arms around her waist. "I guess you could say that." He nuzzled her neck. "I'm late. I need to stop at the office first." Pulling back, he brushed his lips over hers. "I won't be home until later tonight."

Lily slumped her shoulders and blew out a breath. *Great.* She'd have to deal with the gossip on her own. If only she had more energy to handle the whole stupid situation.

Chapter 36

Work waited but, knowing what awaited her, Lily wasn't in a hurry to arrive. Abe would update her on all the gossip regarding the wedding, or he'd express his desire to be the godfather. A continuous stream of people would come into the station, asking all sorts of questions, and despite her denial, she knew they'd persist in their quest. With Ben gone, she was left to deal with this mess.

Settling herself into a kitchen chair, Lily tapped her fingers on the table, searching for a viable excuse to escape work. *Sick? No, Ben won't buy that argument.* She ran a finger along the edge of the placemat. *Doesn't need me?* An image of her desk, piled with reports needing her attention and notes tacked to the front of her computer, flashed through her thoughts. *Nope. Can't use that reason, either.* She propped her cheek on her palm and sighed.

Peri entered the kitchen.

Lily swiveled. Peri rarely woke before noon, and almost never before nine in the morning. "Are you going somewhere?"

"I made plans with Maybelline." Peri strolled over to the cupboards. She opened and closed every single door, slamming shut the last one. "We have nothing to eat."

Lily smiled. Lack of food was hardly a reason to

miss work. However, the excuse was decent enough. "Hey, you want to go to Betty's?"

Peri leaned against the counter. "Don't you have work?"

Lily shrugged one shoulder. "I do, but I could be late."

"Excellent." Peri shifted from the counter and strolled out of the kitchen. She stopped in the doorway. "Give me five minutes. I'll call Maybelline and have her meet us."

Five minutes and another twenty-five passed, and still, Peri wasn't ready. She marched up the stairs and into Peri's room. "What's taking so long?"

Peri studied Lily through the mirror. "Hey, a girl needs time to look her best."

Lily rolled her eyes. "Are you finished now? I don't have all day, you know."

Peri scrunched her face. "Yeah, I know. Work."

Lily stepped into the café.

All conversation ceased, and everyone's gaze swung in their direction.

Coming to Betty's is definitely not my best idea. She turned to Peri and glared. "Do you see what I'm dealing with because of you?"

Peri fluffed her hair. "I made you royalty here." She sashayed to the counter. "You should thank me."

Betty smiled. "I expected you earlier."

"I know. Abe's gonna be mad I'm late." Lily glanced at Peri, before turning to Betty. "Because of his coffee, not me."

Betty chuckled and patted Lily's hand. "Tell him you're not feeling well. Nothing he can do about morning sickness."

Peri propped a hip against the counter. "She has many long months ahead of her."

Mrs. Peabody joined them. "Oh, isn't that the truth. All three of my babies kept me awake most of the night, rocking and rolling. I don't think I ate more than a bite or two each day for the first six months of my pregnancy." She slid a pointed glance toward Lily's tummy. "Once you have them, they don't let you sleep, either."

Lily stiffened. *Babies. Up at night? What the heck?* She glanced toward Peri.

Happily leaning against the counter, Peri followed the conversation with avid interest.

She shot her sister a glare.

Peri lifted one shoulder and waggled her brow.

Sally Maple joined the group and stood next to Lily. "Little Sammy never slept. He was too busy either crying or causing trouble. I'll tell you, he gave us a run for our money."

"Kids." Shaking her head, Peri sighed. "What can you do?"

Grabbing hold of Peri's arm, Lily pulled her aside. "What do you think you are doing?"

Peri ripped free. "I'm making conversation."

Frustration licked at Lily's already frayed nerves. She glanced over toward the group of women. They were busy discussing their children. She turned back. "You're acting like I'm pregnant."

"Jeez. Relax. If I knew you'd be touchy, I would have stayed home." Peri walked back and grabbed their coffee. She headed toward the condiment stand.

Tossing a ten on the counter, Lily grabbed Abe's cup. Glaring at Peri's back, a slow anger burned inside.

Right now, I wish you would have. She stopped at the stand.

Flicking a glance in Lily's direction, Peri opened a pack of sugar and sprinkled the white crystals in her cup. "I don't understand. What's the big deal?"

Lily forced back the urge to pull her hair and scream. Lifting the plastic lid, she poured a small dollop of cream into the dark brew. "The *big deal* is I'm *not* pregnant, and Ben and I are *not* getting married." She glanced over her shoulder.

The women at the counter were in deep conversation.

Turning back, Lily lowered her voice. "The only reason I'm not admitting the truth is because of the election."

Peri swirled a stir stick in her coffee. "So, you'd rather make Ben look like a liar than honest?"

"No. Of course, not." Waving a hand, Lily bit her lip. "I just want to help Ben win."

Peri tilted her cup. "You really want to help him?"

Lily nodded.

"Then marry him."

Lily's stomach lurched.

Pivoting, Peri glanced over her shoulder and smiled. "*That,* sweet sister, will surely get him elected."

But, he doesn't want to get married. Gritting her teeth, Lily waved goodbye to Betty. *I've put myself into a terrible predicament.* She glanced at Peri. "I'm buying donuts for Abe. Do you want to come?"

"Of course. You promised breakfast."

Lily stepped out of Betty's Café. A soft, warm breeze tugged at her hair. She tucked the strands behind her ear and walked along the sidewalk. "They only serve donuts at Dainty's."

Peri shrugged. "Exactly what I want."

Maybelline met them on their way to the donut shop. "Oh, here you are."

"You want to go with us to Dainty's?" Peri sipped her coffee.

"Sure, why not? I'm not eating a donut, though." Maybelline rubbed a hand against her stomach. "Gotta lose weight, you know."

Lily skimmed her gaze over the shorts Maybelline had stuffed herself into. *Maybe foregoing a donut isn't a bad thing.* She continued toward Dainty's.

Maybelline groaned softly. "Oh no. Here come's trouble—"

Lily spied Karla Sweet sauntering toward them. As usual, she was dressed in another provocative, body-hugging outfit. The bright yellow sundress was better suited for a nightclub than a stroll through town. Her cinnamon hair held loose beachy waves.

Karla narrowed her gaze.

The low smile splitting Karla's face caused dread to settle in the pit of Lily's stomach. The desire to run flared inside. However, she refused to cower. She'd stand her ground, even if the effort killed her—which, from the triumph on Karla's face, it just might. She turned to Peri and Maybelline. "Don't say a word. I'll deal with her."

Coming to a stop, Karla slid her gaze over Lily. "I'm glad I spotted you."

Shoving aside Lily, Maybelline dropped pudgy hands to her ample hips. "We wish we could say the same."

Karla smirked. "Looking to lure back John?"

Maybelline stiffened. Her face colored to a deep red, and her mouth pulled down into a fierce scowl. She lifted her chin and glared. "I'm too good for him."

Running her gaze over Maybelline's form, Karla snorted. "Really?" She turned to Lily. "How's Ben doing today?"

Refusing to be intimidated by the arrogant smile on Karla's face, Lily returned the stare. "He's doing fine."

Karla widened her smile and fluffed her hair. "I'm sure he is after last night."

Lily shrugged. "He had a city council meeting."

Karla patted her hair. "Is that what he told you?" She tsked, brushing past. "Interesting."

Lily snapped back her head. *What the heck does she mean?* Frowning, she watched Karla stroll away with her head held high and a sassy sway in her hips. *Did he discover he missed their shared past and stopped over last night to renew their relationship?*

"Who does she think she is?" Peri snapped.

Lily pulled her attention to Maybelline and Peri. They glared at Karla.

"Seriously, did you hear her insult?" Maybelline narrowed her gaze at Karla's departing back. "Trust me, I deserve way better than John."

"Not *him*." Peri tilted her head slightly and wiggled her brows in the direction of Lily.

Grimacing, Maybelline waved a hand. "Oh, right. Don't listen to her. She's just causing trouble. Ben would never be with Karla again."

Lily's heart plunged. "Again?"

Stiffening, Maybelline shot a glance toward Peri.

Peri thinned her gaze into tiny slits and pinched tight her lips.

"What?" Maybelline threw wide her arms. "It's not a state secret. They used to date. Although, once he discovered Karla cheating, he ended the relationship."

Walking toward Dainty's, Lily replayed Maybelline's words. Her heart felt heavy, like it was weighted down with cement bags. Karla and Ben had a past she hadn't known. The memory of him with Karla outside Martinis all those weeks ago returned with vivid clarity. He insisted they were friends. Now, she wondered if he told the truth. She kept her voice casual. "Do you know if City Council had a meeting last night?"

Whipping her attention toward Lily, Peri glared. "Oh, come on. You don't actually think Ben lied?"

Lily didn't know what to believe. She offered a weak shrug. "No." Her voice held little conviction, though.

Peri flung out a hand. "He wouldn't lie."

"She's right." Maybelline opened the door to the donut shop. "He's too ethical, which is exactly why the town loves him."

Today, Shelly stood behind the counter. Folding the top, she held out the oil-saturated white paper bag. "Here you go. Two grape-filled, powdered donuts."

"I'll take two, as well," Maybelline told Shelly.

Frowning, Peri turned to Maybelline. "I thought you didn't want donuts."

"I didn't." Maybelline shrugged. "But, I realized I hadn't eaten my fruit, yet."

"You want anything today?" Shelly wiggled her brows in the direction of Lily's stomach. "The baby might be craving a chocolate-filled. We just made them…"

A note of enticement laced her voice. Lily shook her head.

"The baby might not want them, but I sure do." Peri pointed to the display case. "I'll take two."

Shelly filled the order and handed Peri the bag.

Diving into the bag, Peri dug out one of the donuts and bit into the pastry.

Lily glared at Peri. "Look at you. You have white powder all over your face." She handed Shelly a five-dollar bill, before turning and leaving. Outside, she swiveled and faced Peri. "Stop telling people I'm pregnant."

Peri dusted the white powder from her face. "You want to teach Karla a lesson? Stuff a pillow under your shirt to show her you're pregnant. Or better yet, actually become pregnant."

"*Ooh,* pregnancy *would* teach her a lesson." Maybelline licked the sugar from her fingers.

Lily's knees buckled. "I am not getting pregnant just to spite Karla." She glanced down the side walk. Her heart thumped.

Parked in front of Alexis' shop was Ben's distinctive black vehicle. Moments later, the door swung wide. With a suitcase in one hand, he held open the door.

Alexis breezed out of the boutique. Side-by-side, they strolled toward his vehicle.

Whatever she said caused him to smile.

Stiffening, Lily dug fingers into the curled flap of the paper bag. *Why is he with Alexis?*

Tossing the luggage in the back, Ben offered a hand and helped her into the passenger seat. Minutes later, they sped from town, neither noticing the women staring from down the walkway.

Maybelline wrinkled her brow. "I wonder what Ben's doing with Alexis."

Peri shifted her gaze to Lily. "Don't jump to conclusions."

Lily ignored the warning in Peri's voice. "I'm not jumping to conclusions. You witnessed the same thing as I did. I'm not surprised. Alexis is the type of women he needs."

"What?" Peri threw open her arms. "Do you hear yourself? Ben doesn't love Alexis. I'm telling you, he loves you."

"Let's face it, though—" Maybelline reached for another donut. "Besides Karla, his only other serious relationship was with Taylor."

Lily's heart plummeted. *Ben was in a serious relationship?* She pivoted. "What?"

Munching on her donut, Maybelline wiped a hand across her mouth. "He met her this past Christmas." She bit the donut and chewed. "Actually, just before New Year's. He was in full swinger mode then. Never stayed with a woman for more than a date—two at the most, and only rarely. Of course, this behavior happened after the whole Karla break-up. But for some reason, he really clicked with Taylor. They were pretty serious for a while. He kept running down to the city to see her." Pausing, she swallowed her bite. "I'm telling you, once he started dating Taylor, everyone thought he'd finally settled down. Then things kind of fizzled, and he went back to his old ways—"

Maybelline's voice faded to a dull buzz. The urge to throw up her hand and cover her ears, burned through Lily. She didn't want to hear the words spewing forth, confirming her worst fears. Instead, swallowing back the pain, she remembered the trail of women fawning over Ben.

So, not just Karla, or the dozens of other women, but some Taylor, who did the impossible and attained Ben's heart. Lily gripped tighter the bag. *Again, I'm just another woman, tantalizing and desirable, but not worthy of commitment.* She bit her lip and closed her eyes. *He's worse than Eric. At least, Eric gave the illusion of permanency. Ben only wants a moment, a summer, but not forever.* She stumbled forward, forcing her feet in the direction of the station. *I need to escape, to leave before my heart shatters further, never to be whole again.*

Clutching Lily's arm, Peri stopped her. "Lily, Ben and Alexis are friends." She glanced at Maybelline. "Like siblings, really. Right?"

Maybelline shrugged. "Yeah. Sure."

Lily shrugged free. She wasn't a little girl. She didn't need to be shielded from terrible news. Especially since they all witnessed the evidence. Refusing to permit the knife hovering above her heart to slice downward, she stifled the pain. "Only they're not siblings. Sometimes friends make the best relationships."

Maybelline licked her fingers. "My mother always said you must be friends first."

Peri thrust an elbow into Maybelline's side.

Scowling, Maybelline clutched her waist. "Well, it's true."

"I doubt he's *with* Alexis." Glaring, Peri confronted Lily. "You need to trust him. Ben isn't Eric."

Lily's heart missed a beat, and her stomach lurched. *Why did she bring up my ex? Of course, Ben and Eric are different. Well, almost different.* She fisted her hands. "I realize he's not."

Peri flung out an arm. "You need to give him a chance to explain."

Stopping at the traffic light, Lily pivoted and narrowed her eyes. "No, I don't."

The light changed.

Leaving Peri and Maybelline behind, Lily hurried through the crosswalk. The words Ben spoke earlier swirled through her thoughts. He didn't say what kind of appointment he had, just that he needed to go. *Did he and Alexis have a rendezvous planned? But, if so, why not here?*

The answer was obvious. With the gossip in town, he wouldn't risk the chance of getting caught. She jumped the curb and forced her legs forward. Reaching the steps of the police station, she looked up. From the window, she spotted the back of Abe's balding head. Flexing her fingers, she heaved a sigh, and trudging up the steps, entered the police station.

Frowning, Abe shifted his attention from the puzzle book. "Where the heck have you been?" He snatched the bag and the paper cup from Lily's outstretched hand.

Shoving aside the images of Ben, Karla, and Alexis, she dropped into her chair and focused on the stack of work. Unfortunately, the events of the morning refused to leave her thoughts. She gave up and turned to Abe. "Do you know why Ben went to Albany today?"

Abe didn't glance up from the puzzle. "Said he had an appointment. Probably won't be back until tomorrow."

Lily snapped up her head. "Tomorrow?" The memory of him with the overnight bag flashed through her thoughts. *Why did he say he'll be back tonight, then?* "Why overnight?"

Scowling, Abe looked over the edge of the book. "I have no idea." He sniggered. "But from my experience, his trips to Albany always involve an overnight stay."

Lily slumped in the chair. *So, then, he does have plans with Alexis.* "Will he be alone, or with someone?" She held her breath. Despite what she'd seen, she still didn't want to hear the answer. Somehow, hearing the truth would make the pain all the worse.

"What do you think I am? His secretary?"

Staring down, she curled the edge of a paper. "Do you know if City Council had a meeting last night?"

Abe shifted gaze and frowned. A glob of grape jelly clung to the edge of his lip. "Nah." He waved a hand. "They only have them once a month, on the third Tuesday."

Lily swallowed. "I see." Her heart squeezed and her eyes filled with tears. Ben lied.

Chapter 31

As nine approached, Claire paced the bedroom, her nerves stretch taut. A thousand questions ran through her thoughts. What if she was wrong? What if she ruined everything? What if Ben didn't love Lily?

Claire discarded the last thought. Even though he didn't share his feelings, she wasn't stupid. The fact he had remained with the same woman longer than a date or two was proof enough.

Voices sounded on the stairwell. Claire dashed from the bedroom to see Maybelline and Peri climbing the stairs.

Peri glanced toward the top and stumbled. "What the hell?"

Claire frowned. *You'd think they'd never seen a woman with her hair tucked under a black knit cap and her face painted black, green, and brown.* She beckoned. "Hurry up."

Reaching the top, Maybelline pinched her nose. "What the heck is that smell?"

"Deer urine—" Claire ushered them into the bedroom. "So they don't detect me."

Peri waved a hand in front of her face. "How could they not? You stink."

"The smell is part of the scheme." Claire grabbed the bundle of clothing off the bed and tossed it to Maybelline. "Put on this outfit while I tell Peri the plan."

Wrinkling her nose, Maybelline clutched the mound and frowned. "When I asked for help, I didn't expect to be a burglar."

Claire snapped down her brows. "For goodness sakes. Ben's the police chief. You're not robbing Lily. We're scaring her." She rammed a hand against Maybelline's arm. "Now go. We don't have all night."

Maybelline glared. "Fine." She stomped from the room.

Pivoting, Claire turned and scowled. Peri had stuck her head out the window. She pressed together her lips and marched across the room. "Shut the window. Do you want your sister to see you?"

"Right now, I don't care." Peri scowled. "Your smell is making my eyes water. I'm gonna puke."

Claire wasn't in the mood to listen to Peri's issues. Peri had precisely two choices—be guillotined by the sash or endure the stench. She didn't care which one Peri chose, as long as Lily didn't spot her draped from the ledge. Reaching forward, she nudged the sash.

Peri yelped and yanked back her head.

The window crashed against the sill.

Glaring, Peri rubbed the back of her neck. "Boy, your sweet lady routine is a real lie."

"You need to listen." Pinching down her brows, Claire dropped her hands to her hips. "So, here's the plan. Maybelline and I will be in your backyard, acting like burglars." She pointed. "You will be consoling Lily." She wagged a finger. "*And* when you hear us, you need to ramp up your fear. Make her think someone is trying to break in. She'll want Ben, then."

Peri frowned. "I don't know. I can't see Lily

calling him. She's too upset. She thinks he's with Alexis."

"Bah…" Claire waved a hand. "Alexis isn't Ben's type."

"Yeah, well, you didn't see them together." Peri pulled her mouth into a frown and fisted her hands. "They looked like they were excited to be together."

"Nonsense." Claire shrugged. "Alexis and Ben are friends. Nothing more. Now, will you do what I tell you or not?"

"I kind of had plans for tonight." Peri pinched two fingers against her nose. "I have it on excellent authority one exceedingly sexy fireman will be at Martinis, and I plan on spending some quality time with him."

Claire rolled her eyes. "You can be with Dax another time. Right now, we need to concentrate on your sister."

Peri frowned. "You should know I'm terrible at consoling."

"What do you think?"

Claire turned at the sound of Maybelline's voice.

Maybelline swept across the room with a pirouette.

Claire and Peri burst into laughter.

"What?" Maybelline tugged the black ski cap low.

Peri laughed. "The outfit is a bit tight, don't you think?"

Maybelline's hand dropped to her hip. "Well, *excuse me* for not being tall and thin like a model."

Claire thrust a can at Maybelline. "Put on this paste."

After opening the can, Maybelline sniffed. Gagging, she shoved aside the canister. "I'm not wearing that slime."

Peri leaned in to smell the contents and retched. Wiping her eyes, she wrinkled her nose. "What the heck? The odor is worse than yours."

"Minnie lost one of her cans of deer urine, and the other had just enough for me. I had to create my own. I didn't have much to work with, so I dug in the garbage and found some rotten food. I pureed everything and added some rancid grease. I figured they'd do the trick." Grabbing Maybelline's wrist, she flattened the can against her palm. "Rub some under your arms, around your neck, and behind your ears. We need to cover your scent."

"But I like my scent." Maybelline gave the jar another hesitant glance. "John bought me the perfume. It's incredibly chichi."

"Will you forget John already?" Claire flicked a hand. "He's not good enough for you."

Scowling, Maybelline scooped out a glob. "He's better than this junk."

Claire sighed and ran a shaky hand over her face. "Maybelline, I can only deal with one problem at a time, and right now, I need to make certain Lily doesn't leave, and Ben doesn't hate me." She closed her eyes and mumbled a few words. When she finished, she snapped open her eyes and fixed her gaze on the women. "Tonight, I have a very good chance of ruining two people's lives. Let's pray that I don't."

Chapter 38

Lily wasn't tearful. No, she was furious. Fisting her hands, she paced the small confines of the room. She edged around the bed, only to turn back and follow the path again. A fire burned low in her stomach, and all the mistakes she'd made played through her thoughts.

How foolish am I? She knew all along Ben would find someone else. Why had she allowed herself to fall for him? Well, she might love him, but she'd be darned if she'd stay to witness his revolving door of women. She wasn't a number at the deli, waiting her turn.

Just because the plan was to stay through the summer didn't mean she *had* too. Besides, if she remained here any longer, she'd go crazy. The town was dull and filled with gossip. The people weren't kind, either.

Only, as much as she wanted to believe this lie, she couldn't. Sure, Mitch and Suzette Bird hadn't welcomed her with open arms, but they allowed her to help on the donut committee, and she appreciated their kindness. Of course, Karla and Jenny were envious. She didn't blame them, though. Had the situation been reversed, she'd be jealous, too. The truth was, she *was* jealous. She couldn't fault them for feeling the same.

The rest of the people, though, welcomed her. Papa, from Papa's Pizza, always provided free food for her and Peri. Claire, Maybelline, Betty, Mr. Waverly, even Alexis, had been kind.

The gossip, though, drove her nuts. Although, if she was honest, most of the talk was curious rather than malicious. Plus, the excitement exhibited by the community had been palpable with the 'presumed' engagement and subsequent 'pregnancy.'

Pacing the room, Lily worried her lip, remembering the articles in *The Aberdeen Times* and *Aberdeen Almanac.* The few glimpses she caught were sprinkled with charm and romance, and as much as she hated to admit it, the writing was persuasive enough to make her believe Ben did love her. Why, she'd even miss sour, grumpy Abe.

As the truth settled inside her, her knees buckled. She dropped onto the bed. Somewhere along the way, she'd fallen in love with the town and all its faults, just like she'd fallen in love with Ben. She wished Peri was here, instead of out, so they could leave before her heart broke further.

"What are you doing?"

Lily turned.

Peri lounged against the door jamb, staring.

"I thought you were at Martinis."

Peri stepped into the room. "I was bored."

"On a Thursday night?" Lily arched a brow. "Tonight is Ladies Night. I swear I heard Maybelline say Dax would be there."

"I'll have other chances." She dropped to the bed. "Are you okay?"

She heard the worry in Peri's voice. Tears welled in her eyes. She refused to let them fall. "I'm fine." To cover the lie, she stood and walked to the closet. Throwing open the doors, she stared at the row of Ben's clothing. She trailed fingers across one of his suits. The smell of his cologne filled her nostrils. Lily closed her eyes and squeezed back the tears. She'd need to let Claire know to pick up his clothing. Right now, her emotions were too raw to deal with seeing him. Dropping her hand, she cleared her throat. "You need to pack."

"What? Why?"

Lily tugged one of his shirts off the hanger. *What the heck? He wouldn't even miss it.* Without turning, she piled a few of her shirts over it, effectively hiding the dark fabric from her sister's sharp gaze. "Because we're leaving." She peered over her shoulder and, smoothing a hand over the pile, eyed Peri. "Tonight."

Peri rushed across the room. "We can't leave. Summer isn't over."

"I know, but I need to find another job."

"No, you don't." Peri stood in front of the closet. "You have one at the police station."

Lily nudged aside her sister and walked to the bed. *Where did she get such a crazy idea?* She dumped the clothing into the open luggage. "My job is temporary. Besides, Ben will find someone to replace me. I've seen the line of women."

Peri stepped back and flung out a hand. "You're jumping to conclusions. You need to hear his side of the story."

Lily remembered Peri's words from earlier. *Am I treating Ben the same as Eric?* She didn't believe so, but uncertainty plagued her. "Why? Abe already told me the truth about the council meeting."

Peri shrugged. "Are you sure? He's not exactly on top of events."

Arguing with Peri's logic was impossible. However, given Abe's insistence on the meeting and Karla's suggestion, the conclusion was obvious. "Positive." Lily scooped a handful of panties from the drawer and dropped them into the luggage. The white teddy landed on top. A knife pierced her heart. She lost the opportunity to wear the outfit for Ben. Now, she never would. Blinking back the tears, she stuffed the lingerie beneath a stack of clothing. "Ben's a free man. He never suggested otherwise, and today, I witnessed the proof."

Peri leaned over and scooped out the clothing. "We don't know what happened."

Slapping away Peri's hands, Lily deposited the clothing inside, then smoothed a hand over the top. "You witnessed the same thing I did." Swallowing past the lump in her throat, she flipped shut the top of the luggage. "You better start packing."

"Did you hear that noise?"

Lily glanced up.

Peri's fingers were weaved together, and her gaze darted to the window and back.

Just another fanciful notion to prevent us from leaving. "I didn't hear anything."

Peri pointed toward the window. "I'm telling you, someone is outside."

Zipping shut the luggage, Lily straightened. She strained to hear any unusual sound. Only the soughing of wind and the Waverlys' dog barking filled the night. She strolled across the room and reached for the curtain. "I'm certain no one is out there."

Grabbing Lily's arm, Peri dragged her away. "What are you doing? You'll make yourself a target."

She's lost her mind. Breaking free, Lily walked toward the door. "Don't be ridiculous. The noise is probably raccoons."

Peri hugged her arms across her chest and shuddered. "I hate raccoons."

Lily rolled her eyes, and opening the door, reached for the light switch. Ben's warning rang through her thoughts. *No one is outside, but still...* She dropped her hand. "Even so, raccoons can't break into the house."

"Oh really?" Peri lifted her arms and wiggled her fingers. "Have you seen their hands?"

Hurrying across the kitchen, Lily lifted the curtain on the back door. A sliver of moonlight shone through the break. She peeked over her shoulder. Peri's mouth gaped, and her eyes were as wide as saucers. Under other circumstances, she'd laugh at her sister's fear. Right now, though, nothing was humorous. She peered into the darkness. Nothing moved, and no threatening sound broke the night. "They're harmless."

"Harmless? I don't think so." Peri ran toward the door, pressed her back against the hard wood, and glared. "Who knows what they'll do if we ruin their plans?"

"Raccoons don't have 'plans.'" Lily dropped the curtain.

Reaching out, Peri caught Lily's wrist. "Don't!"

Lily whirled and frowned. "Why are you yelling?"

Swiveling her gaze, Peri fanned a hand. "I'm just…" She bit her lip and glanced at the door. "Scaring them."

Yanking free from Peri's biting grip, Lily grabbed the door knob. "Relax. I'm just going outside to frighten them."

"What if the noise is from a burglar?"

Turning, Lily burst into laughter. "A burglar? Here?"

Peri crossed her arms over her chest. "Well, guess what? For your information, Maybelline told me the other day, some man snuck into Mrs. Shapiro's backyard." Shuddering, she wedged herself between Lily and the door. "When she opened the door, he hit her on the head and knocked her out."

Mrs. Shapiro robbed? Ben never told me. Her heart thundered, and instinct warred with common sense. Lily pressed a hand to her mouth. "I hadn't heard."

With her back pressed against the door, Peri glued her palms to the surface. "Maybe we should turn on the light to...uh..." Her gaze darted to the door. She turned back and arched a brow. "Scare them."

"Them?" Lily frowned. "How do you know there're more than one?"

Peri bit her lip. "I...uh, just figured there must be."

Lily rolled her eyes. *Okay, now I know she's nuts.* "A gang of burglars?" Shoving aside Peri, she reached for the door knob. The sound of a man's voice, indistinct and muffled, sounded. She stilled. Her pulse raced, and a whirlwind of terrifying thoughts scurried through her mind. "Someone *is* out there."

Stiffening, Peri wrung together her fingers. "I told you." She bit her lip. "What do we do?"

Leaning against the side cabinet, Lily crouched. She cupped her palms, pressing them against her chest. "I don't know."

Peri squatted. "Call Ben. He'll help."

Yesterday, maybe. Tonight, hardly. She ignored the knife twisting in her heart. "He's busy. Remember?"

"You are *so* stubborn." Peri flung out her arm. "Where's your phone? I'll call him if you won't."

Lily held a stiff finger to her lips. "Be quiet. The burglar doesn't need to know we're frightened." Raising an arm, she trailed her fingers across the drawers next to her until she found the one she wanted

"But we *are* scared," Peri hissed.

Glaring, Lily opened a kitchen drawer.

Peri leaned close. "What are you doing?"

"Getting a weapon." The confidence in her voice belied the fear churning within. With fumbling fingers, she touched a familiar object and extracted the long, serrated knife—sharp enough to hurt someone. As she gripped the weapon against her chest, she couldn't keep her hands from shaking. *Be brave...* She took a deep breath. "You open the door, and I'll run out."

"Are you crazy? You'll kill someone." Peri crossed her arms over her chest. "Which by the way won't make Ben happy. The last thing he wants is a wife who's a convicted murder."

Lily darted a glance toward Peri. "He doesn't want a wife." She licked her lips. "Besides, it's either them or us. If someone is getting hurt, I'd prefer it to be them."

"I'd prefer it not to be anyone," Peri mumbled.

The doorknob rattled.

Peri whimpered.

Closing her eyes, Lily tightened her grip.

Metal scraped against metal.

Lily stood and poised her body for the oncoming attack. Her pulse raced, and her heart thundered. Holding her breath, she lifted the knife above her head. *You're fearless...*She didn't have the strength to take down a man, and she certainly wouldn't outweigh him. Her only advantage was the element of surprise. *When the door opens, I'll lunge.* With her heart thundering and her hands shaking, she pressed her back against the wall.

Peri grabbed the back of Lily's shirt.

The door opened.

Shrieking, Peri jerked back.

Lily lost her balance, slamming into Peri. The knife slipped from her fingers and clattered to the floor, useless.

Chapter 39

Ben flipped the light switch. He slid his gaze from Lily to the floor then up. "What the hell? You nearly killed me."

Lily bit back a sigh at the familiar silhouette. Her heart thudded. Ben's arms circled her waist. She broke free and stepped back. His face looked tired and his gaze, worried. "What are you doing here?"

"A call came into the station, so they notified me." He knitted together his brows. "Besides, I told you I would be back later."

"Oh please." Peri shoved her way in front of Lily. "We caught you today leaving town with Alexis."

Shrugging, he shifted his gaze between the two women. "So?"

Peri dropped her hands to her hips and her mouth gaped. "You actually admit you were with her?"

Closing her eyes, Lily silently prayed to hear words other than the truth.

Ben leaned against the counter and stretched out his long legs. "Why would I deny it?"

Lily slumped her shoulders and dipped her head. *The truth hurts more than I expected.*

Narrowing her gaze, Peri threw up her arms. "That's it. The wedding's canceled."

Lily clamped a hand over Peri's mouth. "We're not getting married."

Peri shoved aside Lily's hand. "Well, now you're not. You can't marry a man who's an admitted cheat and liar." Tapping her foot on the floor, she eyed Ben. "And you can just forget about seeing your baby, too."

Flaring his nostrils, Ben faced Lily. "What the hell is she talking about?"

Peri pointed. "She fell in love with you, and you broke her heart."

Heat crowded Lily's face. *Why the hell would Peri tell him such a thing?* She vowed the minute she and Peri were alone, she would explain the meaning of having your sister's back—which included keeping secrets. "No, you didn't."

"Not true." Peri turned to Ben and glared for a second, before returning her glare to Lily. "If you didn't, you wouldn't care if he went on a date last night with Karla, and then today with Alexis. You certainly wouldn't make us go back to Buffalo tonight."

Ben jerked away from the counter. "I *what*?"

Peri dropped her hands to her hips. "Oh, don't try to deny it."

Arching a brow, Ben swung his gaze to Lily.

Discussing his dates, or her broken heart, was not an option, and in no way would she admit she'd stupidly fallen in love. Her heart wobbled, and a lump formed in her throat. Peering at the ground, she threaded together her fingers. "Karla told us."

Jamming her hands against his hips, Peri confronted Ben. "Why would you want Karla?"

Lily snapped up her gaze and searched Ben's face. *Why her and not me?*

Peri flung wide her arms. "She'd be terrible as the mayor's wife. She's too cocky and talks too much."

Leaning back, Ben rested his hands on the edge of the counter and held Lily's stare. "I couldn't have possibly been with Karla. I was at the City Council meeting last night."

How dare he lie. Lily stiffened. "No, you weren't." She jabbed a finger in the air. "I asked Abe, and he said there wasn't one."

Ben narrowed his gaze. "For God sakes, why did you ask him? The only thing he pays attention to is his word puzzles."

Peri leaned into Lily's side. "He has a point. The man does have an inordinate fascination with those stupid magazines. I mean, really, who wants to spend all day figuring out words? Sounds boring." She lifted her chin and glared at Ben. "But…you still haven't explained your rendezvous with Alexis today…*with* luggage…"

The muscle flexed in Ben's cheek, and the twitch in his eye returned.

Both were a sure sign an explosion was near. She considered warning Peri then decided against the idea. Her sister would find out soon enough.

Flinching, Peri took a step back. She glared for a moment before throwing up her hands and stomping to the kitchen door. "Fine. I'll leave." Stopping, she turned and scowled. "You should know, though, I don't appreciate you breaking my sister's heart."

Ben fixed his gaze on Lily. "If she didn't jump to conclusions, her heart wouldn't be broken."

Lily's stomach tumbled, and a niggling of doubt flitted through her thoughts.

Peri gasped. "I told her the very same thing." She swiveled her gaze to Lily. "Time for you to figure things out."

Reaching out, Lily caught Peri's arm. "Wait. Where are you going?"

Peri flicked a glance toward Ben.

Seaming his lips, he raised a brow.

Peri peered out the kitchen window. A smile spread across her face. "To get ready. I've got some plans of my own." She pivoted and left the room.

The living room door swung shut with a quiet swoosh.

Lily turned and faced Ben. His gaze held a note of concern.

Bending low, Ben scooped the knife from the floor. He studied the sharp edge for a second, before placing the weapon on the counter and sighing. "You're leaving?"

Her stomach wobbled. She dropped into the kitchen chair and stared at her hands. "It's time."

Ben gripped the counter edge. "I hoped you'd stay."

The tender tone in Ben's voice nearly undid her. Lily lifted her chin. "I've been cheated on before. I won't allow any man to hurt me again."

****

"Ah, right." Leaning back against the counter, Ben stretched out his legs and crossed his arms over his chest. His throat tightened and his chest hurt. He forced out the painful words. "I forgot I'm dating other people."

Lily straightened her shoulders. "Leaving is for the best. You'll have the freedom to do what you want."

Taking a deep breath, he sighed. "And you only want what's best for me?" Since when had he given the impression he wanted his freedom? Sure, in the beginning, he considered her an exciting diversion—an extension of his time with Taylor—short-term and not destined to last. But somewhere along the way, the challenge of seducing her changed to needing her.

"Of course." Nodding, she wrinkled her brow. "Although, running for mayor, you'll need to find the perfect woman to help your election. If you asked me, I'd say Alexis is that woman."

She's confused. If I needed a wife to get elected, I wouldn't run. Being mayor was a temporary career. Being a husband was a lifetime commitment, and one he didn't take lightly. *I need to make her understand.* Shoving away from the counter, he took two steps and encompassed her in his arms. He rested his chin on the top of her head, while circling his thumbs across her lower back. "Alexis is a friend. She's *Ellen's* friend."

Lily looked up. "Which makes her perfect. She's already a part of your family, and she's from here. The residents expect you to marry a local."

"Perhaps." He sighed. "You're right, though. I was with Alexis today."

Lily tensed.

Releasing one hand, Ben brushed a finger against her cheek. "She needed a ride to the airport." An image of Taylor driving away flashed through his thoughts. As painful as losing her had been, he endured. However, he wasn't certain he could say the same if Lily left. "I planned to go to Albany anyway, so, I offered to take her." Reaching for her hand, he kissed her palm. With his free hand, he dug into his pants pocket and drew out a black, velvet-encased box. He flipped open the top. Inside flashed a large diamond set in a platinum band.

He slipped the ring from the box.

Lily dropped her gaze and gasped. *A ring? An engagement ring—for me? From Ben?* Her pulse raced, and the sensation of tingles washed over her flesh. With her heart hammering, she lifted an arm. Unable to stop her hand from shaking, she brushed a finger over the stone. A mixture of coolness and warmth mingling with the soft, velvety fabric scraped across the tips. Moisture rimmed her eyes. She reached up and swiped at a teardrop.

Pressing a finger to her chin, he forced up her gaze. "I hadn't planned on proposing this way." He traced a line over her finger and stared into her eyes. "Lily, I don't want someone from here."

Biting her lip, she fisted her hand. "But, your election…"

He stared into her eyes then licked his lips. "I don't care about the election. I love you." Uncurling her fingers, he slid the band on her finger then pressed her hand to his lips. "Will you marry me?"

A smile brushed her lips. "How can I say no?"

"You can't." He grazed his lips over hers then leaned back. "Haven't you learned anything about me? When something is important, I don't stop until I achieve my desire." He brushed his thumb over the ring. "You make me a better person."

Epilogue

Lily stood in a small antechamber. Through the church walls, she heard the organ music swell, echoing softly into the room. Her stomach tightened at the knowledge that in only a few minutes, she'd step out of the room and face the crowd.

Glancing down, she stared at the glistening diamond. She took a deep breath, and with a shaking hand, rubbed a finger against the metal. The platinum band felt warm and solid against her touch—just like the man waiting at the altar. Her heart bumped. *I still don't believe it…Ben actually wants to marry me.*

Nearly two months had passed since he asked for her hand. Since then, she barely had time to wrap her brain around the whole idea of her engagement, let alone marriage. With all the wedding planning and supporting Ben's efforts for the election, she hadn't time to dwell on today.

Closing her eyes, she pressed together her lips and inhaled, enjoying the solitude. Moments earlier, her mother, Mari, left to take her place in the church, and Peri—well, who knows where Peri went. *Probably eyeing Dax.*

She smiled. Besides herself, Peri had been thrilled with the engagement. Although, she suspected Peri's excitement had more to do with spending additional time in Aberdeen pursuing Dax, and less about the wedding.

A soft click sounded.

Popping open her eyes, Lily pivoted.

The door swung open.

Peri stepped into the room. The hem of her copper-colored dress swished softly against the deep, red carpet.

"How's Dax?" Lily smoothed a hand over the strand of pearls circling her neck.

Reaching up, Peri carefully arranged a lock of Lily's hair. "Looking quite handsome in that black tux." She leaned back and smiled. "Ben's not too shabby either."

Lily snorted. In the time she'd known Ben, he'd always looked incredible.

Swiveling, Peri glanced toward the door before turning back. "So, are you ready?"

Her heart fluttered. Lily slid a glance toward Peri and grinned. "Yes."

"You should be." Dropping her hand, Peri stepped back and winked. "I told you a while back you were destined to marry Ben. He's perfect for you."

Lily smiled. "I know."

Walking across the room, Peri grabbed a bouquet of white roses sprinkled with lilies and greenery. A soft copper-colored ribbon with an ornate bow circled the stems. She pressed the bouquet to her nose and looked up.

Frowning, Lily studied her sister. "Are you crying?"

Peri slashed a hand across her eyes. "No."

Lily arched a brow.

Sniffling, Peri chuckled. "Okay. Maybe a little."

She strolled across the room and held out the spray of flowers. "I'm just so happy for you."

Lily brushed her fingers across her sister's arm before accepting the arrangement. "Yeah, I am too."

Peri fidgeted with the sleeve of Lily's dress, smoothing out a crease. "You look beautiful, you know."

Pivoting, Lily glanced again in the oblong mirror tucked into the corner of the room. The white satin gown embellished with delicate lace hugged her curves in a way that was both demure and elegant before flaring softly just above her knees. The dress had cost a fortune, but the minute she spied the outfit, she knew this dress was the one. She hoped Ben was as pleased. Shifting her gaze, she studied her sister's reflection in the mirror. "Well, you're next."

Stepping back, Peri flung up her hands. "I don't think so." She darted a glanced toward the door. "There's one man I still haven't conquered yet."

Lily arched a brow. She knew exactly whom her sister spoke of—Dax Moore. "Not giving up?"

Peri smoothed a hand down her copper-color dress. "Nope." She winked. "And I expect tonight might be special for me too."

Laughing, Lily ran a hand over her hair. "Oh yeah? Why's that?"

Shrugging, Peri nudged Lily's hand to the side. "Weddings are romantic. I'm thinking with me as maid of honor, and Dax as best man, we just might get an opportunity to connect."

Lily rolled her eyes. Today, she could be generous. After all, her dream had come true. Why not let Peri have hers? "Well, for your sake, I hope you get your wish."

Peri waved a hand. "Oh, don't worry. Things work out as they're supposed to." Sweeping her gaze over Lily, she sighed. "You can thank me any time you want."

Lily arched a brow. "For what?"

"Well, don't forget. I was the one who suggested we come to Aberdeen." Peri lifted her chin. "If it wasn't for me, none of this..."—she fanned a hand—"would be happening."

Can't argue with that logic.

Lily smiled. "Thank you." She meant the words too. If Peri hadn't been so persistent, things might have ended differently. She drew Peri close and pressed a soft kiss to her cheek. "I love you."

Stepping back, Peri wrinkled her nose. "Now, don't get all mushy on me." She swiped a hand to against her face. "You know, you've made a lot of women miserable."

Tilting her head to the side, Lily frowned. "Yeah?"

"Yup. I heard Jenny was so distraught over the fact she lost Ben, that her father sent her for an extended vacation to Europe." Peri snorted. "I heard her tell some woman at Betty's Café that she planned on finding her Prince Charming—as if..."

Lily laughed. She didn't believe in fairy tales, but if she did, then she figured she'd gotten hers when Ben asked her to marry. "Well, I hope she does."

Dropping down on the gold brocade chair, Peri tapped fingers against the armrest. "Karla flew to Hawaii for vacation. She refused to see Ben get married."

Good. I'm glad. She nearly ruined things for me

and Ben. She grazed a finger over a petal. "I know."

"She'll probably find some guy to marry." Peri ran a finger along the arm of the chair and studied Lily. "Did you ever think you'd marry someone like dad?"

Dropping her hand, Lily peered up. "How so?"

Lifting one shoulder, Peri fanned a hand. "Well, Ben's just like dad. He's devoted to you, and he's a solid, upright guy." She waggled her brows. "You know, you could have done worse."

She's right. An image of Eric flashed through Lily's thoughts. Cheating, deceiving Eric. She shuddered. *And to think, I thought I loved him.* With Ben, she found someone committed, dedicated, and faithful. "You're right. I did get lucky."

Peri wagged a finger. "Remember, always listen to your sister."

Laughter burbled from Lily. "I'll remember that fact in the future."

The door opened.

Ellen rushed in. Like Peri, she was dressed in a copper-colored dress. Her hair was swept up in a French knot, and a dazzling diamond necklace circled her neck. She hurried over and pressed a kiss to Ellen's cheek. "I've never seen my brother so nervous." Sliding a glance in Lily's direction, she twisted the diamond stud in her lobe. "He's actually pacing the front of the altar. I don't think he'll calm down until the marriage is official."

"He should be nervous." Peri scowled. "If it weren't for Claire's cunning and my interference, he'd have lost Lily."

Nodding, Ellen swiveled her gaze toward the closed door. "The church is packed. They've even put speakers on the sidewalk and a large-screen tv for those who couldn't come inside to watch."

Lily's stomach lurched. "Really?"

Ellen nodded. "This wedding is a big deal. Everyone loves you as much as Ben. They want to see their happily-ever after."

James, Lily's father, stepped into the room. He looked handsome, dressed in in a deep-gray tuxedo. Hurrying across the room, he kissed Lily's cheek. "Your mother and me are so happy." Stepping back, he swiped a hand across his eyes.

Peri strolled over, and narrowing her gaze, scowled. "Are you crying, Dad?"

Tugging out a kerchief from his pocket, he wiped his nose. "A father's prerogative." He stuffed the kerchief back in his pocket and turned to Lily. "You ready?"

Lily clutched her father's arm and took a deep breath. "More than you can possibly know." Swiveling, she eyed the door. "How's mom?"

Her father rolled his eyes. "Crying like a baby." He shook his head. "What is it with women and weddings?"

Chuckling, Lily patted her father's arm. "Don't know, dad. Must be the romance in us."

James scoffed. "Women and their fanciful notions." Huffing a sigh, he waved his free hand. "Can we go now?"

Smiling, Lily nodded. "I'm ready."

"Well, then, let's make the town happy." Peri grabbed her bouquet and walked out the door.

Ellen followed.

Clutching Lily's arm, James started forward.

Lily stopped him.

He turned and frowned. "What now? Did you forget something?"

Lily smiled. "Yes."

Dropping his hand to his hip, he gritted his teeth. "Oh, for goodness sake." He waved a hand. "Well, hurry. You don't want to keep your future husband waiting, now do you?"

Lily giggled. Peri was right. Ben and her father were almost identical in demeanor. "No. I don't." She trailed a finger across the tip of a white lily and studied the man who taught her so much. "I just want to say thank you."

James jerked back and widened his eyes. "For what?"

Smiling, Lily caught her father's arm. She squeezed gently. "For providing the perfect example of what I want in a husband." Her father's cheeks turned pink, and his eyes filled with moisture.

Dipping his head, he grabbed the kerchief from his pocket and wiped his eyes. "Aw…now, why did you have to go and say such a thing?"

Lily laughed. "They were good words, Dad."

He stuffed the kerchief in his pocket and pressed a hand to her cheek. "I know." Sniffing, he tugged on her arm, drawing her toward the door. "Come on. Your future husband is anxious. I don't want to make him more worried than he is right now."

Taking a deep breath, Lily swept into the vestibule and gazed around the crowded church.

Music, drifting softly from the organ, ebbed and swelled in rhythmic cadence. Golden flames flickered and glowed from the candles on the altar, and colorful light rippled through the stained-glass windows lining the perimeter walls. The smell of lilies and roses competed with the scent of perfume. Suddenly, as if on an unseen cue, the spectators stood. Swiveling, they pinned their gazes toward the back.

Lily's heart thumped, and her stomach squeezed. She tightened her grip on her father's arm. *Be brave.*

Gilding upon the white runner paving a trail to the altar, Ellen led the procession.

Peri followed.

James stepped forward.

Lily tightened her grip on his arm.

A soft hush descended in the church.

Turning, James slid his gaze over her face. "Are you okay? Having second thoughts?" He patted her wrist. "You don't have to get married."

Lily's lips trembled, and her pulse raced. *I don't?* She slipped her gaze past Ellen and Peri, past the rows of pews, decorated with ornate bows, the copper-satin ribbon folded and twisted in a flurry of loops, past the curious gazes of the congregation.

She spotted Suzette and Mitch Bird. They stood shoulder to shoulder with their hands clasped together. Mitch caught her gaze and gave her a slight nod. Suzette, tilting her head slightly to the side, smiled. Betty sat beside Alexis. Leaning in, she whispered something, causing a far-off look to enter Alexis' gaze and a soft smile to crease her lips.

Lily slipped her gaze past her mother, who continually wiped her eyes with a scrunched-up kerchief, over Claire, whose eyes held a note of victory, moving beyond Dax, who looked dashing in his black tuxedo, to Ben.

Standing beside Father Frank, Ben looked handsome in the black tux. His gaze, filled with deep, abiding love, was riveted on her. A soft, warm feeling spread through her.

I need him. He's my home.

Pulling her gaze from Ben, she looked at her father and smiled. "Nope. No second thoughts."

Nodding, James guided her up the aisle.

Before she knew what happened, she was standing beside Ben in front of the altar. Her father pressed a kiss to her cheek before releasing his grip and moving behind her.

Father Frank, dressed in all-white, stood in front of two steps leading to the altar. Holding a bible and a rosary, he stood, smiling. Behind him, on the altar draped in white cloth, sat two, tall, white candles, one on each end of the table. Their flames flickered and spluttered, casting the area in a romantic glow.

Peri stepped forward.

Lily handed her the bouquet before turning.

Smiling, Ben clasped her hand between his. A smile, as warm and welcoming as the summer sun, slid across his handsome features. Holding her gaze, he pressed a kiss to her knuckles.

The collective sigh rippling from the spectators matched hers. Her heart swelled, and all the love she felt, nearly consumed her. Her very first encounter with him floated through her thoughts. *How did I ever consider him egotistical and self-serving? And why did I fight my attraction?* Now, these many months later, the idea of avoiding him was ridiculous.

Somehow, her heart knew the very thing she resisted was the very thing she needed. She didn't want her independence or her freedom. What she needed was this man—this strong, dependable, confident, capable, patient man. She closed her eyes and said a silent thank you to her maker, and then turned her attention to the priest.

"Dearly beloved..." Father Frank's voice rang loud and sure through the church. "We are gathered here today, in this sacred place, to bring this man and this woman into holy matrimony..."

Ben squeezed her hand.

She returned the gesture and sighed. *Welcome to Aberdeen, indeed.*

****

The next day in *The Aberdeen Almanac,* Rose Smith declared fairy tales really did come true. Neither Ben nor Lily read the story. They were on their honeymoon, but everyone assured Lily later that Rose wrote the most romantic tale the town had ever read.

A word about the author...

Jules Hahn has been passionate for writing since grade school. She wrote and illustrated her very first book in second grade called *Goober the Squash*.

Always one to live in her head, Jules loves to create stories of love and romance, usually involving herself. *Welcome to Aberdeen* is the first in its series to be published.

Jules lives in Phoenix, Arizona and is married to her high school sweetheart. Together they have two wonderful boys. You can follow Jules' series on her webpage JulesHahn.com.

http://juleshahn.com

~

Another Title by This Author
Hometown Player

Thank you for purchasing
this publication of The Wild Rose Press, Inc.

For questions or more information
contact us at
info@thewildrosepress.com.

The Wild Rose Press, Inc.
www.thewildrosepress.com

To visit with authors of
The Wild Rose Press, Inc.
join our yahoo loop at
http://groups.yahoo.com/group/thewildrosepress/

Lightning Source UK Ltd.
Milton Keynes UK
UKHW020627310520
364100UK00003B/523